Also by Annie Solomon

Like A Knife

Dead Ringer

Tell Me No Lies

BLIND CURVE

ANNIE SOLOMON

WARNER
FOREVER

NEW YORK   BOSTON

Warner Forever is a registered trademark of Warner Books.

Cover design by Diane Luger
Cover photography by Herman Estevez
Hand lettering by David Gatti
Book design by Giorgetta Bell McRee

Warner Books

Time Warner Book Group
1271 Avenue of the Americas
New York, NY 10020
Visit our Web site at www.twbookmark.com

Printed in the United States of America

First Paperback Printing: February 2005

10 9 8 7 6 5 4 3 2 1

To the sisters: Ilene, Jill, and Joan.
And to my brother, Saul, the poor guy
who has put up with us all.

Acknowledgments

I'd like to thank my friend Judy Morris, whose career as an Orientation and Mobility instructor first gave me the idea for this book, and who blindfolded me and taught me how to navigate my home.

I owe a huge debt to everyone at the Tennessee Rehabilitation Center Vision Impairment Services, particularly Director Gale Demick and instructors Jean Ward and Kathleen Dineen, who shared their experience and expertise, plus the many students who shared their stories. Rehab Counselor Paulette Frailie was also a big help.

I'd also like to thank Dr. Meredith Ezell and Dr. David Uskavitch for their help with the medical side of cortical blindness.

Once again, Detective Lieutenant William Siegrist answered all my questions, no matter how trivial. As did weapons expert Steve Doyle, who, thankfully, is always eager to talk about the intricacies of deadly force.

To my editor, Beth de Guzman, and my agent, Pam Ahearn, thanks for encouraging me to undertake this story, even when I wasn't sure I could, and for helping make it the best it could be.

And to Larry and Becca: thanks wouldn't be enough.

BLIND
CURVE

CHAPTER 1

The night was too damn cold to be out on the streets. But the tall man with the knit cap pulled low over his face just hunched inside his green army jacket and stamped his feet to keep warm. A two-day beard stubbled his face and dark, greasy hair hung beneath the cap. On the street he was known as Turq, short for "turquoise," the color of his deep-set eyes.

Half a block from the west side projects, he stood near a burned out streetlight where an abandoned grocery store hulked on the corner. Hidden in the shadows was the gun he planned to buy.

The seller was late, and Turq cursed silently. His neck bothered him. Two nights ago, he'd been popped in the head during a routine drug sweep in the Dutchman's Tavern, and the cold was making it ache.

His cell phone vibrated against his hip.

"Yo," Turq said low.

"What's up, uncle?" The voice belonged to one of his ghosts, stationed across the street and up the block, but still able to trail his every move.

"My date is late."

Footsteps approached.

"Catch you later, dude," Turq said.

The seller rounded the corner. Fifteen at best, he was scrawny, dressed in hip-hop mode with chains and a track-suit hanging on his lanky form. The kid swaggered confidently toward Turq, who groaned under his breath. The young ones were the worst. You never knew what they'd do.

Turq didn't waste time. "You got it?"

The seller eyed him suspiciously. "You got the dead presidents?"

"Two hundred. Cash. That was the deal."

"Yeah, but I don't know you, bro. And I don't do business with peeps I don't know."

Christ. Turq tightened his jaw. First the guy was late, then he started giving attitude. Forcing himself to relax, he stuck out his hand. "Name's Turq. Ah shit. No, it ain't." He grinned sheepishly. "It's Danny." He left off Sinofsky, hoping the first name would be enough. "But don't you go telling no one."

Slowly, the seller shook his hand. "Danny, huh. Now that's about the whitest name I know."

"We friends now?"

The seller shrugged. In the dim moonlight his skin looked creamy and smooth, no trace of beard yet. Danny tasted sadness. Kids killing kids.

"Yeah, okay, Danny," the seller said.

"So where is it?"

"Not here. I got it stashed."

Damn. Changing locations was not a good idea. It meant his ghosts would have to follow in the catch car. If they could follow, and sometimes they couldn't.

Or it could mean a setup. Take the money and run. And he had a lot of money on him.

But an illegal gun was a gun, and already he could smell the steel. "You bring it here, bro. That's the deal."

The kid took a step back. "Fuck that shit. Cops all over the place."

"It's here or no place."

"Then it's no place, dawg." The kid turned around.

Christ. "Hold up!"

Going somewhere else sucked big time, but so was letting another gimme hang on the street where innocent civvies ended up paying the price. The latest vic had been a three-year-old girl.

"Where we going?"

"I'll take you."

"I gotta know where first." If he could alert his ghosts, who were listening on a hidden wire, they had a better chance of keeping tabs.

But the night was not going Danny's way.

"It's a sweet little secret spot. I got me a car waiting."

The kid didn't look old enough to drive. Fuck. "Okay. Gotta have that piece."

"Yeah?" The seller led him around the corner to a rusted 1972 Chevy Camaro that was once gold and now looked like faded dirt. "You got a job in mind?"

Danny gave the kid a long look. "Never mind what I got in mind. I got the bills. That's all you need to know."

The seller nodded, fifteen going on fifty. "You got that right."

Danny got into the car, fingers tingling, adrenaline pumping. He imagined Parnell popping his cork when he found out. He almost grinned, picturing his lieutenant's face.

The car wheezed down Market Street toward the railroad tracks by the river. A century ago, this was the commercial heart of Sokanan. Barges from Manhattan traveled up the Hudson and off-loaded at the dockside warehouses, filling up with light manufactured goods and produce from Hudson Valley farms. Freight trains did the same, going west.

Now the place was deserted, though the upswing in business from the Renaissance Oil deal, which brought a new boom to the town, had started talk of renovating warehouse row into a shopping mall on the lines of Faneuil Hall in Boston.

But all that was down the pike. Right now the place was dark and dusty.

"So where are we?" Danny asked, feeding clues to his ghosts. "Down by warehouse row?"

"You got eyes, don't you?"

The seller pulled off the main drag onto a narrow path heading west toward the Hudson. The car bumped over old cobbles, then parked in a dirt yard fronting a derelict warehouse. Moonlight bounced off the river, creating shadows and gloom. Faded yellow letters at the top of the brick building spelled out its name, but Danny could make out only an M and a C.

"McClanahan," Danny murmured.

"What you talking about?"

Danny nodded toward the warehouse. "The building. See the 'M' and the 'C'? I'll bet that was McClanahan's."

"Who gives a shit?"

Danny didn't tell him.

He got out, scanning the area. Murky and abandoned. No way backup could get there without being noticed.

His palms were sweating but he followed the seller toward the looming structure. He did not want to go into that warehouse.

"Where is it?" Danny asked.

"Inside."

Shit. "Go get it. I'll wait here. That place gives me the—"

The warehouse flickered in front of him. For a second he was in complete darkness. He stumbled, almost fell.

What the f—

A gunshot cracked above him where his head would have been. Someone grunted and his vision cleared. In that split second he saw the boy down on the ground.

Danny dove behind a dumpster as another shot chased him.

"Rounds fired!" he shouted into the hidden wire. "I'm behind a dumpster by the old McClanahan warehouse."

His cell vibrated. He grabbed it. "You got the location?"

"We got you, uncle."

Danny looked around. It would take time for the ghosts to get there and less than that to die. The shot had come from the warehouse roof. An excellent position, it gave the shooter coverage of the entire area, while Danny was pinned down—no vest, no weapon, just a fistful of cash for protection.

Trapped, he banged the back of his head against the bin's metal side in frustration. A shot pinged off the edge and instinctively he ducked.

The young seller lay unmoving facedown on the ground, the soles of his Nikes to the sky. Was the kid carrying? It wouldn't surprise him. In any case, he couldn't leave him out there, wounded and exposed to the shooter.

He crawled to the edge of the blue bin, reached out and got shot at for his trouble.

Shit.

He snatched back his hand, took a breath, tried again. This time, he managed to latch onto one of the boy's feet.

He dragged the body toward him. It jerked as another bullet hit.

When the boy was safe behind the trash container, Danny rolled him over. His eyes were wide open and a black circle decorated the middle of his forehead.

Fuck.

Who the hell was out there?

No time to think about it. He scrabbled over the body and found a fully loaded nine beneath the tracksuit. Wouldn't do much good against the high-powered rifle the shooter had, but it was better than nothing.

He peered around the corner of the dumpster and, once again, his vision sputtered out. He blinked as cars squealed into the area, sirens screaming. Doors slammed, shots fired. Bayliss over the bullhorn. "This is the police! Throw the rifle down!"

Then another voice over that. "Sin! Where are you? Sin!"

Hands shook him. "Jesus Christ, what happened?" It was Mike Finelli, his other ghost. "Danny? Sin? You all right?"

"Yeah, I'm fine. Except I can't see a fucking thing."

"It's called cortical blindness," the neurologist said, her voice so calm and matter-of-fact he wanted to deck her. He didn't know how long he'd been in the hospital, but it felt like years. He'd been shuffled off to doctors and technicians who were a mush of voices with no faces. Now he sat in some kind of armchair; he could feel the shape and the fabric. And from the quiet and lack of movement around him, he sensed he was in a private office. And this doctor—Christ, he couldn't even remember her name—was telling him . . .

"You're kidding. One minute I'm fine and the next minute I'm fucking blind?"

"You had a stroke."

"I'm thirty-two and healthy as a horse. Guys like me don't have strokes."

"I understand you were hit in the head two days ago."

"In my line of work I get hit a lot. What the hell does that have to do with anything?"

"You injured your neck," she said gently. "Tore your vertebral artery. That's the one right at the top of your spine. The tear allowed blood to dissect—to seep—into the arterial wall. The blood embolized. Clotted. The clot traveled to the top of the basilar artery, the main artery at the back of the head. It went from there to one of the posterior cerebral arteries and fragmented, plugging up your cortex."

"Yeah, but why can't I see?"

"Because the messages from your eyes can't get to the cortex, which is where they're interpreted. It's called a bilateral occipital stroke."

The words slid over him like so much fog. His heart was thudding wildly, his mouth was dry. He wondered if he'd been shot at the warehouse instead of the seller and this was a coma dream from which he would eventually wake.

"Detective Sinofsky?"

"Yeah."

"Do you have any other questions?"

He hesitated, feeling lost, adrift. "Am I . . ." He cleared his throat. "Am I dreaming?"

There was a short pause. "No." She spoke the word quietly, with compassion and complete certainty.

He nodded, dread gripping him. "Any chance this will go away?"

Another short pause. "It's possible. There have been cases of it clearing up on its own."

"But?"

"But the damage is extensive. I wouldn't count on it. I'm sorry." He heard the sound of her rising, the swish of clothing, the creak of a chair. "I'm going to set you up with a social worker. She'll get you into rehab. You'll need a mobility instructor."

He sat there, not taking any of this in. A hand touched his shoulder. He flinched.

"How are you getting home?"

He had no idea.

"Are you married?"

He shook his head.

"A girlfriend? Parents, relative?"

His mother was dead, and he didn't want to dump this on his sister, Beth.

"I'll, uh, I'll call a friend."

He'd been in and out of his clothes, his eyes and his head poked and prodded, his body X-rayed. But now he was back in his street wear—the ripped jeans and ancient army jacket that belonged to Turq. Fumbling in the huge pockets, he found his cell phone below Turq's knit cap. His fingers searched the buttons for the correct ones, but his hand was shaking.

Gently, someone took the phone from him. "What's the number?" Doctor whoever.

He swallowed. His brain had stopped and it took a moment to jumpstart it again. But he remembered it at last and told her. A minute later she handed him the phone.

Mike Finelli's voice came on the line, an anchor of familiarity.

"It's me," Danny said, desperate to keep the tremor out of his voice.

"Sin. Where are you? I've been at the hospital all day and they keep saying they're doing tests. What's going on? Are you okay?"

Not really. But he wasn't ready to get into that. "I need a ride home."

"Beth's here. I think she's got that covered."

A phone rang and he heard the doctor pick up and speak softly into it.

"What about her kids?" he asked Finelli.

"I don't know. They're not with her."

"All right. I'll call Beth on her cell and tell her where to meet me."

"She's right here—"

A hand touched his arm. "Hold on," he said to Mike.

"Mr. Sinofsky?" A bright, cheery voice. "I'm Pat Embry. I'll be taking you to the waiting room where your mobility instructor will meet you."

"They're taking me somewhere," he told Mike. "I'll have them call Beth when I get there."

"If you'll just stand for a moment," the cheery voice said. He pictured a plump, big bosomed woman with tightly curled hair—an Aunt Bea type—but her hand, which she kept on him while he complied, was bony and smelled of disinfectant.

"Just a few steps," she told him brightly as if he were three. "Here's your chair."

He felt the leather sides of a wheelchair and something tightened in his chest.

"That's right. Good boy. Comfy?"

His hands fisted.

"Okay, here we go."

*   *   *

They'd all warned her about him. Everyone from the supervising social worker to the nurse's aide had given her a sharp-eyed look, a cautionary word.

But she didn't need a warning because she remembered him.

Someone had wheeled him into the patient's lounge and he'd managed to find his way out of the chair. One arm propped against the wall, he faced the window as though drinking in the night.

His jeans were outrageously worn, faded and ripped. After fourteen years and who knew what life had done to him, she would have thought his wardrobe would at least have improved. His black T-shirt was in much better shape. The sleeves strained over well-defined biceps. A man's biceps to match a man's body. Tall and rangy, he had wide shoulders that tapered down to a lean waist and a tight rear. A jungle cat. Strong, healthy. Young.

Looking at him, even from the back, she felt the opposite.

She stepped into the room, and his shoulders stiffened. He'd heard her.

"Detective Sinofsky?"

He turned and hit her with the full force of his face. Even prepared, she nearly gasped. Age had given him lines and hollows, hardened him into an adult. But he was still dark and intense with a face born of fantasy. Of dangerous dreams deep in the night.

Far away, deep in the recesses of her soul, something stirred. An echo of an echo, so thin and faint it was easy to pretend she hadn't heard it.

His eyes were deep-set and still piercingly turquoise. Clear and transparent as the Caribbean. And healthy-looking. No injury marred the lids or sockets. Nothing at all to signal they were useless.

"Danny Sinofsky?"

"Who wants to know?"

She swallowed, glad he couldn't see the shock and pity she didn't hide fast enough. Would he have recognized her? Half hoping, half dreading, she steeled her voice into the safe rhythms of brisk objectivity. "Martha Crowe." She waited just the merest second to see if her name jarred memories. But he stared expressionlessly at her, and she doused the quick jab of disappointment. "I'm a rehab teacher and an O and M instructor—Orientation and Mobility. I'd like to talk to you about your options."

"Options?"

"We can get started with a cane immediately. But there are other things to think about. A dog. Even some electronic devices."

His face, tough and impossibly handsome, even shadowed by stubble, darkened. "Get lost." The expression was eerie because it looked as though he could really see her. "I'm fine."

Not one for false comfort, she opted for bluntness as a way to cut through the anger. "You're not fine. You're blind."

He tensed, coiled, muscles waiting to spring. "It's temporary."

She looked at his paperwork. Cortical blindness due to a stroke caused by a neck injury. A freak accident but not unheard of. The internal damage had been extensive; there wasn't much hope he'd get back his sight.

"Look, Detective—"

"Are you still here?"

She remembered the rough-edged boy with the smile

that could break hearts. The man he'd grown into scowled at her.

"I know this has been a shock but—"

"I told you to get lost. My eyes are fine. A few days and this will all be a bad dream."

"I hope so but—"

He took a threatening step in her direction. Despite his handicap, she instinctively stepped back.

"Something wrong with your hearing? Get the fuck out of here!"

She inhaled a breath, let it out slowly. Sometimes shock therapy was the only way to get through a shock. "You want me to go? Why don't you come over here and make me."

A flash of panic crossed his face, quickly followed by fury.

"I'm right here," she said using her voice to position herself in the room. "Throw me out."

He leaped at her like a caged tiger. But instead of bars, the darkness held him back. He ran into a row of chairs. Bolted to the floor, they didn't budge and he went flying backward, struck a coffee table, spilling the year-old magazines on the floor. Cursing, he cleared the table and banged his head against a post holding a magazine stand. By this time he was completely turned around and would have headed off in the opposite direction, but she ran over, put a hand on his upper arm just above the elbow.

His arm was hard and powerful, intensely masculine. The feel of it beneath her fingers sent a jolt through her system, yet he was the one who flinched. His whole body shuddered with rage.

Quietly, she said, "Even if you're blind for only a day, you should learn to get around without breaking your neck."

"Fuck you."

"Not likely, but if you'd like to try, my number is 422-2222. Easy to remember. 422-2222."

He shook off her hold as a man hurried into the room. "Sin?"

Danny turned to the sound of the new voice. A lean-faced man with silver hair.

"It's Bob Parnell." The expression in Parnell's face was carefully controlled, but the taut lines around his mouth and the intense way he observed Danny gave his true feelings away: worry, shock, uncertainty. But none of that was in his voice. "How're you doing?"

"Terrific." Danny's tone said otherwise.

"Look, can we sit somewhere and talk?"

Panic surged into Danny's face again. "To your left," Martha said quietly. "Nine o'clock. Three steps over."

His expression hardened, but he followed her instructions and found a seat without mishap.

The new man looked from her to Danny and back again. "I interrupt something?"

She stuck out her hand. "Martha Crowe. I do rehab."

"Bob Parnell. I do police work. I'm Danny's boss. And his friend."

"Good." She gave his hand a firm, curt shake. "He could use one. We're done for now." She turned to Danny, who sat stone-faced. "422-2222. All twos, detective. Except for that four in the front."

She left him. Half of her hoped he called. The other half hoped he wouldn't.

Danny listened for the sound of her retreating footsteps. Was she gone? He prayed she was. Prayed he'd never hear her calm, Goody Two-shoes voice again.

We can start with a cane.

Everything inside him shuddered with panic. The words replayed themselves over and over. A cane. Tapping out every step for the rest of his life.

"Danny. Danny! Can you hear me?"

"I'm blind, boss, not deaf."

A hard nugget of silence greeted that jibe. "Sorry," the head of Sokanan's detective division said. "I was talking to you and—"

"I'm a little distracted."

"Yeah. I imagine you are."

Another short silence. Danny pictured the older man's lean, no-nonsense face. Firm, planted. The calm in the center of the storm. When Danny was a kid, angry and lost and ready for trouble, Parnell had cuffed him, brought him to the station, scared the living shit out of him, and let him go. And every so often, showed up at home. Took him to a ball game. Made sure there was something besides Cocoa Puffs to eat. He'd been the hand that kept Danny from falling over the cliff. When he returned from the army, Parnell had reached out again, pulled him into the department. If there was one person on this earth he didn't want to fuck up in front of, it was Bob Parnell.

"What did the doctor say?"

"I'm blind."

"You want to expand on that?"

Danny pushed out the explanation as best he could, choking on the words "cortical blindness," "stroke," and the other medicalese.

"So it wasn't the shooting?"

"No. It was the pop in the head at the Dutchman a couple of nights ago. Christ, how ironic is that? I can dodge a bullet but don't hit me."

"Is it permanent?"

Danny shrugged. "Not if I have anything to do with it."

Parnell touched Danny's shoulder. He started.

"Look, I can't tell you how sorry I am. How sorry we all are. The whole department. This has hit everyone hard."

Danny's belly turned over. The thought of everyone feeling sorry for him made him want to puke. "I don't need you to feel sorry. I'm going to be fine."

"Danny—"

"I mean it," he said, shrugging off Parnell's hand.

"Hey, Sin. How you holding up?"

Danny steeled his face into neutrality at the sound of the newcomer's voice. Although Sokanan's detective division was too small to be broken into units and everyone was expected to handle a variety of cases, Hank Bonner was usually the division's point man on homicide. If he was here, maybe there was news. Any change of subject was welcome.

"You working on the warehouse shooting?"

"Yeah. I'm digging deep, but I gotta tell you, I'm not getting very far."

He pictured Hank. A couple of inches taller than Danny, he was a big man with a perpetually tanned face from working in his family's apple orchards. He was a good cop who knew what it was to weather personal storms. He'd weathered plenty of his own in the last few years. But Hank's family tragedy had ended with marriage and a new baby, a happy ending that at the moment seemed wildly out of reach for Danny. His personal life was the last thing he wanted to talk about. "You ID the kid?"

"Name's Rufus Teeter, but goes by T-bone. Mean anything to you?"

Danny shook his head, grateful to have his mind occupied by the normal routine of police work. "Any connection to the drug trade or the gangs in Weston?" Weston meant the west side projects where Danny had met T-bone. Recently, they'd seen a rash of drive-bys and armed robberies, which was why he'd been there in the first place—too many weapons bloodying the streets. Danny was one of five assigned to the Neighborhood Recovery Unit, responsible for getting illegal guns off the streets, as well as the players, junkies, hookers, and johns that went along with them.

"Not yet."

"What about Ricky Roda?" He named the key player in Sokanan's drug trade.

"Can't see why Roda would take out one of his own," Parnell said.

"Who knows how guys like him tick? Drugs and money are all they care about. Someone puts the tap on that, who knows what he'd do."

"I don't think so," Hank said. "Kid's a distant cousin of Roda's sent up from Mississippi. I just came from the interview. Women wailing all over the place."

Christ. Danny should be doing the interviews. He swallowed down a rage of jealousy. "Maybe it's someone wanting to get back at Roda. Someone sending a message. Is there someone else from the Bronx trying to move in? Sokanan's just a train ride away. Maybe it's a turf war."

"We're checking that out," Hank said.

"Nothing's popped yet," Parnell added. The two men lapsed into silence, as though turning that thought over.

"What about the gun?" Danny asked, afraid to let the silence stretch. Too much thinking in the quiet. Too many places he didn't want to go. "Kid said it was in the warehouse. Anyone find it?"

"No," Parnell said.

"So what does that mean?"

"Maybe he had it stashed deep, and it'll turn up eventually."

"Or maybe there never was a gun."

Another silence. What were they thinking? Danny would have given anything to see their faces.

"A setup?" Hank said.

"Why not ?"

"Then why take the kid out first?" Parnell said.

The scene played out in Danny's head—the tramp to the warehouse, his aversion to walking into a trap, that brief, weird shutting down of his eyes, his near-fall in the dark . . .

Had the shooter meant to hit him and hit the kid instead?

"If he was after you," Parnell said, "why do it that way? Why not wait until you got inside where they could roll you good?"

No one answered. Probably because there was no answer. Yet.

It was eerie, this conversation. Like lying on his cot in basic training, talking after the lights were doused. Words floating in the dark.

"And you didn't see the shooter?" Hank asked.

"No."

Not that it mattered. He couldn't ID him off a mug shot or a lineup anyway. Not now.

Not ever, a voice in his head whispered.

Another flush of panic swept through him. This couldn't be real. Couldn't be happening to him.

"Okay." Parnell sighed. "I'll keep you posted. If you think of anything else . . ."

"I got you on speed dial."

The rustle of clothes told him the others were rising.

Danny stood, too, praying he'd judged the sounds right and was facing them.

"I'll see you tomorrow," Hank said. To Parnell, Danny guessed. "Sin, you take care." He slapped Danny on the back and left.

Parnell said, "What are your plans?"

"Plans? Get my damn eyes back, that's my plan."

A strong hand squeezed his shoulder. "Good. We're all hoping that one works out. And in the meantime, I've got you on medical leave."

"In the meantime, he's coming home with me." That sounded like Beth. "Hi, Bob."

"How are you, Beth?"

"I'll be better once I get him home."

Danny turned his head toward his sister's voice. "I'm going to my own house. I'll be fine."

She sighed. "I'm not letting you go home by yourself. And there's no room for me and the kids at your place. So you're coming home with me. Don't argue."

Her voice was thick with the struggle to keep tears at bay. It pierced him, that sound, knowing it was there because of him. *Him*. The one who always took care of everything.

Parnell leaned close. He felt the other man's body against his. "Go ahead and let her baby you. Women like that. It'll make her happy and it won't kill you."

The panic threatened to overwhelm him. He just wanted to be alone where no one could see him. But his friend and his sister were two too many to fight at the moment.

Nodding, he rose, searching for obstacles. Without asking, Parnell took his arm and Danny jerked it away.

"Whoa, Danny. It's okay. You need some help. I'm here."

Danny clenched his jaw. He did need help. And it killed him. Curtly, he nodded, not trusting himself to speak.

Parnell took his arm again and walked him through the darkness.

Because he didn't have a clue where he was going, every step was a leap of faith and a struggle with fear. Even with help, Danny still managed to stub his toe, hit his shin, and walk into someone.

It took another hour to get through the hospital paperwork. They loaded him up with phone numbers and pamphlets he couldn't read. There was more discussion of rehab and that Martha woman. Beth made him another appointment with the neurologist and one for another MRI and then they were free to go.

Except he'd never be free again unless he got his sight back. Always helpless. Always dependent on someone.

Beth took his arm, her touch reinforcing his despair.

"What time is it?"

"Five thirty five."

"In the morning?"

"At night."

So he'd been there all night and all day. No wonder he felt keyed up and exhausted.

"Who's with the kids?"

"I dropped them next door."

Guilt swarmed him. He'd been watching out for his baby sister for as long as he could remember. Having her watch out for him set his whole world upside down.

"Look, I can call a cab. You go home and take care of the kids."

"Shut up, will you? Geez. I'm not letting go of you, so get used to it. Nothing you can do about it. Damn stupid man." She muttered the last, but he heard her. "All right.

Here's the door coming up. Two steps. That's right." She talked him through and the sting of winter air bit into his face. He gulped in exhaust and old snow. They were outside.

"Wait here," she told him. "I'll get the car."

He opened his mouth to protest that she didn't have to pick him up like some damned cripple, then didn't. It would be easier and faster for her to get the car by herself.

He stood awkwardly, afraid to take a step in any direction. Someone rushed by him.

"Hey, pal," whoever it was murmured. "Watch where you're going."

He projected himself into the darkness, trying to see himself standing there, hands fisted tight to keep from howling.

A car pulled up, a door slammed. Then Beth was at his side. She led him to the car like he was a child, and he felt his way around the door and seat. She shut the door behind him and seconds later, slid behind the wheel. The car moved off, picked up speed. It was a strange, eerie feeling, hurtling through a void, no way to judge direction, suspended in deep space, running faster than sight.

Silence hovered between them. He didn't know what to say and he imagined Beth didn't either. It was all too unbelievable.

"The social worker at the hospital said she was setting you up with some kind of instructor," Beth said at last. "Did she?"

"Someone came around, yeah."

"And?"

"And what?"

"And what did you arrange?"

He hesitated. He knew he was in for another fight and didn't have the energy. "I didn't."

"What do you mean?"

"I don't need any damn instruction. This is temporary. I'm going to be fine."

Beth didn't respond, but that was response enough.

Ten minutes later, the car slanted up a slope and stopped. The garage door scraped open.

"I'm going to pull into the garage," she said. "Wait there and I'll come get you."

But he was sick of being led around by the nose. Once the car was parked, he got out himself.

"Danny, wait—"

But he was already feeling his way along the wall. He ran into something that fell over with a metallic crash.

"Oh God," Beth said. "Are you all right?" She was beside him again. "There are rakes and shovels here. Hold on while I clear a path."

Holding his hand and creeping slowly, she guided him into the house. He pictured the narrow back hallway with the washing machine and dryer on the left. If it looked the way it usually did, there'd be a laundry basket somewhere on the floor, dirty or clean clothes spilling over. His toe hit it, and Beth pulled him to the left to avoid it.

"Up a step," she said and he smelled old coffee and cooked onions. They were in the kitchen. Two more steps and he groped for a chair. Collapsed into it. He was sweating.

"I'm just going to call Debbie and ask her to bring the kids over."

"Look, you don't have to check in with me every minute."

"I'm sorry. I just . . . I just don't know how to behave. What to say. What to do."

Her voice clogged with tears and his chest contracted again.

"I don't know either, babe," he said softly.

Was she staring at him? He turned his head away but she put her arms around him.

"I love you, Danny."

He held her tight and sighed. "Go get the kids." His voice came out rough and choked.

He heard them the minute they came in the house. Nine-year-old Josh and five-year-old Katie. A whirlwind of sound, of voices, footsteps, and energy.

"Is he here?" Josh was asking.

"Do his eyes hurt?" Katie said.

"Shh, now we talked about this," Beth said in a low voice. "Don't be rude."

"But I want to see," Katie said.

He braced himself for the onslaught. "I'm in here!" Footsteps pounded as the children ran into the kitchen.

"Josh, Katie!" Beth called after them.

"Uncle Danny!"

Before he could say anything Katie scrambled onto his lap. He didn't know where Josh was.

"Come on, now, Katie, get down," Beth scolded.

Katie ignored her and he let her settle. Small hands brushed his face.

"They're still pretty," Katie said, her little fingers tracing his brows.

"You really can't see?" That was Josh. His voice was close as though he'd stopped just short of Danny's chair.

"God, I'm sorry, Danny," Beth said.

"It's okay," he said to Beth. And to the kids, "The eyes are fine. It's my brain that's messed up."

"Wow," Josh said solemnly.

Katie knocked on his head. "Are you going to be stupid now?"

"Katie!" Beth said.

"I hope not," Danny said. "It's just that the part of my brain that sees things is plugged up."

"You should get Drano," Katie said.

"Is it going to get unplugged?" Anxiety tinged Josh's voice. "You promised to teach me how to pitch this summer."

A small vise grabbed hold of him and twisted sharp. "Summer's a long ways away, Josh. We'll see."

"You won't," said Katie with a giggle.

"Okay, that's enough," Beth said, and lifted the little girl off his lap. "Go wash your hands. Dinner will be ready in ten minutes. You, too, Josh."

Dinner proved a minor disaster. He knocked over the milk carton, then spilled his coffee and heard Josh yelp in pain. Instinctively, he leaped up to help, overturned his chair, got tangled in it, and went sprawling.

Katie laughed, but Josh burst into tears and while Beth went after her son, Danny sat on the floor, helpless and angry.

"You're funny, Uncle Danny." He felt her crawl onto his lap and put her head on his shoulder.

"Yeah, Katie, I guess I am." One big, fat, blind joke.

Beth returned a few minutes later. "You've got milk and coffee on your jeans. Take them off and I'll wash them."

"That's okay. I got a spare somewhere. Josh all right?"

"He's fine. Really. He's in his room. He . . . he's just having trouble with all this. He still remembers Frank leaving. I don't know. Your . . . losing your sight somehow brings it all back. Be patient with him."

Danny nodded numbly. "Sure. No problem."

"Katie, why don't you take Uncle Danny to his room," Beth said in an overly bright voice.

"Okay." The little girl slipped her hand into his. "Come on, Uncle Danny."

Between the two of them they managed to get to the room he always stayed in when he slept over. He did that a couple of nights a week. Making sure Beth was all right, the kids okay.

Danny fished his wallet and ID out of his pants and unhooked his cell phone. He slid off the wet jeans and rummaged around the closet until his fingers closed on something that felt like denim. He traced the shape—a waist and two legs. Gingerly, he slipped them on. They fit.

Feeling his way to the bed again, he lay down, every speck of him weary. The usual drill after an undercover buyback was a return to the station—preferably with the gun and the perp—recover his duty weapon and back up, and process the collar before going home. He never went to bed alone. If he didn't have a woman for company, he had his North American minirevolver, a five-shot .22 Magnum, which he never slept without.

But he hadn't made it back to the station. And he hadn't gone home. For the first time in he couldn't remember when, he was unarmed. Naked, exposed, his dick shriveled in humiliation.

And if he did have his mini? A queasy shudder ran through him. Without sight, his judgment would be gone. He'd likely shoot Josh or Beth as an intruder. Or his own foot off.

He closed his eyes, the dark no darker either way. He

forced himself to relive the scene at dinner. Blackness closing in like a suffocating blanket, reaching and hitting everything but what he wanted, spilling food and drink like a baby.

He could have hurt someone. Burned Josh, landed on Katie.

He bit down hard on the rage that wanted to boil up and out of his mouth. Clutching the cell phone, he felt carefully for the keypad. In his head he heard the dry, quiet voice deal out the number.

All twos except for that four in front.

It took him several tries, but eventually his fingers found the buttons.

CHAPTER 2

By the time Martha finished her reports, updated her patient files, and checked her schedule for the next few days, the sun had long set and everyone else had gone home.

Nothing new there. She often stayed late, eventually lugging her purse and a canvas tote filled with files and notebooks down night quiet hallways.

Tonight the bag felt heavier than usual. The encounter with Danny Sinofsky had tired her out. With those hauntingly beautiful dead eyes, his face hovered in the back of her mind even as she tried to forget it.

She got in her car, looking forward to the safety of home. She called to tell her dad to take the chili out of the fridge and start heating it up, but no one answered. She called the shop to find out if he was working late, but no one answered there, either.

A thread of worry tugged at her. It was probably nothing. Maybe he was out playing cards. Or he had stopped by the hardware store and got to talking. There were a thousand and one things he could be doing.

But she dropped by the Craftsman anyway. The dim bar smelled the way it always did—of beer and smoke—and the jukebox wailed what seemed like the same old Johnny

Cash tune every time she came. She stood inside the doorway, all the bad memories converging on her. The necessity of calling a cab because she was too young to drive herself, the embarrassment of the driver always knowing who she was and where she was going, the humiliation of coaxing her father out of the bar and into the cab, the wheelchair always a problem. Her father hadn't been on a real drunk for years, yet she was always on the edge waiting for him to fall off that cliff again.

Quickly, she scanned the bar's occupants, but her father wasn't among them.

"Hey, Martha," said the burly bartender, Cal, a man with a thick neck and a goatee that didn't hide his double chin.

She slid onto a bar stool. Someone had made an effort to honor the season with a couple of jack-o'-lantern cutouts and a big black cat that hung over one side of the bar. On the other side was an election poster that said VOTE.

"My dad been here?"

"You just missed him."

Her heart took a dive, but she bucked up quickly. Face facts. Deal with them. "He behave himself?"

"Oh, yeah." Cal grinned. "Charlie Crowe is always a gentleman."

She snorted. Not a description that often came to mind when talking about her dad.

"He was fine. A couple of beers, that's all. I'd have called you if it looked like he was heading for trouble."

The screw inside her unwound. "Thanks."

"He was in a mood, though."

"A mood?"

Cal shrugged. "Quiet. Like he had something big to think about." He grinned. "Asked me if I thought you were happy."

She blinked. Her father had never seemed to care if she was happy or not. "Me?"

"I told you—he was in a mood. Get you something?"

She let out a long breath. What was Charlie Crowe up to? "No. I'd better get back."

"Long day?"

She nodded, noting ruefully that her day must be written all over her face. Then she caught a glimpse of herself in the mirror behind him and saw why. Half her hair had come undone from its top knot at the back of her head and now hung in a flyaway mass over one shoulder. Black as tar with the texture of straw, it often came loose but she was always surprised to realize it.

Cal left to pour a drink for someone else, and she quickly tucked the cascading hair back into the knot.

Surreptitiously she watched a group playing darts. Fine looking young men with jeans and smiles and muscled arms, their dates lithe and pretty in short, flippy skirts and heeled black boots.

She tore her gaze away. Must be something in the air; she was catching Charlie's mood and she'd given up brooding long ago. That face, that dark, intensely masculine movie star face had brought this on.

For a moment she took herself back. Remembered what it felt like to be eighteen. To long to be noticed. Admired. Sought after.

She shuddered, glad that part of her life was over, and waved good-bye to Cal. She was not going to sit there, stewing. She'd made a fine life for herself. Damn anyone who said otherwise.

She hadn't quite reached the door when her cell phone rang.

"Martha Crowe," she said.

"This is Danny Sinofsky. You said to call."

His voice came through the line, deep and resonant. It sent a shiver skimming up her back, and she stiffened her spine against it.

"I have time tomorrow morning," she said brusquely.

A slight pause, as though he wasn't sure he wanted to do this. She waited. He probably didn't.

"Nine o'clock." He gave her the address and, without another word, disconnected.

Martha stared at the phone, but it didn't apologize for the caller's rudeness.

She pushed through the door and the cold slapped her face with an icy hand. He was not going to make this easy. Either for her or himself.

Her father was still out when she got home, but he'd left a note saying he was playing cards and wouldn't be back until late. At least he was not in trouble.

She heated some of the leftover chili in the microwave and ate it while she watched a rerun of *Extreme Makeover*.

The episode was one of her favorites. It featured a police officer who said her face looked worse than the corpses she encountered. A secret, guilty pleasure, the show was a beast-to-beauty fantasy she couldn't resist, though she'd die if anyone knew it. She watched avidly, her heart beating faster at the end when the drab, homely woman at the beginning came out looking like a superstar.

When the show was over, she went upstairs and washed her face, keeping the image of the beautiful transformed blonde in her head. She brushed her teeth, changed into pajamas, and crawled into bed. From her tote she picked out and reviewed the files she'd need for the next day. Because he was her first client, she read Danny Sinofsky's last. The notes she'd made blurred into a vision of his hostile, panicked face, and she fell asleep dreaming about ocean-filled eyes.

In the morning, she showered and dressed, pulling on the first things her hand touched in the dresser: matching brown slacks and tunic. The clothes slid over her skinny six-foot frame. She pushed her narrow size twelves into a pair of scuffed brown loafers and attacked her hair.

It took her three tries to organize her stiff mane into a neat twist at the back of her head. Forced to confront the mirror, she saw a plain face, straightforward, no nonsense, with everything oversized. She'd long ago given up makeup, daring the world to take her as she was: large eyes, wide mouth, strong nose, long jaw. The Wicked Witch, they'd called her at school. Or Scare Crowe.

She grumbled as once again her hair fell out of its pins. Finally, she gave up and shoved it all behind a blue stretch headband.

Downstairs, her father was hunched in his wheelchair, nursing a morning cup of coffee over the kitchen table. She could smell the smoke on him, and a jab of irritation bit her. Charlie Crowe was past fifty and still behaved like a teenager.

"Morning, Daddy." She wondered where he'd stashed the cigarettes and why he thought he was fooling her.

"Martha."

"Did you have breakfast?"

"No."

She grabbed a box of cornflakes, a bowl, a spoon, and a carton of milk from the fridge, all of which she set down in front of him. She did this automatically, the way she'd done every morning since she was twelve. "Eat."

He grunted, sipped his coffee, and ignored her. His hair, once as black as hers, was pulled back into a long braid and heathered with gray. Her own wide mouth and prominent nose sat squarely on his long face.

"You're starched up this morning," he said. "Where is Generalissimo Crowe going today?"

She ignored the dig, sat down, and poured cereal into her bowl. "I have a new client." She pictured Danny Sinofsky and a rumble of apprehension went through her.

"Ahh," her father said. "Time to batten down the hatches." As usual, he wore a T-shirt with the sleeves ripped out. His arms, tattooed with a skull and crossbones when he was eighteen, and with her own name a year later, bulged with power, in stark contrast to his withered legs.

"Dad, don't start with me."

He held up his hands in surrender, palms outward. The tips on his right were yellowed, nicotine-stained. "I didn't say a word."

"You didn't have to."

"But now that you mention it, I saw Arnie Gould last night and he did say he might be free for dinner." Arnie Gould was one of the new guys down at the bike shop. For the last thirty years, except for the bad times after the accident, her dad had lived and breathed motorcycles. Fixing, rebuilding, and eventually designing. After he'd lost the use of his legs, the shop had saved his life.

"There's still chili left over."

Charlie sipped at his coffee. "I was hoping we could do better than leftover chili."

She stared at him, puzzled, and he avoided her gaze. She put down her spoon. "I stopped at the bar last night and Cal said you were asking him about me. What is going on?"

He shrugged. "Nothing. I just thought I'd invite—"

"Well, then, fine. There's chili in the—"

"You could make that chicken thing. Maybe put on a dress."

A dress. "I see." But she didn't. Not really. Her dad had never been concerned about her social life before. And he'd never, not once, tried to matchmake.

Her father squirmed in his chair. "He's a nice guy. You'll like him. Good job. Never been married."

"Dad—"

"It's just dinner."

Her stomach lurched. It was never just dinner. It was an auction block, a runway competition. "I'm busy."

"You're never busy."

"Trust me, I'm busy." She pushed back her chair, dumped what was left of her cereal into the garbage, and rinsed out the bowl.

She poured her coffee into a travel mug and slipped out of the kitchen. Her father rolled his wheelchair to the doorway, his smoke-tinged voice following her.

"One of these days I'm not going to be around to keep you company, Martha."

"Well, I hope we enjoy the time we have left together then," she called as she got her coat out of the closet and went out the door.

Charlie Crowe watched his daughter go. She was a tall woman, not pretty by any stretch of the imagination. Life might have been easier if she'd been small and fair like her mother, but when was life ever easy? She hacked a damn trail through the world, he'd give her that. Never saw a back straighter, a set of eyes more keen to see things as they were, or a heart with more walls around it.

Not that he could blame her for that. He had plenty of walls of his own. And fences breed fences.

He wished things had been different. Wished he'd been less selfish or less heartbroken.

He reached into his pocket and pulled out a crumpled sheet of paper, which he carefully unfolded and smoothed over his lap. The page was covered in childish handwriting. He'd found it a week ago when he'd run out of cigarettes and was rummaging through all his hiding places. It had been shoved at the back of a drawer, lost and forgotten, and carefully dated at the top: "June 3, 1987," more than two years after his accident and eighteen months after Ginny had walked out the door.

> *Dear Mommy,*
>
> *School is almost over. I have three more weeks. The sun is out now all the time. Daddy likes the sun. He sits on the porch in the sun and smokes. I don't let him smoke in the house because I know you don't like it. The house smells very pretty all the time now.*
>
> *Every night I pick out my clothes and lay them on the chair so I can dress in the morning. I am being very good. I make Daddy breakfast every day and I make my own lunch.*
>
> *I know you will be home soon. I miss you. Daddy misses you, too. He doesn't drink as much.*
>
> *I'm glad I'm here and not with Aunt Nancy anymore. She says my feet are too big.*
>
> *But now I'm home with Daddy and I'm keeping the house perfect so you'll want to come home soon. Me and Daddy miss you.*
>
> *Love,*
> *Martha*

Charlie refolded the letter. It crushed his chest to think what living with his goddamn prissy sister-in-law must have been like. But Martha had needed to live with someone, he was in and out of the hospital and Ginny had left. Her sister seemed the logical choice, though she and Nancy had never gotten along. But calling the kid names. Made him crazy, fucking damn crazy to think about it.

Not that he didn't share the blame. He'd been so full of self-pity and sorrow he hadn't paid much attention to Martha. How long had she clung to the hope that her mother would return? His kid had grown up under his nose and he'd scarcely noticed it.

He hoped it wasn't too late now. He put the letter back in his pocket. He owed her. Big time. He just hoped to God he could damn well make it up to her.

Martha waited for her car to heat up while she double-checked the address. It was in a suburb just outside the Sokanan city limits. Not exactly what she'd expected from the man she'd met the evening before. That man had seemed all city, a night owl, lurking in concrete and shadows. But the address clearly indicated an aging area riddled with subdivisions built in the seventies.

It would take her fifteen minutes to get there, longer if she got stuck in traffic. In the year since Renaissance Oil had remodeled the old GE plant into their corporate headquarters, construction—from new apartment complexes to new office buildings—was everywhere. And the cranes, trucks, and crews could easily complicate the simplest trip.

The steering wheel was icy to the touch, and she thought about running back to the house for a pair of gloves. But that meant facing Charlie again. And she had enough to face this morning without another argument about her social life.

She started the engine, flipped on the radio to drown out

the nervous drone humming inside her, and heard that the national threat assessment had been taken one color higher, though no one would say why. The governor was hitting the campaign trail hard, in what everyone said was going to be a losing battle in the election that was only a few weeks away. Snow was predicted for later that afternoon. She winced. It was the middle of October, too soon for snow. She had a department meeting at the rehab center that afternoon, plus two other home visits. Snow would be a royal pain.

She waited out the news and was rewarded with a Haydn concerto, which took her all the way to Danny Sinofsky's drive. She sat in the car for a few seconds, gripped the wheel, and steeled herself.

God, you'd think she was facing evil incarnate instead of an ordinary man. One she knew at that.

Leaving her tote in the backseat, she grabbed a cane from the trunk and tramped up the walkway. A pumpkin sat to one side of the door and a cardboard skeleton hung down the middle. She rang the bell.

It took him a long time to get to the door, but she waited patiently. She imagined everything would take him a long time until he learned how to get around.

"Who is it?" His deep voice through the door set a metronome thumping in her chest.

"Martha Crowe." She braced herself and the door swung open.

Her breath caught. No matter how much she prepared for it, she was still shaken by the sight of him. Those eyes shone clear and deep against his tan skin and inky hair. They were so magnificent, she would have sworn he could still see with them. His chiseled jaw was clean-shaven today—had he been helped with that? His jeans were cleaner than those of the day before, slung low and molded over his hips. His white T-shirt stretched tight over the beautiful plane of his chest.

"Miss Crowe?" His voice was stiff and his gaze looked above her.

She shook herself out of her ridiculous daze and confronted him coolly, professionally. "You said nine." Immediately, his head swiveled in the direction of her voice. People who were blind from birth didn't always do that. But someone who'd been sighted for years was socially conditioned to face his interlocutor. "I'm a little early."

"Yeah, you are. Like a lifetime." His voice was rough and angry. Just as it had been the night before.

"Excuse me?"

"I've changed my mind."

She blinked, shoved her frigid hands in her coat pockets, and reined in her patience. "Look, it's cold. Do you mind if I come in?"

He hesitated, then with obvious reluctance, stepped back, but only enough to let her slip by. She knew it was because he wasn't sure of his surroundings, but it forced her to slither past, so close, they breathed the same air.

If you could call what she was doing breathing.

She made herself concentrate on the room. Two trucks and a Barbie doll littered the floor. A pair of small shoes rested by the door. An open box of crayons sat on a chair. All that would have to change.

And then it hit her. What the Halloween decorations and the mess meant.

He was married. He had children.

The knowledge sped through her like a river of relief. All at once she felt safe from him, his wife and family a solid barrier.

"How many children do you have?" Rapidly she calculated how much more time she'd have to spend with the family, teaching them as well as him.

"None." The word was crisp, the meaning confusing.

"I don't understand. The toys, the—"

"This is my sister's house. She has two kids. I stayed here last night."

Her body suddenly tensed up again.

"Will you be . . . will you be staying here permanently then?"

"Not if I can help it. I have a small house downtown. Not too far from the station. Just bought it." A trace of bitterness there. "I was going to call a cab to take me home. No point getting comfortable here. Not when I have my own place."

"I'll drive you."

"That's nice of you, but I'll be fine."

"No, you won't."

His face hardened. "Jesus, you don't mince words."

"Do you want me to?"

He didn't answer. Should she back off? But it wasn't like her to give up, not when she knew he needed help and she could provide it. "Look, I'm here. I have a car. It's crazy to pay for a cab. You're already paying me." Or his disability insurance was.

"Not for long."

"Well, get your money's worth today."

He sighed, rubbed two fingers over his brow.

"Headache?"

Instantly, he stopped massaging his forehead, as though it were another sign of weakness. "Nice little leftover from the . . . the stroke. Doc said it would go away in a few days."

"Does your sister have any aspirin?"

"Probably. Somewhere. But I don't need—"

She didn't wait for the rest of his denial. "Wait here. I'll find some."

She located a bottle of aspirin in a cupboard above the kitchen sink and filled a glass with water.

"Here." She grabbed his hand, turned it palm up and thrust the medicine in it. "Three aspirin and water." Without ceremony, she placed the glass in his other hand. "The glass is only half full," she added.

His mouth thinned. "You are one bossy little miss, aren't you?"

"Take the damn aspirin, detective. I promise it won't kill you."

For a moment he stood there, jaw tight. Then he downed the pills. When he was done, he stood awkwardly holding the glass.

"There's a table about five steps to your left. Next to the couch."

He followed her directions, groped for the table, all arms and seeking hands, and carefully set down the glass. He stood with his back to her, rigid, unmoving. Was he afraid of knocking something over?

She opened her mouth to direct him again, but he spoke. "I nearly burned my nephew with hot coffee last night."

His words were apropos of nothing, but she understood. "Yes. You can be a danger to others as well as yourself."

He squared his shoulders and, as if preparing for battle, turned awkwardly and gave her a curt nod. "All right."

She took a breath, arming herself in turn. "Where's your coat?"

He thought for a minute. "I have no idea. Beth did something with it last night."

"Is there a closet I can look? It's cold out."

"In the hallway."

She found the closet, riffled through it, but saw only kid-sized jackets.

"Didn't find anything," she told him when she returned. "Anyplace else it might be?"

His brows furrowed in an impatient scowl. "Look, can we just go? I want to get home."

Beneath the growl, she sensed an edgy nervousness that she didn't want to stretch any tighter. "Fine." She positioned herself next to him and he flinched away.

"What are you doing?"

"Take my arm. Above the elbow. Fingers on the inside, thumb on the outside."

"Why?"

"Look, we can fight over every little detail, or we can—"

"Just follow orders?"

She raised her chin, though he couldn't see. "You'll learn faster that way."

"Yeah, but it's been a long time since my army days."

She repressed a sigh. "It's called sighted or human guide. The blind person holds on, as I've said, stands a half step behind, and the guide leads him or her. You won't trip or fall or bump into anything this way."

"I hold on. Like a baby."

"Like a person who has lost their sight."

"Stop saying that."

"Stop denying it."

They were at another impasse. "If you prefer, we can start with the cane," she said. "That would allow you almost complete independence."

His face visibly blanched.

"Above my elbow." She couldn't help a private smile when he wrapped his hand around her.

His grip was firm, his hand strong on her arm. She was aware of him at her shoulder, his body hard and powerful.

"You're trembling."

Heat flooded her face and she was glad he couldn't note it. "I am not."

"Now who's doing the denying?"

He was looking down at her, an odd little curve to the outer corners of his mouth. She reminded herself he could not see her, no matter how intensely he looked.

"How old are you?" he asked.

She swallowed. "I'll be fifty-eight next February," she lied, her voice as prim as she could make it.

His half smile faltered in confusion. "Getting a bit long in the tooth for this kind of thing?"

"I'm perfectly fine. Ready?"

Once inside the car, he gave her directions, another blessing of which he was probably unaware. Blind people don't drive, so they rarely know how to get from one place to the other. Someone like him, someone who'd been sighted all his life, had a much better feel for the physical world and was one step ahead of those who'd been born without sight.

Of course, they had no adjustments to make, while he . . .

But first steps were usually the hardest and he'd already taken his.

The radio came on with the car engine. Another news report repeating the same news about the governor's reelection.

Thinking to engage him in something other than his own trauma, she asked, "Think Henley is going to win?"

He shrugged. "Doesn't look like it."

"That good or bad?"

"I don't know. Don't imagine I'll have much say in it."

"Why? Don't you vote?"

"Used to."

"You lost your sight, detective, not your brain."

He didn't reply, only stared straight ahead as if he wanted to burn a hole in the windshield.

Another wave of pity shook her, along with a lost memory: Danny lounging against a row of lockers outside her English class, surrounded by a bunch of his friends. She'd passed them by, ducking her head, pulse pounding, hoping against hope that they wouldn't notice her. Or if they did, that they'd ignore her. No such luck. One of them had whistled at her, low and mocking. Someone else had called her Scare Crowe.

But Danny had punched the name caller lightly in the arm. "Cut it out," he'd said, and won her heart.

But though his words had meant the world to her, they'd meant nothing to him — just a passing act of momentary kindness.

God, she thought she'd cremated those memories, incinerated them and scattered their ashes to the winds.

A lot had changed since then. Not the least of which was her. She had taken off her rose-colored glasses and stopped daydreaming. The world was a serious place and she had a serious place in it. People who needed her, who couldn't care less what she looked like.

But still, she couldn't deny the tortured pleasure of having him in the car. To look at him whenever she liked and enjoy the sheer wonder of his face.

Without his knowing.

A sprig of guilt brushed her. She was spying on him. Ogling him behind his back.

To combat it, she broke the silence. "I understand from the medical report that your stroke began with a neck injury. How did that happen?"

Danny sat still, not wanting to talk about it even as the scene unfolded in his imagination. The Dutchman, run-down and seedy, left behind when business moved to other parts of town. The small crowd inside: players huddled in a corner doing a clandestine but steady stream of drug business, petty hustlers hanging by the pool table, lost souls and those looking for direction in a glass hunched over the bar. Murray Potts behind it, gnarled and scrawny, a day's growth of grizzle on his chin, presiding over the whole like an oily wizard.

"I was doing a drug sweep," he said at last. "Things got a little out of control. A couple of drunks decided to stage Custer's Last Stand and fight to the death. We had a bit of a free-for-all, and I got drilled. Don't even know by who."

It was all a blur in his memory. Things had started out calm, he had the suspected offenders under control. Someone came out from the back where the restrooms were; he didn't know who exactly, because he noticed movement only out of the corner of his eye, but it distracted him. And in that moment, all hell broke loose.

"That happen a lot?"

"What?" For a minute he thought she was talking about that momentary distraction, and he tensed. If he'd made any mistakes, that was it. And no matter how many times he told himself it wasn't his fault, the accusation stuck.

But he'd be damned if he took the same from someone who'd never been on the line, never got down in the gutter with the skells and the scumbags, someone who smelled like spring even in the middle of winter.

"Getting . . . drilled."

He'd worked himself up to a good bit of resentment, and her answer took the wind out of him. Ruefully, he shook his head. "Actually, no. First time. Lucky me."

She was silent. "How long have you been a police officer?"

This was starting to feel like an interrogation, her voice floating out of the darkness, insubstantial, bodiless. Meanwhile, the car chugged and hummed, tires spinning over road, hurtling him forward without any sense of where he was going. "Why? What's it matter?"

"I just thought . . . if we're going to work together, it wouldn't hurt to know something about each other."

"How long have you been the blind man's helper?"

If he'd annoyed her, she didn't let on. "Eight years."

"Got a late start."

"Excuse me?"

"You're fifty-eight. Working eight years. Sounds like a late start to me."

"Yes, I . . . I suppose it is." She cleared her throat, sounded uncomfortable, and he let the subject drop. If she didn't want to talk about her late start, what the hell did he care?

Except to wonder at the luxury of taking your time. One he'd never had. He'd been an early bloomer, an adult with responsibilities ever since he could remember. And now what? How the hell was he going to take care of anything now?

"Been a cop for seven years. Did a stint in the army, came home, joined up."

Short, succinct. A few words to describe a lifetime. He

thought of Beth, of the years spent watching over her so their mother could wear herself out working three jobs to clothe and feed them both. He thought of the time after she died, when Beth had been his alone to care for. Thanks to Parnell, Danny had been able to keep Beth with him until he graduated from high school and found a dull but steady job in a trailer factory, stapling chipboard walls together. He'd worked for her, kept her in school, and done it gladly, without thinking. She was his sister, all he had left.

But when she married Frank, Danny didn't waste much time before enlisting. He had four years of freedom, of pleasing himself, before Frank ran off and Beth was alone again, this time with two kids. So he'd come home. And now, Christ, he couldn't think about what would happen if he didn't get his sight back.

"I'm turning down your street now." Martha Crowe's voice sliced into the merciless anxiety.

He conjured up his street. The aging houses built when neighbors knew each other, strolled down sidewalks, and stopped to chat, houses with porches and turrets and thick-trunked trees. Some remodeled, others still in poor condition.

"You've done a nice job with the renovation."

He pictured the porch, which still sagged a bit, and the paint job, which was new—blue, yellow, and white like icing on a cake. He ached to think he'd never see it again.

"Not me. Bought it that way from another guy in the detective division. Hank Bonner. He got married and sold it. Got a sweet deal on it, but he did all the work. I'm not much with a hammer."

"It's very pretty. I'd like to see the inside."

He sat still, refusing to take the bait.

Not that it mattered to the damned woman. Evidently she didn't need an invitation. Her car door opened.

"Wait." He tensed and rammed a hand against the dash, hard enough to crack his knuckles. "Look, can we . . . can we skip the arm holding?"

"It's safer that way." He heard the schoolteacher's reprimand in her voice.

"I . . ." Christ, his throat wasn't working.

"Excuse me?"

"I don't . . ."

"You don't what?"

He pounded the dash. "I don't want anyone to see!"

His outburst brought silence. "It's no shame," she said quietly.

"Not for you."

Martha paused, the truth of that hitting home. She knew what it was like to feel like a freak. It had been a long time, but she hadn't forgotten.

"All right. I'll come around and—"

But he was already opening the door and getting out. When she came to him, he was leaning against the car, huddling in his thin shirt, the wind making a mockery of his dark hair.

She took his arm instead of the other way around, guiding him softly with her voice. "Step here. One more. Three steps to the door."

He fished in his pocket for the keys and she watched him fumble with them. He muttered a curse—he cursed a lot, she realized—and she made a note to help him mark his keys. He didn't ask for help and she didn't volunteer. It was good that he wanted to do for himself. Showed guts and determination.

At last he held one out.

"Is it gold?"

"Yes. Short and stubby."

He felt around the doorknob and fitted it into the lock. The key turned and he smiled.

She couldn't believe what that smile did to his face. His teeth were white against the tan, the eyes sparkling. Such a small thing, to bring so much sunshine.

She looked away and followed him inside.

CHAPTER 3

D anny let Martha work him as long as he could, although he had no idea how long that was. Without knowing where the sun was, what the sky looked like, where the hands of a clock were, time no longer had meaning. His whole world narrowed down to Martha's voice, soft and calm, with a musical lilt he would have enjoyed in other circumstances. Now it overwhelmed, pushing him, badgering him.

"Keep your arm low and trail the back of your hand to judge the contours of walls and the perimeter of the room."

"Curl your fingers inward. Let your knuckles do the work."

"Visualize."

He wanted to scream.

Yet she was patient. And she smelled good. Too damn good for someone old enough to be his mother. The clean, grassy scent, along with her voice, registered much younger than fifty-eight.

Then again, he had no idea how to judge a woman by the sound of her voice or the scent of her perfume. Just one more damn skill he'd have to learn. In the meantime, he walked his house over and over again, mapping it out in his head until he could get almost anywhere without tripping or running into things.

That was a triumph, and she said so, her voice puffed with encouragement. "You're doing very well." He heard the smile and wanted to smash it.

"Yeah. I can actually get around my own house."

"It would be even easier with the cane."

"No."

A short pause. "I'll leave it on the table next to the front door in case you change your mind."

"I won't."

"Fine."

He listened for disapproval and heard only the same calm, straightforward tone that made him want to shout: *I'm blind, you bitch. Feel something. I'm fucking blind.*

He fingered the edge of the couch, the velvety fabric smooth as suede, and made sure it was clear. "I'm tired." He sat. "I've had enough. Go away."

"I really should—"

"Get out."

"Being blind doesn't give you an excuse to be a bastard." The words were stiff, the tone cold.

He didn't give a damn. "Yeah? Well, I think it does."

Her clothes rustled, setting off that strange, compelling scent. Was she arching her back, getting ready to spit at him? "I'll check back with you this afternoon," was all she said.

Her footsteps clacked on the wood floor, then disappeared into carpet. The front door opened and closed, and the silence shut him in.

He leaned forward, resting elbows on his knees, and ran fingers through his hair. When he woke this morning he'd opened his eyes in the vain hope that the darkness would be gone and life returned to normal.

What the hell was he going to do?

Tears and panic choked him.

No such thing as a blind cop.

But he'd invested everything into being a cop. He was good at it. And besides handling a staple gun, it was the only thing he knew.

The thought of sitting here in this house day after day, living off disability, growing moss like he'd seen some guys do, made his stomach writhe.

He pounded the arm of the couch, then hit it again, then again—over and over—violence rising in him until it erupted in a vicious howl. He screamed at the creep who'd hit him, screamed at the universe, screamed until he was panting and shaking uncontrollably.

Abruptly, he stood, tracking the thirty steps to the bedroom on wobbly legs. Sweating and breathing hard, he trailed his hand along the wall, found the closet and, bending down, searched the floor. He visualized the things his fingers encountered—sneakers, cleats, baseball glove, shoeboxes. He upended all the boxes, cursing when he encountered only shoes, until finally he found the one with the .38 detective special.

He pictured it: a small, wicked-looking gun, black with a solid heft and an easy grip. He brought it back to the kitchen, propped himself on a stool by the counter and ran his fingers over the cylinder. He swung it open, so he could feel for the bullets inside. Six shots. A full load.

His body went cold, a welcome numbness. He could end it here. Right now. Wouldn't take but one squeeze of the trigger and he'd be free.

He thought back to the scene at the warehouse. If his

eyes hadn't gone out briefly, if he hadn't stumbled, would all this be behind him now?

He reset the cylinder, heard the solid click that signaled the gun was ready.

Another noise penetrated. A scratching, metallic sound. One he might never have heard if his senses had been overloaded with visual stimulation. Now that he was no longer able to see, his hearing had sharpened.

Someone was at the door.

He groaned. He could not go another round with Mother Crowe.

But if it were Martha, why didn't she knock? Ring the bell?

He stashed the .38 at his back, and trailing walls, edged up to the door. Felt the knob. It was turning. Someone was trying to get in.

Instantly, he froze. He was helpless, blind, running was his only option. But it was too late for that. The door creaked open.

He leaped into the corner, hoping to God he was hidden behind the door.

A heavy step. Cautious, careful. Another.

Not Martha. Her step was lighter. The intruder was a man. And he smelled of cold air and something else, something minty, medicinal.

Danny pulled the gun from his waistband and waited for one more step. Three steps, and the man would be clear of the doorway. Danny inhaled, anchored his hand on the door and stepped out.

"Hands up," he said.

The man's weight shifted and Danny located his position by the sound. "Don't move!" He thrust the gun forward and it was stopped by a hard plane. Back, not belly. *Thank you,*

God. If he kept the man's face away from him, maybe he could maintain the illusion that he could see what he was doing.

Heart thudding, Danny searched, his fingers finding jacket, sweater, empty shoulder holster.

"Throw down your weapon." A second of silence. Danny shoved his gun deeper into the man's back. "Now! Throw it down!" A metallic thud to Danny's left. How far? Too far for him to reach? Christ, he had no idea.

"Hands on your head." Danny placed his hands between the man's shoulders and shoved him hard. "On your knees."

The man stumbled to the floor with a grunt, and Danny grabbed a handful of hair, pulled his head back, and pressed the gun behind his ear. "Who are you?"

The man was breathing hard, Danny could smell the sweat and fear on him.

"Who the fuck are you?"

A footstep from outside. The man stiffened.

A knock and a door opened. "Detective Sinofsky?"

Jesus fucking Christ. Martha.

"I saw someone come in and was wondering if you needed—"

"Martha, don't—"

Too late. The man jerked away. Danny leaped into nothingness, his arms catching air.

Martha yelped. A thud. A body falling? Whose? Danny's heart galloped wildly.

Footsteps pounded down the porch.

The gun was heavy in Danny's hand, but he couldn't see to shoot. What had happened? What should he do? Who was down?

A moan.

"Martha? Are you all right? Where are you? Dammit, where—"

"Here. I'm—"

"Christ, don't move. Stay down." He felt for her, found her feet and legs. She was on the floor.

"I—"

"Stay down!" Cold air washed over him; the front door must still be open. He covered her with his body, wrapped his arms around her, and hoped to hell his back was between her and the door.

An engine roared, tires squealed away.

Silence.

"I think . . . I think he's gone," Martha said in a small voice.

Only then did he feel the curves against him, the small, soft breasts and rounded hips that didn't feel anything like what he imagined a fifty-something woman's body would feel.

Quickly, he released her. "You okay?"

"I think so." But her voice was shaky. "He . . . he hit me, but—"

"He hit you? Son of a bitch," he muttered. "Here, let me—" He was going to say "see," but didn't. Instead, he ran his hands over her face.

"Don't," she said in that same unsteady voice.

"Shut up and sit still."

Her skin was smooth and soft, no wrinkles or sagginess. Not what he expected from someone her age. What did she look like? He tried to picture her, but couldn't.

Her shoulders rose and fell as if she were out of breath. Residual fear or something else? She winced when his fingers traveled over her left cheek.

"Sorry. Anywhere else?"

"No. Really. I'm . . . I'm fine. Let me get up, please."

She was trembling. He wanted to smash something. She'd come here to help him and gotten hurt in the process. How many others would get hurt while he stumbled around in the darkness?

Slowly, he sat back, and she stood. The front door shut.

His stomach clenched. Couldn't even protect an old lady in his own house. "You should put some ice on your face. You're going to have a bruise."

She cleared her throat, as though trying to get hold of her emotions. "How about you? Are you all right?"

"Oh, I'm peachy. Just fine and dandy." But he had to laugh at the irony of it. Minutes before he was ready to off himself, but let anyone else try and he fought like a maniac.

Guess he wasn't so eager to die after all.

He shoved the .38 at the small of his back. "Is there a weapon on the floor?"

"To your right. Three o'clock and then some."

"There are some plastic bags in a drawer next to the kitchen sink. Bring me a couple."

She walked away. "Who . . . who was that man?" He could still hear the fear in her voice.

"You tell me. You're the one with the eyes."

"I have no idea. I never saw him before." Several drawers opened and closed before she returned. "Why was he here? What did he—"

"Got the bags?"

"Yes."

"Use one to pick up the gun and place it inside the other."

The bags rustled. "Done."

She put the plastic bag in his hand. He sealed it and felt the shape of the weapon through the plastic. Was this the sniper from the roof? The fact that someone had gone after him seemed to solidify the theory that the shooter had intended to kill him and not T-bone. But why?

"Can you describe him?" Danny asked.

She paused. He pictured her thinking it over. "I— Yes, I'm sure I can. Big man—"

"My height?"

"Yes, but heavier."

"Okay. So that's six-one, maybe one-ninety, two hundred pounds. Black or white?"

"White."

"Hair?"

"Brown."

"Eyes?"

"Not sure. Dark, I think."

Not exactly brimming with detail. "Scars? Tattoos? Anything strange or unusual?"

"Not that I saw."

The guy could be anyone. Then again, he might be a familiar face to someone who could see. "Let's get you to the station."

"Oh, I don't think—"

"You ID him, we'll catch him."

He was energized, pumped up; Martha could see it in the taut lines of his face.

He found a jacket, stuffed the baggie with the gun inside a pocket, and fumbled his way from the front of his house to the curb. A cane would have made the journey so much easier, but she didn't say so. He wasn't ready yet; no sense pushing him.

He got in the car, and she drove, still reeling from the violence. She'd suffered cruelty, the kind of banal hurt caused by indifference and harsh words, but no one had ever hit her before. She felt immeasurably violated, her world suddenly iffy and unsafe.

But sitting beside her was the man who'd put his body between her and danger. The man who'd protected her. And he was revved up, body straight, forward-leaning. Exhilaration practically poured out of him. For the first time since she'd seen him at the hospital, the desperation was gone, replaced by something else—excitement, purpose.

He was back doing what he knew.

It lit his face. He was devastatingly handsome this way, eager, those glorious eyes so alive she almost believed a miracle had happened and he could see again.

It was all shattered when they arrived at the station.

He couldn't have gotten from the car to the building without help and when he realized it, the excitement mutated into despair. His shoulders slumped, the light in his eyes dimmed.

He directed her to park in the employee lot behind the building. It was a place she was sure he was familiar with.

"Visualize," she told him quietly.

"I am fucking visualizing."

"Take my arm."

"No fucking way."

"You know, I'm tired of that word."

"Fuck you."

"I'm going to get you a dictionary."

"I won't be able to read it."

"On tape."

He tried to go it on his own, but nearly ran in front of a car. Martha screamed, brakes squealed, and a horn blasted. An angry head poked out of the window.

"What are you, blind?"

"Yeah, pal, I am." His hands fisted into tight knots. "Want to do something about it?"

The driver's face colored in embarrassment, and he backed off immediately. "No. Sorry. No problem." The car sped away.

Martha's heart was still pumping wildly, but she felt for Danny. His hands were balled; he was itching to hit something.

She eased one fisted hand open. "Please." She slipped her hand into his. "You're going to give me a heart attack. And at my age . . ."

He didn't answer but he didn't take his hand away.

When they got to the station door, he held out a slim wallet. "There's an ID in there. You'll need it to get through."

She opened the leather case, saw his ID and badge, the shape worn into the leather by time and use. She slid the card through the electronic lock, the door opened, and they stepped inside.

He stopped abruptly.

"What's the matter?"

He stood stiffly, his face suddenly pale. "Maybe this wasn't such a good idea."

"Why not?"

"I . . ." He ran a hand over his mouth as though he wanted to stop the words.

"You'll have to face them some time," she said quietly.

"Yeah," he said with a curt laugh, "and at least I won't be able to see the pity on their faces."

"See? There are advantages."

That elicited a small smile. "You're making jokes?"

She repressed a smile. "Better laugh than cry."

"Easy for you to say," he grumbled.

But he seemed to have regained some of his confidence, and she took advantage of it by pressing on. "Which way?"

"To the left."

She guided him down a long hallway to an open area divided by cubicles with a door leading to an office on one side.

The place was standard institutional, concrete bricks painted beige, linoleum floor, fake wood accents. A whiteboard hung on one wall with names and dates and other information written in red—cases, she surmised—some crossed off, but many others blaring out their unfinished status. File cabinets and bulletin boards filled with paper notices were scattered about. Bold black words like FEDERAL WARNING, NOTICE OF ALERT, and photocopied pictures of nasty-looking men leaped out at her. The place smelled of disinfectant, sweat, and burnt coffee.

Men and women with guns strapped to their waists milled about. Someone looked up and elbowed someone else. One by one the room fell silent as Danny came in.

He tensed beside her, and she squeezed his hand.

Then as quickly as the silence had come, the place erupted.

"Jesus Christ, Danny!"

"How the hell are you?"

"Sin, my man!"

Everyone gathered around, slapping him on the back, touching him, talking at once. Danny shook their hands: Tim, whose baby face and long, stringy hair made him look like he belonged in high school; Anita, a towering, sloe-eyed black woman; Hank, a big-shouldered man with laugh lines around green, sun-kissed eyes. Hank. Hadn't Danny said he'd bought his house from a recently married detective named Hank?

Others whose names she didn't catch crowded around. Most with relief plain on their faces: Danny didn't look like a monster.

No, he looked perfectly normal, as though he could see them.

But of course, he couldn't.

She sensed the strain in him and said, "Could I sit down, please?"

"Leave it to our Sin to keep the ladies standing," said Anita, with a wink at Martha. Her voice was low and smooth. She was so tall, taller than Martha, and she carried herself with pride and ease. Martha watched, fascinated.

"Hope you're not referring to yourself, Bradley, since you don't qualify." Danny grinned at the crowd.

"Hoowee, Danny boy," Anita mocked. "You watch yourself. Don't wanna be taking me on."

Danny held up his hands, palms out. "You are so right, girl." And the group laughed, clearly more comfortable with jokes than anything else.

"Shut up, everyone," Danny commanded. "This is Martha Crowe. And she'd like to sit down."

More talk as people made a place for her. In the midst of it, Danny said, "My desk is the second from the right." As surreptitiously as possible, she led him there and sat in the chair while he perched on the edge.

"What's going on, Sin?" A lean man with laughing brown eyes and short, sandy hair punched Danny in the arm and leaned next to him against the desk.

"Hey, Mike. Martha, this is Mike Finelli. Mike— Martha Crowe." She noticed he didn't bother explaining who she was.

"You're looking good, Sin," Mike said, and the opinion

was eagerly matched by everyone else in the room. Too eagerly.

In the midst of the embarrassed choruses of "he looks great, doesn't he look great?", Martha spoke. "Someone attacked him."

A hush followed. Anita and Tim exchanged gazes. Hank's eyes narrowed and focused.

"Where?" Hank asked.

"My house," Danny said.

Anita pursed her lips. "Right there, in broad daylight?"

"Well, I guess he thought the time of day wouldn't matter," Danny said with a slight edge to his voice.

The group shifted their feet, looked away.

But whether or not Danny sensed the tension, she didn't know. He pulled out the gun they'd bagged and held it up. "Took this off him. What is it?"

Mike examined the weapon through the bag and whistled. "Not sure."

"Why not? You're the weapons expert."

Some of the officers crowded around. "Not a Glock," Anita said.

Martha didn't understand. "Isn't there a brand somewhere?"

"Not that I can see," Mike said.

"What does that mean?" Martha asked.

Danny shrugged. "Probably nothing. Some creep filed it off, try to make it harder to identify."

"But you can identify it, can't you?"

"Mikey here will send it to our ATF liaison. They'll trace it."

The man she'd seen at the hospital came out of the side office. "Hey, Danny. Good to see you." He grabbed

Danny's hand and pumped hard. "How are you holding up?"

"I'm okay." She could see something between the two men. Respect, friendship. Something deeper than colleagues.

"Someone tried to get at him, boss." Mike Finelli held up the baggie. "With this."

The other man took the gun, looked with concern from it to Danny. "Same guy as the warehouse?"

Danny shrugged. "Tell you one thing. The guy at the house today reeked. Kind of medicinal. Like liniment."

"Liniment." Parnell pursed his lips and looked over the group. "Who uses liniment?"

"People who work out," Hank said.

"Boxers," Anita said. "Martial artists."

"Bodybuilders," said Tim.

"I'll check out the local gyms," said Mike.

Danny held up a hand. "You may not have to. I've got a witness. Martha?"

All eyes turned to her.

"She was there. She might be able to ID him," Danny said. "Can you set her up with some books?"

Before she knew it, they'd led her into a small cramped room and piled books of faces in front of her. Danny disappeared, stumbling in the wake of the other two men. She winced as he hit a chair that sat against the wall, blocking his way.

"Let me help you," she heard the older man say.

"I'm okay," Danny's words were clipped, anger and humiliation in three syllables.

She remembered going to the movies with her cousin Stephanie. It was during that first year after the accident when her father was in and out of the hospital and her

mother had disappeared from their lives. Martha had been
left to the mercy of Aunt Nancy and her daughter,
Stephanie. She of the chestnut hair and jade green eyes, of
the stylish clothes and perfect teeth. Under protest
Stephanie had agreed to take Martha to the movies, but
she'd run off to stand in a clutch of giggling girls while
Martha bought her own ticket. On the way to join them
she'd tripped over something. Stephanie had said, "Oops,
watch out, Big Foot," and everyone had laughed.

No one was laughing at Danny, but she'd bet millions it
felt that way to him.

She pushed the pity away and went to work shuffling
through the piles of books they'd placed in front of her. Her
cheek throbbed and she would have liked to put the attack
behind her, push away the image of that fist smashing into
her face. But picture after picture of evil-looking faces
made for a forbidding and scary reminder.

Half an hour later, there was a light knock on the door.
"Can we see you a minute?" Mike Finelli stood in the doorway.

"Sure." She rose and followed him. "Mike, right?"

He nodded and gestured her to precede him down a
corridor.

"Have you known Danny long?"

"Since we were rookies. Drove a patrol car together before making detective."

"What's he like?"

"A hard-ass. But he always watched my back."

She noted the loyalty his statement implied. On both
men's parts. "Has he ever been married?"

He grinned. "Sin? Nah. What for? Women like him too
much."

She could imagine. "What about a girlfriend? Anyone serious?"

Mike gave her a pointed look and she flushed. "I . . . uh . . . I should talk with whoever he'll be interacting with on a daily basis."

He quirked his brows as though he didn't quite believe her. "Well, you can cross girlfriend off the list. Says he has too much going on for a girlfriend. Girls, yeah, friends, sure. But never anything steady. The only woman he's steady about is his sister."

She remembered the house that morning. The toys and kid things scattered around. "What do you mean?"

"I mean the way he looks after her and her kids, you'd think he was their mother, father, and grandfather rolled into one."

"You sound like you don't approve."

"I think it's fine." But something in his voice made her wonder. He paused outside a door and lowered his voice. "Of course, things will be different now." He shook his head. "How's he doing? Any chance of him seeing again?"

"I don't know. I'm not a doctor. As for how he's doing, ask him."

Mike gave her an ironic grimace. "He's not Dr. Phil. He doesn't exactly talk about himself. I'm asking you."

"He's blind. It's a huge adjustment. He needs time and patience. And friends."

He digested that, then opened the door and she found herself back in the squad room. Mike led her to the side office. Danny was in the corner facing the window, arms crossed, his back stiff with angry tension. Something was up. She looked from him to Mike to the third man present, the one who had come to the hospital the evening before.

"Lieutenant Parnell," he said, extending his hand. "We met last night."

"I remember." She shook his hand and looked around. "Problems?"

"Well, maybe a small one." Parnell scratched the back of his neck, a gesture that seemed intended to mitigate whatever he was going to say next. "Evidently, someone is trying to kill Detective Sinofsky."

The bald words took her aback. "The . . . the man at the house."

"We think he could be the same man who shot and killed a boy last night."

"What? What boy?" She flipped Danny a look, but he didn't turn around.

"A warehouse shooting." Parnell said. "Detective Sinofsky was making an undercover gun buy. A sniper killed the gun seller."

"If he wasn't after Sin to begin with," Mike said.

Martha reeled with the news. No wonder Danny hadn't looked like a cop last night, but like someone who prowled the streets. Guns, undercover operations, violent death— this was the stuff of television and movies, not life. Not her life anyway. Absently, she touched her bruised cheek. At least, not until now. "Why would someone want to kill Detective Sinofsky?"

"We don't know yet," Parnell said. "But cops make enemies. It's inevitable. We take threats against our officers very seriously. And with Danny unable to see—"

"Unable to protect myself," Danny said without turning around.

"Whatever." From the tired tone in Mike's voice, she knew they'd been arguing about this for a while.

"With Detective Sinofsky unable to see," Parnell

continued, "I'm putting him in protective custody until we find whoever is after him. And you're going with him."

"Me?" Her brows rose in astonishment.

"You're the only one who can identify the attacker."

"But I couldn't. I mean, none of those pictures . . ." Alarm pounded in her head, and not just for her physical safety. "I . . . no, I couldn't possibly. I have clients, meetings, people who depend on me."

"I'm afraid they're going to have to depend on someone else for a while," Parnell said gently.

"Welcome to my world," Danny said.

Was she really in danger? Once again, she felt the crack of the fist against her cheek. Her stomach flopped. "Look, I understand your concern, but do you really think this is necessary? I mean, I barely got a glance at that man."

"One glance is all it takes," Mike said. "He saw you just as clearly."

"If you refuse to cooperate, they could put you in jail," Danny said.

"What?"

"As a material witness," Mike said.

"Look, this is outrageous."

"My thoughts exactly," Danny said.

She glowered at them. "I am not going to jail and I'm not being locked up with Detective Sinofsky."

He turned around then, leaned negligently against the windowsill, his head turned in her direction, his gaze off center. "Used to be, women would fight over that privilege. But now . . ." He raised his arms in mock helplessness.

"Don't be ridiculous. Your eyesight has nothing to do with it." She looked over at Danny, and it was like looking at the sledgehammer that would bring down her carefully built walls. He didn't know what he was asking of her, couldn't possibly understand. "I just . . . I just . . . can't."

"I'm afraid you have no choice," Parnell said.

"Can't you, I don't know, assign someone to follow me around?"

"Like the Secret Service?"

"Why not?"

Parnell spread his hands in a gesture of apology. "No manpower. I put someone on you and someone on Sin, that's two men down. We're a small department. I can spare one man to watch you both, but not two."

"Look," Danny said, "I don't like this any more than you."

"Well, gee, thanks."

"But it's safer than leaving you out there for some creep to grab."

"Come on, Martha," Mike said, "it won't be so bad. Me, you, Sin over here. One big happy family."

"I already have a family," Martha snapped.

"Well, this is a good way to make sure you get back to them."

CHAPTER 4

Parnell sent someone to pack a bag of clothes for Danny and do the same for Martha. They each handed over a list of what they needed, and while they waited at the station, Danny called Beth and sketched in what had happened.

"I'm okay," Danny reassured his sister for the third time.

"I don't like not knowing where you are."

And he hated not being where she could reach him. A cloud of black dread floated up from his belly, and he recalled his vow at his mother's funeral. Well, it hadn't been a funeral. Not really. They couldn't afford a coffin or a burial site, so she'd been cremated. A few people had shown up: Parnell and his wife, a couple of waitresses from the restaurant his mother had worked in, the night boss of her office cleaning team. They'd trooped to Riverfront Park on a bright and sunny May afternoon. It was pretty enough for a picnic, and he'd felt betrayed by the weather.

As they stood around the riverbank, Beth had slipped her small, fourteen-year-old hand into his and together they'd emptied the box they'd gotten at the crematorium in the water. As air and water took all that was left of his mother he'd vowed that neither of them would end up breaking their backs the way she did.

He'd kept that vow. He chose his women carefully, only going out with those who wanted what he did—no obligations, promises, or strings. He had no wife or children of his own to disappoint and discard. Only Beth. And now she was alone with two kids, and he was blind and useless to her.

He closed his eyes and pressed a palm to his forehead where a headache was beginning to form again. "I'm sorry," he said, because he didn't know what else to say, and because it was true. "It won't be for long."

"What about your doctor's appointments?"

"Cancel them."

"But—"

"Look, I'm okay. Stop worrying."

Beth let out an exasperated sigh. "You're kidding, right? I get to worry about you, Danny. I get to take care of you, just like you took care of me."

Danny's jaw tightened. "No one's taking care of me, Beth. Not you, not anyone. I'll call when I can." He disconnected before she could say anything else.

He rubbed his forehead, wishing for another dose of aspirin, and heard Martha on the phone.

"I told you, I don't know where we're going." Her voice was low with annoyance. "I can't do that. They won't let me. They wouldn't even let me pack my own bag. Daddy—"

Daddy? At fifty-eight she was still calling her father Daddy? Danny didn't know whether that creeped him out or cheered him up.

"I don't know for how long. No one's saying. There's chili in the fridge, two casseroles in the freezer. Don't forget to eat breakfast. And no smoking. I know you have cigarettes stashed around the house. No, don't get all innocent with me. And don't think you can sneak around and smell up the house when I'm not there."

Looked like Danny wasn't the only one she bossed around.

"I have to go. I've got appointments to cancel. A meeting I'm not going to make this afternoon. This is a real mess. I will. I promise. Yes. As soon as I can." She hung up the phone with a sigh.

"Trouble in paradise?"

"No more than yours," she said stiffly. "Who's Beth?"

"My sister."

Paper or pages started being flipped. Was she looking through a book? A notebook?

Absently, she said, "Yes, I heard you were close."

She did? From who? "Who's been talking about me behind my back?"

"Mike."

Big mouth. "Oh, that son of a bitch. Don't believe a word he says. He resents me."

"Really?" A pen scratched against paper. "I didn't get that impression."

"It's true. I'm a better cop than he is." Or was. Before he could dwell on that, someone came into the office.

"You're a better cop than who is?" Mike.

"You." Danny repressed a smile.

"That's bullshit."

"No it's not. You resent me."

"I just wish you'd let go of your sister so I can have a chance at her."

Danny held up his hand in mock outrage. "You're on your own there, pal. I'm not in your way. She just knows a loser when she sees one." This time, he let the grin go wide.

"A loser?" Mike whistled. "Talk about the pot calling the kettle names."

Paper ripped. "I'm glad to see you two are getting along so well, but I still have a life to rearrange," Martha said.

Someone else came in. "Okay, we're all set." Parnell. "Danny, I'd like to talk to you. We can go into one of the interview rooms."

Danny tensed. Moving around was a bitch, especially in front of the guys.

As if she'd read his mind, Martha said, "Why don't you stay here? I have a few more phone calls to make. I can use the phone on Detective Sinofsky's desk. Detective Finelli can show me the way."

Deftly, she maneuvered herself and Mike out of the room, and Danny sent her a silent thank-you.

When she was gone, he turned to where he thought Parnell was. "Whaddaya got?"

"A farmhouse on Route 3 in Old House. Used to belong to the chief's grandmother. It won't be five-star, but it's serviceable, and very few people know about it."

Five-star or hovel, Danny wouldn't know the difference. "Thanks. I think."

There was a short silence. He didn't hear Parnell moving. "You still here?"

"Yeah," Parnell said softly. "I'm still here. I got . . . I got one more thing to ask you."

Danny's hackles rose. He could hear the bad news in Parnell's voice. Carefully he said, "Okay."

"It's the thirty-eight you're carrying at your back. I'm asking you to leave it here. With me."

The blood seemed to leave Danny's body. "You taking my badge, too?"

"No, no. It's not like that. I'm not taking anything. I'm

asking. You can't . . ." He cleared his throat, and the sound made Danny think Parnell was having as much trouble saying this as Danny was hearing it. It nearly shattered his tight control. His hands started shaking and he had to shove them in his pockets to hide them. "You can't use it, Danny. And it would be too easy for someone to take it off you and use it against you."

Danny set his mouth. Parnell was right, but Danny didn't want to admit it. "I used it just fine at the house."

"You got lucky."

And he hadn't stopped that mope from hitting Martha.

He reached around his back and pulled out the revolver. He rubbed its hard edges, felt its solid weight in his hand.

"It's temporary," Parnell said. "I'll put it in your locker and it'll be there when you settle in, figure things out." Euphemisms for "when you can see again," but Danny didn't call him on it. "But for now, as a favor to me and Jackie, let me hold it for you."

The mention of Parnell's wife, Jackie, turned the screws even tighter. Danny's throat constricted. Slowly, he held out the gun. Parnell took it, and without its weight Danny's hand felt light and defenseless.

Parnell cleared his throat again, shuffled his feet. "You're going to get through this, Danny. Just like you got through everything else."

Danny knew he was talking about the years of neglect while his mother struggled to keep them all alive, then her death and the hard years taking care of Beth.

"Yeah, but this time meatloaf and mashed potatoes aren't going to help much." Couple of times a week, Parnell used to check up on them. He never came empty-handed.

"At least I won't have to make sure you heat it up before you eat it."

He paused, and in the quiet Danny remembered the times Parnell and Jackie had schlepped their three kids plus Danny and Beth to a week at the beach. The prom dress Jackie had helped Beth buy. The Ranger games Parnell had sat through, though he didn't even like hockey that much.

"I'm here," Parnell said quietly. "The department's here. We're not letting you slip away."

"Sounds great on paper, but what the fuck am I going to do?" His greatest fear, said aloud for the first time.

"I don't know yet. But whatever it is, you'll be damned good at it."

"Or?"

"Or I'll disown you."

Danny couldn't help a small smile. That's what Parnell had been saying to him since he first caught him stealing CDs when he was thirteen.

"About the only thing it looks like I'll be good at is being blind. And trust me, right now I'm not even good at that."

By the time they arrived at the farmhouse, snow had blanketed the air with an unnatural hush. Danny inhaled the sharp freshness, turned his face up so the flakes drifted onto his skin, a quick sting of cold that melted away.

"Is it sticking?" His voice sounded different, the timbre muffled by the snow.

"Yes." Martha tightened her grip on him, and he knew she was nervous about his refusal to use the correct hold. But he'd be damned if he'd let Mike see him being led around like a lapdog.

"Wait up."

"We should get you inside, Sin," Mike said.

"In a minute. How close are we to the front door?"

"We're parked in the drive a few steps from a walkway leading up to it."

"What do you see?"

"Everything looks clear. No tags, no watchers. So far, so good."

"Sketch it out for me."

"One-story, white clapboard, needs a paint job. Two entrances, front and back. A porch opens onto a backyard that leads to a plowed field. Country road about ten yards down from the front. A wood railed fence marks the property boundary."

He mapped it out in his head. "What's between me and the house?"

"You got a driveway right here. Gravel. A concrete walkway bisects it to the left. Grassy front yard with a big tree in the center."

"Fancy."

"Only the best for our guys." There was a grin in Mike's voice, but Danny didn't respond to it. He was too busy trying to picture the scene. But he had no idea if what he saw in his head was accurate.

Dread fluttered up like a girl he wanted to avoid. Until now he'd been in familiar surroundings. Places he knew and could see in his head. Now . . . He bit down on the anxiety, that queasy feeling of helplessness.

"Ready?" Mike asked.

He took a breath. "Okay, let's go."

They started off, Martha steering him like a boat through water. Her slim fingers clutched his arm, her tall, willowy body swayed beside his. For a crazy half moment, the enticing feel of hips and curves intruded, and despite the age difference, he responded to it.

Maybe she was one of those women who aged gracefully.

Maybe the stroke had done more to his brain than mess with his vision.

He concentrated on his footing. On the feel of the gravel, the sound of it crunching under his feet, on the time it took to cross the drive. He paused at the beginning of the smooth walkway.

"Is this the walk?" He felt for the spongy edge of grass on either side.

"Yes," Martha answered, and brought him to the door like a tugboat towing a barge.

Mike escorted them inside, the slap of his heavier tread preceding them. The place smelled musty, as if it hadn't been open for a long time.

"Wait here." Mike's voice was terse, a tense command.

Danny stood awkwardly, embarrassed that he was the one following orders, not giving them.

"Where's he going?" Martha asked in a careful, low voice.

"To check the house. Make sure it's clear."

"Oh."

He heard unease in that single word, and for some reason felt compelled to reassure her. "It's standard procedure. I'm sure everything is fine."

The prediction proved true when Mike returned. "House is okay. I'll bring in your bags and the case files."

Danny nodded, and the front door opened and slammed shut. Beside him Martha's body relaxed and he wished he could do the same. But the thought of Mike fetching and carrying for him made him crazy.

"You should familiarize yourself with the layout," Martha said.

God, he wished for one moment he could take control and just see the damn place. But he couldn't, so he waited for Martha to begin. The silence stretched.

"So?" he said at last. "Are you going to tell me what it looks like or not?"

"Not," she said.

"You're kidding."

"You won't always have a sighted person around. Figure it out for yourself."

Unbelievable.

He began trailing the walls with the back of his hands, fingers curved inward, as she'd showed him.

"What do you see?" Martha asked.

Not a damn thing. But he knew what she meant. "Table in the left corner just inside the front door." The wood bumped and rippled under his fingers as though the piece was old and worn with use.

"Yes. For keys and gloves and things. What else?"

He skimmed the room's outer rim. "Long narrow room. Doorway to the left about nine o'clock."

"That leads to a bedroom. Beyond it is a hall. I think with more bedrooms."

His knees ran into a piece of furniture, and Martha gasped but said nothing. Swallowing a curse, he felt the contours, wide arms covered in bumpy fabric. "Armchair?"

"Yes. And use your protective stance, so you won't hurt yourself."

Mentally, he flipped her the bird, but moved on.

"Sofa," he said curtly, outlining square arms, cushions, and more bumpy fabric. His shin hit against something solid. Wood, or something like it. "A table in front. Another chair." A metal tube, fabric hat. "Standing lamp?"

"Yes."

Open space between the lamp and the wall. He continued trailing until he hit a barrier. Molding?

"Another doorway," he deduced. "Right side corner."

"The kitchen."

Before he went through the door, he traced the space he'd just been through in his head. Doorways on either side, armchairs, sofa. "So we're what—in a front room? A living room?"

"That's right."

"And it leads into the kitchen."

"Yes."

He nodded, committing as much of it as he could to memory, and stepped through the kitchen door. Almost immediately his hand encountered cool metal. A wide, tall rectangle.

"Fridge."

"Yes."

He continued, fingers curled, the backs of his hands doing the work. "Small counter, stove, sink." He hit a corner, turned with it. "Some kind of door?"

"Leads to the back porch."

He passed it and continued. A draft of cold that stopped as he walked on. "A window?"

"Very good."

A large obstacle that hit him in the stomach. Christ. He backed off, trailed around it. "A table. Round. Chairs with high backs."

"Ladderbacks. Yes. How many?"

He counted as he went. "Five."

"Yes. And to the left of the table?"

He turned the corner, felt empty wall, then a structure. It resolved itself into a recognizable shape. "Counter. Cupboard above and below."

He trailed the counter, and when his hand hit empty air, he stepped cautiously, his arm now bent in front to protect his body.

But he encountered nothing but more wall.

His hand hit a barrier. Like plaster molding. Then empty air. Then the molding again.

"Another door?"

"Yes." He stepped inside. Martha followed.

Her light, spring scent came with her. It spoke to him silently, fecund, female, and once again he had a sudden, sharp flash of desire. Did going blind make him especially susceptible to any woman, no matter how old?

He stopped abruptly. Maybe old women were the only ones who'd be interested in him now.

"You okay?"

His sex life used to be one thing he never worried about. Used to be.

"Yeah. Fine."

"I guess you'd call this a parlor." Her voice lost and gained volume as though she were turning around, checking out the room. She had a distinctive voice, not husky or operatic, but with a low, musical quality. The sound vibrated inside him as though she were in his head. Becoming his eyes.

"Watch for a sofa on the right flanked by two armchairs. Across the room is one of those collapsible card tables and a TV on a metal stand."

He swore silently. He would not become a calf tied to its mother.

"I'll figure the room out later." He needed to break this off, cut the rope binding them together. "I need to get the basic layout first. I can handle it myself."

"All right." Was there an edge of hurt in her voice? Despite it, she backed off, her scent drifting away. He felt both relieved and abandoned.

He returned to the living room as the front door slammed shut. Mike coming or going? A thud, something heavy landing on a surface.

"That's the lot of them," Mike said.

"The case files?"

"Every last fricking one of them." He let out a huge breath and collapsed somewhere. A sofa probably: the furniture sighed under his weight.

"I don't know about you two," Mike said, "but I didn't have lunch. What do you say to an early dinner? I brought food with us."

"Works for me," Martha said.

Sin said nothing. The word "dinner" conjured up the fiasco of the evening before. A slow, shameful burn ran up his neck. Truth was, he hadn't eaten all day, too afraid of what he'd do if he tried. He was starved, but he didn't think he could swallow a mouthful. Not in front of Mike.

He busied himself with tracking the hallway to the left of the living room. Four bedrooms and a bath lined up like a row of tin soldiers. Mike had put their bags in the rooms on either side of the bathroom, first Danny's duffel, then Martha's square suitcase. Without Martha it took him longer to figure out the spatial relations, but that gave him something to think about besides the coming meal.

Alone, he took his cell phone from its belt holder and fumbled with the buttons until he reached Beth at home. "You okay?"

"I'm not the one in protective custody. I'm fine. How about you?"

"I'm here. Wherever 'here' is. Looks . . . *feels* . . . fine. Just wanted to let you know."

"I appreciate it."

He paused, picturing Beth in the kitchen getting dinner ready. "Where are you?"

"In the kitchen."

A surge of satisfaction to know he'd been right. "I'm . . . I'm sorry about before. About hanging up."

"You have the right to be cranky once in a while." A smile brightened her voice. "As long as it's once in a while. Wait a second." Her voice went away. "All right, Josh. I'll see." She came back on the line. "Can you talk to Josh for a minute?"

He thought of his nephew's reaction the night before, and his own humiliation. He swallowed it down. "Sure."

Sound rustled as the phone switched hands.

"Uncle Danny?"

"Hey, pal. You doing okay?"

"Are your eyes better?"

His heart sank. "They're about the same, boss. But hey, that means they're not any worse. That's something, isn't it?" He cringed at the fake heartiness in his voice.

"Are you taking me trick-or-treating?"

Oh, Christ. He'd completely forgotten. Halloween was two weeks away. Maybe he'd catch a miracle and this would all be over by then. "We'll see, Josh. I may have to work."

"You promised."

"I know, pal. I'll do everything I can to be there. Put your mom back on."

Beth came back on the phone. "I'm sorry about that. Don't let him pressure you."

Easier said than done. "He's a kid. He wants things. He's too young to learn he's not going to get them."

"We weren't."

A wave of sadness washed over him. "Yes, we were."

She didn't reply, and in the silence he remembered that Halloween when she was eight or nine and desperately wanted one of those chintzy princess costumes from Wal-Mart. No one was going to spend good money on a costume, but that was all she talked about for weeks. He was too young to drive, and by the time he conned a ride to the store, there were none left to steal. So he'd talked her into going as a ghost, stuck a pillowcase over her, cut out holes for arms, eyes, nose, and mouth, and took her to one of those fancy subdivisions with the stone pillars and the sign in the entrance. Mayfair or Swansdowne or something like that.

The place was across town and they had to walk and take two buses to get there, but it was warm, not like this year at all, so she didn't mind. She insisted on wearing her costume, though, which meant he had to swallow his embarrassment and sit on the bus like a freak next to this little lump of white. On the way back, he lost the bus transfer and without money for the second bus they had to walk home. But she shared her candy the whole way back and by the time they got there, she had only two pieces left. He found one in his lunch the next day.

"Danny?"

He swallowed rising emotion. "Yeah, I'm here." His voice came out husky, and he cleared it. "I gotta go. I'll keep in touch, but don't worry if you don't hear from me. You sure you'll be all right? I can have Mike or one of the guys stop by, see what you need."

"Look, Danny, I'm not fourteen. You're not responsible for me anymore. Just watch your own back, okay? You come home safe. That's all I care about. We'll be fine here."

By the time dinner was ready his stomach was knotted

tight. Mike had brought steaks from a take-out place. The smell was indescribable. Sin's mouth watered, his stomach grumbled.

Mike knocked on the bedroom door and opened it without an invitation. "Come on, pal. I got you set up at the table." He half-pushed, half-pulled Danny into the kitchen, placed a knife and fork in his hand. "Sit down. Dig in."

Danny stood for a second, mortified. He couldn't even cut the meat. Not without using his hands and fingers. The picture he saw of himself, tearing at his food like an animal, made him sick.

The only other option was to have someone else cut up his food. He couldn't bear that either.

"I'm not hungry."

"What?" Mike said. "But—"

Mike cut off his protest, but Danny didn't wait to find out why. He left the kitchen, fumbled back down the hallway and into his bedroom. Closing the door behind him, he leaned against it, lungs choked, sweating like a pig. The panic he'd kept at bay all afternoon came lurching back.

A knock.

He closed his eyes. "I'm not hungry."

"Neither am I," Martha said.

His breath roared in his ears.

"Since I'm not eating either, I thought we could talk."

Talk. Christ, he couldn't manage a single word.

"Danny. Open up."

He leaned against the door, not budging.

"I'm not going away. So you can let me in or listen to me yak at you through the door where everyone else can hear, too."

She sure knew what buttons to push. Self-pity fled in a

flood of anger. With a growl he stepped back and flung open the door.

"You know, you are one giant pain in the ass," he told her.

"It's one of my most endearing qualities."

She sailed past him, and he smelled food.

"I told you I'm not hungry."

"Well, I thought it a shame to let this hamburger go to waste."

She'd moved beyond him. Something squeaked. A bed? Was she sitting on it? He turned to the sound, hoping he'd got it right.

"If I don't want steak what the hell makes you think I'd want hamburger?"

"You don't have to cut up a hamburger, Danny." She spoke in that quiet tone. The one that said she understood completely without him having to say a word.

He stilled. There were fucking tears in the back of his throat.

"I'll teach you how to cut a steak. I'll teach you how to cook one. But right now, you need to eat something. Sit down. The bed is directly in front of you. Maybe four steps."

He made the cross slowly, distrustful of open space. But he found the bed, felt along the edge, and sat beside her. She put something in his lap. A plate.

"Sandwich at six. Bag of chips at noon. Tough luck if you don't like ketchup and mayonnaise on your burger."

The warmth of the plate seeped into his legs, the smell drove him crazy. His stomach was doing somersaults of anticipation, but he sat still, reeling in the emotions.

"I, uh . . ." His tongue was thick, the words a jumble. "You . . . this is—"

"You're welcome," she said, taking the pressure off. "There's a Coke on the nightstand." The bed creaked again as she got up. "I'll leave you to it."

"Wait." He groped for her hand, caught her wrist. Her skin was smooth and soft. "Don't go."

Martha hesitated. She needed to keep this professional and how could she do that sitting beside him on a bed? But there was a warmth in his face she hadn't seen before, and she couldn't resist it. She sat back down, and he bit into the sandwich. He closed his eyes in an expression of unadulterated contentment.

She smiled. "Good?"

"Fantastic." He paused to chew and swallow. His throat worked, the muscles sharp and powerful, and she watched, enmeshed in the utter masculinity of it.

"So if I'm eating your dinner," he said at last, "what will you eat?"

"Yours."

He took another bite, nodded with mock solemnity. "So this was all a plot to get at my steak?"

She couldn't help laughing. "Absolutely. Self-interest is the way of the world."

At least it was right now, while she watched him eat. God, what was wrong with her? She turned away, determined to change the subject.

"Danny . . ."

"Yeah?"

"This man who attacked you. Any ideas about who he could be?"

"Not yet. But that's why we brought the files."

"How are you going to read them?"

He smiled, teeth blazing white in his tan face, and once

again, the expression hit her like a tidal wave. "I'm not," he said. "You are."

"Me?" Her eyes widened in surprise. "Aren't they confidential?"

He shrugged. "I haven't worked on anything top secret. For the last two years I've been assigned to the Neighborhood Recovery Unit. We do a lot of undercover work. Drug buys, guns, prostitution stings. Street crime mostly. Skells and mopes."

"Skells and—?"

"Mopes. Punks and thugs."

"Sounds . . . delightful."

"It ain't routine, I can tell you that. But it's not rocket science either. The files reflect that. Besides, I'm blind, remember? Someone has to read to me. If you want to make it official, we'll call you a police aide."

Martha recalled the way he'd looked when she first saw him. "You had just come from work when I saw you in the hospital."

He nodded, his face a kaleidoscope of emotion—regret, nostalgia, grief. "That was Turq. My street name." He pointed to his eyes. "Short for 'turquoise.' How's that for irony?" As if he were shaking off the gloom, he rose. "Look, why don't you eat while I finish this. We can tackle the files after."

An hour later she was ensconced with Danny in the parlor off the kitchen. Like the rest of the house, this room had the feel of neglect, as if life inside it had stopped somewhere around 1972. The ancient TV didn't work, the oncewhite curtains were filmy with age. But the couch was covered in still-bright sunflowers, and the coffee table in front of it was serviceable. Danny lifted the first banker's box of files onto it.

She opened it and found piles of folders and binders—depending on the complications of the case—all filed by victim or complainant name. She started with "Andrews, Marcella" and spent the next few hours combing through the paperwork, reading everything the pages captured about each case.

She was awed by the sheer weight of wrongdoing. Junkies and dealers and a mile-long list of paraphernalia to go with them—"decks" were glassine envelopes filled with heroin or cocaine, "slabs" were heat-sealed baggies of crack. She reviewed weapon names, calibers, and ammo loads; knives of various sizes and types; and pimps, hookers, and johns. She read strings of CIs—confidential informants—and a host of other lingo that Danny had to explain to her. EDP meant "emotionally disturbed person," SCB meant "Sokanan Central Booking." There were 52s—complaint forms, which described offense, offender, and victim; DDRs—Domestic Disturbance Reports; and OLBS—Online Booking Sheets. A world as alien to her as Mars.

"How do you do it?" she asked.

"Do what?"

"Swim around in this muck?"

He gave her an odd, wistful smile. "Because the muck is . . . shit, I don't know." He paused, searching for a way to make her understand. "It's like a river, see? Alive, pumping, full of amazing sights. On one bank are the people who work their butts off to pay the rent and buy their kid a new pair of Nikes. On the other are the people who are so fucked they'll do anything for a hit, who suck the system dry, or are just plain scumbags. And I keep them apart. Or try to. Some days it feels like a flood—too many of them and not enough of me. And some days, I collar up and feel like I'm actually doing something decent. Something I'm good at it." He paused. "Or was."

The love of his job shone through the words, and something like heartbreak welled inside her. Knowing he might have to give it up must be killing him.

A car rumbled outside and headlights cut through the darkness. She tensed.

"That a car?" Danny's hearing was adapting quickly. More quickly than even he probably realized.

"Someone's pulled up."

Danny signaled her to rise. "Give me your hand." He spoke in a low whisper, and she complied, feeling the strength in his fingers. He pulled her close, shielding her behind him.

"Shift change," Mike called to them from the living room where he'd stationed himself.

The tension in Danny's body relaxed, and she stepped away. But blind or not, she was glad he was beside her.

A few minutes later, Mike entered the parlor, accompanied by a thin, wiry man with a boxer's lumpy nose.

"It's Bayliss," the man announced so Danny would know who had entered.

"What the hell are you doing here, Sergeant?" Danny stuck out his hand. "I thought they were going to let the uniforms babysit."

Danny's hand was off center, but Bayliss adjusted his position and took it. "You know me. Any excuse to get out of the house."

"I know your wife, and that's bullshit."

The other guy looked sheepish. "Well, I'm not supposed to say anything but everyone in the unit volunteered to take a shift."

A beat of silence, then, "Shit." Danny looked down, clearly stunned and uncomfortable.

Into the awkward silence, Mike spoke. "This is Martha Crowe. Martha, Sergeant Mel Bayliss."

Bayliss gave her a friendly nod. "Finelli treating you okay?"

"Oh, Mike's been great," she said. "It's Detective Sinofsky who needs taking down a peg or two."

"Who—Sin?" Bayliss grinned. "Who'd ever believe that?" He turned to Danny and clapped him on the back. "So sit the hell down and fill me in."

They resumed their seats on the couch. Bayliss perched on the arm of a chair, Mike hung over the back.

"We've been going over the unit files," Danny said, and to Martha, "Read him the list."

Every so often, Danny had her write down a name or a location from a file. This is what she read now.

"Tommy Pelotti."

"Remember that drug bust a year and a half ago?" Danny said. "The guy was out of control, swore up and down he'd come back to get us."

"Yeah, I remember him," said Bayliss. "He was dusted. High as a house. Is he out already?"

"Last month."

Bayliss shook his head. "Who else you got?"

"Antone Linley," Martha said.

"One of Ricky Roda's crew," Danny said. "We got him on possession with intent a while ago, but he pled out. But he sure wasn't happy about being bagged."

"Roda's top of our lead sheets," Mike said. "We're checking on all his people."

"Good. I may want in on that." Bayliss and Mike exchanged a glance as if to say they knew Danny was dreaming. She was glad he couldn't see it. "Who's next?"

"Dewayne Cordell," Martha said.

"One of my CIs. A crackhead, but reliable as far as they go. Hook up with him and see what he knows. But be prepared to pay."

"That's it so far," Martha said.

"I'll see what I can come up with tomorrow when we go through the rest," Danny said.

"I'll get started on these three." Mike took the list from Martha. "Come on, Sarge, let me give you a tour." Mike walked his replacement through the house and when he was done, he came to say good-bye. "I left Mel in the kitchen with a cup of coffee. Bradley and Carstens got tomorrow. I'm not due back until the day after. I've got your cell. I'll call if anything turns up." He shook Danny's hand. "Take care of yourself."

He started to go, and Danny called after him. "Hey! Don't scare my sister to death."

Mike stopped short and turned back slowly, like a kid caught stealing candy. "What are you talking about?"

"You're going to see her, right?"

Mike crossed his arms over his chest, half-belligerent, half-wounded. "Maybe."

"Maybe, my ass. Be nice. I don't want her worrying."

"What do you think I am?"

"You don't want me to answer that."

Grinning, Mike left, and Martha marveled at the friendship behind the mock abuse.

A yawn took her unawares and she wondered what time it was. She didn't realize she'd said it out loud until Danny responded.

"I wouldn't know. My watch doesn't speak to me."

She gathered up the files they'd read and set them aside from the ones still in the box. "We'll have to fix that."

He scoffed. "How? Brain surgery? Let me tell you now, the doctors say it won't work."

"There are lots of gadgets to make life easier for you. Talking alarm clocks, computers, you name it. Be thankful you live in the age of the microchip."

He laid his head against the back of the couch and rubbed a hand down his face. "Yes, ma'am. I'm one grateful son of a bitch."

She rolled her eyes at the sarcasm. "Beware. I've got that dictionary on order."

"I'm shaking in my boots."

She smiled and rose from the couch. "On that note, I'm off to bed."

"Already? It's barely midnight."

She paused, frowning. "I thought you said you couldn't tell the time."

"I'm psychic."

"Really." Her tone was skeptical, but there was humor behind it. He was teasing her in the same way he teased Mike, and she was enjoying it. "So what am I thinking?"

He looked at her. Or rather looked to where he thought she was. Either way, his expression was full of sly, male amusement.

"That you wish you were twenty years younger and could take advantage of me."

She colored but was careful to keep the surprise and embarrassment out of her voice. "Your psychic vibes have shorted out. That sounds like wishful thinking on your part."

He laughed, and she drank in the sight. "If it's shift change, it's got to be sometime around twelve."

"Goodnight, Detective," she said dryly.

"Sweet dreams, Martha."

After Martha left, Danny wandered into the kitchen, found Bayliss still nursing his coffee, and joined him at the table.

"You and Miss Crowe getting along?"

He heard the insinuation in Bayliss's voice, and though it echoed what Danny had just said to her, the suggestion seemed obscene coming from Bayliss.

"Get off it, Mel. She's old enough to be my mother."

Bayliss snorted. "Not unless she discovered a way to conceive in infancy."

"What are you talking about? She's fifty-eight."

Mel spit out what sounded like a mouthful of coffee. "Where the hell did you get that idea?"

"She told—" He thought about it, quickly running over all his contact with her. Her voice, her smell, the youthful feel of her. Slowly he nodded. "She's not fifty-eight."

"Not by twenty-five years or so. She's no babe, at least, not the kind you usually go for. Stringy black hair. Tall. Skinny. Wears those baggy feed sack kind of things. But she's a helluva long way from fifty."

"Sonofabitch," Danny said softly.

CHAPTER 5

———•———

Martha's dreams were anything but sweet. They were hot and dark, and had her running through steamy jungles chased by a sleek panther with turquoise eyes. And the farther away she got, the closer she wanted him to come.

She woke abruptly. Sweating, she threw off the covers as though she could throw off the memory of Danny. Sin.

The name echoed in her head.

Still wobbly from the nightmare, she climbed out of bed and padded into the kitchen. Bayliss was in the living room, playing solitaire, a gun beside the cards on the coffee table.

She didn't know how she felt about the sight of the weapon. Both scared and comforted.

He saw her, nodded, and went back to his cards. Martha found tea in a cupboard, heated water, and made a cup. Grabbing her coat from a hook by the backdoor, she stepped onto the porch.

It was freezing, but the cold washed away the lingering heat from her dream. She cupped her fingers around the hot tea and lifted her face to the stars.

"Can't sleep?"

The growl of Danny's voice came from a chair deep in the shadows.

She started at the sound. "I didn't see you there."

"That makes two of us."

She smiled at the joke but didn't say anything in response. "Couldn't sleep either?"

"Hard to sleep when one time of day is the same as the next."

"You'll get used to it."

"I don't want to get used to it."

She didn't bother telling him that it did no good to wish for things. Better to deal with things as they were.

Despite the cold, the night smelled wonderful. Pine and earth and the fresh scent of snow. Moonlight glittered on the field that stretched out before them. Wind rustled the branches of the bare trees.

"Can you see it?" she asked.

"See what?"

"The wind in the trees." She closed her eyes, blocking out everything but sound. The air whooshed stately and slow, as though the branches were giant, bony ribs, and the earth was breathing through them.

"Yeah," he said at last. "I can see it."

They remained still for a long while, then Danny broke the silence.

"How's that bruise doing?"

Instinctively, she reached for her face. By the time she'd brushed her teeth a few hours ago, her cheek had already started turning purple.

"It's a nice mauve color. With shades of violet and ocher making their way to the surface."

"Ah, a fashion statement." He rose and ambled toward her, more sure of himself in the darkness than she was. "I hate to think of it ruining your pretty face."

Her cheeks heated. *Her pretty face.* She gave him a self-deprecating laugh. "I don't think you have to worry about that. There was never much to recommend it anyway. And now . . ."

"Oh, yeah, now that you're . . . how old did you say?"

She blinked rapidly, unable to remember the exact number of years she'd blurted out that morning. "Fifty—"

"Five, wasn't it? Next June."

She sighed in relief. "Yes, that's right."

He stopped a breath short of where she stood against the porch railing. "Or maybe it was fifty-eight in February."

She panicked. What had she told him? "Uh . . . no, fifty-five. In June."

"You sure?" His hands reached out for her, landing on her upper arms and tracing upward. Through her coat his touch left heat in its wake, a relentless path over her shoulders, neck, and jaw. Finally, his hands cupped her face.

"What are you doing?" Fear and excitement created a drumbeat in her chest.

"Seeing you. Like the wind." His fingers traced the outline of her face, running over her ears and down the length of her hair. He caressed her eyebrows, the line of her nose, then the indentation below it and finally her lips.

The cold disappeared into a rush of fire. She stopped breathing.

"I'll bet you've kissed a lot of men in those fifty-eight years."

His voice was low and husky, and she had to fight not to let it mesmerize her.

"Fifty-five. And yes, I've done my share."

"Really." Why did he sound as though he didn't believe her?

"Danny, don't. Please. Stop." She tried to back off, but

he held her tightly, his strong hands wrapped around her head, his thumbs framing her mouth.

He whispered, "What do you feel like, Martha?"

Her knees were rickety, and everything inside her turned hot and liquid. "Like this should stop."

"Do you want it to?"

He was dark as the night, a great, swooping male who would wrap her in his inky wings, take her to some imagined height, and drop her against the hard ground, a pitiful, broken thing.

And for half a second she didn't care. His head was moving, his mouth getting closer. She closed her eyes, breath clogged in her lungs.

"You two are turning my life into a damn hellhole," Bayliss said from the doorway. "If you want to have a midnight rendezvous, do it inside."

Martha's face flamed, but Danny didn't move. "Your timing sucks, Bayliss."

"Yeah, my wife says the same thing."

Danny stepped back, and Martha fled, a prisoner set free.

Bayliss whistled. "You must be slipping, Sin."

"Oh, yeah. Nothing like a little blindness to set the ladies off."

Bayliss said nothing, and Danny made his way through the darkness to his bedroom. Next door, water whooshed into the bathroom sink. Was she washing her face? Cooling down? Did that mean he'd heated her up?

He didn't know why he'd made a move on her.

She'd pissed him off, that's why.

Made a fool of a blind man. Lied to him.

If he couldn't be a cop anymore, he was still a man.

Could still make a woman's heart beat fast. Didn't he just prove it?

He sank onto the edge of the bed, punched the pillow at the head.

Then why did he feel so goddamn awful about it?

The scream that seemed permanently lodged in his throat threatened to erupt. He forced it down, mangled it, beat it with a stick. And even then he wasn't sure it wouldn't burst out of him when he least expected it.

He eased down on the bed and closed his eyes.

He didn't remember falling asleep, but when he woke, the darkness was still there. An acute pain sliced into him, a machete through his ribs. When would his sight come back?

Terror trembled behind his chest. What if the answer was never? What if he remained blind for the rest of his life?

The questions set off a firestorm within him, a desperation so intense it would drive him insane if he let it.

So he sat up, no idea whether he'd slept ten minutes or ten hours. Was it still night? Or had the sun come up and melted the snow?

He stood, squaring off against the edge of the bed, and visualized the map of the room he'd formed in his head. The door should be straight ahead, a few steps away. He took them cautiously. His knuckles skimmed over ripples of plaster molding, over the series of square indentations in the back of the door. He found the knob, turned it.

Coffee was brewing. And he heard the low blur of voices.

To his left was the bathroom. He trailed the wall, found the door, then the toilet, did his business, and walked to the kitchen.

He identified the speakers before he got there. Martha

and Anita Bradley. Anita was the only woman in the unit, a six-foot-plus Amazon with a deep powerful voice that could call out trouble a block away, clear as a bell. If Anita was there, Bayliss had left, and the morning shift had come. Morning. It was morning.

He paused in the living room, listening to them talk.

"Married?" Anita laughed. "Hell, no. Sin's our playboy. In fact"—she shuffled some papers—"word's already out about what happened to him. These came in last night. Barbie, Debbie, Pattie . . ."

"Doesn't he know any women with complete names?"

She chuckled. "Nah. They all have to end in 'ie' to qualify. And, of course, cup size always beats brain size."

His face heated. "Cut it out, Bradley." He stood in the doorway, hands anchored on either side of the opening. "You're making me sound shallow."

Anita snorted. "If the shoe fits, brother . . ."

He pictured the wiseass look on her brown face and schooled his own into patient forbearance. "Truth is, I like all kinds of women. Even you, Anita." The table was on the left side of the room, so he felt around in that direction. "Despite your cup or brain size."

She hooted in mock outrage.

"And your name doesn't even end in 'ie.' And neither, by the way, does Carol, Pam, or Trish."

"Yeah, but they didn't call."

"Not yet, anyway."

She laughed, the full-throated sound bubbling up from deep inside. "Okay, Sin, I'll leave you and your women alone."

"Why, thank you, Officer Bradley. Seeing as it's none of your goddamn business. And we wouldn't want to give

Miss Crowe here the wrong impression of Sokanan's finest."

Anita coughed, as though she was trying not to laugh again. "Of course not."

He trailed a short wall, then the empty space of the doorway into the parlor, another short wall, then the long counter with cupboards above and below. "I smell coffee."

"Fresh pot." A chair squeaked. Someone was getting up. "I'll get you a cup," Anita said.

"Don't bother." Martha's voice was sharp and aloof. "Try the counter about two-thirds of the way toward the table."

A beat. Then a chair scraped against the floor as Anita sat back down.

He cursed silently, now slowly skimming the surface of the counter until his fingers felt the plastic edge of a drip coffeemaker.

"Cups above," Martha said in that same cool voice.

Christ, what did she have to be so mad about? No one had lied to her.

But he had. Sort of. Last night.

He hadn't told her what he knew. And he'd messed with her.

So, shit, yeah, she had a right to be mad.

But that didn't mean he had to like it.

He reached up, fingered the edge of the cabinet, and fumbled with the door. Inside, his hand bashed against cups and mugs before wrapping around one. He took it down, paused, no clue what to do next.

The silence in the kitchen was loud and heavy. His heart was beating wildly. But he'd be damned if he'd ask Martha Crowe for anything.

He found the coffeemaker again, fingered its shape, and

burned himself on the edge of the warmer. "Jesus Christ." he shook his hand, sucked at the burn. But at least he knew where the pot was. He found the handle, pulled it out, then had to find the cup again.

His hand hit against it, and it skidded a few inches away.

"Fuck," he muttered.

"Use a search pattern." Martha, butting in again. "A grid or a circle."

Up yours, he said silently, and finally found the mug. Now what? How the hell was he going to pour the coffee without spilling it?

He bit down on his pride. "Okay, Crowe. You got me. How the hell do I pour this thing?"

"Are you asking for help?"

His jaw tightened. "Do it or tell me how. Without the gloating."

Her chair scraped back and her delicious scent came toward him. Then she was beside him, her hands on his, her breast on his arm. Intentional or accidental? Was she giving him some of his own back? Either way, he was instantly aware of her. Woman, not teacher. Soft. Curved. Female.

"Can you feel the rim of the coffeepot?" Her voice was low in his ear, her breath on his cheek. Beneath her fingers, his ran over the rim, trapped between the two. The pot was glass, smooth. Warm from the liquid's steam. Her fingers were slim, cool, a different kind of smooth.

Whatever saliva he'd had dried right up.

She guided his hand over the lip. "Here's the spout. Feel the edge of the cup with your left hand and rest the lip of the spout on it." Her hands moved with his in a slow, sensuous dance. "Wrap your hands around the cup and put your middle finger over the edge." She helped him do it, and blood rushed through his chest, down through his belly, and up through his dick. Christ. "Pour slowly. When you feel the heat close to your finger, you know the cup is full."

Like that, her hand disappeared, leaving him to wallow in his own heat.

You sad, sick fuck.

He held his breath, poured the coffee. No overflow.

It was pitiful how happy that small accomplishment made him.

"Breakfast?"

"Those who sleep until noon make their own," Martha said.

"Noon?"

"Well . . . not quite," Anita said. "But close enough. It's ten thirty."

Shit. He'd slept half the morning away. Ignoring the implications, the things he didn't want to think about, like depression and self-pity, he tightened his grip on his mug.

"You hear anything on the gun we turned in yesterday?"

"Maybe this afternoon," Anita said. "Bud's doing the trace."

"Who's Bud?" Martha asked.

"Bud Taylor," Danny said, "our ATF liaison. That's the bureau of Alcohol, Tobacco, and Firearms. They do most of our gun traces." He sipped at the coffee, glad he took it black and didn't have to go through another lesson to add milk and sugar. His stomach grumbled, but making breakfast seemed too big a mountain to climb. Pouring coffee was traumatic enough.

"Well"—a sigh and a chair slid against the floor—"I'm back in the living room," Anita said. "Thanks for the coffee."

"Thanks for the supplies," Martha said.

"Can't have our guests starving now, can we?" Anita

said. She passed him, clapping him on the back. "Come talk to me after you eat."

He nodded and she left.

"Anita bought groceries," Martha said. "There's eggs, toast, bacon."

"You going to hold my hand again?" He heard the edge in his voice.

"I'm not afraid of you, Detective Sinofsky." That tone. As though she'd raised her chin, straightened her spine.

"Sin."

"Danny."

"What's the matter, Martha? Got something against sin?"

"I wouldn't say it's done me a whole lot of good." She sounded Mary Poppins proper and every one of those fake fifty-eight years.

"It's not supposed to do good, Martha. It's supposed to feel good."

And shit, he'd give anything to feel good again.

"Feel good on someone else's time. On my time you can learn how to cook breakfast."

"I know how to cook breakfast. I'm a big boy."

"Glad to hear it. Save me some work." The slide of drawers accompanied her words. They slammed shut, as indicative of her mood as what must be a scowl on her face. Silverware or utensils clattered together and banged on what he took was the counter. The fridge opened and thumped closed, metal clanged against metal. "Everything you need is on the counter between the fridge and the stove. Tell me what you find."

Deciding to humor her—and maybe feeling the smallest bit of guilt for what he'd done the night before—he squared off against the counter and crossed the kitchen. He veered left and ended up in front of the sink, so he trailed right, passed the stove, and found the equipment laid out just where she said it would be.

He traced shapes. "Whisk. Knife."

"What kind?"

He focused his fingers on the shape of the blade and handle. "The kind you eat with, not stab with. Not a steak knife or a paring knife. No stilettos, hunting knives, or axes."

"Good." The word was crisp; she didn't rise to the bait. "What else?"

His fingers slid over a long container, paper or cardboard. He opened it, traced the curved lumps inside. "A dozen eggs in a box." Moving right he encountered more utensils. Long handle, cup shape at the bottom, not metal. "Wooden spoon." His hand brushed against something and it scraped against the counter. He fumbled for it, felt the edge, explored the shape. Round, cold, hard. Metal or glass. He pinged a finger against it, and it gave off a metallic ring. "Mixing bowl?"

"Yes."

He fingered a shallow pan with a long handle. "Frying pan." Finally, a papered rectangular cube. "Butter?"

"Margarine."

"How do you tell the difference?"

"Taste it."

"No thanks."

"You can mark it."

"Mark it?"

"Label it."

His jaw tightened. "I can't fucking read."

"With Braille," she said quietly.

The word hit him like an avalanche. His stomach squeezed, and the coffee he'd just drunk threatened to spew out of him. The ghost of Helen Keller rose up, white-haired, dusty in the way some old people were, her fingers tracing symbols she couldn't see. He might admire that, but not enough to turn into her.

"No. Never."

She sighed. As though she'd had a huge letdown—expected, but still disappointed. Well, he didn't give a fuck about her disappointment. No canes and no Braille. He wasn't going to be blind forever.

"You can use a marking pen then."

"A marking pen? Like a Sharpie?" Was she playing him? He couldn't see anything written with a Sharpie.

"Not exactly. More like puff paint."

"Puff paint? What the hell is that?"

"It's a craft paint. It's viscous and holds its shape. This is similar. You mark things with it. One dot for butter, two for margarine. But it won't take you far when it comes to cans."

Dots. Marking out everything in his life from now on. He swallowed. Pushed the revulsion away. Took out three eggs.

Martha watched him work. She was being a hard-ass, making him cook his own eggs, but he had to learn sometime. Besides, she refused to be intimidated by him.

Or by what had happened the night before.

What kind of guy makes a pass at a woman he thinks is old enough to be his mother?

A guy who has something to prove. Like blind or not he was still irresistible to women.

Yeah? Well, let him prove it with someone else. She was not going to let him get under her skin.

He cracked the first egg against the side of the bowl, but unable to judge the impact, he ended up demolishing it.

"Shit." His hand dripped raw egg.

"There's a towel hanging on the bar across the oven door." She was tempted to find it for him, but resisted. Let him see what it was like to be intimidated. She hardened her heart over her instinctive compassion as he fumbled for the stove, eventually found the towel and wiped his hands.

Then he cracked a second egg. It also smashed open.

"Fuck!"

He cracked open a third egg with no problem, got it into the mixing bowl, but when the fourth egg ended up all over him, he shoved the bowl and stormed off with a howl of frustration.

She sidestepped and blocked his way.

Anita appeared in the kitchen doorway, weapon drawn. "What's going on? Everything all right?"

"Get out of my way," he said to Martha through gritted teeth, eyes glaring sharp as a diamond edge.

"Detective Sinofsky is making breakfast." Martha's calm voice belied the pulse beating in her throat. "We're fine."

Anita paused, evaluated the situation, and backed off.

"How long did it take you to learn to shoot a gun?" Martha asked when Anita had gone.

He only scowled at her.

"Did you hit the target first time out? I'll bet you didn't. Did you give up? Did you stalk off the shooting range? Did you—"

"I get the point."

"Good. There are eight eggs left."

His face was tight, his steps jerky and resentful, but he went back to the counter. He could have walked off. He could have given up. He didn't, and a sneaky bit of admiration stole over her.

It took four more eggs to get two into the bowl, and he cursed his way through the entire process, but he whisked them with no problem.

When he finished beating the eggs, she showed him how to explore the stove, turn it on, and cook them.

Anger lines marred his handsome face, but he followed her instructions and when the eggs were done, he scraped them onto the plate, feeling for the edges to make sure he wasn't serving his breakfast onto the counter.

He did none of it happily, but he did it. And that said a lot about the way he faced the world. Plowing through until he got it right. A gust of pride blew through her. Resistance wasn't unusual for the newly blind, but often it took years to resolve. Her father had spent at least that long refusing to learn how to adapt to his injury.

She took the plate from him and set it on the table. "I assume you remember what a standard place setting is like?"

"Oh, yeah, like it was yesterday."

She pretended she hadn't heard the sarcasm, knowing it was the way he coped. "Sit down. Find the edge of the table with the backs of your curled fingers."

He did.

"Move both hands over the edge and forward, maintaining contact with the top of the table."

She watched his fingers survey the table. Even in cautious exploration, his hands were sure and strong, the skin tanned, the knuckles powerful. For half a second she remembered the feel of them on her face the night before. An unsettling quiver ran through her, and she was glad he couldn't witness it.

His fingers encountered something. "Napkin and fork to the left of the plate." His right hand moved farther. "Coffee cup at upper right. It's warm."

She tore her gaze away from his hands and took refuge in a businesslike manner. "I refilled it. Be careful not to lift your hand above the tabletop and sweep across. That's how glasses and bowls get spilled."

"Yes, ma'am."

She sat down at the table, too. She was almost getting used to being so close to him. Almost. "Salt and pepper?"

"If I could tell the difference."

"You still can. If you ask someone to pass them to you."

"Jesus. Will you just pass the damn things?"

"They're at two o'clock. Find them?"

He grimaced but followed her instructions and avoided spilling his coffee. Another gold star. "Yeah."

"Can you tell them apart?"

He lifted them. "One's heavier."

"That's right. Shake a little of the heavier one into your palm. What's it feel like?"

"Hard. Grainy."

"That's the salt. Try the other one."

"Soft, almost no weight at all."

"That's the pepper. Now, what's on your plate?"

"Scrambled eggs."

"Are you sure?"

"Of course I'm sure, I just cooked the f—"

"Okay. But what if you weren't sure? Or what if you had two strips of bacon on there as well?"

He shot her a look. Like he wanted to strangle her. "By the time we finish with all this, my eggs and nonexistent bacon will be cold."

"Use your fork and tap lightly over whatever is on your plate. That will help identify the type of food and where it's positioned."

He patted his eggs.

"When you want to season your food, shake the salt and pepper into your hand, then sprinkle it on."

He followed directions. Perfect. She smiled, that pride of accomplishment wafting over her again. Without thinking she nearly reached over and squeezed his hand before catching herself.

"So am I a good little doggie?"

"You're on your way to being an independent human being."

"Well, aren't I a lucky fucker."

The corners of her mouth twitched. "Yes, Detective, I do believe you are."

CHAPTER 6

————•————

Two nights later, Danny was in his room, avoiding another session with Martha when a knock sounded on the door. So far she'd taught him how to make his bed and sort his clothes, not to mention various other home ec lessons. Half the time he felt as though he was back in high school. No, make that grade school.

He was about to mouth off at her, but the voice on the other side said, "Hey, Sin, it's me, Tim."

Danny brightened. Anyone besides Martha was a welcome relief. Tim Carstens was the NRU's baby cop. A year older than Danny, he was slight of build with a boyish face that put him closer to sixteen. They used him to infiltrate schools and gangs. If he was there, it meant Anita was gone and another shift change had just taken place. Eight o'clock.

"Come in."

The door opened. "Brought you a present."

Danny stood at the side of the bed, making Tim come to him so he wouldn't have to fumble around finding him. "Hope it's an expensive one."

"Only the best for you, babe." Paper crackled and Tim put a bag in Danny's hand.

Inside the bag was a collection of boxes. Danny brought

one out, opened it up, and sniffed. The strong stench nearly made him gag. Liniment.

"Anything?" Tim asked.

Danny shook his head. "Too much wintergreen."

Tim made a noise. "Knock yourself out. Can't stand the smell of that stuff myself."

He left and Danny emptied the other boxes onto the bed, returning the one he'd opened to the bag. There were five boxes in all. Different shapes and sizes. He went through two more without luck when his cell phone rang. He took the phone off his hip and answered it.

"I got prelims on the gun," Mike said.

A bolt of excitement went through Danny. "And?"

"No markings, no proof marks, no serial numbers. Nothing. It's like the thing was conjured out of thin air."

The excitement waned. "Not likely." He swung his legs over the edge of the bed and rested his elbows against his knees. "Someone made it. There has to be a way to trace it. What's the ATF doing?"

"Sending it to metallurgy to see if they can trace where the steel was forged. If they can find that, they can trace it back to the manufacturer."

"Shit." That could take weeks, time he didn't have. The sooner they had a line on the weapon, the sooner they'd have a lead on the shooter, the sooner they could solve this thing, he could shed his personal trainer, and go back to his own life. As though he ever could. "Tell Bud to push it to the top of the pile."

"Yeah, well, we live in hope. I'll let you know when Bud has an ID. In the meantime, I did some checking on that list you gave me the other night."

"And?"

"Cross off Tommy Pelotti. He's already back inside.

Parole violation. Picked him up a week before the warehouse shooting."

Damn.

"What about Antone?"

"Alibi'ed out."

"Big surprise."

"Could be faked. But I have ten people who put him in the Starlight Club at the time of the shooting."

"Starlight is one of Roda's joints."

"True. But the witnesses are across the board. Not just his own crew. I got a couple of college kids, some locals. Everyone swears he was there."

"Well, that's a shame. Dewayne got anything?"

"Nah. Says he'll keep his ears open and let me know, but right now, he's got nothing."

"So we're back to square one."

"Unless you came up with any new ideas today."

He thought of the long, tense afternoon with Martha. "I've been through almost all the files, and nothing's hit me."

"Okay. I'll keep on our boy Antone. See if I can break the alibi. And I'll nag the shit out of Dewayne. How's everything else going?"

"Trust me, you don't want to know."

"Hang tight. See you tomorrow."

Danny disconnected. Nothing was going his way. Tommy and Antone were long shots, but he'd been hoping they'd pay off. The gun was the best lead they had and for it to yield zilch was too damn much.

He'd never had a weapon that couldn't be traced somehow. Even ground-off serial markings could be identified. What kind of gun came off the line with nothing on it?

A cold shudder went through him.

This was nuts. He wasn't even in a big city, and he'd never had a case with that much at stake. Why would someone . . . ?

He fumbled for the buttons on his cell phone. He was getting better at finding the numbers, but it still took him a couple of tries to punch in the right ones. Eventually he reached Bud Taylor's office, only to find Taylor had gone for the day. Danny left a message.

Unease rippled up his back. Christ, he'd give anything to have the solid weight of a weapon on his hip and know he could use it.

He reached for calm, but couldn't get there. He was useless. Fucking useless. Whoever was after him for whatever reason, he was a sitting duck.

And so was Martha.

He'd like to say he didn't give a shit. That it was fine by him, go ahead and shoot her. He'd like to.

But it wasn't her fault she was mixed up in this. It was his, plain and simple. And he couldn't keep himself safe, let alone her.

A knock.

"Danny?"

The devil herself.

"Yeah?"

Without an invitation, Martha cracked the door. "Want a sandwich?"

He suspected a trap. Some kind of repeat torture of the last two mornings. "I have to make it myself?"

"It's after five. You have the evening off." Was there a tease in her voice?

"Thanks, boss."

"You're very welcome. So, turkey or roast beef?"

"You're kidding, right?"

"Roast beef." She sounded as if she'd rolled her eyes at him. "Cheese?"

"No cheese, no tomatoes. Lettuce is fine. Mustard and mayo."

"Yes, sir." There was a distinct mocking tone in her voice. "Will there be anything else?"

Despite himself, his lips curved up. He had to hand it to her. She was damn good at shoving the bullshit right back at him. "Ice cold Bud?"

"Sorry. No liquor license."

"Well, what kind of place is this?"

"It's a hideout. No amenities."

"Ah. I'm gonna have to talk to someone about that. I'll be there in a minute."

After she'd gone, he fumbled for the last two boxes of liniment. The first was another dud, but the last, a hexagonal jar packaged in a small, square box, was pay dirt. A kind of herby, minty smell none of the others had.

Feeling as though he'd thrown the winning pass at the Superbowl, he trailed down the hall and stopped in the living room.

"Hey, Tim. You here?"

"On the couch."

"What is this?" He tossed the jar of salve in Tim's direction and heard the satisfying thump as he caught it.

"Tiger Balm," he said. "Manufactured for . . . let's see . . . Haw Par Healthcare, Singapore. This the one?"

"That's it. From Singapore? Where'd you get it? Some little Chinese folk doctor who only sold it to two people on the East Coast?"

Tim laughed. "Yeah, that would be nice. Try CVS."

"Well, that sucks."

"Not if your guy bought it in So-town. There aren't that many drugstores in Sokanan. I'll check it out tomorrow."

If the ointment had been purchased in Sokanan. If CVS carried Tiger Balm other stores probably carried it, too. No telling where the perp picked it up. But he didn't say anything to Tim. Likely he knew the odds as well as Danny.

"Want another sandwich?" Martha said from somewhere in the direction of the kitchen.

"I'm good," Tim said. "Thanks."

"How about you, Detective Sinofsky. You coming?"

Danny made his way into the kitchen, where he found the table and sat. From across the room came the sound of food preparation: knives clinking against jars, plastic bags scrunching open and closed, china scraping against the counter. Beneath it all Martha's clothes rustled and swished, and that fragrance drifted by.

What was it? Shampoo? Soap? Perfume? The smell was driving him nuts in all the wrong places.

A few minutes later, her footsteps approached and a plate knocked against the tabletop.

"Roast beef, no cheese."

Another plate landed, a chair slid against the floor and creaked as Martha sat down.

Casually, he skimmed the edges of his plate and the placement of the food, the exploration almost second nature now. Sandwich cut in half in the center, chips at nine, pickle at three.

He bit in. "Good," he said, his mouth half-full.

"Glad you like it."

"You cook a lot?"

"My dad would live on peanut butter and boiled eggs if I didn't."

So she cooked for her dad. All sorts of underlying implications there. Maybe he could use them to put her in the hot seat and worm a confession out of her. "So, how long have you lived with your father?" Not *did* she live with him, a question whose answer could be a lie, but how long, a question requiring a more or less factual answer.

"Most of my life." The shortness of the answer begged him to go no further. *Tough shit, Martha baby.*

"Kind of strange for a fifty-eight-year-old to be still living with her father. He must be ancient by now."

"We've always been close."

"Martha and her dad. Sounds cozy." Was she tempted to tell the truth? He took another bite of sandwich, giving her every chance to come clean. "You've never been married?"

"No."

"Really? In all those long, fifty-eight years you never found anyone special?"

She cleared her throat. Was she squirming? "Sometimes it just works out that way."

"And that's how it 'worked out' for you." He nodded thoughtfully, chewed. Swallowed. Let her stew. "How come?"

"How come what?"

"How come you never found anyone in all those many, many years?"

"Look, my love life is none of your—"

"Too picky?"

"I do have standards, but—"

"Too bossy? Now that wouldn't surprise me."

"There's nothing wrong with a strong woman."

"Don't like sex?"

"I like sex just fine."

"Even at fifty-eight? Or, sorry, was it fifty-five?"

A beat of silence. He pictured her putting down her

sandwich, turning to drill him with a look. "What's this all about?" That quiet thing was back in her voice. Quiet mixed with caution.

"You're not fifty-eight, Martha. You're not even fifty-five."

Another silence. Much longer this time.

"Are you."

It wasn't a question, and she didn't reply.

He added some edge to his voice. "Are you."

"No."

And the truth shall set you free.

He polished off the sandwich, not really tasting it, and dusted the crumbs off his hands, casual and indifferent. "So . . . do you play these games with all your blind friends?"

"I wasn't—"

"What? Lying?" A bit of anger sneaked into his voice and he let it come.

"Playing games." The words came out low and small.

"No? What would you call it?"

"I . . . look . . . I didn't mean . . ." She took a breath, a huge mouthful that came out slow and shaky. "I'm sorry." Her chair scraped back. "I . . . I'm sorry." Footsteps fled.

"Everything okay?" Tim's voice. Probably as she roared by him.

Danny pushed his plate away in disgust and followed her out.

"What's with her?" Tim asked.

"Who knows?"

He strode down the hallway, past his room and the bathroom, the route already familiar. He didn't even knock.

Martha whirled as he entered her room unannounced.

"You're not getting away that easy." He closed the door

and leaned against it, one hand tight on the knob. A jailer with his prisoner.

So big, so dark, so beautiful. And brave. She hadn't forgotten the way he'd put himself between her and danger. Twice now. At his home with the intruder, and a few days ago, when they weren't sure if the arriving car was trouble. Considering how much he had to deal with, he was coping brilliantly. The last thing he needed was her betrayal.

But she hadn't meant it that way. She'd only meant to protect herself. To keep him at bay.

"Why did you tell me you were old enough to be my mother when anyone with two eyes in their head—anyone but me, that is—could tell that you aren't?"

"I . . ."

"You what, dammit?"

She didn't know what to say. How could she tell him the truth? "You're very . . ."

"What? I'm very what?"

She swallowed. "Attractive." The word was a croak, barely heard.

But he heard it just fine. A stunned, puzzled expression vied with the anger in his face.

"You lied to me because I'm . . ." He was trying to figure it out.

"And I'm . . ." She squeezed her eyes shut. She could not say this.

"You're . . . what?"

"Not," she got out.

"You're not . . . what?"

She licked her lips. "A . . . attractive."

He shook his head. "This is making sense, isn't it? I mean somewhere on some planet, someone is understanding this."

"I'm not . . ."

"What? What else are you not?"

"Very good with men. And I thought . . ."

"Yes?"

"I thought that if you thought I was older, you wouldn't . . . that is, I wouldn't . . . I mean there wouldn't be any question of . . ."

"What?"

"Anything. Between us. Other than the rehab. It would be easier."

"So . . . let me get this straight. Me, being like an eleven on the hunk-o-meter, would naturally make some kind of move on you, except that I wouldn't because you're like a minus ten. Am I getting it?"

She nodded, her face hot and, she was sure, tomato red. "Something like that."

A beat. His face was expressionless. What was he thinking? She couldn't blame him for being angry. She'd done a rotten thing, even if it had been done in self-defense. All the progress he'd made—had she tainted it? Would he ever trust her again?

She braced herself for an outburst, but none came.

"You know I'm blind." If anything, his voice was overly patient. As if he were talking to a two-year-old.

"Yes." The word came out slowly, cautiously.

He crossed his arms companionably. "That means . . . well, I can't see."

"I know."

He threw up his hands—suddenly, violently. "So, you could be Pamela Anderson as far as I'm concerned!"

"I'm not."

"That's not the point."

"That's exactly the point. I'm not Pamela Anderson. Or Barbie or Pattie. I'm plain old Martha."

"Well, I don't think Barbie or Pattie could have done what you did."

"Lied to you?"

"Taught me how to scramble eggs."

Her chest tightened and her breath caught. She looked down at her hands, surprised to feel the sting of tears. She never cried. Not in a very long time. But his forgiveness, couched in a compliment, overcame her.

She took a minute to regain her composure, then squared her shoulders. "I'm going to teach you how to use that cane, too."

He smiled. "Not in this lifetime."

"We'll see."

His smile widened. "I will, you can bet on it."

It was a sucker's bet, but she didn't care. "I'm starting to think I should take that bet."

"Smart girl."

He turned to leave, then turned back. "So, Martha, one more thing before I go. What is this stuff you use to smell so good?"

She paused. She hadn't realized he'd noticed. "Sachet. In my . . . my clothes. My mother used it. After she . . . well, I liked it, so I began using it too."

"It's very sexy, Martha." He grinned, and opened the door. "Very sexy." And then he was gone.

Martha stood there, too stunned to move. He'd said she smelled sexy.

No one had ever said anything about her was sexy. But if anyone should know it was Mr. Fantasy Man himself.

Good thing he couldn't see.

With a wrench of guilt, she squelched that thought. She wanted him to see again. Truly.

She—

The door opened, and Danny stepped in. His face was different than it had been a moment ago. Now it was tight, tense.

"Martha?" He whispered it, and instantly she knew something was wrong.

"What is it? What's the matter?"

He extended an arm, reaching for her, and she held out her hand. Pulling her toward him, he put a finger to his lips. *Don't talk.* "Someone's in the house," he said in her ear.

Alarm slithered up her spine. "Shift change?" she whispered back.

He shook his head.

Oh, God.

"Are you sure?" She swallowed, knowing she shouldn't need to point out the obvious. But it would be so easy to make a mistake. "Maybe I should check."

He gripped her tighter, his body blocking the door. "Don't you dare."

"But—"

"I know I can't see, dammit. But I can still hear, not to mention smell. I'm not letting you go out there."

"Where's . . . where's Tim?"

"He can't help us."

A squeak of panic leaked out of her. He put a hand around the back of her neck. It was warm, comforting somehow.

"Everything's going to be all right." His voice was soothing, his expression sure.

Did he believe that, or was he lying to keep her from screaming? Either way, she clutched at it like a lifeline.

"Is there a way out of the room?"

Swallowing fear, she took his lead and concentrated on what to do. "Besides the door?"

He nodded, and she looked around. "A window."

"Go check the drop. Hurry."

He released her and she ran to the window, her pulse leaping. The sun had long set, and she could see nothing but her own reflection. "Wait." She ran back to where he was standing.

"What are you doing? We don't have time—"

"I can't see anything." She flicked off the light and ran back to the window. Peered out. "It's a few feet off the ground."

"Grab your coat and get me over there."

"My coat's by the backdoor." Trying to ignore her stomach, which was somersaulting madly, she steered him to the window.

"Then grab whatever you can to keep warm." Quickly his fingers ran over the window and found the latch.

"What about you?" He was wearing jeans and a sweater. Warm enough for indoors but not much use in the cold night.

"I'll have to make do. Damn." He was tugging at the window. It didn't budge.

She hauled a sweater over her shoulders, already shivering. "It's painted shut."

"Christ."

A footstep. Both of their heads snapped up.

"Do you have a penknife?" His voice was low and hoarse with tension.

She gulped and shook her head, her heart beating faster than she thought possible. Then she remembered and said, "No."

"Something, anything. A letter opener?"

"Nail file?"

"Get it."

A door opened somewhere down the hall. For a minute she couldn't remember what she'd done with her purse. Then her brain unfroze and she grabbed it from a chair in the corner.

"Here." She started to hand him the small, metal file.

"You'll have to do it. Quickly. Just enough to get the window open."

Palms slick with sweat, she began to gouge at the seam of paint gluing the window jamb shut.

"How did they find us?"

"The question of the year."

More footsteps down the hall.

"Hurry."

She redoubled her efforts, hacking at the window, while Danny rocked the housing as much as possible, trying to break the seal. His grunting efforts mixed with the pitiful sound of the file attacking the thick paint.

A crack, and the file broke in her hand.

"What was that?"

"The file broke."

"Jesus Christ."

A door opened. Danny's room? She sucked in a terrified breath. Danny's room was only two doors away.

"I didn't want to give us away with the noise, but . . ." He wrapped the sleeve of his shirt around his hand and punched in the window. Glass flew out. Cold air burst in. Shuddering, she covered her fist with her own sleeve and frenetically helped hack out a space big enough for them to get through.

"Go!" He shoved her forward.

"Wait!" She grabbed her purse and a pillow from the bed, tossed her purse out the window, and placed the pillow over the bottom window edge, covering the jagged glass. Then she stuffed herself through the opening. Glass cut into her shoulder and side, but in an instant she tumbled to the ground and turned to help him through.

"There's a pillow to protect you from the bottom glass." He hoisted himself up, and she gripped him under the arms and around his wide shoulders, heaving him out. His weight pushed her down and they both landed on the ground with a thud, his body pinning her.

He said, "We'll have to try this again sometime." He rolled off, keeping contact with her arm, grasped her hand, and pulled her to her feet.

"You okay?" he said.

Before she could answer, a door crashed open behind them. Someone shouted.

"Get us out of here." He squeezed her hand, and she hauled him forward, racing away. Something cracked around them, snapping and popping.

Gunshots.

God, God. Someone was shooting at them. She nearly wept in panic. Her feet slowed. Her whole body was freezing in terror.

"No, keep going!" He wrenched her arm, pulling her forward and almost unbalancing her.

She righted herself, and he shouted at her. "Where are we?"

"I . . . I don't know." In vain, she looked around.

"You have to know. Concentrate! I can't do this by myself."

Another shot rang out and she yelped.

"What happened?" Her own panic was reflected in his voice. "Are you hurt?"

"No. I just—"

"Then think. Where are we going?"

Her throat was too tight, she was lightheaded, and her stomach was churning. But somehow she made herself focus. "Toward the field." He stumbled, lost his footing, and regained it. If she didn't help him, they'd never get away. "Nothing's in front of you!" His hand was so tight around hers. "Just . . . just keep going. It's open space."

The shots seemed to stop or fade away, she wasn't sure which. They were both breathing hard, and her heart was knocking against her ribs.

"Is there snow on the ground? I hear a crunch."

"A thin coat."

"We're leaving tracks?"

She stiffened. Looked over her shoulder. Moonlight glittered on the outline of their footsteps. "Oh, God. Yes." She turned back in time to see a lone tree up ahead. "Tree!" She jerked him to the left to avoid it, and he almost fell.

"Wait. Wait!" He slowed down to a jog. "Is anyone following?"

"I don't know." Dreading what she might see, she peeked over her shoulder again. "I don't . . . I don't see anyone."

But she heard something. As did he. His head swiveled toward the sound of a car starting up. God, no. They'd never escape a car. Not stumbling around on foot.

"Look, we can't head toward a plowed field. If we're leaving tracks, they know where we're going. And a flat field would make it easy for them to mow us down with a car. We've got to find cover. You mentioned a tree. Are there more? Woods? Buildings, any kind of structure?"

She remembered the wind in the trees on the porch, and looked west. "Yes! Woods to the left."

"Head there. And don't wait for me. If something happens, just keep going."

She refused to even think about that.

Clinging to his hand, she flew toward the trees as though she were dying of thirst and they were the only oasis.

How long it took to reach the cover of the woods, she couldn't say, but it seemed like twelve eternities. Sweat dripped down her back and her legs were so rickety, she thought they'd stop holding her up. Any minute she expected a bullet to carve her back in two. The fear drove her forward, even as it made her want to drop and hide.

Miraculously, they reached the safety of the trees and plunged into the forest. Immediately, Danny hit his head against a low-hanging branch. She slowed, and he hit his shin against a rock. She reduced the pace even further, and another branch slapped his cheek.

After the umpteenth time he bumped into something, he stopped. "This isn't working."

He ran a hand through his hair. Like her, he was breathless, chest heaving. His lips were pale, his face taut as though frozen by the cold. A thin stream of blood trickled from his right cheek, which had so many cuts, it looked as though someone had drawn lines on it with a sharp pen. From the window glass or the trees? Vaguely she wondered what her own face looked like, and was glad she couldn't see it.

"Look, go on and leave me here," he said. "No point in you getting hurt."

Her jaw dropped, and the cold swooped into her mouth. "Are you crazy? I'm not leaving you."

His mouth thinned. "It's better than both of us getting shot."

She was still quivering, little tremors of terror and cold that gripped her uncontrollably. She stamped her feet to conceal them, and not a little bit because what he suggested was ludicrous. "Oh, really. Very noble of you. Not to mention crazy. Why don't we just call someone?"

"Like who—Spiderman?"

She wanted to shake him. Men with guns were chasing them, she was turning into an icicle, and he was making jokes. "I don't know. Mike, Anita. You must know about a million cops."

He shook his head, his expression bleak. "We can't call anyone from the department."

"Why not?"

Crossing his arms over his chest, he tucked his hands into his armpits and hunched against the wind. "The only people who knew about that place were cops."

A shiver ran through her, and it wasn't just the cold. "What are you saying? You think a cop is behind this?"

"I have no idea. I only know the information about where we were had to come from someone in my unit."

She stared at him in horror, the zip of those gunshots replaying in her mind. "Not Mike. Or Anita."

"Or Bayliss or Carstens or anyone else. At least, I hope to God not." His voice was harsh, his face harsher. "But I'm not taking any chances."

"So . . . where does that leave us?" She blew on her hands. "If the police are out, that means we go to friends, relatives. Who can you call?"

"I don't know. Not Beth. I can't get her involved in this."

Rapidly, she ran over the list of people she knew. But she came up with only one name. One person she wanted to rely on but wasn't sure she could. Her father had promised countless times to pick her up from school, and countless times she'd trudged the long walk home. She'd learned not to depend on him, and that habit had continued into adulthood.

She bit her lip, nervous and unsure. But what choice did they have?

She plunged her chilled hand into her purse and fished for her phone.

He must have heard her rummaging because he said, "What are you doing?"

"Looking for my phone."

"Why? Who are you going to call?"

"My dad."

He grimaced. "You're kidding. This is not the kind of situation where Daddy can help."

Her stiff fingers closed around the phone. "This one can." She only prayed he would.

She punched in the number and waited for the line to connect. Charlie picked up before the phone could ring twice.

"Daddy?"

"Martha. Where the hell are you?" His voice was full of worry. "Are you all right?"

She hesitated, then told the truth. "Well . . . not really. No."

He cursed a blue streak.

"Dad, we don't have time."

"Tell me where you are."

"Old House. About twenty minutes outside of town on Route 3. We need a pickup, but we can't meet in the open."

"Wait a minute. I'll get a map."

She waited and the silence alerted Danny. "What's going on?"

"He's getting a map."

"Christ." Danny's shoulders were taut, his face vigilant. She immediately tensed. "What? Do you hear something?"

"An engine."

Her heart picked up speed and she strained her ears, but couldn't hear anything.

"I don't think they've gotten to the woods yet, but it's only a matter of time."

Charlie returned to the phone. "Tell me again. Where are you?"

"In a wooded area in Old House. Off Route 3. It's a farm. We're on foot."

"Dammit, girl. Route 3 is miles long. Any idea where?"

She could have kicked herself for not paying closer attention. "No."

"How close are you to the water tower?"

"The water tower? I don't—Wait, I remember seeing it on the way in. I think we could get there."

"Then meet me there."

"Bring a coat. One of yours and something of mine. And if you find gloves and a hat—"

"You have no coat?"

"We had to leave fast."

The cursing started again.

"Daddy. See you soon." She disconnected, surprised at how quickly he'd acquiesced. And not a little thrilled. Her father said he would come.

Now if he only got there.

CHAPTER 7

If anyone had asked Danny a week ago what he'd be doing now, the last thing he imagined was running through total darkness from some unseen terror, completely dependent on an unarmed and untrained civilian. It was like his own private horror flick.

Martha was adamant about the proper hold. "I'm not improvising this. If you want me to lead you out, you damn well better hold on correctly. There's a reason we do it this way."

"Fine. Fine. Just go."

She wrapped his hand around her arm and they lumbered forward like a huge, ungainly beast.

"Can you hear the car?" she asked.

"Still faint. Behind us. Can you see it?"

She stopped and her body twisted away, letting cold air blast him. "No." She turned back around. "If I remember correctly, the trees end at a field. We'll have more cover on the other side of the road, but that means we'll have to cross it to get there. Think it's safe?"

"Probably not. But it doesn't sound like we have much choice. Let's get as far as we can before trying it. See if we can outrun them."

But instead of falling behind, the engine sound seemed

to follow them. She sped up until they were jogging and the wintry air sliced across his face. Breathless, he felt it going down, a rush of ice in his lungs.

"I can hear it now." Her voice carried an undertone of anxiety.

"Pick up the pace."

He matched his steps to hers as best he could, shortening his longer stride and struggling to keep up with her. Behind them, the car roared closer. Was it at the edge of the wood? A door slammed. Two male voices. He couldn't pick up what they were saying.

"Cross now!" If their pursuers were entering the wood, they wouldn't be watching the road.

Unless there were three of them.

He cursed for not staying longer in the house to tell. He'd heard the strange footsteps, the whispered conversation, a crack, a groan, the thud of a body falling. And the faint icy smell of Tiger Balm. At that point, he didn't wait to see what else he could discover. He had to get Martha out of there.

He stumbled over something at his feet.

"Tree root." Martha sounded winded, her words riding puffs of air. "Sorry." She tugged him to the left. "There's a clear spot here. Let's cross."

Space was a never-ending blackness, every step a test against fear and mistrust. Would Martha let him fall? His dependency ground against him. He should be the one leading. Holding on to her was emasculating, humiliating.

But he stuffed the shame down deep and concentrated on his footing.

"We're at the tree line," Martha said breathlessly.

"Can you see the road?"

"Just a minute." She left and anxiety flooded him, liquid

and fierce. Where were they? Where were the people chasing them? How was he going to get them out of there if he couldn't see his own damn feet in front him?

Branches crackling underfoot signaled her return. "It seems clear."

He forced himself to stop shaking. "No guard? No one watching?"

"Not that I could tell."

He breathed a sigh of relief. "Good. Maybe we'll catch another break."

They stepped forward. "Another?"

"We're moving, aren't we?"

"Got it." She dragged in a breath, shuddering. "Here we go." Almost immediately, the footing changed. The road was smooth, the wind and cold sharper. No trees to act as buffer, he guessed.

He huddled into the wind, imagining the picture they made. A two-headed creature silhouetted by moonlight, scurrying across an inky country road only to disappear into the grotesque shadows of looming trees. More horror movie clips.

Martha's body was stiff and tight. He would have liked to reassure her, but couldn't. If they made it, they'd be lucky.

Seconds later, they were on rough ground again.

"We're on the other side. It's scrub and trees here for a while."

Which meant he'd have to cling to her totally. He shoved that thought away, surrendering to the darkness. At least she hadn't fallen apart. He could almost smell the fear on her, but she kept going. That said a lot about her.

"Bet they never taught you this in blind school."

"What?"

"Running away from guys with guns."

"I must have missed that lecture." Her tone was one of dour amusement, the corners of his mouth twisted up.

"You're doing fine."

She inhaled a shaky breath. "Glad someone thinks so. Me, I feel like a wobbly mess." She slowed down. "Lots of downed branches here. Watch your step."

An understatement at best. Their journey might just as well have been a roller-coaster ride in the dark. She twisted left then right, and his pulse leaped. She led him over knobs and lumps and under things he couldn't name. Sometimes a branch startled him as it brushed his face. Sometimes she identified the obstacle. A fallen tree trunk, a rock. In places she put their twined arms behind her back so he followed single file. But to him it was all movement in the dark, a daring, frightening, unseen path with only her body and her voice to guide him.

Mouth dry, palms sweaty, he struggled with the steps, and with the blind trust it took to hold on and keep going. And all the while, the image of their pursuers hovered in the back of his mind.

Who were they? Why were they after him?

Nothing he knew should put him in peril. He'd been in the NRU for three years. If someone wanted to get back at him, why now? And for what?

The anomaly of the unmarked gun stood out in his mind, but he still couldn't make sense of it.

Then there was the rest. Someone he trusted had given him up. *Betrayal* was an ugly word and his mind skittered over it the way a tongue touches a sore tooth. A jab of hurt. He couldn't conceive of Mike informing on him. And Parnell. God, no. If it had to be someone, let it be one of the others.

But the cop in him knew it was a possibility. A grisly, sick, unbearable to believe possibility.

"Almost there," Martha whispered. "I can see the tower ahead." She paused, breathing hard. He imagined white, moonlit air moving in and out of her mouth. She was shaking. His own legs were none too steady and beneath the cold, he was sweating.

"Do you see the van?"

"Yes. Parked on the far side."

A wash of relief. "Call him. Tell him where we are and to come get us. And keep the line open until we're in the car."

Scrounging sounds. Was she looking for her phone? Faint clicks. Punching in the number?

"Daddy? We're here. On the east side of the tower. Bring the car around. No, I don't think anyone's following. Stay on the line until you get here."

A car engine turned over.

"Is he coming?"

"Yes. Very slowly."

"Good. Keep an eye out."

"I'm looking. Everything seems clear. What about you, Daddy? Okay? Good."

The engine rumble neared. The acrid smell of car exhaust closed in.

"He's here. Ready?"

"Be careful." Danny wrapped his hand around her arm again and they set off. "How far?"

"Ten yards, maybe less. We're heading for the edge of the trees." A few more steps and she said, "We're about to come into the open."

He heard a machine glide, like something mechanical moving.

He dug in his heels. "What's that?"

"The van door opens automatically."

Relaxing a bit, he stepped onto smoother footing. Concrete? Blacktop? Something hard and man-made.

Tires squealed.

"Oh, God," Martha screamed. "They're here!"

"Where?"

She pulled him forward and he almost fell headfirst.

"Run!"

Shouts, gunshots, the hard pound of feet.

"In! In!"

Someone was hauling him over a ledge. The van? He threw himself forward. The van lurched, his legs swung outside. He scrambled, clutched at a rubber floor mat for traction. Someone else—Martha?—grabbed the back of his sweater, heaved. Between the two of them, they hauled him in.

"He's in, Daddy. Get the door!"

The mechanical sweep again. The door closing? Tires screamed. He was on the floor, rocked back and forth by the movement of the car.

More shots.

"Shit!" A male voice from inside. "What the hell have you gotten into?" More rocking, screeching as the driver manipulated the van.

They were moving. Fast. The burr of the engine vibrated through the floor, but it was as if he were in a black box hurtling through space. He smelled stale cigarette smoke, engine oil, and leather.

"Where are we?"

"Still on Route 3," Martha said.

"Can you get off the road?"

"Hell, yes." The driver had a deep, husky voice, and

Danny pictured a big man. Someone familiar with whiskey and cigarettes and, he hoped to God, the rougher side of life.

A wrench. The car had made a sharp turn, and Danny's head knocked against something—the edge of a seat? No, it was cool, hard. He reached around to haul himself away. His hand brushed against metal and a wheel.

"Are they following?"

"They were." Martha's voice was clipped with tension.

"What about now?"

A pause. "I think we lost them," came the prediction from the front.

Another silence. As if everyone strained to hear the sound of the car behind them.

"No, there they are!"

The van turned sharply again, and again Danny was thrown against the wheeled contraption. When the car righted itself, Danny did a quick trace of whatever it was. Metal pads, wheels, leather sides, handlebars. Too wide for a bicycle. Besides, it was collapsed in on itself.

The identity of the shape clicked in his head, and he gasped with recognition.

A wheelchair.

Hackles rose on the back of his neck.

"Martha." His voice was a deadly whisper.

"What?"

"What's this"—he jabbed his thumb in the direction of the chair—"doing here? I don't remember you telling him to bring one."

"Relax. That's not for you. It's his."

Her words hit him like a slap. He lowered his voice.

"He's in a fucking wheelchair?"

"You got a problem with that, son?" The voice of the

driver sounded ominous, and the car wrenched to the left, throwing Danny hard against the door.

He winced. "Yeah, I do, as a matter of fact. We got a blind man, a woman, and now a cripple. How much worse can the odds be against us?"

"A blind man?" The driver's voice was appalled.

"My new client," Martha said. "Detective Danny Sinofsky, this is my father, Charlie Crowe."

"Jesus Christ," Danny said at the same time as Charlie.

"Pleased to meet you would have been just fine," Martha said.

"Look," Charlie said, "what is going on? You've got a bruise on your cheek. Did someone hit you? Who's in that car?"

Martha sighed. "We don't know."

"What do you mean, you don't—"

"Just what she said. We don't know."

"You got people shooting at you and you don't know who or why?"

Danny wanted to punch something, but restrained himself. "That about sums it up."

A stream of cursing came from the front seat. For a moment, Danny marveled at the creativity of the invectives. The man was very good at it.

"Dad! Enough. You're not helping."

"I'm helping myself, girl. God almighty." The car swerved right, and Danny swerved with it.

"Any idea where you'd like to go, kid?" Charlie said in his distinctive hoarse voice. "The Plaza, Waldorf, Motel 6? The sooner we get rid of you, the sooner I get my daughter home safe."

Danny bristled. "Home is the last place she'll be safe. And the name's Sin, not kid."

"Sin?"

"Short for 'Sinofsky,' " Martha said, that dry tone in her voice again. "But he answers to Danny, too."

The van tilted up, slowed, then plunged down, brakes squeaking. Danny's ribs were taking a beating, and his brain was racing in time to his lurching heart. They had a cripple driving them God knew where, and Danny was responsible yet helpless to fix it.

"Why can't I take her home?" Charlie asked.

"Because whoever is after me is after her, too."

"And why the hell is that?" He practically shouted it, and Danny couldn't blame him.

"She saw him. She can identify him. That's the guy who hit her."

"Look, will you stop talking as if I'm not here?"

More brakes, another swing to the right. Danny's belly took a left turn while the rest of him went right. Christ, he wanted to scream and grab the wheel, do the driving himself.

"Well, if I can't take her home, where the frigging fuck can I take her?"

Danny ran through the list of possibilities, desperate to get some measure of control over the situation. "Can you get to the river?"

"What's at the river?"

"A boat. We can take it down to Manhattan. They won't expect that, which means they won't be able to follow."

"How the hell are you going to steer a boat? You're blind, man."

"I'm not," Martha said.

"You've never been in a boat in your life," Charlie said.

"First time for everything," Martha said, and Charlie grumbled.

"What happens in the city?"

"I've got a friend there."

"You're going to need a lot more than a friend."

"He's a federal friend."

That stopped the discussion. For a millisecond.

"I'm going with you."

"Bad idea, Charlie."

"Fuck you, kid. She's my baby, and I'm not leaving her."

"Be better if you drove the van around, make them think you've still got us inside. Lure them away."

The good sense of that plan took Charlie down to a low roar. "If I do that, you've got to promise to call me. Let me know she's safe."

Martha emitted an exasperated breath. "*I'll* call you. I may not have that dangling third leg, but I do have a brain."

"Well, whatever you've got yourself messed up in makes me think you lost it along the way," Charlie snapped.

Danny didn't appreciate that snarl in Charlie's voice. Especially since it was completely undeserved. "Hey, Charlie, cut it out. None of this is her fault."

"You think I don't know that?"

"I don't need you to defend me to my own father," Martha said.

"I was just—"

"I know what you were 'just.' Now listen up, both of you."

"Here we go," said Charlie.

"I'm all ears," said Danny.

"I'm a big girl and I make my own decisions. I'm not leaving him, Dad."

Danny balled his hands into tight fists. "I don't need you to—"

"Yes, you do, dammit." He could almost hear her biting

her lip at the mild curse. The picture took the sting out of her words. "And Daddy. You're not getting any more involved than you already are. Lose the car. Take us to the river. We'll be fine. I'll call you when we're safe."

"But—"

"No more arguments."

What was it about this woman? She'd shut Charlie up like a clam. And he was no better, yes ma'aming her to death.

"Okay?" Softer now, but he could hear the love below the question.

Charlie sighed. "Okay."

"Danny?" Something edged into her voice, but he couldn't tell what, except the tone was different from the one she'd used on Charlie. For some reason, the distinction left a little hole inside him.

"Yeah. Sure. Fine by me."

Through the van windshield, the river was a strip of black shimmer. Martha shrugged into the coat her father had brought and hugged it to her. He'd come. He'd shown up just as he said he would. The thought warmed her almost as much as the coat.

"Anything happens to Martha, I'm coming for you." Charlie half-turned in his seat and pointed a finger at Danny, as though he could see it.

They'd ditched the car fifteen minutes before by hiding in a turnoff until their pursuers passed by. How long the trick would fool them, no one knew, but for now, they were parked beside the dock in the Hudson River marina in Sokanan. A few lights gave off a low glow, illuminating the boats and the river beyond them.

"Anything happens to her, I'm already dead," Danny said.

"Stop it. Both of you. Here"—she handed Danny her father's leather jacket—"put this on. Nothing's going to happen to me. No one is dying. Got it?"

There was a beat. A pause that meant the two of them didn't believe the confidence behind her words. She couldn't blame them. She hardly believed it herself.

"Got it?"

"Yeah, sure," Danny said, struggling with the zipper.

"You better be right," her father said.

"I am." She put her hands over Danny's to help him, but he jerked away.

"Don't."

She bit her lip. Any sign of dependency was always difficult for him. But now, in front of her father . . .

"Let's go." She kissed her father on the cheek.

"Call me."

"I will."

"Soon," he ordered.

"I will," she insisted.

He opened the door, and she spilled out. Danny slid after her, his feet feeling for the ground before he stood. "Watch your back, Charlie. If you have some place besides home to stay for a few days, you might think about going there. Just in case they made the van."

Charlie harrumphed. "I don't need no pretty boy telling me how to take care of myself. You just watch out for Martha." Then the door closed, and he roared away.

She plunged her hands deep into the pockets of her coat. It was her old one, the lining ripped in places, the edges frayed. But the black wool was warm and heavy, the collar huge enough to cover her neck and tuck under her throat.

"Grab on."

He placed his hands on her upper arm. "You like this, don't you? Leading me around."

She sniffed, not wanting him to know that she did indeed like the feel of his hand on her arm, the closeness of his hard body. "I'm not leading you anywhere. I'm just helping you get where you want to go."

"Oh. I get it. Like a map. My own private GPS."

She wished he had come up with a more feminine metaphor. Or spoken with less derision. "If that's what works for you." She changed the subject. "So, where's this boat?"

"To the right. Halfway down the dock. It's a small white fishing boat. *The Sinful*."

She laughed, and as they walked, boats washed and hammered against the dock, swaying to the rhythm of the river.

"What's so funny?"

"Come on. *The Sinful*?"

"Yeah. Okay. So me and a couple of buddies were drunk when we painted the name on."

"Let me guess. You don't do much fishing, at least not for fish."

"You think you know all about me." His tone was bland, his expression almost pleasant.

"Anita filled me in."

"Anita doesn't know crap."

"So you do fish?"

"No." He grinned, and in the moonlight, his teeth gleamed white. "I take girls out on it."

" 'Girls'?" She was ashamed of the way the word came out—snotty, mocking—but there it was.

"Yeah, girls. Women. Females."

"Oh. Bimbos. With half-names and full breasts."

He squeezed her arm and leaned in. "Jealous?"

"Yeah, right." But she pictured it. Him and his latest blonde. Small, curved, beautiful. Crawling all over him. *Oh, Sin. Sin.* In that breathy, Marilyn Monroe voice.

"Judge not, lest ye be judged."

"I'm not judging."

"I can hear your disapproval a mile away," he said. If anything, his grin had gotten wider.

She pushed at him, her hand flicking against his muscled shoulder. "Shut up."

He didn't budge much. "Shut up? Come on, Martha, you can do better than that." He leaned close again and whispered low. "Wanna take a ride in my boat?"

"Do I have a choice?"

His grin faded a bit. He turned his face away as though staring at the boats knocking against the dock. "What if you did?"

Her heart caught. What if she did?

She was saved from answering by the appearance of *The Sinful*.

"This is it," she said.

Small was right. But even in the dim light, the boat gleamed. The hull shone, the windshield—the only thing protecting passengers from the elements—was clean. The bucket seats for driver and passenger looked less than new, but well maintained. A coil of blue nylon rope lay neatly stowed. Someone—Danny she presumed—took good care of the craft. An image of him flashed across her brain— shirtless, muscles rippling in the sun, lovingly polishing the chrome the way her father polished a fender. Charlie would have been impressed, but in an entirely different way from her. The image sent a bolt of electricity through her, and she stepped into the boat eager to forget it.

Extending a hand, she gripped Danny's and helped him over. The boat wobbled and she half gasped before biting her lip to suppress it. But he paused, got his bearings, and came forward, groping and bending low to trace the outline of the interior. Slowly, he led her to the helm.

"Here." He fished his keys from his pocket and handed them to her. "It's the second smallest." His fingers traced the dash. "The ignition's somewhere . . ."

"I see it." She put a hand over his and guided him there. His fingers wrapped around hers for a moment.

Neither of them said anything. Martha wasn't sure she could have managed a single word anyway. The air off the river stung colder than in the woods, but their touch generated a liquid heat that swirled in her stomach and dove lower.

"Give me the key," he said softly.

He felt for the ignition and showed her how to turn the boat on. The engine bit and purred in the quiet night. Slipping into the driver's seat, he held the wheel steady while she ran to the rear and unleashed the ropes anchoring the boat to the pier. Then he slid back to the passenger seat so she could take over.

"Easy," he said. "Take her slow. We have to get away from the pier and the other boats before we pick up speed."

As the unfamiliar drag of the hull pushed against the water, her hands clung to the steering wheel in a death grip, the weight of responsibility heavy.

"Remember, it's the opposite of a car. The stern—that's the back—turns first and changes your direction."

She followed his instructions as though they were one creature. His voice, her hands. Water lapped as the boat cut through it. Slowly, they slipped into the center of the black river.

"Can you see the buoy? It marks the channel."

"We passed it."

"Okay. Punch her up."

He put his hand over hers, guiding the throttle forward. Then they were chugging down the river. The wind blew back her hair with icy fingers. Her hands froze on the wheel.

"How are you doing?" he shouted over the growl of the engine.

"Okay," she shouted back, her true feelings too complicated to describe. She was driving a boat in the middle of the night, the river was dark and dangerous, and so was her passenger. Who would have believed it? The situation was fantastical, like a dream, and terrifying, like a nightmare.

"Anyone following?"

"No." Her voice sounded calmer than she felt, and in a distant corner of her mind she wondered how she'd managed that.

"Any traffic?"

"The way is clear."

"Keep her steady. Not too fast. If you want to stop, pull back on the throttle and shift into reverse."

She nodded absently. If they just kept going straight and all she had to do was keep her hands on the wheel, she'd be all right. Anything else . . . She shuddered and concentrated on not running into the bank.

She tried to settle into the rhythm of the boat, swaying with the water, fingers still wrapped knuckle-tight around the wheel. In the distance black shadows hinted at cliffs and banks thick with trees.

She glanced at Danny. His face was lit by moonlight, his

eyes closed against the harsh breeze and the sting of river spray. Posed like that, he seemed a piece of night, sculpted by shadow and darkly beautiful.

She returned to the task of navigating, then found her gaze creeping back to him, knowing he'd never know.

"Is there a moon out?" he asked.

"Yes." His eyes opened, his head turned up as if searching for it. "And stars, too."

"A clear night."

"Yes."

"And cold. Are you cold?"

"Freezing. You?"

Instead of answering, he stood, felt for the back of her seat and used it to guide him toward her. From behind, he wrapped his arms around her shoulders.

"Better?" he said in her ear.

God, her heart nearly fell out of her chest. "I . . . yes. Great."

"Tell me what you see."

She peered around, glad for the distraction. "The river is wider than I thought. It's inky dark, but here and there the moon lights it up. I can barely make out the bank."

As she talked, he rubbed hands up and down her arms, and even through her coat his touch burned.

"The moon is full." Her voice came out breathy. Now who was doing a Marilyn? "Neon white. The face looks as though it's laughing at us."

He nuzzled her neck. "Probably is."

She swallowed. "The stars are sprinkled over the sky. Glittering. Like sequins on a party dress."

"Pretty." The way he said it . . . as though he wasn't just talking about the sky.

His warm mouth traveled up toward her ear, over her

cheek. His hand journeyed down her arm to the throttle, and he pulled it back just as his mouth found hers.

Oh, God.

The boat slowed, and he kissed her.

His hands cupped her face and his mouth captured hers, his tongue hot and sweet. She was starved for the taste of him, ravenous, and she surrendered to his lips, completely, totally.

She heard herself moan, the sound coming from a distance as though someone else uttered it. He smiled against her mouth, and she pulled away to see his jeweled eyes staring down at her. Was that amusement in them? They were so alive, she had to remind herself that he couldn't see her.

She stiffened. "Why . . . why did you do that?"

He ran a finger down her cheek. "I wanted to find out if you taste as good as you smell."

She looked away, down at her hands as though he could truly see her. See the heat flood her cheeks, the embarrassment wash her eyes.

"We need to—"

"I know. We do." But he was turning her, shifting her body to face his, pulling her up out of the seat.

"But we can't stay here in the middle of the—"

"No. We can't."

Then he kissed her again, and her breath vanished, her body melted, thighs sinking into knees and knees sinking into feet.

She was disappearing into heat, a blaze of sensation. His lips, his tongue, the scratch of his beard, and those long, strong fingers that held her chin, caressed her hair, pressed her shoulders so she couldn't escape.

Not that she wanted to.

That moan floated up from deep inside her again. And

like that, she remembered where they were, what they were doing.

Escaping.

She pushed against his chest, gasping for breath. "Wait," she panted. "We have to—"

"Go. I know." His eyes were closed, his voice a rough whisper.

"Danny." He still held her, but his arms were loose around her now.

"When I kiss you I think I can almost see. Everyone kisses in the dark." He dropped his arms, opened his eyes. A hint of bitterness stole across his face. "I'm as good as I always was."

So that's what the kiss was. A chance to feel normal again. It hadn't been about her at all. A wave of cold reality shook her, and she pulled herself together. "Try not to think in terms of good or bad. Different is just . . . different. Not better or worse."

He fumbled for his seat again. "Ahh, Mary Poppins. Turning lemons into lemonade."

"Just dealing with the facts on the ground."

"Right." He nodded brusquely. "Let's go."

She sent the boat forward and the wind picked up again. Chilled as it was, the slap of it felt good. Shook the regret out of her. Was she sorry the romantic mood had been broken? The dreamer in her was. That Martha could pretend he really wanted her, and not just the only female around. But the realist was just as glad to have it over and done. He was her client. A personal relationship was wildly unprofessional.

Besides, would he have gone near her if he could see?

The question rattled inside her, and she settled back into her seat. Shapes on the banks resolved themselves into buildings, a light in a window here and there pricking the blackness with a yellow glow. Warning lights on top of a radio tower blinked red and hot against the night as though trying to tell her something: *Stay away. Stay away.*

She wished she could. She'd be safer that way. At least, if no one tried to kill her.

Danny was a different threat, especially if she let herself get dreamy about him. But how to keep her distance when she was a prisoner in this boat, in his life, unable to flee?

"How long will it take to get there?" she asked, wishing she could sprout wings and fly.

"At twenty knots or so, three, maybe four hours."

God, half the night. The boat could go faster, but she couldn't. Not with her all but nonexistent navigational skills. She sucked in a breath, gritted her teeth, and hunkered down in the cold.

They passed beneath the Mid-Hudson Bridge, and later, the Newburgh-Beacon Bridge, truss lights gleaming. The river narrowed around West Point, where the walls of the military academy and the fortifications of Constitution Island were dim in the moonlight.

Two hours into the trip, a blaze of light appeared on the left. She looked over at Danny. He hadn't said much since he'd kissed her except for terse instructions when she asked for them. She'd left him alone, too confused by her own emotions to talk to him. Now in the reflected sheen of whatever was coming up she saw a brooding expression on his face. She bit her lip, not sure she wanted to make contact, then couldn't help herself. Anything to wipe that look off his face.

"There's a large structure on the left. Lit up like Disneyland."

His mouth compressed into a tight, wry smile. "Not exactly Disneyland. Indian Point, most likely."

"The nuclear power plant?"

"Yup."

It wasn't far from Sokanan, yet she'd never seen the plant, though like most people, she'd heard about it. They chugged by the long, flat structure topped by a many-sided second story with a tower. Beyond the large structure, reactor domes curved ominously against the night sky.

She turned away, fascinated and repelled at the same time.

"If we're at Indian Point," Danny said, "we should be hitting the Tappan Zee soon."

"How much farther after that?"

"An hour more or less."

She was numb with cold and stiff from holding tightly to the wheel. But she could hold out for another hour.

Thirty minutes later, as Danny had predicted, the Tappan Zee loomed out of the night, mere dots of light in the distance that grew brighter and larger until the bridge took shape, connecting two counties on either side of the Hudson.

"I see the bridge," she told him.

Named for the Tappan Indians, who first lived there, and for the Dutch, the original settlers of New York, who referred to the Hudson River as a zee or "wide expanse of water," the bridge started high on one side and sloped down to scoop the water on the other. Right now with the lights outlining its span, the bridge looked like a string of diamonds curved on the neck of the river.

"The Hudson is at it widest here," Danny said. "The breadth sometimes makes for wind and chop, so be careful."

As if on cue, the wind picked up, and the boat shimmied in the water, bucking against waves. She gasped, clutched the steering wheel. Danny reached over and felt for the wheel, placing his hands on top of hers to steady them.

"Hold tight," he said, as if she needed that advice. She was holding as tight as she could.

The boat rocked wildly and the wind battered her ears until she couldn't feel them. They had just passed under the bridge when the boat lurched, and for one heart-sickening moment, they were knocked backward. Their hands flew off the wheel, abandoning the craft to the mercy of the water. It listed and bounced in a dizzy, stomach-heaving polka. Icy water crashed over the sides.

Her heart leapt out of her throat. Terror, primitive and sharp, froze her body. She struggled to regain her balance and sit up, but found it impossible, as though a huge black monster held her down.

"Get control back!" Danny cried, hitting her shoulder as he lunged for the wheel.

"I'm trying!" Was that *her* mouth screaming those words?

She grappled with the wheel, which twisted and turned as though it was possessed. Finally, she threw herself over it in a frantic embrace, using her arms as well as her hands to seize the helm. Without knowing how, she managed to hold on.

Sweating, mouth a desert, she wrenched hard, and miraculously, the boat obeyed. Vaulting over the chop with a sickening slap, it returned to the desired direction. She sat back, body shaking, heart galloping.

"Good!" Danny shouted. "You did good!"

If that was good, she'd hate to see what bad was.

She licked dry lips and wiped river water from her face.

Eventually the wind died, and the boat steadied. Her breathing slowed. The lights of the George Washington Bridge came into view. They were almost there.

"Okay," Danny said when they were through the bridge. "Ease back on the throttle. I need to talk to you."

She didn't like the sound of that. "About what?" The air chilled her throat, but it warmed as the boat slowed.

"About docking. I don't have a permit, so technically, I can't tie up at Seventy-ninth Street, which is where we're heading."

"Who's going to know?"

"There's always security. A watchman. Someone who works for the parks department."

Terrific. She was stuck in the middle of the Hudson River with no way forward and no way back except the way they came, and she wasn't eager to repeat that trip. "Then what are we going to do?"

"Sneak in."

"How are we going to do that? The engine's not exactly silent." Her voice squeaked in panic. What else would she have to get through tonight?

"Relax. You're doing fine."

"Don't tell me to relax."

He shrugged. "Okay. Work yourself up. Be my guest. What time is it?"

Perversely, she forced herself to calm down and held her watch up to catch the moonlight. "Three."

He nodded thoughtfully. "I've been to the boat basin. There's an office in the middle, but at this time of night probably only one man inside."

"One man is all it takes to get caught."

"He can't be everywhere at once, can he?"

Painstakingly, he instructed her how to maneuver the

boat so they had a view of the flat-roofed vinyl-sided building in the center of the docks. The building was well lit and above it, an American flag flapped in the breeze. They cut the engine and hid in the shadows just beyond the first pier. Wind whipped the water and slashed her face, blowing her hair in a dozen different directions. Water slapped against the boat, which rocked beneath her. Ahead of them the docks rolled, squeaking and bumping against one another. Metal ties linking the wood piers banged. Overhead a helicopter chugged.

At last, a light bobbed as it exited the building. The watchman was holding a flashlight.

"He's coming," she whispered.

"What direction?" Danny's voice was also low.

She gulped. "Toward us."

"Okay, we're fine, right? Behind the pier."

"I think so."

"Don't think, know."

She looked from their position to the approaching man. Could he see them? She reached over the boat, stretching madly for the post that held up the pier. Cold air invaded her neck and up her sleeves. She lunged, missed, and the boat rocked wildly.

"What are you doing?" Danny's whisper was frantic.

"Trying to pull us in closer."

"Sit tight," he ordered.

But she was already trying again. This time she caught hold of a nail sticking out of the post. She used it to pull the boat against the pole, as far out of sight as possible.

"I told you—"

"Duck!" She pulled Danny's head down as a flashlight beam flashed in their direction.

"What the—"

"Quiet. He's here."

They hunched over together, not moving. In the darkness the sound of her heart beating seemed louder than the incessant squeal of dock and clang of metal, and she was sure it would give their location away.

Danny gripped her wrist. "What's he doing?"

She peeked over the edge of the boat. Her heart sank. "Lighting a cigarette."

"Shit."

She'd second that emotion.

They sat in their awkward positions, heads bent together, shoulders crunched. She concentrated on the acrid smell of the cigarette smoke, and wished that someone would pass a law banning smoking from the face of the earth.

A plop and a hiss. She peeked again. The watchman had flicked the butt into the river.

"He's done," she said softly.

"Is he walking away?" Danny asked.

"Yes." She let out a huge breath. "It's clear." Slowly they straightened up. She rubbed the back of her neck where the muscles had cramped.

Danny was rolling his shoulders to unglue them. "Tell me when he reaches the far side."

The flashlight's beam bounced as the man walked. "I can't see all the way down there."

"Then tell me when you can't see the light anymore."

She waited until the beam was out of sight, then counted to ten just in case. "Okay. Now."

"Start the engine. Throttle up, but slowly. We just need enough to slide home."

Danny talked her through every step, and somehow she got the boat into a slip. When he felt the boat bump against the edge of the dock, he smiled. "Great job, sailor. Now, tie up."

She found the rope she'd untied at the marina in Sokanan and Danny told her how to knot it around the hook embedded in the dock.

"How's our man doing?"

She looked south and still couldn't see the flashlight. "Still gone."

"Maybe he'll smoke another cigarette."

"We should be so lucky."

"Come on." He gestured toward the dock. "We can't stay here."

But now that she could, she was reluctant to leave the boat. She'd survived the river. Who knew what would happen on land?

Danny stood and groped the edge of the boat, looking for a way off. The craft swayed with his fumbling steps, and she scrambled out.

"Here. Grab on to my hand."

And like the stubborn man he was, he ignored her and found his own way onto the pier.

CHAPTER 8

———————•———————

O nce they were off the pier and through the black iron gate that separated the docks from the rest of Riverside Park, Danny had Martha get the number for the New York office of the Terrorism Control Force.

She gasped. "Terrorism? Oh my God, you're kidding. You think—"

"I told you I had a federal friend. That's where he works. Ask for Jake Wise."

"Surely he won't be there this time of night."

"You never know. And we can leave a message."

She put the call through, but as suspected, he wasn't in.

Danny shoved his hands into his pockets. "We better get inside. Gotta be a bar close by that stays open late. Let's get away from the water."

But after the hours-long boat trip, the wind etching new lines in her face, she was bone-tired and numb. Her hands were screaming stiff, tear tracks had crusted on her face, and her feet felt like blocks of ice.

"Can't we go to a hotel? I feel like I could sleep for a week."

"No hotel. Too easy to track us."

She blew out a huge breath that was half groan. "How

about a doorway then? A nice, simple doorway. At this point I don't even care what it smells like."

Danny's mouth thinned into a hard line. "You will. Come on."

He proffered his arm, and she frowned. Why couldn't he just accept the proper hold? "Are we going to do this again?"

"We're out in the open."

"So?"

"So we don't have to do the blind man's dance here. Take my arm."

She grumbled. "If you'd let me show you how to use the cane, no one would have to hold on to anyone."

His jaw tightened. "I'm not advertising my vulnerability. We're going to look as normal as possible."

A flicker of fear ran up her back. "You don't think someone is watching us?"

"I don't know, but I'm not risking it. Predators look for weak targets. We're not giving them one."

She surrendered to this logic and stepped forward, her hands tight around his arm. He was tense and attentive, his head turning constantly as if his sightless eyes were scanning the area. She suspected he was listening hard for noise, straining to sort out every clue his working senses could process.

She remembered the first time her orientation and mobility instructor had blindfolded her. All she had to do was find her way from the classroom at one end of the hall to a table at the other end, pick up a piece of paper, and bring it back. No curbs to trip over, no streets to cross, no vehicles to avoid. It sounded so simple, but when the darkness descended she was terrified of taking a step. Of bumping into something, falling down the stairs. There were no cliffs in the hallway, yet it felt as though any moment she would step off one. It had taken many tries to get to that table without hugging the walls. Danny amazed her. Every step was an act of bravery.

She huddled against him, reluctant to admit she was grateful for the warmth of his body. He looked at home in her father's leather jacket, the embodiment of bad-boy fantasy, his face unshaven, his black hair blowing in the sharp breeze. Even knowing better, she couldn't help the small thrill that cut through the cold and burned inside her.

From the Hudson, Seventy-ninth Street led up through a series of ramps and tunnels under and around the Henry Hudson Parkway. They walked together, the traffic on the parkway droning overhead, even in the middle of the night.

She'd never been in the city this late. Once her mother had taken her to see *Cats* on Broadway. It had been summer and the sun was still up when they got there, but it was full dark by the time the show was over. There was a huge crush of people, other theaters close by letting out at the same time. She'd inhaled the tang of perfume along with car exhaust, enjoyed the click of high heels on the pavement, tingled with the excitement of theater lights and neon and the little signs on top of the cabs that glowed in the dark. She'd held her mother's hand and they'd swung arms and walked to the train station together. She was proud to be with her pretty mother. Happy to belong to her. It was one in the treasury of memories she'd held in secret, never talked about or acknowledged. When she was young, before she realized her mother was never coming back, she used to take them out, one at a time, and polish them in her mind like jewels.

Now she held on to a different arm, and the city took on different shades. Streetlights gave off dim life, making monsters of empty boxes piled at curbside. Traffic lights splashed red, then green across the wash of blacktop, and occasionally the hot flash of headlights exploded into the dark: yellow cabs scuttling by as though afraid to be caught.

They passed a woman at the edge of the park, high-booted with a tiny leather skirt, a short, furry coat that couldn't have helped much in this cold, and too much makeup. She sized Martha up, found her wanting, and made a joke to Danny about "showing him a better time."

"Not possible, babe," he called out as they passed, and to Martha, he spoke low. "Keep going, and get that broom-stick out of your butt. Everyone's gotta make a living."

But it wasn't prudery that made her bristle. It was the fact that even a hooker felt superior enough to take a jab at her. "Not at my expense they don't. Besides, I thought you arrested them back home."

"Cost of doing business. They know it and so do I. And we're not in Sokanan anymore, Dorothy."

They crossed Riverside Drive and West End Avenue with their sedate apartment buildings, then Broadway with its red-and-white striped Filene's Basement awning on the corner. She shuddered with cold as they tramped one block more to Amsterdam Avenue, turned downtown and found a bar on the next block. The windows on either side of the entrance were dark green. On the left, a white Budweiser logo sat inside a neon green shamrock. On the right, a pink neon champagne glass danced side to side.

"Parkview Bar and Grill," she told him. "Know it?"

"No. But I'll bet there's no view of the park."

"You'd win."

She guided him through the door and was assaulted by the familiar smell of beer and liquor. The place was lit by low amber light, not much different from the streets, except warmer. It was long and narrow, with the bar on the left and booths on the right. Beyond the booths, a few tables were strewn around the back.

A couple of men sat at the bar. One in a rumpled suit, the other in a tracksuit, as if he'd just come from the gym. But he was so bloated she couldn't imagine him doing anything approaching the athletic. Both men looked up as Martha and Danny came through the door. She saw their red-rimmed eyes bleary with drink, and looked away. She knew that face. Had grown up with it.

Beyond the men sat a woman in fishnets with cocoa skin and frosted blond hair, her red sweater tight and low across her breasts. As Martha guided Danny past, the woman edged close to the man in the suit, laughed, and kicked back her drink.

Danny trailed what he could as they went, doing it casually, but he stumbled into a bar stool sitting too far out in the aisle, and muttered a low curse.

"Easy," she whispered. "Almost there." She stopped at a small table buried in the corner. "Okay. Here is good."

He felt around a seat, found its contours, and slid in. "Where are you?"

She touched his hand. "Right across from you."

He leaned in. "Is there a back way out?"

She glanced over his shoulder toward a dangling neon sign.

"Possibly. The restrooms are behind you. There's a narrow hallway back there."

"Go check it out."

"No door," she said when she returned. "Just the bathrooms."

"Okay. That means the front door is the only way out."

He didn't look happy about that, which sent a bolt of anxiety through her.

"Should we go? Find someplace else?" She shivered inside her coat, which she still hadn't removed. The last thing she wanted was to go out in the cold before she'd had a chance to warm up.

"No. But keep your eyes open. We don't want to get trapped here."

He'd ordered while she was gone, and now the bartender brought two cups of coffee and two whiskeys.

Danny sipped at the coffee, then poured some of his whiskey into it. She admired the way he did it, neat, no spilling.

He leaned toward her again. Spoke low. "Tell me who's here. How many people. Men or women."

Surreptitiously, she peered around. "Two men at the bar. A suit and a sweatpants. One woman, blond wig, big breasts, stiletto heels. Your type."

His blind eyes twinkled. "As opposed to you?"

"Never mind me," she snapped. "Everything isn't about me."

For a quick half-second she peeked at the woman at the bar. What would it be like to put sex on the front burner? To wear tight clothes and poufy hair and long, pointy heels? To be obvious and brazen, instead of shrouded and discreet?

A sliver of envy slunk through her, which she quickly repressed.

God, she was envying a barfly in a dive.

But still, she imagined herself in stilettos and a stretchy sweater. She wouldn't fill it out half so well. And she'd feel like a clumsy giraffe in the heels.

Face it, she wouldn't know what to do with herself.

"Okay. Sounds normal enough for a bar in the middle of the night."

"Normal?" She snorted. "What are you calling normal? Invisible people shooting at us for invisible reasons?"

"They're only invisible to me."

She stripped off her coat but slung it over her shoulders, still too chilled to do without. She had just seen herself in the restroom mirror, a sight that left her feeling even more raw and bruised. Her hair looked like a wild woman's, tangled from the boat ride, her nose was red from the cold, cuts on her neck and jaw left trails of blood like Frankenstein scars. She was in no mood to feel sorry for him. "Get over yourself. I don't know who they are. I didn't see any of them back at the house. And I have no idea why they want to kill us. They might as well be invisible."

"Point taken. Let's not split hairs."

She bit back a reply. Her eyes were grainy, her legs burned and itched from warming up. She'd give anything for an hour of sleep, and everything she said came out scratchy and bad-tempered. She took a breath and wrapped her hands around her coffee cup. "This friend, this Jake Wise. You think he can help?"

"If he can't, we're in bigger trouble than I thought."

Terrific. Just what she wanted to hear. "Does this mean you have some ideas about who these people are?"

"Nothing that makes sense."

"What about what doesn't make sense?"

"Look, until we get to Jake it's a big mystery. No point speculating. It'll just freak us both out."

"I'm already freaked."

"Then let's talk about something else."

"What? No one's ever shot at me before."

"How about your dad?"

"My dad? Oh, God, I'd better call him." She found her phone and punched in the number. "Daddy?"

"Where are you?" Charlie's voice boomed into her ear.

"Calm down. I'm fine."

"Calm down? You want me to calm down? You have men with guns shooting at you and you want me to calm down?" He went into a stream of invectives, his voice turning hoarser as it grew louder.

She moved the phone away from her ear and gave him a few seconds to vent.

"Daddy. Daddy!"

He stopped in mid-sentence, and she knew he'd suddenly remembered who he was talking to.

"We're fine, okay? We're—"

"I don't give a damn about 'we.' As long as you're all right. Where are you?"

"Somewhere in the city. A bar."

"He get in touch with his friend?"

"Not yet. Too late. I left a message. What about you? Did the car find you?"

"Yeah. I drove around for a while leading them out of town. Then I lost them again. Accidentally on purpose and hopefully for good."

"Thanks. I appreciate it." She hesitated, not sure it was any of her business, but needing to know. "Did you go home?"

"Nah. I called Arnie."

Was that another subtle pitch for improving her social life, or had Arnie Gould just been handy? She didn't ask, not wanting to know. It was odd having her father pay so much attention to her.

"You keep in touch," he said, proving her point. "And tell that kid I'm here to help."

"I will."

"You take care of yourself, Martha girl."

Unsettled, she ended the call. Her father hadn't called her Martha girl in years.

"So?"

"He said the car found him, but he lost them again."

"Good."

"Says he wants to help."

"Great." The tone was sardonic, the look on his face equally so. "When there's something for a man with no legs to do I'll let him know."

She stared at him, disbelieving her ears. "That man with no legs just saved your life, you ungrateful—"

"Whoa. I didn't mean—"

"At least he's not moping around feeling sorry for himself." Suddenly she was shaking with fury.

"What's that supposed to—"

"He's made a productive life for himself. He has a job, a home—"

"Okay, okay." Danny held up his hands in surrender. "He's a regular superhero and I'm a slimeball for suggesting otherwise."

"You got that right."

Silence loaded with fury descended. She poured the whiskey into the coffee with shaky hands and gulped it. The heat felt good and the whiskey burned going down. Between the guns and running away, and the cold, and the guns. . . . A sob stuttered in her throat, and she swallowed more whiskey-laced coffee to drown it out.

Danny said, "Give me your hand."

She gave him a suspicious glance. "What for?"

"Because I can't see to find it, and if I could, I'd hold it. Apologize. Mean it."

She slid her hand across the table until her fingers touched his. He covered them with his own.

"I'm sorry."

She stared at their twined fingers, at the bony length of hers, which were still smaller and more delicate than his larger, darker ones. Before she could start liking the way they looked together, she slowly disengaged hers. "Apology accepted."

He nodded, blew out a short breath. "So . . . what happened to him? How'd he lose his legs?"

"Motorcycle accident. And he still has his legs. They just don't work anymore."

"Shit." An expression of horrified wonder crossed his face. "That must have been tough. I'm sorry."

She thought back, the pain blurred by years of living with it. "It was a long time ago. I was twelve."

"That's rough. How did he handle it?"

She snorted. "Badly. Not so different from you."

He pulled back his head in annoyance. "What's that supposed to mean?"

"Refusing to deal with the facts on the ground. Took him a long time to figure out he still had a life to live."

He frowned but didn't pursue her little dig. "And what were you doing while he was figuring this out?"

"I stayed with friends. Family. Mostly my aunt Nancy, my mother's sister."

"Why? Where was your mother?"

The question was casually asked, an acquaintance making conversation. But it brought back things she didn't want to talk about. She stirred her coffee, mostly to stall. The spoon clinked against the china in a repetitious circle, which must have irritated him because he put a hand on her wrist, stopping her.

"Where was your mother?"

"I don't know." She sighed. "She left." Why did she always have so much trouble admitting it?

His hand felt warm for the few seconds he left it on her skin. "What do you mean, 'she left'? Mothers don't leave."

"Mine did."

"She just took off?"

"To parts unknown."

He seemed astonished, which shamed her, but also made her wonder about his family, his mother.

"Why did she leave?"

A question she'd asked so many times the words actually grated against her ears. "How should I know? Because she was selfish, immature, wild, evil, rotten, irresponsible." She ticked off the answers she'd accumulated over the years, leaving out the one lingering suspicion, that Martha just wasn't lovable enough, even for her own mother. "I guess she wasn't interested in taking care of a paraplegic or a little girl."

He was silent for a long moment. "Funny. I used to wonder why my mother stayed."

"With you? Why? Were you such an awful child?"

He grinned. "I wasn't the easiest pick of the litter. Kind of wild and rough-edged."

She remembered that boy. The way he always seemed to be in trouble. The way he could smile his way out of it, too.

"There were two of us—me and Beth—and only one of her. Don't know what happened to my father. I must have one somewhere, but he was never around. She worked her ass off for us and dropped dead before she was forty."

He said it flatly, but she sensed the control beneath the words. So, he, too, knew what that loss was like. That they shared something between them made her look at him differently. "You must have missed her."

He smiled again, and this time it was thoughtful and dreamy. "She used to make us breakfast in the mornings. Even if all we had in the fridge was milk, she made us sit down together and drink it. We were in school during lunch and she worked at nights so we didn't see her for dinner, so she always made a big deal out of breakfast."

"Sounds nice."

"Nice?" His black brows furrowed. "Jesus, it was awful." He seemed to catch himself, then think about it. His face cleared. "Yeah, I guess it was nice." He swallowed a gulp of coffee. "How about you? You never saw your mother again?"

"Nope."

"Not even a postcard now and again?"

"Not even."

He seemed to digest that, which was fine with her. She took refuge in her coffee cup, hoping the interrogation was over.

No such luck.

"So . . . you grew up in Sokanan?"

An innocent enough question, but one that made her stiffen, suddenly aware they could be heading for rocky ground. "Yes."

"Which means you went to high school there. North?"

She sipped at her coffee, suspense making her shoulders tight. Would he put it all together? "Yes."

"What year did you graduate?"

"Ninety-one."

There was a small silence. "Me, too."

She gazed down at the coffee to avoid looking at him. "I know."

"You knew we went to high school together?"

There was accusation in his voice, and she defended herself. "We went to the same school at the same time. I wouldn't say we were anywhere near together."

"You're splitting hairs again." His face became thoughtful. "So I know you."

"Not really."

"Martha Crowe." She could tell he was thinking back, trying to place her. She didn't know which was worse, that he would remember or he wouldn't. Finally, he sighed and shook his head. "Sorry."

A ripple of relief ran through her. "It was fourteen years ago."

"But you remembered me."

"Everyone remembers the cutest boy in high school."

He smiled, and in the middle of the dark bar, it lit up the world. "You think I'm cute?"

"Haven't we already established that? Look, at the risk of expanding our off-limit topics of conversation to two, can we talk about something else?"

"I don't know. I'm kind of liking this."

"I'll stand up and announce to the world that you're a helpless blind man."

"You wouldn't."

No, she wouldn't, but she didn't tell him that. "Not if we change the subject."

"You're a hard woman, Martha Crowe."

"It's a hard world, Detective Sinofsky."

He didn't argue that. "What time is it?"

She checked her watch. "Almost four."

"Still too early for Jake."

"Doesn't he have a home phone? A cell?"

"Probably. But not listed. And I forgot to bring my Rolodex. We'll just have to wait."

The bartender arrived again. "Last call. Can I get you folks anything else?"

"Another round," Danny said.

The door opened and a man walked in. He had shaggy dark hair, a mean black mustache, and looked like a bear who'd been rousted out of hibernation and wasn't happy about it.

He perused the bar, rejected it, and cruised the tables. His gaze caught on hers and he glanced away, then back again.

A frisson of fear ran through Martha. Why would someone come in just as the bar was closing? Unless he wasn't interested in beer.

The man started toward the back and their table. She froze.

"Someone . . . someone just came in. He's . . . he's watching us."

Danny tensed. "What kind of someone?"

"Scary-looking."

"That doesn't help much, Martha."

"He's big, dark. Unshaven."

"So am I. What's he wearing?"

"A peacoat with the collar turned up."

"Where are his hands?"

"Inside his pockets." The questions were raising her anxiety level. "I think we should go. One round is enough for me anyway." She started to rise. Danny reached out for her, his hand landing on her hip, and tugged her back.

"Sit down. Relax. What's he doing?"

"Who?"

"The guy."

She sneaked a peek. "Sitting down."

"Where?"

She swallowed. "A table to your right."

"Behind us?"

"Yes. Are you sure we can't go to a hotel?"

"Very sure."

"We'll find someplace else then."

"It's too cold for a park bench. Is he still watching us?"

"Yes," she hissed. "He's staring at me." She yanked at his hand. "Come on, I want to go."

"All right. But slow down. We can't leave without paying." He pulled a wallet from his back pocket, then stopped and muttered a low curse under his breath. She understood. He wouldn't be able to identify the correct amount.

She took the wallet from him. "I'll teach you how to handle money. It's not hard. But right now—" She pulled out some bills and slapped them down.

The bartender was heading their way with their second round. "Change your mind?"

Danny grinned and shook his head. "Women."

"I hear you, bud."

"Money's on the table," Martha said, not appreciating the slur, but understanding Danny's intention. Act normal.

"Have a good one," the bartender said.

"You, too," Danny replied. "Come on, babe. Let's go home."

She knew this was the signal to wrap her hand around his arm. As best she could, she guided him out the door.

Outside, the cold encased them, hard and icy. She looked right, then left, not sure where to go. In her mind, the man from the bar got up and clumped toward the door. And them.

"Is he following?" Danny asked.

"I don't know. We're just outside the door."

"Keep walking away from the river. Find the nearest plate-glass shopwindow and turn us toward it."

"Why?"

"Just do it. And don't look back."

The command heightened her tension. "What if he's following us?"

"We'll find out. Just don't look back."

Her breath jammed in her lungs, and she was quivering all over again, but she followed his instructions. They passed an antique store, a restaurant called Chic!, and a deli. All had iron security gates across their windows.

"Everything's barred." She heard the panic in her voice.

"That's okay. We've gone far enough. I don't hear anything behind us. Is someone following?"

She stole a look over her shoulder. "I don't think so. I don't see anyone."

"Good." Danny slowed. "False alarm."

Relief swooshed through her, making her legs wobble, and she clutched at one of the security gates to steady herself. Only then did the embarrassment come. She had panicked. Over nothing. "I'm sorry."

He shook his head. "If I could have seen the guy . . ."

"I thought . . . I thought it better to be safe."

"It's all right." He put an arm around her shoulders and squeezed her briefly.

"Should we go back?"

"No. That would look funny. Let's walk for a bit. Maybe we'll find someplace else that's open."

They walked ten blocks without success, hunched against the cold. Then the rain started.

It came down without warning, just opened up and poured. It carved into her face like an icy razor and found a way past her coat to her neck. The wind whipped across her legs where the coat ended.

"Jesus Christ." Danny put an arm around her, pulling her close. They bowed their heads against the weather, but it found them anyway. "How are you doing?"

"Fine." But her chattering teeth gave her away. "Okay, so I'm lousy. It's freezing. It's wet. We can't wander around all night like this."

"I know this place."

"Hallelujah. Why didn't you say so?"

"It's pretty raunchy, but we won't have to register."

"I don't care if it's the city dump. As long as it's inside."

"Okay, but don't say I didn't warn you."

They hustled down to Seventy-second street, and took the subway to Canal, which at least got them out of the rain. Wet and dripping, shivering in the aftershock of the squall, Martha bounced around as the car rocketed through the dark tunnel, wheels chomping over the track. The noise was deafening and she wondered what the ride was like for Danny, with only the clack and snap of steel and the whoosh of speed for clues. She closed her eyes and tried to experience it, but knowing she could open them again made it less real.

When they arrived at their stop, they tramped up the steps to the street and emerged into the chilly wet downpour. Danny lifted his collar and directed her a block east and then south for two more, where a sign above a door beckoned like a haven, winking neon yellow through the slashing rain. The Yellow Butterfly.

Despite the name, it didn't look inviting. The windows were barred and the glass in the front door was grimy. But it was warm inside and she ignored the fact that the desk was caged with bars, the person behind it barely visible.

"We'd like a room." Her hair was drenched, her mouth stiff with cold.

"Hey, Jenny. You're new around here." The clerk had a wizened face and an aging voice. He sounded close to ninety, but when she got near enough she saw he was a good forty years younger.

"My name isn't Jenny and I—"

"Oh, I call all you girls Jenny. Too hard to keep the faces straight."

"Look, pal," Danny interrupted. "We need a room, not a conversation."

"Sheesh, back off, son. You'll get yours soon enough." He shuffled inside his cage and came back with a key and a set of sheets. "Twenty bucks an hour, seventy-five till noon. In advance."

She pulled Danny away from the desk. "I've only got forty. How much do you have?"

"I don't know. Last time I remember I had maybe sixty bucks. How much did we spend at the bar?"

"Ten."

"Give the guy your forty. Maybe Jake will be available by then."

She handed over the bills and the clerk gave her the key to a room on the fifth floor. She peered around for an elevator, but he laughed.

"Got to take the stairs, Jenny. No conveniences here." He nodded toward a worn staircase with a heavy iron railing. She pulled Danny in its direction, murmuring tips on where to step and hoping the guy behind the cage didn't hear.

"Told you it wasn't the greatest," Danny said as they climbed.

An understatement if she ever heard one. "How do you know about this place anyway?"

"Working on a case. Tracked someone here."

"I'm beginning to think we were better outside."

He gave a mock sigh, undercut by the twinkle in his voice. "The grass is always greener with you women."

She was huffing by the time they reached the fifth floor and used the key to open the door. Inside stood a bed and a nightstand, one armchair that looked as though it had been there since the Revolutionary War, and not much else.

Clearly the bed was the main attraction.

And if she had any doubts, a rhythmic banging came through the paper-thin walls. It was quickly followed by a man's rising groan, lots of "yeah, baby"s and then a bellow of fulfillment.

Heat crawled up Martha's neck. Danny paused in his exploration of the space and furniture.

A long, long silence filled the room.

Then Danny spoke. "You still here?"

"Uh-huh."

"Blushing?"

"No," she lied.

He grinned. "You want the left side or the right?"

She stared. She could hardly think. What was he talking about?

"The bed," he said. "Which side of the bed do you want?"

The heat in her face redoubled. "I didn't—"

"I thought you said you were tired. 'Sleep for a week' was your exact phrase. Sorry, but you'll have to make do with a couple of hours."

"Yes but—"

"Come on, Crowe. I'll let you take the outside so the roaches have to get past me to get to you."

She licked her lips. She *was* tired. But how could she sleep knowing what was happening on the other side of the wall?

Her gaze was locked on the bed when Danny's hand on the back of her neck startled her.

"I won't bite," he whispered low in her ear.

Sadly, that's what she was afraid of.

They didn't bother making the bed. They shook off their wet coats and used one of the sheets to towel off. She spread the other sheet over the mattress, leaving the ends loose, and Danny crawled in as promised. She turned off the overhead light and lay down next to him. It occurred to her that they were equals in the dark. Both blind and fumbling.

His body lay beside her like a heat shield, glowing, pulsing. The banging started again next door and the sound sent a spear of liquid lust between her legs. She stiffened against it, fighting her own body's response. But even though she knew the transaction next door was strictly financial, the raw sounds of sex stimulated her. Was Danny feeling the same?

Her arms at her side, she lay on her back stiff as a corpse, hands fisted against the mattress. The one between them accidentally edged against his, and she realized he was clawing the mattress, too. As if in concert, their fingers moved together until they were holding on to each other, gripping tighter and tighter.

The moaning rose, the banging on the headboard increased. Danny was squeezing her bones into fluid heat. She was rigid with tension.

When at last the cry of completion came, her fingers were nearly crushed.

And like that, he relaxed his grip. Her body eased, softened. But the throb remained, and the heat lingered, and she wondered what it would be like to satisfy that need.

Here. Now. Her own private fantasy.

She whispered his name.

"Yeah?"

She swallowed. She was making a fool of herself.

It wouldn't be the first time. Like a condemned man's, her romantic life flashed before her. The endless blind dates that went nowhere, the phone calls that never came. When she was twenty-five and just finishing grad school, she was attracted to a guy from the business school, who seemed to return her interest. He brought her flowers, took her to dinner, told her she was pretty and made her believe it. She let her guard down and her hopes up. But once she slept with him, he stopped calling. He ignored her on campus, too, as though all of a sudden she was invisible. Later she found out she'd been his monthly pity pick.

The hurt had been so fierce, the pain had cauterized a part of her.

But now, for the first time in a long time, she felt completely alive again. Connected. Desirous. She couldn't remember the last time she wanted anyone.

It felt good.

She had no illusions. This would be one time. One night. She'd be breaking all her rules for one dream to hold in memory.

But a dream was better than nothing.

So she turned to him and said, "Kiss me."

CHAPTER 9

Danny stilled. "Oh, Miss Crowe. You are one dangerous woman."

"Kiss me."

He turned toward her. Through the room's odors he caught her familiar meadow-in-spring fragrance and knew she was close enough to kiss.

But not here. Not in a flophouse.

He found her face, stroked her cheek. "I don't think that's a good idea."

She stiffened. Under his hand, her face turned away. The rest of her followed. "Why . . . why not?"

He heard hurt in her voice and rushed to dispel it, turning her face back toward his own. "I don't think I could stop with a kiss."

She lay still, as though absorbing the meaning of his words. Then his fingers felt her mouth curve upward. She was smiling. He'd made her happy and a whoosh of warmth rushed inside him.

She inched closer, her warm breath on his mouth now. "Who's asking you to?"

And before he could answer, she kissed him.

It was an awkward kiss, full of nerves and insecurity, but

her lips were warm, sweet with coffee and whiskey. Only a better man could have resisted.

Danny wrapped his arms around her, pulling her toward him. Her lips parted, and the unexpected touch of her tongue sent a bolt of electricity shooting through him.

She moaned, deep and low as though it came from the core of her soul. "Oh, God. Danny."

He shifted her leg so it rested on top of him, and pressed her ass so she fit against his erection. She didn't have a lot of flesh on her. Her rear was small and round, her thigh slim against his hip. But the valley between her legs was snug against him. Perfect. He was so hard and she felt so good.

He ran his hands up her back, over her shoulders and down her long, narrow arms. She quaked with his touch, inciting him further. He found her breasts. Small buds, they molded to his palm, the nipples already hard and pointed.

He shuddered with wanting her, with knowing the universe had not taken this away from him. That blind or not he could still please a woman.

He slipped a hand under her sweater. Her skin was smooth and soft, her breast begging for his mouth. He lifted her clothes, licked the nipple and she moaned, arching into him. He reached for the waistband of her slacks and as his fingers closed on the zipper tab, the banging next door started again.

And he remembered where they were.

And who he was with.

Not just any woman. This woman. This prickly, bossy, self-deprecating woman. This woman who had somehow gotten to him in a way no one else ever had. This woman whose job it was to teach him. To make him feel better about himself.

"Martha." He forced her away, forced air between their

bodies. "Martha, wait." He unwrapped her arms from around his neck.

She was panting, the rhythm of her breath rising and falling in great gasps. His own heart raced like a demon.

"What?" Her voice was fogged, sluggish. "Don't stop." She gobbled down air. "Why . . . why did you stop?"

He scuttled down the bed and sat at the end, hunching over his knees.

"I don't—"

"What?" The bed creaked. She was moving. Her hand touched his back.

Her fingers sent a blaze through him. "Don't. Stay back there." God, he didn't know how long he could play the white knight if she kept touching him.

Her hand fled as though he'd bit it. "I don't . . . I don't understand. I—"

What was she doing? Christ, if only he could see her face.

"I'm throwing myself at you." She spoke quietly, a world of embarrassment in her voice.

"I know what you're doing. A little therapy for the blind man you feel sorry for."

"No. Danny, that's not it." Again, her hand rubbed his back.

He flinched. "Don't do that."

"I like touching you. You're so . . . so beautiful."

"Am I?" He shook his head, resentment working its way to the surface. "And what if I wasn't? What if I was some short, fat, ugly guy?"

"But you're not."

"But what if, Martha? What if I were? Would that make a difference?"

It took her a while to answer. "Probably," she said at last, a wry, rueful tone in her voice.

"So you're no better than the rest of us mortals."

The banging next door rose in crescendo. Grunts punctuated with "Oh, God, fuck me."

And even though he wanted her, he couldn't take her. Not here with the drunks and whores. And not because she pitied him.

He rose. There was a chair here. Somewhere. He stumbled off, tracing the outline of the bed until he got to a wall. He was in a black box, a cave, darkness so complete he hadn't known it existed before. He projected all his senses into the tips of his fingers and trailed the wall.

"What are you doing?" Martha asked.

"Looking for the chair."

"It's over—"

"I'll find it," he snapped.

He found a window instead, the glass cool to the touch. His foot slammed into something. He swore, ignored the burn and felt the obstacle's shape. A table. Round. A lamp on top. Then some kind of lumpy material. A chair arm.

He fingered the chair, found the cushion, made sure it was empty, and sank into it. "Get some sleep."

He closed his eyes. Not because he needed to; the darkness was there whether or not his eyes were open. But he closed them anyway. For Martha. To preempt whatever argument she might make. As his lids clamped down, the guy next door came with a bellow.

In the ensuing silence, Martha's voice floated toward him. "I don't feel sorry for you, Danny."

* * *

An hour later, Jake Wise called. It felt like a couple of centuries, but Danny knew it was an hour because he asked Martha the time as she put the cell phone in his hand.

"Sin!" The playful pleasure in Jake's voice cut through Danny. All of a sudden he realized what contacting his friend meant. He'd have to tell Jake what happened. Show him the blind man. Dread thrummed a sickening beat.

Jake rippled on. "Jesus Christ, what the hell have you been up to?"

Too much, way too much to talk about. "You wouldn't believe me if I told you."

Jake laughed. "Yeah? Still crawling around in those local sewers, wearing last year's jeans and needing a haircut?"

"Some of us don't need fancy clothes to get laid."

"Don't I know it. Some of us just bat our turquoise eyes."

The good-natured jibe was nothing Danny hadn't heard before, but now it bit into him. "Yeah, that's right."

Jake must have heard the edge in his voice. "You okay?"

"Sure. Fine."

"So what's with the wake-up call?"

"I need to see you."

"And how's that gonna work?"

"You tell me."

Jake got the silent message. "You underground?"

"In a semi-sort of way."

"And the babe? God forbid you're without a babe."

"There is no—" He stopped short, realizing how what he was going to say would sound to Martha. Instead he admitted, "She's a witness."

"A witness." Jake snorted. "Only you, Sin."

"Look it's not—" He couldn't explain what Martha was

to himself, let alone to Jake. "We're out on a limb. We need a place to stay."

"Where are you now?"

Danny gave him the street coordinates.

Jake took a minute to consult a map or a colleague, Danny wasn't sure which. "That pretty much sucks, Sin. The governor's coming this morning for a big rally. NYPD's got the streets blocked off for half a mile in all directions to make room for his motorcade. I can get through with a siren, but don't know if you want that kind of attention."

"Definitely not. We'll have to hoof it."

"A restaurant okay? There's a coffee shop on Mercer. Can you get over there?"

"Half an hour?"

"See you then."

Thank God Jake was Jake and hadn't asked too many questions. He held out the phone, and Martha took it from him.

"What did he say?" Her voice was cool, matter-of-fact even, but that didn't mean she wouldn't have plenty to say about what had happened between them. Women always wanted to talk, analyze, pick things apart like army ants until not even crumbs were left.

He only hoped she'd hold off until he got things straight with Jake. "He wants to take us out for breakfast. We're meeting him at a coffee shop. Get your coat on. We have to walk there."

"Can't we call a cab?"

"We could if there were any. But the streets are blocked off for the governor's motorcade. He's doing some kind of last-minute election rally."

He heard the rustle of clothes. Was she standing? Putting on her coat?

"You didn't tell him much."

"Thought it was better to do that in person. I'm sure the phones are okay, but it doesn't hurt to be cautious."

"Is that why you didn't tell him you're blind?"

Her voice was quiet, but he still couldn't hear the word without his stomach heaving. "What was I supposed to say? Hey pal, guess what? I can't see a fucking thing?"

"I would have done a little editing, but yes. Something along those lines. It's going to be a shock."

Danny sighed and rubbed his forehead. "I don't know why I didn't tell him."

"Scared?"

The word sent a shaft of anger through him. "I'm not scared of anything."

"Except being blind."

Instinctively, he took a step toward her. God, he wanted to shut her up. "Don't say—" His knee slammed into the end of the iron bedstead. "Jesus fucking—"

A fist pounded the door. "You in there!"

"Are you all right?" Martha was all over him. He shrugged her away.

"I'm fine."

"Hey! You staying, you owe me another twenty bucks."

"We're leaving!" Danny called out. "Get lost."

"Not without the money or seeing your back for sure."

"Here." Martha shoved her father's leather jacket at him and opened the door. From the strain on the hinges it sounded as though she'd ripped them open. "That's enough. We're leaving."

"Okay, okay. Just doing my job."

"Do it someplace else," Danny said, and waited to hear the clerk's footsteps. "Go on."

"Not until I see you heading out."

She came back for him and took his arm. Head up, he felt for a clear path, trying to look as normal as possible. She stopped and the room door closed behind them.

"We're going." Martha's voice was a cool huff. "Here's the key."

The man made some kind of confirmation sound in the back of his throat. Finally footsteps retreated.

"Ready?" Martha asked.

"Yeah. Sure."

Truth was, he was anything but. Martha had been dead-on in there: He was scared to see Jake. Scared to show up as anything less than the man he used to be. Scared of Jake's pity.

Danny should have told him. But the words had stuck in his throat.

He held on to the wall and took the stairs cautiously. When they reached bottom, Martha led him across an open space—the lobby, he presumed—then a blast of cold air hit him. They were outside.

He struggled with the zipper on the jacket, cursed, but finally got the two interlocking pieces to fit. Jesus Christ, he couldn't zip up his own jacket, how the hell was he going to keep himself and Martha alive?

They proceeded slowly, ponderously. Street noises had doubled in the few hours they'd been inside. Once they got out of the blockaded area, car horns blared, brakes squealed, buses rumbled. Every so often Martha moved him to the left or right. A couple of times, people bumped into him, and she murmured a low "Sorry."

He knew that was less likely to happen if he held on to

her the way he should. But he couldn't make himself walk into that coffee shop clinging to her.

"Who is this Jake Wise? How do you know him?" Martha's hands wrapped tight around his arm as if afraid to let go. But the closeness warmed them both. The sun was up; he felt it on his face. And though the air was still vicious, the extra heat took the knife edge out of the cold.

"We were in the army together. Trained for Special Forces at the same time and ended up in the same unit."

"Are you good friends?"

"We don't darn each other's socks if that's what you mean. But we do go to Knicks games together."

"You think he'll be able to help?"

"He's smart, well-trained. I have high hopes."

It took them the allotted time to get to the coffee shop. The minute they walked in, Danny realized they were in for complications. Martha didn't know what Jake looked like, and he sure as hell couldn't point him out to her.

"A man is waving from a booth in the back," Martha said. "Could that be him?"

"What's he look like?"

"Light brown hair. Suit. That's about all I can tell. Wait a minute—he's getting up. Coming forward."

"Sin!"

At the sound of the familiar voice, Danny's gut twisted tighter. "Hey, pal."

A hand grabbed Danny around the neck and pummeled his back. "Good to see you. Got a booth back here. Come on."

Martha tugged on Danny's arm, pulling him forward, probably to the booth.

"I've been waving my arm off at you," Jake said.

Danny licked his lips and forced a smile. "Well, I didn't see you."

"Don't know how you could've missed."

Martha squeezed his arm. A little signal that said, go ahead, tell him. It's going to be all right.

Easy for her to say. "The thing is, Jake, I . . . uh . . . I don't see much of anything these days."

"We're here," Martha murmured, and somehow manipulated his arm so he was up against the outside of the booth.

She let go and he was able to feel his way onto the bench seat. The material was smooth and cool. Leather or leatherette. He slid in and Martha came after him.

Jake didn't say a word. Danny imagined he was taking it all in. Martha moving him this way and that, him fumbling around. All he needed was a sign around his neck.

"What happened?" Jake's voice was sober, serious, and Danny would have done anything to get the old hectoring badger back in Jake's voice.

"You want it in professional or layman's terms?"

"He had a stroke." Martha's no-nonsense voice cut through. "He's blind." She turned to him, her body twisting so one breast hit him in the elbow. In an instant he was back in the flophouse, his hands all over her. The two things melded together. Her pity, Jake's.

"I'm sorry, Danny." Her voice was low, softer now. "But best get it over with."

He nodded, his jaw tense, his throat so raw with holding back emotion he wouldn't have been able to answer her if he wanted to.

"A stroke," Jake said slowly. "Jesus Christ." A few seconds of silence and then a low chuckle vibrated from across the table. "Sin, my man, you will do anything, I mean anything to get women crawling all over you. I've heard of desperation, but this beats all."

For a moment, Jake's words didn't register. "What are you talking about?"

"Come on. You think I don't know a sympathy ploy when I hear one? Look at the poor, helpless blind man." Jake imitated a woman cooing. "Ooh, maybe he needs help. Maybe he needs someone to hold his hand, rub his head, stroke his—"

"Okay, that's enough. I get it." The tautness inside Danny relaxed. He could never have handled condolences and he was thankful to God he didn't have to.

"Not that you ever need help, but if you wanted attention, I can think of a helluva lot of better ways to get it."

Danny nodded, felt a grin start. "Yeah, me, too."

"So, who's your friend?" And that was it. The subject of blindness breeched and conquered. Time to move on to more important things.

"His *friend* is Martha Crowe."

A week ago Danny might have been surprised at the blunt way she spoke up, not bothering to wait for an introduction. But not now.

"Jake Wise."

He felt movement. Were they shaking hands?

"So fill me in, Sin. What's going on?"

"Coffee?" An unfamiliar woman's voice.

"All around," Jake said, and the clink of china merged with the gurgle of liquid.

"So what's for breakfast this morning?" the waitress said. She took their orders, and when she'd gone, Danny began to brief Jake.

Martha added cream to her coffee, and while Danny brought Jake up to date, she took the opportunity to observe the newcomer. He was smaller than Danny, wiry where Danny was broad, with a lean, square jaw set off by close-cropped sandy hair. He wore a dark, sleek suit, a conservative maroon tie, but the businessman's attire couldn't hide his steely edge. Laugh lines bracketed his mouth and fanned out from his eyes. Or were they squint lines, as if he'd spent a lot of time gazing out into the sun searching for enemies?

And yet those same eyes held a curious, teasing sparkle. He'd been absolutely fantastic about Danny. She hadn't missed the way Jake's face had drained of blood when she'd blurted out the truth about Danny's eyes. Nor the pinched set to his mouth. Yet Jake had responded just right. She would respect him for that alone, but his keen intelligence as he took in everything Danny said also won her admiration.

"So you think what? That Ricky Roda's smuggling unmarked guns into the country?"

She remembered Ricky Roda from the case files. According to Danny, Roda was a major player in the Bronx and lower Hudson Valley's drug and gun trade.

"An untraceable weapon is an advantage any scumbag would pay top dollar for," Danny said.

So this was what Danny had been speculating about. God help her, in the incredible rush of feeling from him holding her, touching her, she'd nearly forgotten what had brought them together.

"Then why involve me?" Jake sipped at his coffee. "The ATF handles gun-related crime."

Danny overrode Jake's objections. "Our guy in the ATF is stuck. He sent the gun for a metallurgy analysis, but who knows how long that will take. Meanwhile, our asses are on the line."

"You think this ties back to Roda's operation? Why would he kill his own cousin?"

Danny leaned forward, as though eager to answer. "If the kid was stealing from Roda—selling these guns on the open market to any unvetted skell—he's a liability. The last thing Roda wants would be attention drawn to his business. He has to be careful how he disposes of these weapons. The kid had to be selling them on the sly, and Roda might have been forced to take him out. But he couldn't just kill him, so he made it look like a hit on me."

When had he time to figure all this out? "I don't understand," Martha said. "If the original shooting wasn't an attempt on your life, what was the man at your house all about? Not to mention whoever broke into the farmhouse."

Danny shrugged and cupped his hands around his coffee mug. "Maybe it was all a cleanup job that went bad. The shooter at the warehouse was supposed to take out me and the kid. He screwed up and had to correct his mistakes. He keeps making the same mistake—"

"So he keeps coming after you," Jake finished.

Danny nodded. "Exactly."

Martha shuddered. What was it like to live with that kind of violence and danger? In a million years she never would have thought she'd know.

"What about the leak in the department?" Jake asked.

"Maybe Roda got to someone."

"Who? How?"

"Damned if I know."

Jake turned to Martha. "And you're the witness."

"I saw the man who came to Danny's house."

"That where you got the—" He nodded at her face, circling his own eye.

She touched the lingering traces of bruise on her cheek. "Yes."

His mouth tightened. "And you can ID him?"

"I know what he looks like, but I couldn't find his picture in any of the books at the police station."

Their breakfast came, and Martha dug in as though her she hadn't eaten in a week. Jake passed the salt and pepper to Danny, and out of the corner of her eye she watched him season his eggs as she'd taught him, and as casually as if he could see. His hands encircled the plate briefly, he patted its contents with his fork, surfed the table for his coffee, and did it all without spilling anything, and without hesitating in embarrassment.

Two gold stars, Detective.

They paused to eat a few bites, then Danny said, "We need a place to hole up while I figure this out. A safe place."

"I can help with that. Off the record, at least for now. I can't act officially—I don't have jurisdiction over guns. And the leaky boat—that's a local problem. The Feebies should handle that. But I can stow you somewhere and put you in touch with a few people who can help. People I trust."

An hour later Jake proved good as his word. Their hideaway was a small apartment in a nondescript building on the Upper West Side, ironically not too far from the Parkview Bar and Grill. Utilitarian in design, it contained only the bare minimum: a living area with couch and a couple of armchairs all in early motel, a tiny kitchen with stove, fridge, and a sink. The best thing about it was the two bedrooms. With doors. Her relationship with Danny was too confusing at the moment. One bed would have sent her over the edge. The last thing she wanted was a repeat of the night before: her throwing herself at him, him throwing her right back.

She watched silently as Danny mapped out the space. Did he really think she'd asked him to kiss her out of pity? Her attraction to him was so obvious she would have thought he could smell it. Her face heated, and she ignored it by focusing on Danny's exploration. He trailed the walls, felt for furniture, doorways, appliances in the kitchen, and she watched closely, safe in her professional role.

Jake didn't say a word as Danny investigated the space with his fingers, but his face spoke volumes. Taut with some emotion—anger or regret—he stood rock still, as though forcing himself to look. Then Danny disappeared into the bathroom and Jake turned to her.

"How did you—" He cleared his throat, blocked by whatever he was feeling. "Christ." He swallowed and shook his head. "How did you get involved with Sin?"

"I'm a rehab and mobility instructor. Danny is one of my clients."

"That's why you were in the house during the attack?"

She nodded.

"Is he—" He licked his lips. "Is he going to get his sight back?"

"I don't know. Maybe. But the doctors say probably not."

Jake nodded, absorbing the information. "Okay." He said the word with finality. Subject closed.

Danny came out of the bathroom into the silence between the two of them. He leaned against the side of the entryway into the living area and gave them a crooked grin. "Been talking about me?"

Jake gave a curt laugh. "Jesus, Sin. Blind or not, you

sure as hell know what's going on. Yeah, I asked a few questions."

"Got your answers?"

"Yeah," he said softly. "I did."

Martha looked between the two men. Volumes went unspoken. They'd have a freer hand without her. "I . . . I'm beat. I'm going to lie down."

"Take the second bedroom," Danny said. "I've already scouted the first."

"I should go, too," Jake said.

"Hold up a minute," Danny said.

Carpet absorbed Martha's footsteps as she passed by, but Danny heard the swish of her clothing and waited for the sound of the bedroom door clicking shut. Then he fumbled for the couch in the living room, felt the tweedy fabric, and made sure no one was already there before sitting down.

"Jake, you still here?"

"I'm here, Sin." His voice was quiet, low. Danny heard the edge of compassion and his back went up.

"We going to have the sympathy talk?"

"Not unless you want to."

"Good."

The couch sank under Jake's weight. "Then what's on your mind?"

"I want to talk to Roda. I want you to arrange it."

A long silence followed. Danny knew what he was asking. Jake couldn't act officially, so he'd have to work around the rules. And that could mean trouble for him. Was the bond of their shared service still strong enough to hold?

"I'll see what I can do," Jake said at last. No questions about how a blind man could run an interrogation, no protests or objections. Just the trust that Danny could still act on his own behalf.

He swallowed the emotion rising in his throat. "Thanks."

"I'll let you know," Jake punched Danny lightly on one knee, the gesture expressing what words hadn't. Confidence. Friendship.

Danny had one more test of that connection. "Something's still bothering me. The gun."

"Uh-huh. I'm with you."

"I didn't want to say anything in front of Martha, but—"

"What if it isn't Ricky Roda?"

The question hung between them like a gaping hole. "That's a sterile gun, Jake. I haven't seen one in a long time."

"Not since the army."

"You know what those guns are used for."

"Black ops. Wet work."

Silence while that sank in. Danny picked his words carefully. "Maybe the gun is exactly what it's supposed to be. A weapon for assassination. One that can't be traced."

Jake moved, but Danny couldn't tell what he was doing. Scratching his jaw? Running a hand through his hair? Just getting more comfortable? "Look, I'm all for raising the threat alert, Sin, but let's face it, you're not exactly a high-profile target. And neither is Sokanan. Why would someone send that kind of muscle after you?"

"That's the part I haven't figured out yet."

"Which is why the Roda theory plays a whole lot better."

"I'm just putting it out there, Jake. Something to chew on in the dark."

Another brief silence. "That a blind joke?"

Danny pushed through the bitterness. "Can't put nothing past you, pal."

A beat of silence. Then Jake said, "Remember the closet?"

Danny smiled. He remembered the closet all right. No one who'd been through Special Forces forgot that training exercise. Two guys locked together in a dark closet, no weapons, forced to fight their way out using anything except sight to do it.

"You made it out then, Sin. You'll make it out now."

CHAPTER 10

———•———

The plan to put Danny in touch with Ricky Roda was a simple one. Grab him and run.

There were a few complications, like bodyguards with guns, but Danny figured he could get around that.

If only he could get around Martha.

"No." Her voice was emphatic. "I'm not putting my father in danger again."

"He won't be in danger," Danny said. "Not like last time. No one will be shooting at us. It'll just be like a Sunday drive."

"Right."

The kettle boiled, shrieking holy hell into the kitchen. They were perched on stools at the counter that formed the outer edge of the room and separated it from the living room.

Martha's seat scraped back and a second later the screeching stopped. Door and drawers opened and closed. "Tea or Maxwell House?"

"Coffee." He needed something to keep him awake. If he let himself, he'd fall flat on his face. But they had to move fast and tying up this key loose end was important. "He told you he wants to help. Here's how he can help. We need a van."

"You can have his van. But not him. Let Jake drive." Something clicked in front of him. "Coffee's up," she murmured.

He eased his hands over the edge of the counter until he located the mug. "We need Jake for other things."

"No."

"I'll just ask him myself."

"You don't know his phone number." Her voice had gone away, then come back again. The other stool moved, and he assumed she'd filled her own cup and sat back down. "And I'm not giving it to you."

"Are you kidding? I've got the resources of the mighty TCF behind me. Phone numbers are nothing."

She grumbled, the sound like a frown deep in her throat. "If anything happens to him . . ."

"Nothing's going to happen to him."

Before he could close the deal, his cell phone rang. He brought it out of his pocket and fumbled for a button to push.

"Danny?"

He recognized the voice. "Beth?" A zip of fear. Why was his sister calling him? "Is everything okay?"

"Oh, my God, you're alive. He's alive!" She spoke off the receiver, and a cheer went up. Male voices in the background.

"Are you all right? Where are you? Mike and Bob Parnell are here. They said something ha-happened. That you might be—" Her voice started to break.

"I'm all right," he said quickly. "I promise." Guilt replaced the fear. Of course the department would contact Beth and scare the shit out of her. He should have called her himself.

"But where are you?"

"I'm safe."

"Let me talk to him." That sounded like Parnell. Danny tensed, not wanting to believe the betrayal at the farmhouse could lead right back to him, but knowing it could.

"Are you all right? What the hell happened at the farmhouse?"

Danny debated how much to reveal. He was shooting in the dark, and didn't know who to trust. "Two men. Maybe three. I don't know exactly. But our friend was there."

"The friend who paid you a house call?"

"One and the same."

"How do you know? Did Miss Crowe see him?"

Danny bristled at the lack of confidence the question implied. "I smelled him."

"You—"

"Smelled him. That's right." He pushed through the embarrassment. "I can still do that, and this guy reeked. Tiger Balm."

"What's that?"

"Some kind of Chinese liniment."

"Chinese? Like from a hole in the wall in Chinatown?"

He wished. "Made in Singapore, but Tim got it at CVS. He was going to check the stores around Sokanan."

"I'll put someone else on it."

"How is he?"

"Alive, but barely." A rush of relief. That was good. "Not talking yet." That was bad. Tim might have seen something useful. Then again, if he had, would Parnell tell him? Danny gave himself a mental slap. Of course he would. Parnell would tell Danny anything he needed to know. Wouldn't he?

"How'd you manage to get out?"

And yet . . . "A little luck, a little help from my friends."

"Well, that's cryptic." Parnell waited, but Danny didn't explain. "How about Miss Crowe? Can you be more specific about her? Is she all right?"

"She's fine. I've got her with me."

"And where's that?"

Danny didn't answer and Parnell made a sound of frustration. "How am I supposed to protect you if I don't know where you are?"

"You can't. That's the idea. Someone knew where I was at the farmhouse."

Parnell paused. "Those men would lay down their lives for you, Sin."

"I used to think so."

"Whoever attacked you almost killed Tim. We want to get him as much as you do. Besides, you can't go this alone." Danny heard the unspoken thought: *You're blind, powerless.* "Look, you've got friends here. Let us help you."

With friends like that . . . "I'll think about it. Tell Beth I'll be home soon." He disconnected.

Lieutenant Parnell ended the call to Danny and gazed grimly at Mike. The two of them were in Danny's sister's living room, Beth anxiously gazing at them. "He's not talking."

Mike Finelli nodded, equally grim. "Yeah, well, no surprise there. Not after what happened."

"He'll be all right, though, won't he?" Beth looked from Parnell to Mike and back again.

"He'd be better off with us behind him," Parnell said.

Beth put a hand on Mike's arm. "You'll let me know if you find him?"

Mike squeezed her hand. "You bet. Look, how about I come by tonight, make sure you're okay?"

She nodded. "Thanks. But the important thing is to make sure Danny's okay."

"Absolutely," Parnell said, and walked with Mike to the door. "We'll keep you posted. The kids are all right?"

"Fine."

"You let Mike or me know if you hear from Danny. And if you need anything."

She kissed Parnell on the cheek. "I will."

"See you tonight," Mike said.

Outside, Parnell stopped on the front stoop and turned his collar up against the cold. "Reach out to Mr. Crowe. Maybe his daughter contacted him and he knows where they are."

Mike nodded. "Will do. What about the possibility of a leak?"

Parnell's mouth tightened into a hard line. "I'll handle that."

Charlie Crowe didn't exactly dislike the police. He just had a natural distrust of authority. Though much of that skepticism had been blunted by time, it hadn't been completely obliterated. So when Detective Finelli showed up at the bike shop, Charlie was more inclined to say nothing than to tell the truth.

But Finelli kept driving home the one point that had been bothering Charlie all along.

"I've known Danny a long time. He'll do everything he can to keep your daughter safe. But we both know that right now his resources are, well, limited at best."

"You mean the guy's blind." Charlie wheeled himself around the detective and pushed the button that lowered the worktable to lap height. He was working on a custom job for a collector in Philadelphia—a tribute bike to the Spirit of '76—and the red, white, and blue handlebars had just arrived.

"Well, that is a drawback."

"Some guys think not having legs is a drawback." He cut open the packing, pulled the handlebars out, and laid them on the table next to the gleaming, neon blue motorcycle frame. Without the bars the machine looked like a creature without its head.

"We're not talking about playing football here. We're talking about your daughter's life. If she contacted you, if you know where she is, believe me, she'll be safer with the police behind her."

He snorted. "The damn police got her into this in the first place."

Finelli shifted his weight, an uncomfortable expression on his face. Charlie was right and Finelli knew it. "Then let us get her out. She's practically alone out there."

Charlie sighed. Despite the phone call from Martha, he'd been sick with worry all morning. He knew what it was like to have the world think you were less than a man, and he didn't want to doubt this Sin character just because he was blind. But he'd be damned if he risked Martha's life for the same reason.

He peered closely at Finelli. The guy looked bona fide, but Charlie didn't go in much for looks. On the other hand, things could go just as wrong without the police as with them. Seemed like the odds would tilt a bit more in her favor with them.

He scratched his jaw, giving himself one last chance to change his mind. "I picked them up at the water tower on

Route 3 last night. Someone was chasing them. Someone with guns."

"Did you see who?"

Charlie shook his head. "Too fucking dark and things happening too fast."

"Where'd you take them?"

"The Hudson marina in Sokanan. Your boy said he had a boat that would take them into Manhattan. I got a call early this morning that they got there. That's all I know."

"Why Manhattan?"

Charlie set the handlebars in place, inserted the bolt, and began to tighten the torque. "Something about a friend he wanted to look up. A Fed."

Danny gulped at his third cup of coffee. It tasted of chemicals, but he needed the jolt to help get his brain around the possibility that one of his fellow cops was a traitor.

Footsteps. "I'm making toast," Martha announced. "Want some?"

"No, thanks."

Plastic wrapping crackled, toast went down.

"Look, if you're going to brood, do it out loud."

"I'm not brooding."

"Really? You've been sitting there drinking coffee for over an hour. What would you call it?"

"Thinking."

"About?"

"Why someone in the NRU would leak our whereabouts."

The stool next to his moved. Martha sitting down?

"Any conclusions?"

He shrugged. "Blackmail. Gambling debts. Secret sexual perversions. Envy. Greed."

"Anyone fit any of those profiles?"

"Not that I know of."

He smelled the bread browning, and his stomach rumbled. For the thousandth time he caught himself wondering what someone else was thinking. It was eerie to be suspended in uncertainty with no visual cues. He tried picturing her face but didn't know where to start. Was she frowning or just sitting thoughtfully? What color were her eyes, her hair? Was she pale with freckles or dark and olive-skinned?

"What color is your hair?"

"What?"

He sent her what he hoped was a deadpan look. "Don't tell me you're deaf. We can't afford to lose any more senses. What color is your hair?"

"I—my—" Her voice stumbled, got that funny embarrassed tone he found oddly charming. "Why do you want to know?"

He shrugged, stringing her along. "No reason. Because I can't see for myself."

"It's . . . it's black."

"Catherine Zeta-Jones black?" He pictured a deep, rich color.

"More like Wicked Witch of the West black."

He nearly choked on a mouthful of coffee. "Oh, that's attractive."

"It's the truth." Her voice firmed, as though she'd stiffened her spine.

"You don't think much of yourself."

"I think a lot of myself. I just don't sugarcoat things."

"Just the facts, ma'am?"

"That's right."

He tried to conjure up an appropriate image but couldn't make the color work in his head. To him she would always be a spring meadow, and how could that be anything but pretty?

"And don't think you can get around me by telling me I'm the next best thing since J-Lo."

He couldn't help a small laugh. "Man, you are so suspicious."

"I still don't want my father driving that van."

"Well, you know what Mick Jagger says. Want and need. Two different things."

"You don't *need* my dad to drive the van, either."

In the distance a cell phone rang. Martha scraped back her bar stool and left the kitchen.

Danny picked up his mug in one hand and used the other to trace the outline of counter and cabinets until he found the sink. He put the mug there, neater than he'd ever been, and made his way to the bedroom he'd staked out. His shoulders felt like two boulders above his arms and despite the coffee, his head was starting to fuzz. The lack of sleep from the night before was taking its toll.

He pulled off his sweater, realizing vaguely that the only clothes he had were on his back. Or off, as the case may be. Carefully, he folded the sweater, sure he was just mashing it into a mess, and laid it on top of what he assumed was a dresser. He removed his sneakers and socks, placed them next to the sweater, then edged his way to the bed and lay down.

Usually, going to sleep was hard because he knew he'd wake up having forgotten he couldn't see, and would have to relive the shock all over again. But now, after the night he'd had, sleep was welcome. He was drifting off when a knock sounded on the door.

"Danny?"

He'd recognize that voice anywhere. "Come in."

When she opened the door, Martha blinked at the sight that greeted her. Danny, lying in bed wearing nothing but a pair of jeans. Even last night, when her hands had been all over him, she hadn't seen much of his body; they hadn't gotten far enough. And now here he was, long legs and a hard, muscled chest, abs rippling as he sat up, shoulders and arms taut and powerful.

"Martha?"

"Uh . . . yes?" Her brain wasn't working.

"Did you . . . want something?" He spoke patiently, as if to a child.

Did she want something? The question struck her as ridiculous. She wanted him to want her, not just need her. Without her begging or throwing herself on top of him.

Fat chance.

But chance wasn't why she'd come.

Why had she come?

She looked down, away from the beautiful body on the bed, so she could concentrate. Her hand came into focus. She was holding something.

A phone.

She was holding her phone.

"My . . . my father wants to talk to you."

His brows quirked up with a satisfied look and she snapped at him in a low voice. "No, I didn't ask him."

He held up a hand in mock supplication. "Okay, okay. Down girl."

She bit her lip. Why was it so difficult to talk to him sometimes?

"The phone?" He held out his hand, and she had to walk over to give it to him. Had to stand close enough to touch, to stroke, to run her hands down the strong plane of that magnificent back.

"Sinofsky," he said curtly. He listened, a frown slowly forming between his black brows. "Christ," he muttered, and listened more. "Well, the damage is done. No, I don't know if they know my friend's name. Finelli might. But it won't take long to figure it out. Look, you want to make it up to me? I got a favor to ask."

Martha tensed as Danny told Charlie what he wanted, but it was clear from the conversation that her objections were all overruled.

Danny disconnected, then punched in another number, quickly getting Jake on the phone and alerting him that Charlie had told the police about him.

"Someone from Sokanan PD could be snooping around so watch your back."

When he was done, he handed Martha her phone.

"That means trouble, doesn't it?" she asked. "If they find Jake, they could find us."

"Jake's a pro, and he's been warned. He'll take proper precautions."

"All the more reason to keep my dad out of this."

"Look, I know you didn't want me to get Charlie involved, but he'll be okay. He's a tough bird."

She nodded. "But not indestructible."

"I don't know. He's done all right so far."

She had to give him that. Reluctantly. "He's my father," she said quietly. "He's all I have."

He groped for her arm and tugged her down beside him. "I know. No wonder your dad is so possessive."

His touch sent a tremor through her. Fear and need all mixed up together. "I wouldn't call him possessive. At least not when it comes to me."

"He seemed plenty upset in the van. And eager to help."

"It takes someone shooting at me to get him to pay attention."

"And yet, you live with him."

"He'd suck on cigarettes and coffee all day if someone wasn't there to look out for him."

"So you're elected?"

"There weren't a whole lot of volunteers." The truth and an excuse at the same time. She'd been so anxious to hold on to the family she had left.

"And now the two of you, you're what—an old-fashioned spinster and her father?"

His words would have hurt except she saw a teasing light in his eyes.

"Just don't tell me you have six cats crawling around your house."

She repressed a smile. "No, no cats."

"Because I'm not much of a cat person."

"Neither is Charlie."

He gazed at her—a long, penetrating look made even more disconcerting because he couldn't see her face. Yet it felt as though he was staring at something she'd rather no one saw.

"I think you like taking care of people, Martha Crowe."

She couldn't tell if that was a compliment or a criticism. In either case, it embarrassed her. "I've been taking care of my father since I was twelve," she said coolly. "It's a hard habit to break."

"Is that why you do what you do? Habit?"

"What do you mean?"

"I mean, how did you get into the blind business?"

She squirmed a bit, not sure she wanted him to know so much about her. "I didn't know what to do with myself after college. I could get a free ride if I did a master's program in rehab at Val State."

His brows rose in surprise. "You little mercenary."

"Well, rehab was something I was very familiar with. It was a good fit."

"And no one could see you."

She narrowed her eyes. "What's that supposed to mean?"

He dismissed her wariness with a shrug and a yawn. "Nothing. Just an observation."

A little too acute of an observation, but she didn't say so.

He yawned again and plopped down on the bed. "God, I'm tired."

He did look tired and drawn. His jeweled eyes glittered deeper in his face, and the cuts from the woods and glass were scratched into the stubble on his jaw and cheek. She probably looked no better. She'd tried to clean up a bit in the bar restroom, but no amount of dabbing could obliterate the traces of the bruise that still lingered on her cheek.

"Come here. Lie down." He patted the bed beside him. "I can hardly think straight. You must be exhausted."

She inhaled a sharp breath. Was that an invitation?

"Don't worry, I'm too bushed to make a pass."

He closed his eyes and she watched him hungrily, foolishly, half of her relieved and half of her disappointed. Against her better judgment, she slid in beside him. He tucked an arm around her so her head rested on his shoulder. She stared at the ceiling, too afraid to look at him. Her free arm lay tense and unmoving at her side.

"It will be all right," he murmured. "I promise." And she understood suddenly that this wasn't a pass but an attempt to soothe her. Comfort her. And the thought that he cared enough to ease her fears made her believe.

"Okay."

"So relax. Go to sleep. Nothing will happen to your father. Trust me." He held out his hand and slowly she placed hers into it. Fingers entwined, he set their hands on the center of his chest, his atop hers. She felt warm skin, the pulsing of his heart. Her own matched the rhythm, like a swift rush of thudding water.

"Mind if I ask a personal question?" His voice was low and sleepy, his eyes still closed.

What in God's name could he want to know that he couldn't ask outright? She swallowed, primed for embarrassment. "Sure."

"Why did your parents name you Martha? It's, well, kind of old-fashioned."

The unexpected question took her by surprise. "No 'ie' on the end?"

His mouth curved in a small smile. "Yeah. No 'ie.'"

On the scale of personally threatening questions, this one ranked pretty low. She relaxed, her body softening against his. "You know the Beatles song 'Martha, My Dear'? My mother's favorite."

He paused. "That song's about a dog."

She smiled ruefully. "Yeah, I know."

He snuggled her closer against him. "I like dogs. Now cats . . . like I said, I'm not much for cats. Thank God they didn't name you Garfield. I might've had a problem with that."

She laughed and punched him in the side.

"Woof, woof, Martha."

And that was the last thing she heard before drifting off to sleep.

* * *

On Wednesday, Charlie left the shop at five, made a big production out of waving good-bye to Arnie Gould, lifted himself into his van, folded his wheelchair and placed it where he could get at it later, and got into the driver's seat.

None of this was new or different; it was a routine he'd been following for years and was second nature. The only thing out of the ordinary was the way he kept checking the parking lot. Quietlike. Not turning his head, but using his eyes to make sure no one was watching him. He was pretty damn sure he was in the clear, but he wasn't going to take chances, not with his daughter's life at stake.

He lit a cigarette, took a nice drag, felt the smoke settle comfortably in his lungs, and watched out the side view mirror. If the fuckers were there, he sure as hell couldn't see them.

He inserted the key in the ignition and used the hand controls to get the van rolling. He pulled into the street, watched for a tail, and made sure to drive slow and steady, all his turns as deliberate as he could make them.

Ten minutes later, he was at the Craftsman. He pulled up to a space in front of the bar and reversed the routine he'd used to get into the van, using his arms to maneuver himself out of the vehicle and into the chair. He pressed a button on the remote and the door locked. Carefully, he rolled himself into the bar.

The place wasn't too crowded. A couple of guys at the bar and none at the tables. Then again, it was early. He waved at Cal, ordered a beer, and perched himself at one of the tables across from the bar.

"How you doing, Charlie?" Cal set down the beer and nodded toward the coat Charlie had left on. "You coming or going?"

"I'm warming up. Not even November and it's fucking

winter out there." He dug into his pocket and tossed some bills on the table.

Cal picked them up. "No tab today?"

"Pay as I go," Charlie said. "Less temptation that way."

"Speaking of temptation, I saw Martha in here a few days ago. She doing all right?"

"Sure," Charlie said, hoping it was true. "She's doing just fine."

"Holler when you're ready for another round." Cal went back to the bar and fussed with the cardboard black cat that had fallen over and was covering the VOTE poster. Between Halloween and the election, the place was a fucking decoration nightmare.

A drumbeat took up residence inside Charlie's chest, a sign of rising excitement and nerves that he ignored as best he could. To everyone else he hoped he looked perfectly calm, perfectly normal, sipping the one beer like a damn fruit fly for a full fifteen minutes.

"Hey, Cal," he called when the time was up, "you got any new graffiti in the can?"

"Just the same old jokes, Charlie."

"You should hire someone to scrawl you some new ones. Be kind of like a new attraction." Charlie rolled his chair toward the men's room at the back, and when he was out of sight, made a small right, and went out the backdoor. Waiting for him was the company van that Arnie Gould had parked there the night before. The company van that had been fitted with hand controls, so Charlie could use it.

He unlocked the door, got himself situated inside, and pulled the van into the back alley and down two blocks to Rossvelt, where he made a right and headed for the parkway. A few minutes later, he was on his way to the city.

* * *

Ricky Roda had a standing date. Every Wednesday, he and two of his boys drove from the Bronx to Yonkers to visit Ricky's girlfriend, Judith Ashanti. Judith started life as Juditha Tompkins, working her way up from the streets, where she and Ricky first met. A few years ago she left her name and the streets behind. Now she ran a small art gallery featuring African and African-American artists. She was tall and willowy, with hair cropped close to her well-shaped head and smooth, black skin that showed off large silver earrings. She was beautiful and smart, except when it came to Ricky Roda. But she refused to see him unless he left his posse home, so every Wednesday, the boys drove their boss to Yonkers and sat in the car while Ricky drank wine and got his rocks off with Judith. He rarely stayed the night, though sometimes he didn't show up at the car until two or three in the morning.

This Wednesday, the boys dropped Ricky off and left him at the elevator as usual. Ricky got off at the fifth floor and noticed WET PAINT signs on the wall. A man in painter's overalls was capping a paint can, finishing up for the day.

Careful not to touch the wet wall and ruin his latest Burberry suit, he turned his back on the working schmo and headed toward Judith's apartment.

He didn't hear the man behind him until he had him by the throat. The needle barely pinched him.

CHAPTER 11

———————•———————

The dark alley seemed to close in on the van; Martha had the impression that she would be crushed in an avalanche of waiting. Minutes stretched into eternities, the heavy silence broken only by Charlie, who tapped the steering wheel in a steady annoying beat. He probably wanted a cigarette.

Behind her and Charlie, Danny sat on a carton in the back, still and ominous as the brick walls surrounding them. She could just make him out in the faint glow of a distant streetlight that filtered through the windshield.

"Where is he?" she said at last, unable to keep dread at bay.

"He'll be here," Danny snapped. He'd been testy all day, chafing at sitting on the sidelines while someone else carried out the action.

Charlie just continued to tap the wheel.

A man appeared in front of the van, a flashlight illuminating his form, and Martha jumped. Covered by white painter's overalls, he looked eerie and unearthly, an alien materialized from space.

"That's him." Charlie pressed the control that opened the van door.

Jake disappeared around the side and through the open

door she saw him carrying a body over his shoulder. "He looks like a runt, but he's a heavy son of a bitch." Jake grunted, dropping Ricky Roda's upper torso onto the van floor. The body thumped, arms flopping, and Danny felt around, found Roda's shoulders, and pulled him inside.

Jake jumped in after and as the door glided shut shrugged off the painter's overalls. Beneath he wore faded jeans slung low on slim hips and a navy T-shirt stretched over taut muscles. The shirt had CIA emblazoned across the back and underneath, in smaller letters, CULINARY INSTITUTE OF AMERICA. A private, federal joke, he'd told her earlier at the apartment when he'd come to pick them up. She'd frowned, not understanding how anyone could joke about anything at that point. Or this.

The engine started, and the van left the protective cover of the alley. Charlie turned right and eased into traffic, instructed to keep driving and hopefully confuse Roda as much as possible about their whereabouts.

"Make the call," Danny said.

Martha unfolded the paper with the phone number on it. She pressed the numbers, fingers less than steady. A woman answered, her voice low and throaty.

"Ms. Ashanti?" Martha tried to make her own voice sound as officious as possible.

"Yes."

"This is Sookie Wade from the Starlight Club." Danny had given her the name and explained that Roda owned the Starlight, and it would be the most believable venue for this ruse. "I'm calling for Mr. Roda. He asked me to let you know that he's been held up and will be late."

"How late?" The question was hard and unhappy.

"I'm sorry, he didn't say."

"Well, you tell Mr. Roda that I have better things to do than wait around for him."

Martha's heart thumped. If Judith Ashanti left her apartment, Roda's men would see her and know something was wrong.

"I . . . I'll certainly tell him." Her brain was racing, desperate for a reason to keep her home. "But he did ask me to say that if you wait, he'd have a surprise for you. To . . . to make it up to you."

She grunted. "Huh. You tell him it better be an expensive one."

"I . . . yes, I'll tell him. So you'll wait?"

Judith sighed, clearly put upon. "Oh, all right. But he better call me himself next time." She hung up, leaving Martha staring at the phone, relief pumping through her.

"Everything all right?" Jake said.

She swiveled around to face the back. He was busy tying Roda's hands and feet.

"I think so. She said she'd wait for him."

He put a blindfold over Roda's eyes. "Good."

"How much longer until he wakes up?" Charlie asked.

Jake checked his watch. "Not too long. I didn't give him much."

As if to prove his point, Roda groaned, and Martha bit her lip.

Ricky Roda was a small man, slim and lithe, with dusky skin pocked with acne scars. He wore what looked like an expensive suit, sleek and silver and very dandified, with a pink silk handkerchief peeking out of the jacket pocket. His head lolled back and his mouth was open, his dark, slicked-back hair mussed, a hank hanging over his forehead. He didn't look particularly threatening at the moment, but Danny had told her he was a key suspect in three drug-related murders in the Bronx and one in Sokanan last year, though no charges had stuck. Yet.

Jake had propped Roda up on the floor, his hands tied to the wheel of Charlie's chair. She knew the minute he regained consciousness because the groan turned into a gasp and he jerked against the bonds holding hands and feet together.

"What the fuck! What's going on? Where am I?"

"Calm down," Jake said. "You're safe. No one's going to hurt you."

"Who the fuck are you?"

"We're just going to have a little chat," Danny said, "and then we'll let you go."

Martha hoped that would calm the situation, but Roda snarled at Danny.

"You want to chat, you make an appointment."

"Your secretary was out," Danny said smoothly. Now that everything had started he seemed in complete control, and she wondered how he remained so composed. Then again, this was what he did, what he was trained for and good at. Danger or no, there must be a certain comfort in being back in this familiar world.

But if Danny was feeling comfortable, Roda wasn't.

"I ain't telling you squat."

"Then you'll be here a while," Jake said.

Danny wiped his hand across his mouth. "Look, we apologize for the inconvenience, but it was necessary."

"Yeah, why's that?"

"We could tell you," Jake said, "but then we'd have to shoot you."

"Fuck you."

She and Charlie exchanged a look; things weren't going well.

"It's about T-bone." Danny's sharp words cut to the heart of the matter.

Roda stilled. "What about him? You have anything to do with messing up that boy, I'll tear you apart, bro."

"He was your cousin?"

"Who are you? Cops? This is illegal, that's what this is. You can't haul a citizen off the street, drug him, bag him up—"

Jake smiled but with a deadly edge that sent a shiver up Martha's back. "Then maybe that should tell you something, *bro*."

"You Clarence's boys? You tell that motherfucker I'll break his ass."

Clarence? Who was Clarence?

"You have to get out of here first," Jake said.

"Let's get back to T-bone," Danny said. "He was your cousin."

"Yeah? So what?"

"So what was he doing selling guns on the street?"

"I find out Eddie Clarence popped that cap on T-bone—"

Jake slapped Roda on the side of the head, and Martha started. Suddenly she understood the other "things" Jake was supposed to do instead of drive.

"Why was T-bone selling guns?" Jake asked.

Roda growled but answered. "Boy was trying to impress me."

"What kind of gun was he selling?" Danny asked. "A nine, a four-five?"

"How the fuck should I know?"

"Where'd he get it?"

"Maybe he jacked it, huh? Not from me, I tell you that. Stupid baby prick. Aunt crying all over me, sister dissin' me all the time . . ."

She heard genuine grief and regret in Roda's voice, and wondered if he was telling the truth.

"You know what a sterile gun is?" Danny asked.

"We playing *Jeopardy* now?"

Jake hit him again with a sickening crack, and Martha flinched a second time. Everyone had tried to convince her not to come, and now she wished she'd listened to them.

"Answer the question," Jake said. "What's a sterile gun?"

"I don't the fuck know. Something a doctor uses?"

"You keep up the jokes," Jake said. "We got all the time in the world. Do you?"

Danny said, "We think you know what a sterile gun is, Ricky. We think you have a supplier. We think little T-bone got hold of one and thought he'd make a mint selling it on the sly. And we think you took him out because of it."

Roda exploded, surging up like a feral dog. Instinctively, Martha jerked away, but Roda didn't get very far, pulled back by the length of his leash. "What the fuck you talking about? You a crank? Some junkie base head? I loved that little guy."

"Yeah, I'm sure you did," Danny said. "Loved him to death."

"Who are you? I'm not saying nothin' till you tell me who the fuck you are."

Jake looked at Danny as though waiting for a clue about how to proceed. But of course Danny didn't know it. He just stared off as though looking out a window that wasn't there, his blind eyes dark and unfocused.

Slowly he turned his head, leaned into Roda. "Listen, you little scumbag runt." His arm shot out and he groped until he had Roda by the throat.

"Hey, what you—"

Danny shook him. "The last few days of my life have been a shit hole. I've been shot at, chased, almost froze to death. Not to mention certain other liabilities I won't go into now."

"Off! Hands off me!"

Danny tightened his grip, and Martha nearly leaped out of her seat at this new and different Danny. She shot a desperate glance at Jake. If Danny didn't ease up, he'd kill Ricky Roda. Jake shook his head, warning her not to speak.

"I want that shooter." Danny was choking Roda, throttling him. It was as if all the rage he'd felt since losing his sight was focused on the hands around Ricky Roda's throat. "If you're telling the truth, you want him, too. That puts us on the same side."

"I don't even know who you are!"

"I'm the guy that's going to get that asshole even if I have to go through you to do it." He threw Roda back against the floor. He bounced against the wheelchair and the seat, coughing.

"Jesus Christ." Roda hacked out the words. "Look, I didn't off T-bone. I didn't. On my mama's grave I didn't. I don't know nothing about no whatchamacallit—sterile guns. I run a nice, clean drug business. I got a few girls on the side, maybe a few other side deals, but that's it."

Silence descended. Charlie made a right and she caught his eye as he made the turn. Was Roda telling the truth?

"What do you think?" Jake asked at last.

Danny shook his head. "I don't know."

"You believe him?"

"Word. I'm speaking truth, for chrissakes!"

"Yeah?" Danny's eyes could have cut through steel, if only he could see to do it. "Prove it."

"Prove it? Can't even see where the fuck I am. How'm I s'posed to prove it?"

Danny laughed, short and gruff. "I'm familiar with that scenario. But that's your problem."

Roda lashed out again, and Jake hit him in the head again. Roda took the punch cursing. His jaw clamped, the muscles tense. He sat still, breathing hard, buying time, thinking things over.

Martha closed her eyes. How much longer would this go on?

"Someone paid T-bone to hook up with that cop." Roda's voice was hard and angry, but the words made Martha's eyes fly open. Suddenly, the air seemed to vibrate with energy.

"Who?" Danny's voice was keenly edged.

"I knew that, he be dead as you, I get out of here."

"You're a big talker for a guy all tied up and blind-folded," Jake said.

Roda didn't respond.

"Look, Ricky, we both want the same thing." Danny's voice was quiet now, even soothing.

"So you believing me now?"

"I'm inclined to, yes. But that still leaves a lot of questions between us."

"Like who the fuck you are."

"Like who tapped your cousin and why. You have any leads?"

"I got my boys working it."

Danny took a piece of paper from his jeans pocket. It was a phone number for a prepaid cell phone bought for this purpose. He stuffed the paper into Roda's pocket, the one with the pink hanky. "They come up with anything, I'd like to know."

"Yeah? Why?"

Danny hesitated. "Because I'm the guy the shooter set T-bone up for."

"Trust." Danny leaned back against the van wall, trying not to let Roda's words reverberate in his head. *Someone paid T-bone to hook up with that cop.*

"Trust?" Martha's voice squeaked in panic. "What does trust have to do with it? He knows who you are now."

They were driving back to the apartment after leaving Ricky Roda back in the alley, another injection keeping him from identifying the rest of them or the van.

"She does have a point," Jake said dryly.

"You have to give a little to get a little." Danny spoke slowly, trying to keep his voice calm. The last thing he wanted was to scare Martha even more, though she had every right to be terrified. "If we want Roda to let us in on what he finds out, he has to trust us. Letting him know who I am tells him I'm trusting him with important information, just like he can trust me."

"That's a big fucking gamble," Charlie said. "Especially with Martha in the mix."

Didn't he know it.

"Dad, this isn't about me, it's about D—"

"It sure the hell is about you. Why else did I agree to this?"

"Look," Danny said. "I didn't tell him about the rest of us. Just me. It's just me on the line."

"And anyone who gets too fucking close to you," Charlie growled. "You think I'm stupid? Someone put a hit on you. What happens if they miss again and hit Martha?"

The thought cleaved Danny in two.

"I'm taking her with me." Charlie barked the words, no

argument invited. "We'll go someplace. Florida, Arizona. I don't give a rat's ass as long as it's far away."

A pang of loss surprised Danny. He ignored it. "That's a good idea."

"Don't even go home," Jake said. "Just leave now."

"You're doing it again," Martha said.

"Doing what, Martha girl?"

"Talking about me like I'm not here." Her voice was taut, thin, as though she was speaking through gritted teeth.

And now came the real battle.

"Your dad's right. At this point, getting as far away from me as possible is the safest thing you can do."

"And what about you?"

"What about me?"

"What's safe for you?"

"Finding out who's after me and why."

"I hate to point this out to you, Danny, but you're newly blind. You've refused to learn the cane, so you can't even get around by yourself. You can't handle money, you can't tell the time. You don't even know how to cross a street safely. How are you going to investigate this by yourself?"

He felt as though he'd been bitch-slapped. Beaten down by the one person he trusted.

"I'll manage." The words came out tight, lips barely moving.

"I'm sure you will," she said quietly, "but not without help. A year from now, you'll be fine. But there's too much you don't know at the moment." A swish of clothing as though she'd turned around in her seat. "I'm not leaving him, Dad."

A spate of cursing.

"Dad—"

"You'll fucking well do what I tell you!" Charlie roared,

braking the car with a squeal. Danny was thrown forward, then back against the side of the van.

"I won't. And yelling isn't going to make me."

"I'm still your father." His growl carried a threatening undertone, but she ignored it.

"I know that. But I'm not leaving Danny."

"I don't fucking need you." Danny spit it out, hoping the vehemence would convince her.

"Hey, Sin." A hand on Danny's shoulder. Jake? Saying without words, cool off, calm down. She doesn't deserve that.

She didn't deserve to die for him, either.

"I don't want you." The words were clear, distinct, and filled, he hoped, with everything he couldn't say. *In my mind, in my bed, in my life.* Something ripped in his chest, the lie like a knife slicing into him. He waited for her gasp, for some sign that she believed him. Nothing but silence.

"Want and need, Danny." Martha spoke at last in that maddeningly prim way. "Two different things."

A half hour later, a resigned Charlie dropped them off at Jake's car and he drove them back to the apartment where Martha disappeared into her room.

Danny fumbled with the six-pack of beer Jake had brought earlier, putting out two bottles and edging his way back to the living room where he'd left Jake. Danny almost sat on top of him, before feeling his way to the empty space on the couch at Jake's left.

That alone should have told him Martha was right. Couldn't even damn sit down without screwing up.

He handed Jake a bottle of beer, twisted off the cap on his own, and chugged down the cold liquid. Getting drunk sounded like a great plan.

Jake chuckled. "I don't know how you do it, Sin."

"Do what?" He guzzled another swallow.

"No matter what the situation you always manage to have some woman crying over you."

He tensed. "She wasn't crying."

"Figure of speech." Jake swigged his beer, and the sudden coil in Danny's gut relaxed. "But she does care about you."

"I'm her fucking patient. That's what she's paid to do."

"You don't believe that. Not really."

Danny sighed. "I don't want to think about it. I wish she'd gone with Charlie."

"No, you don't."

He shook his head with a short laugh. "Part of me does. Part of me—"

"Yeah, that part can be pretty damn demanding."

Danny laughed, remembering the feel of her under his hands, the soft curves and long, slim limbs. "She keeps telling me she's not very pretty."

"She's not." He said it in a matter-of-fact way that cut through whatever denials Danny might have made.

"Says her hair is witchy black."

"Well, now that I think about it, yeah, she's right." The couch shifted as Jake changed positions, leaning back. "But her skin . . . her skin is nice. Milky. And she has fine eyes. Green, with a little brown in them."

He tried to picture it, but couldn't.

"She's too damn bossy."

"So I gathered."

"Not to mention blunt."

"Yeah, she doesn't suck up much."

Danny hesitated, then spit it out. "I like her."

"I know." The words gentle, sympathetic.

"I don't want her hurt."

"I know." Gentler still.

A beat, while that confession hung between them. Then Danny moved to safer ground.

"You think Roda was telling the truth?"

"Sixty-forty, yeah. Any ideas who wants you dead?"

Danny shook his head. "I handle street crime. Drugs, hookers, and guns. No one with the kind of weight who'd put out a hit."

"What's the last case you worked on?"

"Gun buys. We had a spate of street killings. I was doing an undercover buy when this happened." He gestured to his eyes.

"And before that?"

Danny thought back. "Routine stuff. A drug sweep a few days before. That's where I got popped in the head and this whole thing started."

"You pick up anyone interesting there?"

"Same old, same old."

"What's the place like?"

"The Dutchman? A hole in the wall. Used to be a big deal twenty years ago. Politicos, wheeler-dealer meeting place. The GE plant took the business to the other side of town. And then the plant closed and there was no business except for the lowlifes and street dealers."

"What about your other cases?"

"Been through every goddamn case I worked on for the last five years. Nothing."

"What about Eddie Clarence?"

"Don't know much about him. Bronx rivalry, I think. Got a contact in NYPD. I'll check it out."

Jake rose, the couch creaking with the release of his

weight. "In the meantime, we wait and see what Roda does."

Danny rose, too, turning toward the sound of Jake's voice. "I'm getting sick and tired of waiting."

Jake clapped him on the shoulder. "You don't have much choice, Sin. And besides, I'm sure you can find plenty to keep you occupied."

Danny bridled at the amusement in Jake's voice. "It's not like that."

"You can't see the way she looks at you. But hey, I can always stick around and chaperone."

"No thanks."

Jake laughed. "Yeah, I figured that's what you'd say."

Danny didn't know why he bristled, but he did. "Look, I'm not going to—"

"Yeah, sure. I know you, Sin. Blind or not, you can't resist. Just promise you'll let her down easy. She's what John Wayne used to call a good woman. She's not one of your bubble girls. She's a grown-up. Treat her like one."

"Thanks, Dad."

"You're welcome. I got one more thing to lay on you. Didn't want to say anything before we jammed up Roda, but you were right about Sokanan PD asking questions. I heard from a Mike Finelli. Know him?"

"Like the back of my hand."

"Trust him?"

"With my life. Or I did until the farmhouse. He's one of the guys in the NRU, so who knows? What'd you tell him?"

"Deny, deny, deny. But that doesn't mean he bought it. We may have to move you."

The thought of getting used to another space made his skin crawl. "Let's give it a few more days, see how things go."

"Okay, pal. I'll see you tomorrow. Let me know if Roda gets in touch."

The door opened and closed, and Danny was alone.

And suddenly, like a bomb exploding in the darkness, he could see.

CHAPTER 12

———•———

I t was all there before him. The Dutchman, clear as day. The bar with the men hanging on to it. Murray Potts behind it, his skinny little weasel face scowling. The picture was frozen right there in front of his eyes, and he stopped breathing.

Danny scanned the bar, reveling in the sight of it.

The sight of it.

He started to quake.

"Martha. Martha!"

Footsteps came running. "What? What's the matter? What happened?"

He swallowed. Opened his mouth. Couldn't talk.

"What is it?" She shook him, and darkness returned. But for a moment, for a single, bright, wonderful moment, he could see.

"Danny," Martha snapped. "Talk to me. What's going on?"

"I . . . I saw something."

"You what?"

His lungs gained strength. His mind started clicking. She was holding on to his arms and he reversed their position, running hands up her arms until he found her shoulders and grabbed them. "I saw something!" He shook her. "Christ almighty, I saw something. With my eyes. I saw it."

"What? What did you see?"

He was shaking with excitement. "The Dutchman. The night I did the raid. I saw the Dutchman. Everything. The bar, the men, the bartender, the dust in the light, the jukebox in the corner. Oh my God, I can see. I'm going to be all right."

He wiped a shaky hand over his mouth. He had to sit down. Stumbling around, he looked for the living room and the couch. His brain wasn't working and he couldn't think straight. Where was everything?

"Here." Martha took his arm and tugged him in the right direction. He was so overwhelmed, he didn't utter a word of protest.

He sank into the couch, his legs wobbly, his chest icy cold, then hot, then cold again.

"Danny, try to calm down." She sat beside him, put a hand on his arm. "Tell me again what happened."

"Jake left. And then . . . out of nowhere . . . I saw the Dutchman. The bar. I'm telling you, I saw it. Clear as day!"

Martha said nothing. A great, glum silence settled over them.

"What?" Danny demanded. "What the hell's wrong with you? I'm telling you I saw something. It was real."

"You saw a bar in Sokanan. We're here in Manhattan. You couldn't possibly have—"

"I'm telling you, I did."

Another brief pause. "Think about it, Danny." She spoke quietly, her hand still on his arm. As if he were a child, a crazy person. He jerked his arm away.

"I don't have to think about it. I know what I saw."

"You're a smart man. How is that possible?"

"I don't fucking know! I just know I saw it. And if I could see that, I can see anything."

"Danny." There was something in her voice. Not anger, beyond patience. Something . . . sad. Like tears. Why was she crying? She should be howling for joy.

But she wasn't, and that sent an avalanche of cold through him.

"Listen. Please." Her voice cracked. She paused, then continued in that same quiet tone. "It was a visual memory. Something from . . . from before your injury. I read about cortical blindness. These kinds of . . . of illusions can be a side effect."

He sat still, her words turning him to stone.

"You may have others. You may think you're seeing odd things. Bricks on the side of the road. A tree in a yard." She gripped his hand. "It doesn't mean you can see, Danny. It's just a . . . a leftover from when you could."

He stood, rigid with wanting to smash her and her words. Smash something. Anything.

Stiffly, he made his way from the living room to the hallway, past the bedrooms and down the never-ending corridor of darkness to the bathroom at the end. He fumbled for the knob, pushed in the door, felt around for the toilet, and threw up.

Martha swallowed the tears in her throat. Through the bathroom door she heard Danny retching. She wanted to vomit herself.

Not only for Danny and the loss of that shining look of hope on his face, but for herself. For the narrow, selfish rush of panic when he'd first said he could see. And the horrid bud of gladness that he couldn't.

It was evil, that first, desperate impulse. Evil to wish him blind forever. She didn't. She'd swear it on a stack of Bibles.

But that dark voice persisted inside her head. If he could see, he'd see her.

No babe. No boobs. No "ie" on the end of her name. Just plain, honest-to-a-fault, Average Josephine Martha.

And then what?

He certainly wouldn't need her anymore.

A blast of guilty awareness blew through her. Had she been using that need to bind him to her?

God, she was an awful, vile woman.

A door opened, then closed with a click of finality, as Danny left the bathroom and went into the bedroom. The sound of his defeated, shuffling footsteps broke her heart.

She was tempted to go to him, see if her presence could ease his grief. But she didn't move, afraid what she really wanted was to hold him, touch him, use her body to make him forget and give herself a memory she'd always remember.

She didn't know how long she sat there. Outside the windows, night enfolded the darkness. Across the way, light filtered through blinds in a window in an anonymous building, leaving the rest a shadowy black wall. She rose at last, feeling old and dried up, and a little surprised. It had been days since she'd felt that way. Not since . . .

Not since she'd seen Danny again.

The corners of her mouth quirked up in a small, bitter smile at the irony. She brushed imaginary lint off her sweater, straightened her shoulders, and made her way to her own bedroom. She didn't bother turning on the light, finding her way to the bed in darkness. She lay down, staring at what she knew was the ceiling, but couldn't see.

The human heart had its own darkness. Places that

should remain unlit and unexplored. That no one should see. Not even herself.

She drifted off into a restless doze, waking then sleeping then waking. She came up to consciousness again and heard someone moving around.

Danny.

She discovered him half-perched on a stool at the kitchen counter, an unbuttoned shirt hanging loose over his bare chest. Like the rest of him, it was beautiful. Hard and muscled with barely a whisper of dark hair. She looked away, focusing on the counter where a couple of empty beer bottles sat. He was working on a third.

At the sound of her footsteps, he turned in her direction. "Let me guess," he said. "Typhoid Martha, bearer of bad news and destroyer of worlds."

She sucked in a breath at the cruel edge in his voice. "I only told the truth."

"Yeah. Far be it from you to dodge the almighty truth."

She looked down at her hands, away from the lines that bleakness had carved in his face. "I'm sorry."

"Are you? I don't think so. Not really." He took a swig off the bottle. "You know, hope can be a powerful motivator, Martha."

"It can also lead to delusion, and decisions made on false information can lead to disaster. And I am sorry."

"Sometimes a little delusion goes a long way."

"And sometimes it's just an excuse, a reason not to face reality." She thought of herself. Of the long, desperate years she'd waited in vain for her mother to return. And the moment when she knew, unequivocally, that her mother was never coming back. The pain of that realization, the sharp, cutting edge of it, hot and stinging, had been like a brand, marking her forever. She never wanted to feel that anguish again. She never wanted anyone to feel that anguish.

"You're not God, Martha." He spoke softly, one hand tracing the outline of the bottle. "You don't know what's going to happen. I could get my sight back. It could happen."

"I'd be the last to deny that. I just don't think you should plan around it. If it comes, fine. In the meantime, play the hand you're dealt."

"I'm trying. Christ." His voice cracked. "But I need something. Some hope, some comfort. I'm dying here."

Tentatively, she reached out and touched his face. His cheek was warm and rough with stubble. "It wouldn't be real."

He grabbed her hand and used it to pull her close. "I don't care anymore."

And then his mouth was on hers and she didn't care, either. Not that he was needy and couldn't see and if he could he would never turn to her in this way. Not that he was using her, because she was using him. She didn't even care that the pretense was childish and born of her own delusions.

His lips were hot and demanding, and his hands moved fiercely over her, kneading, pressing. He tasted of beer and man and like nothing she'd ever tasted before.

He stood, turning them around and pushing her against the stool until she was the one sitting. He nudged open her thighs and inserted himself between them, his hands in her hair, his mouth on her neck, biting, nipping.

In an instant, her sweater was gone and she shuddered with the surprise of cold air and the flush of heat his hands created. She gasped as he found her breasts, fingers squeezing her until it hurt.

And then one of those hands slipped into her trousers. They were loose knit with an elastic waist and he had no trouble getting through. She cried out when his probing fingers stabbed into her and found her wet and ready.

"Jesus, God," he groaned. He lifted her slightly so the slacks could come off, then pulled her forward on the stool. She didn't even hear his zipper open.

He was inside her so fast, she barely had time to gasp. She was slick and wet, and he was a rocket going off, fast, furious, and desperate. His fingers dug into her shoulders, his body slammed into hers again and again. He grunted, gritted his teeth and shuddered, his body quaking as he came.

Finished, he sagged against her. Through the lingering, unfulfilled heat, she saw the kitchen, the beer bottles, the sink complete with dirty dishes. Saw herself on the stool, and Danny, who hadn't taken off a single stitch of clothing. Her body throbbed, and a tear leaked down her cheek.

With a shaky hand, she wiped it away. Disengaged herself. Pulled up her trousers and turned away while Danny did whatever he did. Neither of them spoke.

She stumbled out of the kitchen to the bathroom, where she cleaned herself up. Finished in the bathroom, she crept into the bedroom and curled up in her bed, drained.

Numb with shock, Danny heard Martha's footsteps retreat from the room. Slowly he sank to the floor between the two stools, his back against the wall that held up the counter.

He dropped his head into his hands, fingers clawing at his hair. What the hell had he just done?

But he knew what he'd done.

He groped his way back up, leaned into the counter, arms extended and braced. He remembered Jake's parting advice, heard Charlie's half-meant threat to cut his arms off if he didn't take care of Martha.

And his own voice. Berating, punishing. He'd never taken a woman in anger before. Never.

Then again, he'd never been blind before.

A howl rose up inside him and he lashed out, sweeping away whatever was on the counter. Glass shattered, the universe splintering into thousands of jagged shards.

He stood still, picturing the mess he'd made. He couldn't even clean it up.

Maybe not the glass. But the other . . .

Slowly, he felt his way out of the kitchen, into the living room and down the bedroom hallway. He knocked on her door.

"Go away," she said.

He opened it. "I'm not going away."

"Yes, you are." Something hard hit him in the shoulder.

"What was that?"

"My shoe. Leave."

"Not until I say what I came to say."

"Then say it and go."

He took a breath. Was she watching him? He imagined she was, so the apology could be more complete. "I'm sorry."

"Yeah, I'll bet you are."

He made his way to the bed, cautiously feeling around the unfamiliar space.

"What are you doing? I told you not to—"

"I was angry. Messed up."

"You're full of excuses." The words were cool and resentful, and he knew he deserved them.

"Not an excuse. An explanation."

He located the edge of the bed and sat. The bed creaked

as she moved away from him, but he found her anyway. It was funny about fingers. Now that they were the definers of his world, his were unstoppable. And though she squeezed herself as far away as possible, his fingers explored and sought until they encountered the curve of a shoulder and told him her back was to him.

She stiffened at his touch, but he didn't let that stop him. Gently, he stroked her back. "I didn't mean to hurt you. I'm a bastard, and I'm so, so sorry."

He traced the ridge of her taut spine. "You want to hit me? I won't see it coming. You could get in a pretty good slug."

She elbowed him in the gut. He grunted and coughed. "Not bad, but could be better."

The bed moved, squeaked. Was she getting off? Suddenly hands attacked him. Pushed, slapped, punched.

"You want to fight?" she cried. "Come on, blind man, you against a girl. That should even things up."

"Stop. Stop!" He groped wildly, listened hard for the rustle of the bed, trying desperately to locate her position through the angry windmill of thumps and cuffs. She landed one on his face, then shoved at his chest, then pummeled his arm. "I don't want to hurt you. Stop it!" He ducked beneath the fury of her assault, found a knee, used it to locate her leg, and twisted.

She unbalanced and landed with a bounce on the bed.

A long raggedy breath, as though she was sucking in tears. The sound cracked his world. He lowered himself to the bed and pulled her against him. "I'm sorry. I'm sorry. I'm sorry."

And then he was kissing her, his mouth trying to say what words couldn't. She was warm and sweet and he wanted to make everything up to her. The danger he'd put her in, his inability to protect her, his own part in hurting her.

He didn't think she was listening, but suddenly, like a miracle, she was kissing him back. Pressing herself against him. Something opened inside him, a huge, heavy door letting in light and air and welcome where there had been only darkness.

Then as quickly as she'd responded, she gave a little cry, slammed the door shut, and pushed him away.

Hope sank. He so wanted to make this right. "What's the matter?"

She shook her head.

"Talk to me."

"It's not . . . it's not fair." She was breathless, the air pushed out of her lungs in small pants. "I can't—"

"Can't what?"

"Resist you."

He found her face, stroked her hair, spoke softly. "Works both ways, babe."

She shuddered, and he took that as a good sign. His fingers danced over her neck and collarbone, the edges distinct and intriguing, little mountains and valleys of bone and skin.

He waited for her to stop him, and when she didn't, he ventured lower, dipping toward the vale between those small, tight breasts. She stilled.

"Is the light on?" he asked quietly.

"No." The word was breathy.

"Good." He lifted her shirt, she tugged it down.

Gently, he moved her hand away. "It's all right. Shh. It's going to be fine this time. I promise." The shirt went up and off.

"Danny—"

He placed a finger on her lips. "No talking. No seeing." He rolled her on her side to unclasp her bra and then back again. "No thinking." His hand skated over her breasts, feather light. "Just feeling."

Palms slid to her belly, and slowly he pulled off her pants.

She stiffened. "I don't think—"

"Shh. What'd I say about talking and thinking?" He continued to remove her clothes until they were all gone and she was nothing but smooth, soft skin and clear, sharp bones. Her belly was a concave dip between hip bones, her thighs slim and smooth, the curls between them tight and springy.

She started when he touched her there, and he leaned over, whispering into her ear. "It's all right. Relax."

"I . . . I can't."

"Close your eyes." He stroked fingertips over her eyes, checking that they were closed. "Just breathe. Do nothing but breathe."

From her face, he traced a soft line over neck and breasts down to those springy curls at the base of her thighs. Slowly, gently, he stroked her, barely touching the skin below. She gasped, and his dick, already stirring, shot to attention. He ignored it.

"I'm not some charity case you have to feel sorry for." She stuttered the words. "Oh, God."

"I thought it was you feeling sorry for me." He kissed her to shut her up. "This is for you, Martha. Lie back and enjoy it."

Martha moaned, her head roaming side to side on the pillow. She was entirely naked, her body exposed to him. And yet he couldn't see it. And in the room's blackness, neither could she.

There was freedom in that. As though invisibility gave permission to do anything, feel anything. No judgment, no shame or insecurity. Just pure sensation.

His hand stroked her breast, softly caressing, the thumb circling the tip. And then out of the darkness his mouth was there, licking and pulling, each tug answered with a jet of heat between her legs.

As though he felt it himself, his hand stroked up her thigh, gently pushing her legs apart. His fingers found her opening, dipped in and out. In and out. His hand covered the sensitive nub, bringing her higher and hotter.

Her hips jerked to the rhythm and she groaned, lifted her knees, and spread herself wider. His mouth moved from her breast, down her belly, leaving the air to cool the wet trails. She anchored her hands in his hair as he slid lower and lower until his mouth replaced his hand and his tongue replaced his fingers.

He held her up, hands beneath her bottom, sucking, licking. She was floating on sensation, floating on heat, rising in a liquid pool of desire.

"Oh, my God. God." She clutched at his head, nestled between her thighs, and the greedy intensity built. She was taut with pleasure, a strand of delight spun finer and finer. God, what he was doing. There, right there. Yes. Coming. It was coming. So good, so good, so g—

She exploded into pieces of night.

Danny kissed the inside of her thighs, feeling her little aftershocks of pleasure quake against his mouth. He was intoxicated by the taste and smell of sex, so hard he was desperate to ram into her.

But he was also damn pleased with himself.

She moaned, shifted on the bed, and he slid up, resting

his head on her belly. He couldn't stop touching her. His hands moved over knee, thigh, hip, the skin like velvet under his fingers. She stroked his hair, massaged his scalp, her movements languid and weak at first. Then gaining strength, her hands roamed over his neck and shoulders, her nails leaving wicked shivers in their wake.

"Danny," she whispered. "Hold me."

He slid up her body, took her in his arms. But she pulled away and pushed his shirt over his shoulders. He removed it, threw it somewhere into the room, and settled back beside her.

They lay together, touching. It was sweet and so different from anything he'd ever done. Usually it was all fun and games with his women. Lots of laughs. A romp. Nothing either of them took too seriously except for the momentary pleasure it gave them both.

What had Jake called them? Bubble girls. Pretty but empty. He'd been happy to make no commitments, happy to find partners who felt the same. Shallow? Maybe. Truth was, he already had enough people depending on him. He wasn't looking for more.

So what was he doing with Martha? She was the real deal. An adult. A serious woman meant for serious things.

A voice inside him blared a distant warning, but her hand moved over his chest, her lips trailed kisses down his shoulder to his belly, and drowned it out. He groped for her head, entwined his fingers in her long hair, remembering the description, picturing a black, black witch's brew, and not seeing it. Seeing only how good she felt.

He was engulfed in darkness but she was beside him, her presence like a light in his mind. He pulled her up, kissed her softly, sweetly.

"You are so beautiful," he whispered.

She stilled. "Don't. Don't say that." Her voice was sharp, and her unnatural fear sent a twist of sadness through him.

His hand roamed over the smooth plane of her stiff back, the little bumps of spine like pebbles in a stream. "Why not?"

"It's not true. If you could see, you'd know it's a lie."

Down his hand slid, gliding through silk over the curve of her waist, up the hill of hip and the soft mound of her ass.

"I don't need to see. I can feel. And you feel beautiful. So soft. So pretty in my hands."

She relaxed a bit. "You're very good at this, aren't you?"

He smiled. "I have had a lot of practice."

"I don't know how I feel about that," she said glumly.

"Grateful?"

She slugged him. He grabbed her hand and rubbed it over his chest, up his neck and face, kissing the palm.

"It's not a line, Martha. Maybe you're not a great beauty. Maybe you underestimate yourself. How would I know? I see you through different senses. You smell like spring and you feel amazing. Isn't that beauty enough?"

She was silent and he didn't know whether she believed him.

Then her fingers were at his zipper, and she was tugging at his jeans.

"Show me, Danny. Make me feel beautiful."

The night washed over his bare body, cool and hot at the same time. Slender fingers wrapped around his erection, and he groaned at her touch.

"Jesus, God, Martha." Blood thundered in his chest and in his ears.

"Come inside me. I want to feel you."

He swallowed, tense with trying to control himself. "One round without a condom is risk enough."

"I don't have any diseases. Do you?"

She stroked him from root to tip and he gritted his teeth.

"Christ, no, but—"

"I'm on the pill."

That surprised him, but before he could react she reached under to cup him, then back around to stroke. He shuddered with the pleasure and barely got the words out. "Have you been hiding something behind that prim facade?"

"It's to keep me regular. And I'm not prim."

"You are prim." He reversed their positions, putting her beneath him. "And thank God for irregularity." Then he slid into her.

Slowly this time, oh so slowly. She was wet again, ready for him. She closed around him like a soft fist, fleshy and warm. And God, so tight.

He was lost in the darkness, in the smell of her. Flowers and May and the tang of sex.

And for the first time in days he forgot he couldn't see. Forgot someone was trying to kill him. Forgot fear and doubt and helplessness and embraced the darkness, the pleasure of her body so keen and sharp it lit up his soul.

CHAPTER 13

———— • ————

Inside his dark blue Taurus, Mike Finelli sat in the shadows and chewed a thumbnail. Through the windshield, he had a clear view of the Breakout, where the light of the cop bar's blue-and-white sign illuminated the departing figure of his sergeant, Mel Bayliss. Mike switched on his engine and a few minutes later, Bayliss pulled into the road. Mike geared up to follow.

Bayliss turned left on Route 9, went a couple of miles, and exited onto Van Buren. Down ten blocks and into his own driveway.

Mike parked under a tree across the street three houses down. From there, he could still see the front of Bayliss's house. He reached into the glove compartment, pulled out a box of Jujubes from a stockpile of candy, and popped one of the sticky candies in his mouth.

This was his second tail of the day, his third all week. It gave him a head cramp to suspect his own guys, but that was the only conclusion that made sense. No one else had known where they'd stashed Sin.

So far, Bayliss, like all the others, had led him nowhere but to nights like this. Freezing his ass off in his own car, ruining his teeth on Jujubes.

He hunkered down behind the wheel, watching his

breath puff out in the moonlit dark. Shadows danced behind the curtains of the Bayliss house, but Mike couldn't tell who they were. With three teenage boys, there was probably a helluva lot of chaos inside the small Cape Cod.

He wondered what Sherry Bayliss had made for dinner. She was a good cook, and Mike's stomach grumbled at the thought of pot roast and mashed potatoes. Or pork chops and mashed potatoes. Or just mashed potatoes. He'd had dinner there a couple of times. The kids had all talked at once and mounds of food had disappeared in front of him.

Now Beth, she wasn't such a great cook. Lots of Hamburger Helper, stuff like that. But she had other things he admired. Loyalty and grit. She hadn't collapsed when Frank ran out. She'd toughed it out and made the best of it.

Of course, Danny had helped. A lot.

The two of them . . . He popped a fistful of candy in his mouth. They were suffocating and endearing at the same time. In comparison, Mike's family was a disaster. His mother didn't talk to his father, his brothers didn't talk to each other. Everyone had a gripe.

Danny and Beth never whined about each other. Shouldn't that be the way families worked?

The garage door opened again. Mike sat up straight, ditched the Jujubes, and turned on his engine. Bayliss's car zoomed out like a cat with its tail on fire.

Mike whipped his car around and followed.

Five minutes into the tail, Mike's cell rang. It was illegal to hold a cell phone and drive in New York State, but he always wore a small headset that allowed him to keep his hands on the wheel. He flicked it on.

"Finelli."

"Christ, Finelli, they got Anita." The driving voice, charged with anger and emotion, belonged to Tito Oviedo, the newest guy in the NRU, and Danny's temporary replacement. A substitution everyone knew might be permanent.

"What are you talking about?" He pictured the squad's chocolate-skinned Amazon. Her six-foot frame was powerful and indestructible. He couldn't imagine anything happening to her.

"Anita. She's dead."

In Martha's bedroom, night crept unnoticed into day. Danny wouldn't have known the difference except that Martha had mentioned the gray morning light seeping through the edges of the window shade. They'd been up most of the night, making love and sleeping and making love again. If he let himself think about it, he'd get all worked up again, so he blocked it out, concentrating instead on the three coins she dropped in his hand.

"How much?" She lay beside him, still sharing the darkness, naked and seemingly oblivious, a pile of bills and coins on her belly.

His fingers rubbed against the loose change, feeling for the small, distinctive markings she'd pointed out. "This is a penny. Smaller than the other two, raised edges but no serrations." The coins clicked together in his hand as he jiggled them around, picked out another. "This one's larger, has serrated edges. A quarter. And this"—he moved his thumb and forefinger over the metal surface, comparing and contrasting—"a nickel. Larger than the penny but no serrations. Thirty-one cents. Do I get an 'A'?"

"Mm. An 'A' plus."

She hadn't bothered turning on the light or lifting the shade, and for some reason he was grateful for it, as though the darkness equalized them somehow.

It didn't. It never would. But he could pretend, couldn't he? Pretend that the sun hadn't risen, and the light he couldn't see wasn't grooming the world for common sense and realism, and the need to plan their next move.

Truth was, he didn't want to plan. He wanted to continue pretending it was only the fact that she hadn't turned on the light that kept him blind.

He rolled over and sucked on a breast. She squirmed in pleasure. "We'll never get to the bills if you keep doing that."

He groaned. "You are such a taskmaster."

With a sigh, he turned onto his back again and ran a hand over her bare belly, enjoying the smooth span of skin and scattering change. He groped in the sheets, located one of the wayward strips of paper that represented cash, and held it up.

In a singsong, school-kid voice, he said, "Teach me, Miss Crowe."

"How you identify the bills is up to you, but a common method is to leave the ones flat." She took the bill and placed it on the center of his naked chest.

Seizing her hand before she could remove it, he kissed her wrist. She twisted free, her hand sliding up to his face, and then her mouth touched his.

"I thought you wanted to talk about money," he whispered, their breath mingling.

"I do."

"Then stop distracting me."

"Me?" She sputtered, then laughed and cleared her throat. "So, the ones are—"

"Flat."

A crinkle of paper followed. "Fold the five in half." She

handed him a folded bill. He opened it and folded it again, letting his fingers adjust to the action and the shape.

He put the five on top of the one. "Okay. I got a one and a five here. What happens with tens, twenty, fiftys, hundreds?"

"Hundreds?" Her voice expressed mock astonishment. "How often do you carry around hundred-dollar bills?"

"In my line of work, you never know." It was out of his mouth before he thought about it, followed immediately by the cold realization that if he wasn't dead first, he would soon be out of that line of work.

Stark, sudden silence imprisoned them.

Then her hand was on his face again. "Whatever you do, Danny, you're going to need money to do it." Her voice was gentle, the sharp edges of her pragmatism softened by the tone.

She was right. He knew she was right. Knew he had to learn a whole new way of being. But, Christ, he wished she were wrong. Wished he'd find a miracle and the hot ball of anguish that lived inside him could dissolve. He swallowed and nodded, and her hand went away.

"So, let's start with the tens." She was back to being his Annie Sullivan, his practical, crisp teacher. He pictured her naked, his proper Miss Priss soft and available, and the contrast eased the pain in his chest. "Fold the tens in half twice, so they're half the size of the fives." She placed a folded bill in his hands, and he refolded it. The twenty, she folded lengthwise, and he did the same.

"If you have a fifty, fold it lengthwise twice. A hundred, well, I don't know."

"Little origami swans maybe?"

She elbowed him in the ribs. "Laugh all you want, pal. It works."

He groped for her body, feeling the familiar slope of hip and belly, the sweet curve of breast. She groaned and stirred under his hand.

"When are you going to call me Sin?"

She shoved his hand away. "When you stop trying to sidetrack me and pay attention."

"I am paying attention." He put her hand on his growing erection.

"To handling money, not me."

"But you're so much more interesting." He rolled on top of her and slid inside, her body warm and inviting.

"Danny, Sin. Oh God."

And then he was lost inside her, whole and strong once more, while the coins jingled and danced to the rhythm of their bodies.

Hours later, the phone finally woke them. Martha came up out of deep sleep to the sound of a tinny ring, and it took her a moment to realize what it was.

Danny was faster.

"The phone," he said before she quite knew where she was. Then the importance of the call shot through her. That was the prepaid cell phone. Only Jake and Ricky Roda had that phone number. Which one was it? She tensed, the ringing suddenly ominous with meaning.

He reached over her for the bedside table. Sometime during the night, he'd carefully placed the phone there, but now he grappled for it and knocked the phone to the floor.

"Fuck," he muttered, and Martha leaned over the bed, stretching to pick it up but the light was too dim to see it. There was a lamp on the nightstand, and she switched it on.

"What are you doing?"

"Turning on the light so I can see what happened to the

phone." She found it on the floor, handed it to him, considered it a small victory that he didn't berate her for not letting him do it himself. "Here."

He punched in one of the buttons, suddenly taut and in command, the cop again. "Sinofsky."

He rubbed a hand over his face, wiping sleep away. After a few minutes, Danny's face hardened, and his turquoise eyes went dark. Their expression would flatten someday. But not today.

"That's a tall order. I don't know if I can do it. Not without knowing what you have." A pause. "What kind of name?" Now he looked thoughtful. "Give me your number. I'll get back to you."

He ended the call and lay back down. Slowly, as though considering something. Her pulse picked up.

"Who was it?"

"Roda. Says he has a name."

"A name?"

"A contact. Someone set up the warehouse. If we get a lead on who it was, we could get some movement on the case."

"So that's good, isn't it?"

"Except he wants a deal for one of his homeboys in exchange." He threw off the covers and sat on the edge of the bed. "What time is it?"

She checked her watch. God, the day was almost gone. "Five."

His brows rose. "In the morning?"

"Evening."

He blew out a breath. "Okay. Where are my clothes?"

She gathered them up and handed them to him. Wordlessly, he pulled on his jeans and tossed his shirt over his shoulders, covering up the hard, muscled body she'd touched and caressed and lain with all night. It was strange to see the reality of his compelling face again, those glittering eyes, the attractive shape of him.

He stumbled out of the room, turned left toward the bathroom, and a few minutes later the shower turned on.

She thought about joining him, then didn't. The light had brought with it the old world, and yet she was new, different, and the difference sat uneasy inside her. Part of her scurried away, embarrassed, shy. But the other part wanted to hold on to the night's magic. She felt like a surfer who'd caught the Big Wave. She was riding its crest, reveling in the wind blowing back her hair, the salt spray, the exhilaration of the balancing act to stay upright and ride the water to its end.

She smiled at her own insanity. The smile widened and widened. As if she'd never stop smiling.

She pulled on her own clothes and plopped backward on the bed. Spread-eagled, she kicked and writhed in triumph. Yes, yes, *yesss.*

And though a tiny bead of worry rested in a distant corner of her mind, she shuttered it, nailing it up tight for now. What happened when the wave ended and the ride was over? It didn't matter. She wouldn't let it.

She went into the kitchen and saw the broken glass on the floor. How had that happened? She bent to pick it up, adding cleaning to the list of things Danny would have to learn.

When the floor was clear she made a pot of coffee. One thing this place had was plenty of coffee. She was about to pour a cup when Danny barked at her from the bathroom.

"Martha!"

She hurried to him, afraid he'd had another vision memory. But he was standing at the sink, towel wrapped around his waist and a razor in his hand. Steam fogged the air, and through it his hair gleamed black. He looked like some pagan water god, slick and damp, and apparently at ease.

"Yes, master?"

He grinned, his pretty eyes crinkling at the corners, and for a moment her heart stopped. His eyes were so alive, so lifelike, she had to remind herself he couldn't see her.

"I like a woman who knows her place," he said.

"No, you don't."

Like hers, his smile widened. "God, you love an argument. Come here."

No argument there. She slipped into his arms and felt the strength of his back beneath her fingers, his skin warm from the shower. He kissed her, rocking her down to her toes. She didn't know if she liked that. He was an earthquake, always shaking her up.

"Is that why you ordered me in here?" Her voice came out low and husky.

"Not exactly, although it was a nice, unintended consequence." He held up the razor. "Help me with this. If I do it myself, it'll take half an hour."

She hid her surprise. This was the first time he'd ever asked for help. Did that mean he was taking a cautious step toward acceptance? Or did he just want to get shaved and out of there?

"Okay. Sit down."

He located the toilet and sat on it while she shook up the shaving cream Jake had brought along with some clothes for Danny and meager supplies.

"Tilt your head back."

She began to apply the foam to his face. The stuff was soft and sensuous and smelled like him. Her hand spread it over his skin, caressing the blades of cheekbones, the strong jaw, his chin and neck. She melted. The sight of his bare torso, shoulders wide and powerful, recalled the feel of him above her, the groans of pleasure in the darkness, the way he'd made her feel. Wanted. Beautiful. *So pretty in my hands.*

She licked her lips, picked up the razor, put the edge to his neck. Her hand was shaking, and he grabbed her wrist.

"That's my jugular, sweetheart. You okay?"

She looked down at his worried face, unable to resist teasing him. "Don't you trust me?"

"Don't have much choice, do I?"

She pressed the razor closer to his skin, smiling, though he couldn't see it. "Do you trust me?"

"Yeah, all right. I trust you." He let go of her wrist, and she began to scrape it against his beard.

"This was your idea," she said.

"Don't remind me."

She finished and used a warm, damp washcloth to wipe away the remnants of shaving cream. "Okay, sir. That will be fifty dollars."

"How would you like it folded?" She was standing in front of him and he pulled her into his lap. Another kiss, another moment of pure shuddering instability.

"Whoa," he said softly, upending her. "Better stop this now or we're never going to stop."

She ran an unsteady hand through her hair. She needed a shower. A nice, long, cold shower. "I made coffee. Why don't you help yourself while I take a shower?"

He seemed to think about it.

"What?" she asked.

"Well, if it's a choice between coffee and you in the shower, I'll take—"

"Coffee." She pushed him out the door. "Or we'll never get anywhere, remember?"

He laughed and let her close the door on him.

Fifteen minutes later, she was clean and refreshed, her wet hair wrapped in a towel. She went into her bedroom and rummaged through the clothes her father had brought. The scent of sachet wafted over her. She'd made sure to ask her father to pack one of the small, perfumed bundles with her things. But despite the fragrance, all her clothes seemed suddenly dull. She wished she had something tight and sexy. Something black that would make Danny sit up and take notice.

Mentally, she shook herself. First off, Danny couldn't take notice. Second, she'd feel like a fraud. Like she wasn't herself, but one of Danny's "ie" girls. Third, he'd already taken notice, hadn't he? All night long.

She pulled on a pair of her ubiquitous knit slacks and long tunic sweaters, this one in green. She stared at the mirror. Why did she feel so dissatisfied? The clothes were soft and comfortable. What more could she want? She peered closer. Truth was, they hung loose and baggy and hid every curve. She looked as though she was wearing a green potato sack. She frowned. At least the color set off her eyes.

The reminder slammed into her again. It didn't matter what she wore. Not the color or the style. Not to Danny. As long as he couldn't see, it didn't matter what she looked like.

As long as he couldn't see.

She stuffed the implications of that disturbing thought deep in a closet in her mind and locked the door.

By the time she finished dressing, Jake had shown up. And brought dinner if her nose was any guide. She finger-combed her damp hair, leaving it loose to dry, and joined him in the living room.

"Hey, Jake."

He stood as she came in. Danny was in the kitchen fiddling with a couple of beers.

"You're looking all clean and perky." Jake winked, and her face flamed. Was the whole night written all over her face?

He laughed and put an arm around her shoulder and squeezed briefly. "It's okay," he whispered. "I've got your back. He gets out of line, you call me."

"How—how did you know?"

"Danny's grinning like a six-year-old. Telltale sign."

She glanced over at Danny. He was feeling for the bottle tops and twisting them off. And smiling. Without looking up he said, "What are you two whispering about?"

"You," Jake said, enjoying himself.

"He's a federal agent, Martha. That means he's full of lies."

"I don't think he's lying," Martha said, grinning in turn.

Danny ambled into the living room and held out a bottle to Jake. "That's the thing about the Feds. You don't know they're lying until it's too late and they've suckered you in."

Jake ignored the ribbing and took the beer. "So Roda called?"

With those three words the atmosphere changed. Tightened. Danny felt around for the arm of the sofa and perched on it. "About an hour ago."

"What's he want?"

"A deal for one of his homies who got collared up two days ago. Says he'll give us T-bone's contact in exchange."

Jake whistled. "Can he do it?"

Danny shrugged. "Don't know."

"Can you?"

"If Sokanan has him, I could make a recommendation to the DA. Maybe she'll go for it, maybe not. Either way, I'd have to surface to do it."

Martha went still, a flame of fear shooting through her. Jake, too, was silent, but Danny barked a short, curt laugh.

"Fuck it. What the hell. It's only life, right?"

Two large paper bags sat on the kitchen counter. Unable to just stand there, Martha began to unpack the cartons of Chinese takeout, stacking them haphazardly without paying attention to what she was doing. She set out plates and silverware, fingers moving automatically. Every fiber was fixed on Danny as he made his phone call to the DA's office.

It didn't take long. Five minutes later, he disconnected.

"They're checking into it," he said.

They ate while they waited, a meal Martha picked at without tasting.

Danny patted the food on his plate, speared a piece of kung pao chicken. "I heard from our ATF liaison."

Surprised, she swiveled to face them. "When?"

"When you were in the shower."

"They got an ID on the gun?" Jake said.

Danny nodded. "Something called a Samokres. Ever heard of it?"

Jake shook his head, then said quickly, "No. Sounds Russian."

"Croatian. A modified Browning, semiauto. Bud—Bud Taylor, he's our liaison—says they were made for use in the Balkan War in the early nineties, but never went on the market. Most of the initial stock was stolen. At least, that's the story the manufacturer gave out."

"Or sold on the black market."

"Either way, Bud says it's not something you see much here. He's got feelers out to the dealers who list them. He'll let me know what he finds."

Martha listened with odd fascination. It was like eavesdropping on foreigners talking about their country. A place she'd never been, where language, vocabulary, and custom were worlds apart from hers but entirely familiar to them.

Jake shoveled a forkful of fried rice into his mouth, and Martha wondered how he had the stomach to eat. "What about Eddie Clarence? You talk to your guy?"

"Yeah. Clarence and Roda came up through the gangs together. There's some kind of grudge match between them. Clarence just finished doing a bullet at Riker's that he blamed Ricky for."

A bullet? She asked, and matter-of-factly Danny explained, "A year in jail."

Jake took a swig off the beer bottle. "So maybe you just happened to fall into Roda's sewer. Clarence wanted payback, he takes out the kid. He has to take out you, too, but you manage to get away."

"Only one problem. Clarence is EOT."

She opened her mouth to demand another explanation, but Jake forestalled her.

"End of tour," he said.

"Dead," said Danny. "Sometime last night. Bronx is liking Roda for it, but they're still working it up."

If Roda was responsible, did Eddie Clarence's death have anything to do with the chat in the van? No one said so, but they could all put two and two together.

Martha gave up pretending to eat. "So where does that leave us?"

"Can't lean on Eddie Clarence for one thing," Danny said. "Which means one less place to go to for answers."

"But I still don't understand. I thought you said you didn't see the person at the warehouse. If you can't identify him, why would he keep coming after you?"

"Maybe he didn't know about my eyes. Or maybe he didn't believe it. Some guys don't like loose ends."

"But what about the gun? Where would Clarence get a sterile gun?"

"Black market, Internet. Plenty of dark holes out there for people buying and selling illegally."

"At least we have a motive," Jake said. "Something that hangs together."

She still didn't understand. "Roda said someone set Danny up. If Eddie Clarence was after the boy, why would Danny be involved?"

The question seemed to puncture the discussion's forward movement.

Danny banged a fist on the table. "Shit."

Jake pushed his plate away. "I've got more bad news. Been waiting for the right time to tell you, but there probably isn't a right time."

"Tell us what?" A nervous burr ruffled Martha's skin.

Jake paused, looking from her to Danny and back again. She saw regret and distress behind his eyes, and the burr increased to alarm.

"What?"

"He's leaving," Danny said flatly.

"Leaving? He can't leave." She turned to Jake, numb horror robbing the words of sense. "That's not true, is it?"

Jake's mouth thinned. "I'm afraid it is."

"But why? Where are you going?"

"Out of the country. There's been a break in a case. I have no choice."

"But what about—"

"It's okay," Danny said quickly.

Anger lit her. Jake was deserting them. "It's not okay. You can't do this by—"

"It's okay." Danny's voice was hard and edged with warning. "Look, I expected this." He turned to Jake. "I appreciate everything you've done so far. We'll be fine."

Fine? Was he crazy?

"I've made arrangements for you to stay here as long as you need to," Jake said.

Danny nodded. How could he be so calm?

"And here." He slid a credit card across the table. "You'll need food and supplies. I set up an account you should be able to use without anyone tracing it back."

Martha picked up the card. Through a blur of disbelief the name on the front swam into her vision. Bobby Brook.

"I figured Bobby could go either way, male, female." He slid across two other pieces of identification. "And, in case you need them, Bobby's driver's license. One for each of you."

Martha couldn't make herself pick up the license. It was too real, too much proof that Jake was walking out the door and leaving them alone. "Will we be able to reach you?"

Jake shook his head. "Not by phone."

"Where are you going, the moon?"

Jake hesitated, and Danny replied for him. "It's NTN, Martha. 'Need to know.' And you don't need to."

She frowned. "That's NTK."

"Technically, but NTK has no rhythm." Danny grinned, and Jake returned the smile.

"You can't dance to it," he said. As though it was an old joke between them.

"You think this is funny?" Martha jerked out of her chair, yanked her plate from the table, and stalked to the kitchen. Things were hard enough, and now, without Jake's experienced eyes . . . Her back to the two men, she leaned against the sink, the edge cutting into her stomach to stop her rising hysteria.

Behind her the talk continued in low, sober tones.

"When?" Danny asked.

"Tomorrow."

Tomorrow. The word thudded in Martha's ear like a prediction of doom.

"How long?"

"I don't know. I'm sorry."

"Hey, them's the breaks. Don't worry. I'll figure it out."

"You won't have to do it alone." He got up, and Martha turned around in time to see him place some kind of briefcase in front of Danny. Jake snapped open the fastenings. "I didn't want to leave you totally isolated, so I borrowed a laptop. Check it out."

Danny put his hands on the machine, then withdrew them. He looked winded, as though Jake had punched him hard and low.

Martha stared at Jake in astonishment. What was he thinking? A computer wasn't much good to someone who can't see.

"Thanks, but I don't think—"

"Try it out," Jake plowed on, overriding Danny's half-spoken objection.

"But—"

"Go ahead. Just press something."

Danny shook his head, and with obvious irritation,

pressed down a key. The letter "g" appeared on the screen and at the same time a robotic voice said, "G." Danny stilled.

Martha looked at Jake. He smiled back at her.

"What is this?" Danny said.

"It's a screen reader," Martha said, familiar with the technology. "Special software that translates text into speech."

"We call it Mr. Ed," Jake said.

"Mr. Ed," Danny said, more statement than question.

"Yeah, you watch *Nick at Nite,* don't you? Mr. Ed's the talking horse. This is the talking computer. Go ahead, write something."

Slowly, Danny picked out a phrase. The machine voice spelled it out as he went. "G-o t-o h-e-l-l."

Jake clapped Danny on the back. "I love you, too, pal," he laughed. "I've already programmed in an e-mail address where you can reach me. The rest is pretty standard stuff. You can surf the Net, send and receive e-mail. The software reads everything on the screen and translates it into a voice. It's a little confusing at first, but you'll get the hang of it. Oh, there's a pair of earphones so you don't drive Martha crazy."

The cell phone rang, cutting into the conversation like an executioner's ax. Jake exchanged a look with Martha while Danny answered, listened, agreed to whatever was said, and hung up.

"Okay," he said into the expectant silence. "They'll go for a lesser charge if the information is solid."

"Only one way to find out," Jake said.

Danny picked up the phone again and punched in another number.

He spoke without introduction. "I got your deal working. You know the drill. If the information scans, your boy will be out in two instead of doing the whole nickel."

Once again, the jargon stumped her, but Jake mouthed "five years" in explanation.

"So," Danny said. "What have you got?"

CHAPTER 14

———•———

Danny adjusted his mirrored sunglasses and huddled deeper into Charlie's leather jacket, shoving his hands in the pockets to keep warm. Somewhere, Martha was sitting on another iron bench, huddling like him against the cold. A thin wire from his right ear to the phone on his hip was the only thing connecting them. They'd stopped on the way and, in addition to the glasses, had bought two hands-free headsets with Bobby Brooks's credit card. The kind with a simple earpiece and a microphone embedded in the wire. Now her voice in his ear was also his eyes.

"Anything?" he said softly.

"Who knows? There are a lot of people here."

"Not very comforting, Martha."

She'd described the setting to him, but they hadn't had time to explore the space and all he could picture was a scene from a movie he'd once seen on TV. An inner city concrete playground with high, wire-mesh borders, chipped and faded hopscotch boards painted onto the concrete, and naked basketball hoops. It was all black-and-white in his mind, like the movie had been. Cold, gray, and speckled with litter.

He would have preferred to do this in a more familiar

territory, but Roda had set up his little meeting in territory familiar to him: the South Bronx.

There had been much argument with Martha about it for the last twelve hours, much slamming of doors and turning of backs, and no amount of reassurance had soothed her.

"Wait until Jake gets back," she had said.

"That could be a year from now."

"What if it's a trap?"

"What if it isn't? I can't sit around, waiting and hoping no one finds us. Running when they do. This is our best chance for a lead. I'm taking it."

"Take it by yourself, then." He pictured her face. Angry? Hurt? Worried? It was all there in her voice. He imagined arms crossed, stiff back turned. "I'm not helping you kill yourself."

Danny put a tentative hand on her shoulder, found she had, indeed, turned her back. "I'm not asking you to."

She jerked away. "Then you'd better learn the cane."

He gritted his teeth. "I'm not advertising my weakness to whoever's out there."

"Then how do you expect to find the meeting place, let alone whoever you're supposed to meet?"

"You're going to help me."

"I just said—"

"I know what you said. And if you think I believe for a minute that you'd let me do this alone . . . You talk tough, Martha, but it's just talk."

That lit a small fire under her. "You think you know me?" she screeched.

"Yeah, I think I do. And not just in the biblical sense."

Slam.

Remembering, he smiled to himself. He would have

liked to keep her out of it. Liked to keep her as far away as possible. But he needed her. It bristled, that need.

But not as much as it used to.

Now he sat in his perpetual darkness while traffic buzzed like an orchestra warming up, dissonant and arrhythmic. Occasional bursts of laughter told him Martha was right; he wasn't alone. Someone shouted in Spanish, footsteps pounded by him, a passing boombox thudded the latest from 50 Cent. Danny's heart jolted with every unexpected sound.

"What was that?" He scratched his nose, hiding his mouth behind his hand.

"I don't know. Just a kid."

"You gotta tell me when someone's getting close."

"Sorry. If I knew I was going to do this, I wouldn't have cut all those spy classes."

"Very funny."

"Are you sure we can't go home?"

"Are you sure there isn't a bunch of men standing around watching me?"

She was quiet. "No, I'm not sure. Everyone looks suspicious. Like you said, we're not in Kansas anymore."

He wiped his mouth with the back of his hand and slouched deeper into his coat. Beneath him the bench's solidity helped shore up his nerve. He was stuck in a black cavern, the foolish goat, sitting, waiting, unknowing while the lion approached on silent feet, teeth bared, blood lust up. Did Roda have men watching, guns drawn, knives sharpened? He tensed, braced for a blow that could come from anywhere, and slipped the knife he'd filched from the kitchen down his sleeve. Not much use against a gun, but at least it was something.

He closed his eyes, straining to pick out the important

sounds from the unimportant ones, and not succeeding. He fingered the blade hilt. He'd have to get close to use a knife. Very close.

"Someone's approaching," Martha's voice was low and tense. "Your left. Two boys, one maybe sixteen, one younger. They're heading straight for you."

He stiffened. *Two of them? Christ.*

"Are you Turq?"

Danny snapped to his left, where the high and childish voice had come from. He licked his lips, willing his heart to settle. "Little Man?"

"Yeah."

"The older one is across the way," Martha said in his ear. "On a bench ten feet to your left. He has a good view of you."

Danny's pulse rate jumped. The deal was the boy came alone. No backups, no weapons. Where were the older kid's hands? In a pocket, fingering a weapon? Danny would give anything to see, to scout him out. But he couldn't even ask Martha without giving himself away.

Danny nodded to his left, praying he got the direction right, and glad his eyes were covered. He'd refused the black glasses—too Stevie Wonder. The mirrored lenses seemed more threatening, which was why he chose them. "Who's that with you?"

The kid hesitated.

"You were supposed to come alone."

Martha's words echoed in Danny's head. *What if it's a trap?*

"My brother wouldn't let me come without him." Little Man's voice was truculent. "I told him I ain't no buster, but . . ."

A buster was a gangsta wannabe. Danny let out a held

breath, relaxed the grip on the knife. Christ, what was he going to do anyway—stab a kid? "That's okay. You got a good brother there." Provided he wasn't packing.

Martha said, "He's not moving. Just sitting there, watching."

"Don't tell Ricky," Little Man said.

Danny wished he could see the kid. The gang slang told him something about his background, but beneath the bravado Danny heard a hint of fear. A little boy's fear.

He thought of Josh, of the difference between his nephew's life and Little Man's, and not for the first time since Danny had lost his sight, the panic rolled free. How would he manage to shield Beth and her family from Little Man's hard world?

"If your brother stays where he is, it's between you and me." He patted the bench. "Sit down."

Instead of obeying, Little Man said, "Wuzzat?"

Danny froze. Was the kid pointing to something? "What's what?"

"That wire. You some kind of cop?" His voice was all nerves now.

"Relax, kid. It's my phone. See?" He held up the wire, showed how it was attached to the phone at his hip. Didn't mention that Martha was there on the other end. "Frees up my hands in case you don't tell me what I want to know." He put a little edge in his voice. "Now, sit down."

Clothes shuffled, a leg bumped his.

Danny kept his gaze straight ahead, tough, indifferent. "Ricky tells me you know something about T-bone."

"Maybe."

"You going dry on me, Little Man? Ricky won't like that." Casually, he flexed his hands. "Neither will I."

Beside him, the kid stirred.

"You're scaring him," Martha said in his ear. "Stop it."

He ignored her, and Little Man spoke low. "Don't be dropping this dime, Ricky didn't say it was cool."

"But Ricky did. So stop playing me. What do you know about T-bone?"

"He was a real bama, 'kay?" The voice hadn't changed yet; he could be anywhere from ten to thirteen. Not that youth was any reassurance of safety. Not anymore. "But we clicked up."

The kid started swinging his leg; Danny felt the swish of movement against his. That meant the kid's legs didn't reach the ground. Danny revised the age downward from thirteen.

"Yeah? How come?"

"He told good stories."

Not exactly the answer Danny was expecting, but not too surprising when he remembered Little Man was just that—little. "What kind of stories?"

"About fishing and pigs on a farm and swimming in the creek. Boring bama shit, but I be down wit' it. We don't have no creeks here. Sometimes in the summer the fire hydrant goes and we fool around in that, but I ain't never seen no tadpoles in the fire hydrant."

"Bama" was short for Alabama, and meant loser, bumpkin. Danny remembered that T-bone had been sent up from Mississippi. Despite the negativity, his life must have sounded exotic to Little Man. It probably would have sounded exotic to Josh, too. A pang went through Danny. Of regret and loss for futures extinguished.

"So why was T-bone shot?"

"Heard him talking once. Said a white guy was looking to hook up a gun buy. A deuce and deuce."

Danny's attention sharpened. "He said that? A twenty-two?"

"'Swat I heard. Cracker said he'd pay two Cs to set it up and T-bone could double his money by lifting the same from the seller."

If Little Man was telling the truth, their theory about T-bone moving one of Ricky's sterile guns didn't play out. Sokanan PD had never found the gun T-bone had been set up to sell, but a .22 was hardly a special ops weapon.

He crossed his arms, scratched his jaw, hoping he looked thoughtful. "T-bone do much street time?"

"Nah. I told you, he was just a bama. A BG wanting to prove himself." A baby gangster was one who hadn't shot anyone yet.

"You get a look at the guy pushing the sale?"

"Nah."

"Ever smell him?"

Little Man guffawed. "Smell him? Shit, no, I ain't never smelled him. What's he smell like?"

Danny quickly moved on. Only dogs experienced life through their noses. Dogs and him and the rest of the blind world. "How about a name? T-bone ever mention one?"

"Snake. Called him Snake."

Snake? Jesus, what was that? Some kind of street name, like Turq? Or was it descriptive—the guy looked like a snake?

"Said he talk funny."

"Funny? How funny?"

"Like he wasn't from the neighborhood, y'know?"

Danny frowned. That could mean the guy was from any-where between Boston and Beirut. "That it?"

"'S the dope."

"Okay. You can bail." The boy's clothes rustled as he slid off the bench. "And, Little Man—"

"Yeah?"

"You tell Ricky you did good."

The kid moved off and as agreed, Danny stayed where he was. If Roda had men out, Danny didn't want them to see him stumbling around. This gave Roda extra target time, but that was a risk Danny had to take. He put his hands in his pockets, let the knife slide down until he had a firm grip on it.

"They're leaving," Martha said. "Brother's looking over at you. Nod or something."

Danny turned in the general direction of left, nodded.

"Good," Martha said. "They turned around. They're going."

"Anyone else looking my way?"

"Not yet."

He strained his ears, listening for anything that hinted at unseen danger. All that came back were the sounds of the yard and the traffic.

And then someone sat next to him.

He stilled, then smelled who it was.

"All clear. I think." Martha's low, cautious voice no longer came from the phone, but from the same place on the bench Little Man had been. "Can we go now?"

He removed the earpiece and unplugged the wire from the phone, handing all of it to Martha. "You in a hurry?"

"Don't fool around, Danny. I want to get out of here." She stood and tugged at one of his hands to pull him up. When he'd found her arm and wrapped his hand around it, she sailed away at a fast clip, pulling him along in her wake.

"Whoa, where's the fire?"

"I told you, I don't want to hang around."

Her voice sounded off. "In general, or is there something specific?" An alarm began to sound in his head. "Something scare you?"

"No. It's . . . it's nothing. I just want to get back to the apartment. There are men drinking in a vacant lot. People are staring at me. I don't like it here."

Traffic noise increased. Someone whistled and shouted, *"Ese vato!"* They were at the street.

She was walking fast, and he tripped. "Hold up," he said through gritted teeth.

She did, but her tension was palpable. "I don't see the car." They hadn't been able to convince a yellow cab to bring them here; no one wanted to go that far north. In the end they called a gypsy who picked them up an hour ago and promised to take them back.

"We in the right spot?"

"I don't know." She shuffled uncertainly as though she were looking around. "I think so."

"Call and see what the problem is."

She did and was told the car was on its way.

"Fine. We wait." He stood next to her, uncomfortable, uneasy, a tree sticking up in the desert.

A group of boys—teens or young men—came by, hooting and whistling. "Hey, *flaca*," a male voice said, making kissing noises as they passed. She tightened her hold on him.

"Can we take a bus?"

"You ever figure out the buses here? Express, local, alternate Tuesdays in the rain. Might as well learn nuclear physics."

"What about a subway?"

"You see one?"

"No."

"Which means we'd have to tramp all over looking. Not something I'm good at."

"How about a place we can wait inside? A lobby of one of the apartment buildings."

He didn't want to move, it was too hard. But Martha was clearly feeling as exposed as him. "Okay, but call the damn car. Tell him where we are. Find out where the fuck he is."

She tugged him to the left and then left again. Some kind of Latino hip-hop slammed against his ears, a car horn honked and brakes screeched behind him.

Inside the building, Martha noticed the group of young men who had passed them by a few minutes ago. They were milling around in a corner and looked at her with cool predatory eyes—a pack of wolves assessing dinner. She glanced away, a pulse pounding in her throat, and edged close to Danny, not feeling any safer than she'd felt outside. Where was the car? She peered out the door to the street. No car pulled up.

From her right a cadaverous creature shuffled toward them. She thought it was a man, but his chest was so sunken she wasn't sure he was human. She backed away.

"What?" Danny whispered. "What is it?"

The man eased closer. "*Ese,* you got money?" He whined the question, his eyes glazed and unhealthy.

"No," she said coldly. "No money."

"Wassa matter, you let your lady talk for you?"

"Get lost, pal."

The group in the corner watched disinterestedly. The skeleton glanced over at them and then back at her and Danny. He crept closer, smiled. He had brown, rotting teeth.

"*Ese,* I think you got money. Let's see what you got."

Without warning, he leaped and put an arm around Martha's neck. She screamed.

"Martha!" Danny turned around wildly.

The skeleton put a hand over her mouth so she couldn't answer. "Your money! Or I cut the lady!"

"Martha!"

She squealed beneath the hand and struggled against the man's hold. From nowhere, a knife appeared in Danny's fist. He slashed with it, but nowhere near her captor. The group seemed interested in this. They started to come closer.

The skeleton laughed. "What's wrong wit' you, man? I'm over here."

One of the group snuck up to Danny, whipped off his glasses.

Oh, God.

Danny struck out, but the thief easily danced away.

Throat tight, heart racing fast enough to fly out of her body, she jabbed her captor hard with her elbow, an attack that wouldn't have foiled a healthy man but vanquished him. He dropped her, howling like a sick cat.

"Martha! Are you all right?"

The group began to close in. She gulped in air, turned frenetically in the slowly narrowing circle. "Danny!" She seized his arm, and he yanked her close. They were both shaking. "There's a group here," she said in a low, unsteady tone. "Surrounding us."

Danny had a white-knuckled hold on the knife. Her mouth was dry, her hands damp. She looked around for escape, for help. Nothing appeared.

"Touch us and Ricky Roda will hear about it!" she shouted as loud as she could. A couple in the group faltered. "I swear, you hurt us, you'll answer to Ricky."

One of them held up a hand. He seemed young, insignificant, a soft mustache just beginning to form above his upper lip. But the rest obeyed him, and leisurely—far too leisurely for her thudding pulse—the group broke up.

"Hey, *chivero*." The leader strutted over to the skeleton, who was still moaning. "The guy is blind."

"So?"

"So you want a fix, find someone else to bankroll it." He kicked the guy in the rear.

"Chingate," the skeleton sneered.

"Fuck you, too. *Con sofos*."

The leader watched until the junkie had slunk out of the lobby. Then he turned back, eying them with menace. "You, too. Friends of Ricky or not, we don' like your kind here."

Martha's jaw tightened. "Blind people?"

"White people." He jerked his head in the direction of the door.

Martha took Danny's hand, and they walked out with as much dignity as possible.

"They hurt you?" Danny asked once they were outside. "They fucking hurt you, I'll—"

"No!" Because what could he do? "No. I'm . . ." She swallowed hard, afraid the fear she'd kept bottled up would burst out in a torrent of tears. "I'm fine."

Danny pushed through the darkness, stumbling, groping, every step a leap of faith into thick, black nothingness.

He'd been useless in there. Worse than useless.

The car turned up, and they managed to get back to the apartment. When he finally stepped inside, he sagged against the door.

He was going to get her killed. If he didn't know it before, he sure as hell knew it now.

Clothes rustled. Was she taking off her coat? The couch or a chair creaked as she sat down.

He trudged toward the kitchen and put the knife back in a drawer where it clattered against the other silverware, a harmless utensil once again. For a long moment, there was nothing but silence. Then a muffled sob came at him. A gulp like stifled tears, and Martha's steps fled the room.

He followed her muted sounds to the bedroom, where he found her with a pillow held tight over her mouth to drown out the noise of weeping.

Gently he removed the pillow and drew her into his arms. She shuddered against him, long, shaking, bone-cracking sobs. The aftermath of terror.

He dug in his heels to withstand the storm, holding her, gentling her, telling her she was safe now. But inside his head she screamed over and over, and all he did was slash at air.

Slowly, the sobs abated into hiccups. "I'm . . . I'm sorry," she whispered.

"Shh. No need." He put a finger over her mouth to stop her apology, then felt her quiver against him.

"Oh, God," she said, tears starting again.

The sound nearly broke him, and to stop it, he kissed her. Her mouth was soft and warm. "It's all right," he whispered, and kissed her again.

And suddenly, she was kissing him back, and the gentle comfort turned into something else, something hot and electric. And safe, so very, very safe. To have her body next to his, to think about nothing but the feel of her under his hands, to know this was one thing he could do for her, and to want to, desperately.

Frantic to feel the solidity of his hard muscled body, Martha yanked up his shirt. Her fingers found his skin, tracked his back, felt his chest rise and fall as he took her mouth with his. He was warm, so warm and alive.

Pictures flashed in her head. The park with its graffiti-covered concrete, the skeletal man with his bony hand covering her mouth, the sharklike awareness in the faces of the young men. And Danny. So strong and helpless at the same time. She closed her eyes, clutching him tighter, as though the reality of his living, breathing body could banish fear.

"I need you, Danny." She was panting, breathless, afraid even now that something terrible would take her away from him. "God, I need you."

She pulled him to the bed, unsteady hands wrangling with his clothes, then hers, driven to forget, impatient to remember that no matter what had happened earlier, they were here now, alive and together.

His mouth found her breast. His tongue flicked the nipple and she groaned. Every thought, all fear, vanished in a haze of pleasure.

She gasped as he sank into her, home at last, his arms enveloping, his mouth a welcome cave of heat. Above her, his body was a shield, safe and protective, and as he moved inside her, withdrew, and slid back in, the rhythm echoed in her head. Alive. Alive. Alive.

"Wrap your legs around me," he said, his voice hoarse with tension.

She did as he asked, and he slipped his hands beneath her rear, tilting her up. And suddenly he was penetrating deeper, so deep he touched her soul, the very heart of her.

And it was like nothing she'd ever felt before. Wild, she spiraled into a heated ecstasy. Each time he touched that spot deep inside she gasped with a kind of rapture so intense she thought she'd lose her mind. She *was* losing her mind; there was nothing but sensation, nothing but him and his body winding her tighter, setting her on fire, the blaze good, so good.

She was surrounded by a scorching pit, pulsing with desire. She wanted to make it last, wanted to stay forever in the liquid blister of passion. But he pushed inside her, the strokes searing and deep, and suddenly she couldn't stop herself.

She soared off the cliff, screaming with pleasure, plunged into shattering space, quivering, quaking. In the distance she heard a roar like thunder, knew it was Danny joining her in her staggering flight.

And as the shudders receded, the tears came again. Softly this time, and whether from fear or joy or sheer, unadorned gratitude for living she couldn't tell, her emotions were all mixed up. But she was glad Danny couldn't see them.

He pulled her close, saying nothing. What was there to say? They were alive, and she was grateful.

And then she remembered what she hadn't told him. The thought cooled her ardor, which must have translated into some small movement she wasn't even aware of.

"What?" He spoke softly, still holding her.

She didn't want to ruin the moment with hard reality, so she said, "Nothing. It's nothing."

Danny's hand tightened around her shoulder. The skin was smooth as marble, and he imagined it that way—creamy and lit from within by a secret glow. Was she having regrets? Because that was just about the best damn sex he'd ever had.

If only he could see her face, study what was in her eyes. "Something's the matter."

"God, no. Are you kidding? Everything is . . . is perfect." Perfect? Oh yeah, except for the fact that she'd been attacked under his nose, and he'd just stood there swinging at nothing.

"It's just . . ." She hesitated. "It's just that I've—"

"Never been mugged or knifed before. Yeah," he said harshly, "you've had a lot of exciting new experiences since you met me."

"No. It's not that." She swallowed, and his nerves jumped. Bad news was coming. "I have something to tell you. I didn't want to tell you there, at the park. That's really why I wanted to get home quickly. And, God, I don't want to tell you now, not after—"

"You're killing me here, Martha. What are you talking about?"

"Your friend Anita from the NRU."

He frowned. That was the last name he expected to come out her mouth. "What about her?"

"I was pretending to read the paper on the bench, like you told me to. An article in the regional section caught my eye. She's dead, Danny. Anita's dead."

CHAPTER 15

———•———

H ank Bonner pulled up to the small ranch-style home Anita Bradley had shared with her sister, Bea. Between them they raised Anita's daughter, Jessica, who was seven. Bea was a familiar figure at department picnics, another tall, chocolate-skinned woman, but softer, without Anita's hard body. He knew Jessica, too. She always ended up in the group of kids that included Hank's niece, Amanda. Last time he'd seen her—at a July Fourth barbecue—she'd just had a visit from the tooth fairy, and proudly showed off her wide, gap-toothed smile to anyone who'd pay attention.

He sighed as he got out of the car. Anita's death would be devastating to the small family. A familiar ache jarred him. He'd experienced that kind of loss himself and had only come to terms with it in the last year. His wife, Alex, had been instrumental in helping him find peace.

Hank trudged up the walk to the house, sick with what he was about to do. Probe Bea for every dark corner of her sister's life. It wasn't going to be fun for either of them, but it had to be done. Someone had shot a cop, and no one would get a pass until they caught the bastard who'd done it. At least he'd waited until the evening to visit Bea, when Jessica might be in bed and out of the way. He'd had trouble reaching Anita's sister. She worked part-time as a teacher's aide, but had called in sick that week. She didn't answer the phone at home and evidently didn't own a cell.

Bracing himself for the grief that haunted the edges of his job, he ambled to the door and rang the bell, noting that no one had turned on the house lights. There were no lights inside the house, either, and the place looked dark and ominous. He waited a few minutes, knocked, and waited some more. No answer.

A rope of alarm grabbed him and twisted. Had something happened to Bea and Jessica, too? Refusing to go there yet, he scouted the outside of the house, peeking into the windows, but the curtains were all drawn.

Anita died yesterday. Was her sister already dead or hurt inside? Chest thumping, he took off his coat, wrapped it around his hand, and punched in a pane of glass on the backdoor. In two seconds, he managed to undo the deadbolt. Two seconds more, he was inside.

The place was dark and empty. "Bea!" No answer. He called again. Nothing.

That rope around his gut tugged harder. He switched on a light with his elbow, careful not to leave prints. He was in the kitchen. The fridge was stocked. A coffee cup and a cereal bowl were in the sink. They looked like they'd been there a while. Since yesterday morning when Anita left for work? He walked through the house, checked the bedrooms and closets. All full.

He scrutinized the living room, searching for anything that could hint at what had happened here. Everything looked normal. No sign of stress or struggle.

He let himself out and jogged next door, where lights told him someone was home. An elderly woman answered the door. Gray hair, brown skin that sagged beneath her chin, two large gold hoops that pulled down her ears like heavy weights. She wore a loose dress over wide, flabby hips—what his grandmother would have called a house-dress—and on top of it, a faded yellow apron.

She gave him a mild, curious look. "Can I help you?"

Hank showed her his shield. "Sorry to bother you, Mrs.—"

"Newman," she supplied. "Paulette Newman."

"I'm Detective Bonner, Mrs. Newman. Sokanan PD. I'm trying to get hold of Bea Bradley."

Her face crumpled. "Is this about her sister? I saw in the paper that she was killed. Awful. Just awful the things that happen today."

He couldn't agree more, but he didn't have time to discuss it. "Yes, ma'am. Have you seen Bea lately?"

She clucked her tongue and shook her head as if Hank's question hadn't registered. "And with Bea and Jessica gone and all."

Hank's awareness sharpened. "Gone?"

She nodded, wiping her hands on the apron. "Oh, yes. They left about a week ago."

Hank raised his brows. Anita hadn't mentioned her sister going somewhere. And with Jessica. "Left? Moved you mean?"

"Went somewhere. Piled the car with suitcases and left in the middle of the night. I don't sleep so good no more. Woke me up."

"That's strange."

"I thought so, too, but Anita said they wanted to get an early start on their road trip. Said they were taking a few weeks off to go to Florida. A vacation."

A vacation? In October? A cold wind was blowing through Hank, but he smiled, all friendly to keep her talking. "Well, that must be nice. My niece and nephew would kill to go to Florida. Of course, they have school. Funny her taking off like that in the middle of the school year."

Paulette Newman shrugged. "I guess. Didn't think about it at the time. When your kids are grown you get out of the habit of thinking about school. Then again, not everyone appreciates education the way they should." She sniffed as if to underscore her point. "Anything else I can do for you? I got supper waiting. Mr. Newman sure don't like it cold."

Hank handed her a card with his name and contact information on it. "If you hear anything about Bea or where she and Jessica went, let me know. Everyone in the department would like to support her at a time like this."

"Be pleased to. Something terrible, what happened." She clucked her tongue again. "Something terrible." She put the card in her apron and closed the door.

Hank turned up his collar against the cool night air. "Something terrible" was right, and he had a terrible feeling about it.

Anita died and her sister and daughter vanished. Not exactly what he'd call a coincidence.

Danny made dinner, adding bacon to his repertoire of culinary arts. If he could only live on eggs for the rest of his life, he'd be fine. Tomorrow, though, one of them would have to go out for groceries, and he'd have to move beyond eggs.

Tomorrow.

The word spun visions of today over and over in his head. Martha screaming, him fighting air.

He licked his lips, steadied his hands. He'd become too attached. Way too attached. What shitty timing, with this dangerous darkness he swam in now. His entire future, not to mention his life, hung like a noose in the wind. Not a time to develop relationships.

He shouldn't have touched her. Shouldn't have gone anywhere near her.

Too late now, bro.

He thought about the sex they'd just had. At the memory, a blaze of heat raced through his body like a wildfire. But he fought it. He knew what the sex had been about: forgetting. It may have been terrific, but only because it had come out of such intense desperation to wipe out the memory of fear.

But it couldn't be wiped out. Shouldn't be. He'd been defenseless, incapable of keeping her from harm. There was a lesson in that.

While she cleared the table and washed the dishes he groped along the bottom of the counter until he located Mr. Ed. He wanted something else to think about besides Martha Crowe, and there were a whole list of things crowding his head. Anita Bradley, for one.

The article Martha had read provided scanty information. Just that Anita had been found by two kayakers in the shallows of the Hudson off Sokanan. She'd been shot, and the police weren't speculating on motive.

Was Anita's death connected to the attempt on him? Was everyone in the NRU a target?

Then there was the name Little Man had given him. Where would that lead?

He hauled the laptop onto the counter, clicked open the case, and lifted the lid. Light exploded out of the blackness, and once again, his vision filled.

This time it was his mother, standing in the doorway to their kitchen in the apartment on Brower. She wore the orange-and-white uniform from Janko's 24-Hour Pancake

House. He could even see her name tag: BARBRA. Like Streisand.

His hand started shaking.

Hello, Ma.

She said nothing, did nothing. Just stood there, tired and familiar, her feet in those thick white shoes she always wore to the restaurant. A still picture, like a postcard from the past.

Yet she seemed to be looking at him. Hard. Was she trying to say something?

He knew she wasn't real. Knew the sight of her was just a trick his brain was playing on him. Yet he drank her in, tears filling his eyes. He was afraid to move, afraid to speak. He sat frozen, hands clamped to something hard that bit into his skin.

And then, like morning fog, his mother was gone and darkness returned.

He remembered where he was: Jake's safe house. And what he was doing: opening Mr. Ed. That hard thing he was clutching to keep his hands from shaking was the laptop's cover.

He released his hold.

"What are you doing?" Martha's voice from near the sink.

He cleared his throat, not sure it would work. "Seeing if Jake answered my message about Snake."

As quickly and surreptitiously as possible, he scrubbed the wetness from his eyes and brushed his mother away. But she lingered there in the back of his mind while he turned on the machine. Did her appearance mean anything more than a flawed mix of brain chemicals?

Or was it a message, a further inducement to stay away

from Martha? If he didn't, would she turn into the beaten down picture of exhaustion his mother had been?

The question set unease ticking inside him, so he set it aside to concentrate on the computer. He'd spent the hours before dinner practicing, and could now power up pretty easily, navigate the keyboard more or less accurately, even go online, though that didn't go smoothly yet.

He donned the earphones while the machine booted up, a series of audio signals taking him through the procedure, and once the desktop was established, a beep alerted him to incoming e-mail.

It took him a couple of tries to hit the right combination of keys. That quiver in his hands hadn't gone away yet, and he was all thumbs. But he muddled through until he'd called up the message in his inbox.

In his ear, Mr. Ed's robot voice chirped.

```
To: sinbad
From: jman1
Subject: friends in low places
Message: Inquiry kicked up 3 possibles.
Snaps attached.
```

Attachments. Danny didn't have a clue how to get to them. What key to push? Should he click on something on screen? What and where? He didn't want to get Martha involved; he wanted some time alone without her smell driving him nuts and urging him to throw her on the floor or the couch or the bed or whatever was handy. But he didn't have much choice.

Cursing, he flung off the headphones. "Martha!"

"What? I'm right here." Again, she spoke from somewhere near the sink. Water spit on, then off, and she moved behind him, her hands on his shoulders. She leaned forward, her peach-infused hair brushing his cheek. Silently, he repressed a groan.

"Oh my God, he found him?" She must have read Jake's message.

"Or a bunch of people with the same handle. But I don't know how to download the images yet."

She slid her hands under his, so he could feel what she did as she did it. Her hands were smooth and warm from the hot water, and he was tempted to bring one to his lips.

Carefully, he pulled his hand away. "What's happening? Can you see the pictures?"

"One is up. I don't recognize him. Here comes the second. A pause while the second picture downloaded. "That's not him, either." She gasped.

Third time must be the charm.

"That's him, Danny. Oh my God, that's him."

"Okay, calm down. Let's see who he is."

With painful slowness, he tapped out a message to Jake, Mr. Ed tolling out the words.

```
To: jman1
From: sinbad
Subject: friends in low places
Message: What's behind door number 3?
```

Jake must have been near his computer because he replied within a few minutes.

```
To: sinbad
From: jman1
Subject: friends in low places
```

Message: Savo Kokir. Serbian exmilitary.
Very bad dude. Sit tight. Will call.

Martha clutched at his shoulders. Neither of them said anything, though the fingers digging into him spoke volumes.

"Do you know him?" she said at last.

"No. But Serbia fits with the Balkan-made gun."

"Ever heard of him?"

"Not that, either."

"Then why—"

"I don't know."

"But what do you think?"

He shook his head, the darkness all around him more sinister than ever. "You don't want to know."

The kitchen at Apple House, Hank Bonner's family farm, was in after-dinner chaos. Both his nephew and niece, fourteen-year-old Trey and eleven-year-old Mandy, had social studies projects related to the upcoming governor's election, and they'd scattered presentation boards, markers, scissors, magazines, glue, rulers, and who knew how many pens and pencils on the kitchen table before the dinner dishes had been completely cleared. His son, dressed only in a diaper and still-dirty bib, had grabbed a kitchen chair, pulled himself up, and was banging on the seat, agitating loudly to join the circus.

"Are you going to vote for Governor Henley?" Mandy asked.

"Haven't made up my mind yet." Hank liberated a dirty fork and napkin from under Mandy's elbow.

"Mr. Bell says he's going to lose," Trey said absently,

flipping through an old issue of *Slam,* the basketball magazine.

"Hate to break it to you kid, but Mr. Bell is not a fortune-teller." Hank slid the magazine away from Trey. "And you won't find anything about the election in there."

"Politics sucks," Trey said. "Why can't we ever do anything interesting?"

"Because it's school. It's supposed to be boring."

"School sucks."

"I like it," Mandy said, and Trey rolled his eyes.

"Okay, Johnnie, okay." Hank's wife, Alex, lifted their nine-month-old off the floor and into his highchair before he howled himself to death about not being able to join his cousins. She grabbed a piece of paper and a thick crayon from the pile, and put them in front of the baby.

"Draw us a picture," she said, rubbing her hand over the baby's down of white blond hair.

"No, write me a letter," Mandy said, showing him how to mark up the paper.

The baby grinned at his cousin and drooled.

Hank picked up a pitcher of apple cider and returned it to the refrigerator. "If you want to be helpful, teach him how to use a napkin. That kid needs one."

"He's just teething," said Alex.

"He's just gross," said Trey.

"He's a baby!" Mandy protested.

The phone rang, and Trey jumped up. "I'll get it."

Hank and Alex exchanged a quick glance. Lately, Trey had been getting a lot of phone calls. Mostly from someone named Brittany.

This time, though, Trey was too late. A voice from the den called out. "For you, Henry."

"Thanks, Mom."

Trey bounced back to the table where he slouched in his chair and fiddled with a pen. Hank smiled and picked up the phone.

"Hello?"

"Hank?"

"This is Hank Bonner."

"It's Danny Sinofsky, Hank."

Hank's world suddenly compressed. Like everyone else in the department, he knew about the botched job at the safe house and that Danny had disappeared. "Hold on. I want to take this somewhere private." The phone was an old-fashioned landline, and he let it hang loose from its cord. "Trey." The boy looked up, instantly alert. "Hang the phone up when I tell you to."

Trey nodded, no questions asked.

Hank went into his bedroom, which had been enlarged and redecorated when he and Alex had married, and bore little resemblance to the room he'd once had as a kid living in the old farmhouse. He picked up the phone, told Trey to hang up, and waited for the telltale click.

"Where are you, Sin?"

"Not ready to say. Look, don't want to mess with you at home, but figured you couldn't put a trace on me there."

The guy was cautious. "Okay. But are you safe? What about the woman? Everything all right?" He didn't mention the blindness. He didn't know how to even approach mentioning it.

"We're safe for now. But I wouldn't say everything is all right."

"So what can I do for you?"

"You working on Anita?"

"Yeah."

"Anything you can tell me?"

Hank debated, but since he didn't know where Sin was or who he was with, he came down on the side of caution. "Not really."

"Come on, Hank, don't give me department bullshit. What have you got?"

Hank sighed. "We've got zip, Sin. That's the truth."

"No connection with the warehouse shooting?"

"Why, do you think there is one?"

"It's a little weird that two of us in the NRU were attacked."

"You think someone is trying to take out the unit? Why? Were you putting extra pressure on anyone?"

"Nothing unusual." Sin paused. "Look, I have some four-one-one on the warehouse shooting. I don't know what good it will do you, and I'd appreciate it if you keep it low profile for now. Treat it as a good faith gesture so you won't think I'm going to screw you on anything you give me."

"What's up?"

"Martha Crowe, the wit who saw the attacker at my house, she ID'd the guy. Name is Savo Kokir. Ever heard of him?"

Because of his wife's Russian background and her connections in international business Hank had heard a lot of foreign names in the last two years. "No. Is he Russian?"

"Serbian. Exmilitary."

Hank whistled. "What's he doing here?"

"Still working on that."

"Mob connected?"

"That's one theory."

"Drugs or guns?"

"I'd play guns if I were betting. He left a pretty interesting one behind."

Hank nodded, remembering the unmarked pistol. "Okay, I'll see what I can dig up in that direction. Do you know what Anita was working on?"

"Far as I know, same as the rest of us. But Parnell would have a better handle on that."

"Okay, Sin. Thanks."

"One more thing, Hank. You want to tell me again what you don't have on Anita?"

Hank laughed to himself. Danny Sinofsky was their best undercover. A good UC developed a sixth sense about people. Not much went past him. In the end, Hank opted to tell him what little he knew. Like Sin had said, a good faith gesture. "She was shot in the head, Sin. Execution style."

"Christ." There was revulsion and fury in the one word.

"And her sister and daughter are missing."

Now it was Sin's turn to pause. "What do you mean 'missing'? Like dead missing?"

"Like I don't know yet. Could be. But a neighbor saw her and the girl drive away. We have an APB on the car."

"Okay. Thanks. Keep me in the loop if you can. I'll do the same. I've got an e-mail address you can contact." Hank wrote it down and hung up.

He stared at the framed picture of Alex standing under an apple tree covered in pale pink blooms. It recalled how they'd met, how the murder of a Russian immigrant had led to a much larger story.

Now there was another foreign connection to a case he was working on. But why was an ex–Serbian military guy attacking Sokanan cops?

Hank left the bedroom and headed toward the kitchen. The noise of the kids—Johnny especially—vied with the thumping of the dishwasher and the laugh track of whatever sitcom his mother was watching.

The house overflowed with the sounds of his family, simple sounds that filled him with warmth and peace and love. If only the rest of his life ran so smoothly. Why couldn't he catch a nice, uncomplicated robbery for once?

CHAPTER 16

Danny spent a sleepless night in the living room, too unsettled to stay with Martha. He felt split down the middle. One half ached to crawl into bed with her, hold that long, lean body against him. She called herself witchy, but if so, it was good magic. She made him feel whole again. Brought light into his shadow. Made him forget, if only for a little while, that he was blind.

But he *was* blind. Someone wanted him dead, and they'd take her with him.

The other part of him knew that even if he survived, he didn't have much to offer. His career was over. He couldn't imagine what he could do without eyes. He couldn't even get himself to a job, let alone find someone to employ him. His stomach curled and twisted. He couldn't take on another person's wants and needs. He was too needy himself right now.

And face it, maybe that's what all this with Martha was about. Him needing, taking. What did she get out of it? Her life interrupted, put on hold, and threatened. A nice, neat package.

The phone cut into his thoughts. He fumbled for it, heard the distant crackle of static and then Jake's voice. "You there, Sin?"

He sat up, attention caught. "I'm here. What have you got?"

"This Savo Kokir has a rap sheet longer than the phone book. Assassination, bombings, sabotage, extortion, kidnapping."

Danny felt as though he'd been hit over the head with a rock. What would a guy like that want with him? "What's his MO?"

"He's a die-hard Serbian nationalist who refuses to give up the dream of a greater Serbia. He finances his Balkan operations through a wide network of terrorist activities. He's been implicated in actions in Uganda, the Congo, Sudan, Lebanon, the Balkans, and the various stans of central Asia. Oh, and he's a fitness freak, which might explain the liniment thing."

"What's he doing here?"

"That's what me and everyone else in the TCF wants to know. He's never been tied to anything in the U.S. Until now."

Inside Danny's chest a nervous hum started. "Any theories?"

"If it's terrorism, we've got a whole list of targets. Close to home, there's that new Renaissance Oil headquarters, for starters. You've got three or four bridges in the immediate vicinity. If you want to get really paranoid, there's always Indian Point. Any of those ring a bell?"

Danny shook his head, baffled. "I never go near the RO compound. All my stuff is on the other side of town. The bridges are handled by the state, and Indian Point is your problem."

Jake sighed. "Yeah, that's the hitch. Working you into any of those scenarios."

Danny hesitated, hardly believing the words were going

to come out of his mouth. "Look, we have a guy who does wet work and a weapon to carry it out. What about that? Who's vulnerable for assassination?"

Jake paused, the implications huge with him, too. "What big shots have you come in contact with?"

It seemed bizarre and far-fetched, but . . . "I met the mayor once. And, of course, the police chief."

"Any reason they might be targets?"

"Sure. For some nutcase. Why not? Then again, we're talking Sokanan here, not New York, Chicago, or L.A."

"It would have to be a nutcase with international contacts."

"There's plenty of that coming out of RO."

"Okay, I'll set up a chat with their security team. And with the governor's people. You ever meet him?"

Danny shook his head. "Nope."

"Well, with the election he's the biggest target. I'll alert the appropriate agencies, make sure Henley and all the other possibles have extra protection."

Danny circled back to something much closer to home. "You know, maybe we're looking at this from the wrong end. Maybe the set up *was* for T-bone, not me."

"So Roda got it wrong?"

"Why not? He's not exactly Mensa material. Maybe Eddie Clarence hired Kokir to off T-bone and I was in the wrong place at the wrong time."

That at least sounded credible. But Kokir was the only one left who could confirm or deny.

"Any lead on Kokir's location?"

"Negative. But we're already checking out our contacts. This guy makes everyone nervous. We want him locked down fast."

Danny rubbed the back of his neck. He was so tired of

being in the dark. Literally and every other way. "We have another cop down."

"What? Who?"

"Anita Bradley, a cop in my unit. They found her body yesterday. Shot in the head."

Jake paused. "An execution?"

"Looks like it," Danny said glumly. "Her sister and kid are missing, too."

A heavy silence while Jake absorbed this new information. "Think there's a connection?"

"Who knows?"

"If there is a link, that could mean Kokir is still in Sokanan. Shouldn't be too hard to find a foreign-speaking guy in your hick burg."

"Hey, watch your mouth. That's my home you're talking about. And for your information, wiseass, we've become a lot more cosmopolitan since RO came to town. The Russians brought in a whole cast of international characters. Foreigners in Sokanan are a dime a dozen now."

"We'll have to smoke this one out, then."

Danny knew instantly what Jake meant. That nervous hum grew louder. He thought of Beth and the kids, and everything they needed from him. He thought of Martha and everything she deserved from him. And himself, unable to satisfy either.

But he could do this. Even a blind man could do this.

"Hey, bro." Jake's voice cut in. "What's going on there? What are you thinking?"

Danny peered into the endless, heavy darkness, and saw nothing but more of the same. "I'm thinking it takes bait to catch a rat."

*　　*　　*

Martha surfaced slowly from the thick fog of sleep. Was someone calling her? She groaned softly, shifted in her dark cocoon. A weight on her shoulder. A hand.

Danny.

She jerked, a fuse of alarm exploding her awake.

"What is it?"

"Shh. Everything's all right."

The room was pitch-black but his voice was calm. She breathed again, settled back against the pillows. "You scared me."

"Sorry. Didn't mean to."

She groped in the darkness for his hand. "Coming to bed?"

"No."

Maybe it was morning already. She checked the luminous dial of her watch. It was only 2:30. "Been to bed yet?"

"Not really."

She moved over. "Lie down then. See if you can sleep."

"I can't."

"Yes, you can." She ran a hand up his thigh. "I'll help you."

He stopped her, placing his hand over hers. "I only woke you to let you know I'm leaving."

She stroked his hand sleepily. He wasn't making any sense. "Stay." She yawned. "Lie down. Talk to me."

"I'm going back to Sokanan."

She smiled. "Very funny."

"I'm not joking. I have a car and a driver coming. It should be here any minute."

The smile faded. A small chill snaked up her back. She sat up, switched on the light. His face was sober, not even a glimmer of lightness in his eyes. "You're serious."

"You'll be safe here. I called your father, and he's coming to stay with you." He rose, and she grabbed his arm.

"Wait a minute." She scrambled out of bed, hugging her arms in the cool air above the blankets. "You're going home? Why?"

"Savo Kokir is there."

She blinked, flummoxed. "That sounds like a good argument for staying here."

"Not if we want to catch him."

She opened her mouth, then closed it. What was he talking about? "I don't understand. How is being there going to help capture—" Understanding dawned. "Oh my God. You're sticking your neck out, hoping he'll try to chop it off."

His face was hard, his expression flat. He turned, clearly not interested in arguing with her. "I gotta go."

She ran for the door. "Oh, no you don't. Are you crazy? You can't even—"

"Don't say it."

"—get around without help."

His jaw tightened. He reached for the doorknob and poked her in the hip. "Get out of the way."

"You want to put a bullet in your brain? Just pick up a gun. It would be a lot faster."

"Martha, get away from the door."

"You can't tell time, you can't shop for food, you can't—"

"Mike can take the glass off my watch so I can feel the hands. He can bring in ten dozen eggs, which is all I can cook anyhow."

She waved a hand in front of her face, trying to sort everything out. "But Mike's with the department. I thought you said you couldn't trust them."

"If I want to stay hidden. But I don't. Now get the hell out of my way. I'd do it myself, but—"

"You can't see. That's the point. You can't even tackle me, how are you going to tackle Kokir?"

"I don't have to tackle him. I just have to stand still."

A tremor shook her. He was really going. "Don't do this, Danny. Please."

He turned away, then back again, his mouth a firm line. "It will be all right. I promise. I've got Homeland Security and the TCF watching my back. Trust me. Have a little hope."

She started to cry. "You know I don't do hope very well."

"Then just dial down the realism a hair."

"But this is real. It's your life." She sounded like a whiny, girly freak but she couldn't help herself. She wanted to throw her arms around him and force him to stay, but his harsh face and the taut lines of his powerful body were a formidable blockade.

"I can't spend it looking over my shoulder, no pun intended. Kokir is a known terrorist. He's got a reason for being here and no one knows what it is. We have to find him.

"But why you? You're bl—"

He put a finger over her mouth. "The one he's looking for. We have to draw him out somehow."

"But—"

A knock on the apartment door. She jumped, and Danny tightened his hold on her. "It's all right. That's probably Charlie." He turned them around so she was no longer in front of the door. "Let's let him in." Somehow, he got the bedroom door opened and hurried through it.

She followed, fear and disbelief making her steps

ragged. Charlie was already wheeling through the front door by the time she got into the living room.

"Daddy, tell him not to do this. Tell him it doesn't make sense."

"It's the most sensible thing he's done yet," Charlie growled. "Getting as far away from you as possible."

A thin smile played around the corner of Danny's mouth. "Glad someone thinks so."

"I'll go with you," she blurted out.

"The hell you will," Charlie said.

"No," Danny said at the same time.

"How are you going to—"

"I'll manage. I had a great teacher."

"He's a big boy, Martha."

"He can't see! Why doesn't that penetrate?"

"It penetrates," Danny said, and the tone of his voice pierced her. "Deeper than you think."

A leaden silence. Then Charlie spoke.

"Go on." His rough voice was uncharacteristically gentle. "The car is waiting for you at the curb. I told them you'd be down."

"I'm coming with you." She started after him, but Charlie grabbed her arm.

"Let me go, Dad."

"You're not going anywhere." He pulled her onto his lap, his huge arms locking around her like shackles. She struggled but didn't get very far.

"Let go of me!"

"Go," Charlie said to Danny over her protests. "I've got her."

"Danny!"

He walked through the door, and it closed behind him.

"Settle down," Charlie ordered when she continued to wrestle against his hold. "You'll tip us over."

"I don't care. Let me go."

"You don't care if you leave your legless dad flopping on the floor like a flounder on the pier?"

"Oh, God." She wilted abruptly and sucked in a ragged breath. "Why did you let him go? Why?"

"Aw, geez, Martha. For chrissakes. He's a man. He makes his own decisions, he has to find his own way. You know that better than anyone."

"And if he ends up dead?" She felt battered and bruised with dread, but her father only shook his head in disgust.

"He has a whole department behind him, not to mention the Feds. This guy he told me about, the one they're chasing—everyone is drooling over catching him. No one's going to let Sin out of their sight. Why can't you find comfort in that?"

"Because he's at risk, and you helped put him there."

Charlie eyed her balefully. "I know what you're angling here for, girl, and no way on this fucking green earth am I taking you home. You're out of it and you're staying out, and I'm not going to argue with you about it." He dropped his hold and pushed her off his lap. "It's the middle of the night and I'm tired. We can talk about it in the morning."

"I want to talk about it now."

"Where are the beds in this place?" Without waiting for directions, he wheeled himself toward the bedroom corridor. Martha followed.

"Dad—"

"In the morning, Martha." He pushed open the first door—Danny's room—and rolled inside. Martha was right behind him.

"Go to bed, Martha."

"I'm not leaving until we finish this."

"Until you talk me into what you want, you mean. I'm not taking you home, so forget it. What is it with you and this guy anyway?"

"Nothing," she said quickly, her face heating.

"Yeah, that's some nothing making you blush."

"I care about him."

"What does that mean, 'care'? Care like you would a stray dog? Or care like you do me? Or something else?"

She was silent. Her love life was not a topic she wanted to discuss with her father.

"He's blind, Martha. You want to spend the rest of your life taking care of some guy like me?"

"The rest of my life? I—I hardly know him." She spluttered, defending herself and avoiding the details all at the same time. "No one's talking about . . . about some deep, long-term commitment here."

"Why not?" The question rasped against his smoke-tinged voice. "You're not a fly-by-night type, Martha. You're a long-term relationship type. And I don't see long-term in the cards with this guy."

"I never said—"

"You need someone solid and down to earth. With a job and a future, not an endless stream of rehabilitation needs."

"You weren't solid and down to earth, and Mom married you." She hurled the words at him, unthinking, and he hurled them back at her.

"And look where it got her."

Silence hung between them. They never talked about her mother. Never.

Softly, she said, "She could have stayed."

"And lived a half-life with a broken man?"

"You're not broken," she flashed, and his steady gaze refuted her words. "And it could have been a full life."

He looked down at his hands, then back up at her, his expression candid. "She wasn't strong enough. And that's the plain, goddamn truth of it."

"She was a coward." *And she didn't love us. Love me. Not enough.*

Her father peered at her, his expression oddly gentle. "You're wrong, you know, Martha girl. She did love you."

Her face heated. Was she so transparent? "Yeah, so much, she ran as fast and as far as possible."

"She did the best she could until she couldn't do it anymore."

"How can you forgive her like that? She left you. Abandoned me. Right at the moment when we needed her most."

"I haven't forgiven her. I just stopped caring because caring was tearing me apart. And once I stopped feeling sorry for myself I started to understand."

Stubbornly, she stuck out her chin. She didn't want to consider any good thoughts about her mother. "I would have stayed. I did stay."

"It's different. You were a little girl. You didn't have much choice."

"I'm not a little girl anymore, and I'm still here."

He hooted. "And look at you. You're thirty-five, single—"

"I'm thirty-two," she said stiffly. Leave it to her father not to even know how old she was.

"Thirty-five, thirty-two, what the hell difference does it make? The point is you've spent your whole life taking care of me. You don't go out, you don't wear pretty clothes, you have no friends."

She glared at him, the words digging deeper than she cared to admit. "I like my life."

He raised his bushy brows, his face a study in complete skepticism. "Do you? Do you really, Martha girl? Because I gotta tell you, I'm having trouble believing that. I'm having a whole lot of trouble with that."

She turned away from his piercing gaze. "What I do and what I don't do is none of your business."

"Yeah? Well, I'm making it my business. You stayed and took care of me, now it's my turn. A damn fucking sight too late, if you ask me, but better late than never. And more of the same is not what I want for you. And not what I'm going to help you get. You're staying here and leaving Danny boy to whatever fate has in store for him." His face softened into a scowl, his voice into a grumble. He waved her away. "Now, get out and leave me alone." He wheeled the chair around, manipulating it easily even in the tight space, and rolled to the bed.

She left him for her own room, forced herself to breathe, to calm down. What was wrong with everyone? Charlie forgiving her mother, acting like . . . like a real father. And Danny, God . . . was he crazy? The things that could happen to him. She tried not to think about that. Tried not to want to be there, despite the danger. Not to be by his side, be his eyes, be whatever he needed her to be. As long as he stayed alive.

But she couldn't help herself.

Half an hour later she crept out of her room, switched on the hall light, and cracked open her father's door.

Light from the hallway streamed through the small gap in the doorway. Her father lay on his back in Danny's bed, snoring lightly, the wheelchair butted against his bedside so he could reach it easily.

"Daddy?" She spoke softly but clearly. He didn't respond.

With careful steps she sneaked into the room, swept up the clothes he'd tossed on the dresser, and tiptoed out.

In the hallway, she ripped through his pockets, feeling as though she were violating him by going through his personal things. She found the car keys in his pants, but not the ticket from the garage. She tried the back pockets, pulled out a thin sheet of paper, creased many times over. Something about it looked familiar, but distant and faded, like an old memory. Slowly she unfolded it.

Dear Mommy . . .

Her heart lurched and she hid a gasp behind her hand. Swiftly she scanned the letter, remembering the foolish, foolish girl who'd written it. The one who still knew what hope was.

Where had Charlie found it and what was he doing with it?

Unexpectedly, tears filled her eyes. Tears for the child she'd been, for the family she'd lost.

Was Charlie right? Did it all boil down to her mother's weakness and human frailty more than her own unloveability?

Carefully, she put the letter back, the question too weighty to answer at the moment. But it echoed inside her as she searched the rest of his clothes and finally found the parking ticket in his shirt.

Folding the clothes neatly, she returned them to the dresser, even though she risked waking Charlie. She would have left them on the floor by the door, but it would be hard for him to reach them. He was going to be furious enough when he discovered she'd gone; if she left him practically naked, too, he'd probably explode.

She placed a note on top of the pile where he couldn't miss it in the morning. On the back of a check, she'd written:

> *I've taken the van. I'm sorry. You said we all have to find our own way. This is mine. Will be back to get you.*
>
> *Love,*

And she'd signed her name, the letters small and precise and tidy.

She took one last look at him before she left. His wide shoulders in the sleeveless undershirt stuck out above the blankets. He wasn't old. A few years past fifty. But he'd had a hard life full of grief and trouble, and the pain was seared into the lines of his face. It was a strong face, not handsome, but powerful in a brawny way. It suited him, though it sat so uncomfortably on her.

Slowly, she backed out of the room, glad she wouldn't be there in the morning. What came out of his mouth would not be pretty.

The driver, TCF agent Tony Burdock, helped Danny up the walk to his front door. Burdock was no Martha, and Danny mostly fumbled for the steps, understanding for the first time how useful a cane could be. He ground his teeth against the thought, biting down hard on his helplessness, especially in front of a stranger, not to mention a colleague. He felt for the door, groped for the keyhole, but before he could get keys out, it opened.

"Hey, Sin."

"Mike?" He knew someone would be waiting. He had arranged it all before he left the city.

"Yeah, man. It's me." His voice sounded friendly, normal. Good, old, reliable Mike.

But Danny hesitated. Was Mike the leak? Danny didn't want to think it, but he didn't want to think it had been anyone.

Burdock stepped inside, Danny followed. He inhaled the familiar scent of home—old wood and something indefinable but distinctively his.

It seemed as though he'd been gone forever, but it didn't take long to reestablish the layout in his mind. He smelled coffee. Someone was moving around.

"You okay, Sin?" That wasn't Mike.

"Parnell?" Another lethal doubt.

"Yes. And this is Agent Warren Miller, from Homeland Security."

"Good to meet you, Detective." A deep bass voice with the hint of the south in his words.

Danny stuck out his hand in the direction of the voice, and someone shook it. "Agent Miller."

And now he was here, surrounded by friends or by enemies. He didn't know which, and it didn't matter. He was the cheese to catch a rat. He was bound to get bit.

The thought gave him a small measure of comfort. Staying safe was for those who couldn't act, who were damaged and scared. He would not live like that.

Suddenly, he was bone tired. Adrenaline had kept him going, but now that he was here the chemical boost had deserted him, and he felt drained and limp.

"Look, I could use a hit of caffeine. And give me a minute to figure out where I am."

"No problem."

Truth was, he wished he could do this alone. It rankled to think they were all watching him, but he couldn't stand there in the entryway forever. Eventually they were all going to see him trip and stumble and fall. Might as well get it over with.

Someone moved in front of him and to the left. He wasn't familiar enough with their individual footsteps and movement style to tell who it was. He put out his arms, found the wall on his left, and trailed it into the kitchen.

He roamed the edges of his house and made his way into the den in the back, where he was told the team had set up their equipment. He sat on the couch, forgetting to check it was clear, and landed on a pile of papers. He pulled whatever it was out from under him, and hands took the papers away. More hands gave him a cup of coffee. Furniture sighed and creaked as the men sat down.

Danny sipped the coffee. It was hot and strong and hit him hard. "So where do we stand?"

"Sharpshooters on the roof across the way," Parnell said from in front. Danny pictured him in the love seat.

"Surveillance van on the street." Mike was on the left. The brown armchair.

"You got it all covered."

"Kind of short notice, but we'll tighten things up in the morning. We're good for now," Parnell said.

"We've got a plan to go public with this, Sin." Miller. His voice came from the right; he must be in the other brown armchair.

"With what? Kokir?"

"With you. The governor has agreed to do a photo op tomorrow. He's giving a speech about health care and the disabled and looking for a poster child. Of course, we had to inform him of the possible threat and once he heard about you, he—"

"Oh, yeah, a blind cop. What could be better?" His voice registered disgust.

"We need to get your face in the paper fast."

Danny sat rigid with anger. It was one thing to suffer in private, but to have his story splashed across every newspaper in the state?

"I told them this was a bad idea." Mike, in a low voice. "You don't have to do it."

"Yes, he does." Miller sounded as if they'd been arguing about it for days. "It's all set up."

"Like I give a fuck. Maybe Kokir is watching the house and already knows I'm back."

"No one's watching the house," Parnell said. "Except us. We've had guys here since the attack at the farmhouse. It's clean."

"Christ." Danny leaned back and rubbed a hand down his face. "Okay. Whatever. Bait is bait. Not much use if you hide it."

"Good," Miller said. "Better get some sleep. We see the governor at ten tomorrow morning."

A crackle of communication equipment. "Parnell." A pause. "What? Shit."

Danny's hackles rose. "What is it?"

"Someone is approaching the house."

Everyone froze, then clothes rustled, furniture moved. Someone grabbed his arm. "Come on." Mike tugged him away.

"Wait. Where are we going?"

"Shut up and come with me."

"Can you ID the suspect?" Parnell must be talking to the sharpshooter. "Is it Kokir?"

Mike was rushing Danny away.

"What do you mean you can't ID them? You better be damn sure before you shoot."

Danny pulled against Mike's onward rush. "Hold up."

"We gotta get you somewhere safe."

"Dammit," Parnell said. "Okay. Fire the warning shot."

All sound seemed to stop as though everyone was listening to the zip of the bullet hitting the front of the house.

Someone screamed outside.

A bullhorn. "Hands on your head! Down on the ground! Down!"

A pause that lasted a century. Then Parnell spoke. "Secure? Yes, copy that. Everyone all right here?"

"So far," Mike said.

"Stay here," Miller said.

Danny was cold with tension. Mike's hand on his arm gripped tight.

The front door opened. Feet shuffled. Men's voices.

"What's happening?" Danny asked.

"They're bringing him inside."

It sounded like an army doing it. "Can you see who it is? Is it Kokir?"

Hope soared. Kokir caught, not a scratch on anyone. No photo op, no running and hiding. Everything back to normal.

Normal. What the hell was normal?

Doctors, canes, eternal darkness. No present, no future.

A bullet was starting to sound better and better.

He broke away from Mike.

"Hey! Where are you going? Dammit, Sin—"

But he hurried away, too fast to be careful. He hit his leg against something—coffee table, piece of furniture—almost ran into a wall.

"Are you crazy?" Mike caught up to him, but Danny

jerked away again. "All right. All right. Here. The doorway is here." He shoved him through.

Voices intensified.

Miller: "Who are you?"

Parnell: "You should have stayed put."

And that one voice that cut through all the others:

"Danny. Thank God you're all right."

CHAPTER 17

⎯⎯⎯⎯⎯•⎯⎯⎯⎯⎯

They'd handcuffed her, shoved her roughly into the house. Her mouth was dry and her pulse throbbed furiously in her throat, but none of that mattered the minute Martha saw Danny, whole and safe.

"You are insane, woman," he roared. "What the hell did you do?"

She'd been shot at and manhandled, it was the middle of the night, her legs were still quaking, and she was not in the mood for a lecture. "Before you start screaming at me, can you ask them to take off these handcuffs?"

"Uncuff her," Lieutenant Parnell said.

"Wait." Danny raised a hand. "I'm not so sure. Better to cuff her to a chair. It's the only way you're going to get her to do what you want her to."

She held out her wrists. "Ha-ha."

One of the men released her.

An intimidatingly large African-American man in a dark blue suit frowned at her. "Who is this?"

Before she could answer, Lieutenant Parnell did. "Martha Crowe. The eyewitness. This is Agent Warren Miller from Homeland Security."

Martha stuck out her hand and Miller shook it. "You told us you had her stashed, Sinofsky."

"I did."

Miller turned unhappy, narrowed eyes on her. "How did you get here, Miss Crowe?"

"I . . ." She straightened her shoulders. She would not be cowed by their stern faces or their scary guns. "I borrowed my father's van."

"You what?" Danny exploded. "Jesus Christ."

The rest of the men huddled around her, watching with hostile faces.

Danny addressed the group. "Can you give us a minute?"

The men exchanged glances, then Parnell stepped back. "Sure." He waited a beat, as though expecting Danny to take her somewhere. Then he seemed to remember how hard that would be. "Why don't we . . . uh . . . regroup in the den. The rest of you men, retake your places outside. We've got everything here under control."

Miller's lips compressed into a thin line, but he shuffled off into the back of the house. In a few minutes, they were alone, and she braced herself for the onslaught.

"All gone?" At least his first words were pleasant enough.

"Yes."

He nodded thoughtfully. "You going to explain?"

"I should think the explanation is obvious."

"Oh yeah, crystal, babe." He stabbed the air with an angry finger, which was much more like what she'd expected. "You don't trust me. You think I need a babysitter."

But not that. Berating her for putting herself in danger, yes, but this? She held up a hand in protest. "Wait a minute. No. That's ridiculous."

"Is it? Look at you, you can't let me out of your sight."

"Not because I think you're a helpless—"

"Blind man?"

"I don't—"

"Would you have pulled this if I wasn't blind? Would you have willfully compromised a joint state, federal, and local operation, almost got yourself killed, may in fact still get yourself killed, if I wasn't?"

She paused for a millisecond, but the hesitation was telltale.

He sneered at her. "The truth, Martha. It's what you're famous for."

Her face heated, all the way from the neck up. "I . . ." She bit her lip, knew he was right, and refused to admit it. "I don't know!" She threw up her hands in frustration. Why didn't he see that she was just worried? "What difference does it make? You are blind."

"Ah, those illustrious facts on the ground. Well, I know exactly what you would have done. Nothing. You hear me? Nothing. You would have stayed put." His face was lined with fury, his dead eyes hard and iced.

"Okay, fine. You're incapable of taking care of yourself and I'm the queen bitch for reminding you of it. Now what?"

"Now? Jesus Christ. Now I'm goddamn stuck with you."

She raised her chin. "Big problem."

"That's right. You're a fucking big problem. Because I don't need you." He lowered his voice to a cold rasp. "And I don't want you. You and me—we were just part of therapy. The session is over."

A wave of hurt crashed down on her, but she stood her ground, refused to let it drown her.

"There's a guest bedroom off the den," he said coldly. "It's yours for the duration."

"You're going to lock me in?"

"If I have to."

"And while I'm playing Rapunzel, what are you going to do?"

"That's NTN, Martha, and—"

"I don't need to know. Blah, blah, blah." She shoved him. Literally pushed him, as though shifting his body might get his brain to shift in the right direction. She may as well have tried to budge a mountain, but she plunged on anyway. "Do you think I came all the way up here to be shunted aside? You don't want to tell me, I'll just ask your boss, or your friend Mike. Or I'll e-mail Jake. You must have a computer here somewhere." She looked around wildly, as though the machine would appear right there in front of her.

"Fine," he said through gritted teeth, and told her about the plan for the photo with the governor.

She was appalled. "What if Kokir doesn't wait for your picture in the paper? What if he shoots you in the middle of the governor's speech?"

He smiled, and it was small and tart, and as dead as his eyes. "That's what we're hoping for, isn't it?"

She opened her mouth to protest, then stood there gaping at him. What he'd said was so outrageous. He was turned toward her, his gaze in the right area, but slightly off center. Like his thinking.

And suddenly all the puzzle pieces fell into place.

"No, Danny," she said quietly. "It's not what 'we're' hoping for. Although it may be what you'd like."

His black brows drew down in a fierce scowl. "What the hell are you talking about?"

"You know, my dad tried to kill himself, too."

"I'm not trying to—"

"And he had lots of friends to help him, just like you. His best buds were Jim Beam and Jack Daniels."

"You're crazy. It's not the same."

"I'm very familiar with the self-destructive impulse in the newly handicapped."

"Self-destructive? You're the one who walked out of a safe house and barged in here, almost getting your head shot off in the process."

"But I did it out of love for you, not because—" She gasped and covered her mouth. Her face paled. She hadn't meant to say that, hadn't even acknowledged the feeling was there, inside her. Silently, she moaned, exposed and defenseless.

He wasted no time taking advantage of it. "I don't want your love. I don't want you getting hurt for me because you think I'm not good enough to take care of myself. How much clearer can I make it?"

She blinked rapidly, stalling the tears, and forced her voice into its coldest tone. "I'm sorry, Danny, but unfortunately for us both, you've got it. Stay alive and deal with it."

The next morning Mike drove him to Veterans Hall where the governor was giving his speech. He left Martha at home with two men from Homeland Security to keep her locked down. He hadn't spoken to her, though he knew she was there. While he was in the shower, she'd picked out the suit he was wearing and laid it out in an orderly, easy-to-decipher pattern on his bed. Leave it to her to know what he needed and do it without him asking. He didn't thank her, though truth be told, he was grateful he hadn't had to ask Miller or one of the other guards for help.

He was still rocking with anger at her appearance. She'd

put herself at risk for him, a risk she would have never taken if he'd been whole. That knowledge curdled in his gut like sour milk. How many other people he cared about would take risks for him? Beth? The kids?

He'd heard a story once, a funny story, or so he'd thought at the time. About someone's uncle who rushed into the street to save a blind man from an oncoming car only to be killed in the process.

He would not live that way, at the mercy of other people's compassion.

The car jolted over uneven road, and he swayed with the bumps. For half a second he was back on that roller-coaster ride with Martha in Charlie's van as they escaped the farmhouse. In a flash he remembered where that ride had taken him, to the river and the boat basin, and eventually the Yellow Butterfly Hotel.

And suddenly he was overwhelmed by the loss of her, by the necessity of it, and by the huge gulf it would leave. He would miss her. Not just the feel of her bones against his, the delicious porcelain dip of her hips and her collarbone, but the lip she gave him, the schoolteacher bossiness. The way she led with her chin.

God, she made him so furious.

I did it out of love for you.

The words ricocheted inside him. He wanted to hem them in, confine them in a dark corner until he figured out what to do with them.

The car stopped.

"We're here," Mike said.

No use thinking of that now. No use dreaming or planning or thinking about the future. Not when he didn't have one.

They exited the armored limo, and Mike took him

through a back way to the speaker's platform in the meeting room. Like Burdock, Mike was a lousy guide, and Danny tripped over something on the floor—an extension cord, Mike told him—and hit his shin against something Mike didn't bother to identify.

The meeting room itself sounded cavernous, voices hollow with echo, footsteps larger than life. Mike sat him behind a long table covered with a smooth fabric. Tablecloth. White, probably. He smelled coffee and food. Glass and silverware clinked against china. He wondered how many other white-covered tables were scattered around the hall.

He was introduced to several people. The governor's chief of staff, aides, journalists. Someone placed a plate of food in front of him. Eggs Benedict, he was told. He ignored it, too tense to eat. Besides he felt a bud of panic at eating in front of so many people. What if he spilled something? Got egg on his tie?

He wore a Kevlar vest under his suit, and it was hot and uncomfortable. As an undercover cop he almost never wore a vest, so had never gotten used to the feel. But Parnell and Miller had insisted, and Danny would have been a fool to resist. As Martha said, he was an easy target.

Not that he was alone. Between security on the governor and his own entourage he was crowded with protectors. Miller and Mike were on the platform with him. Other officers mingled with the crowd. If Kokir showed up, he'd be spotted.

Unless he was disguised, or sent someone else in his place. A cool wave shuddered up Danny's back.

"All clear so far," Miller murmured behind him.

Danny was sandwiched between two people on the governor's staff. The one on the right leaned over. "Everything all right, Detective? Can I get you anything?"

"I'm fine," Danny said tersely. What was the guy's name anyway? They'd been introduced, but he was just another voice in the void.

"How about some coffee?"

"Thanks, but I'm fine." Robard. Andrew Robard.

"Have you met Marcus Hanson? He's on your left."

"And he is not happy," Hanson said in a acrid tone. "Our numbers are in a downward spiral as it is. Just what we don't need is another spending initiative."

"He's with the governor's reelection campaign," Robard said as if that explained the other man's mood.

"Thanks, Andrew, we've met." Hanson had a thin, querulous voice. Danny remembered the handshake. Pudgy hands, loose grip. "And no offense, but you people think we're made of money."

You people? "Excuse me?"

"Henley's making a big mistake if he thinks he's going to get elected on the backs of the disabled."

Robard gave a little embarrassed cough. "Marc, why don't you let Detective Sinofsky enjoy his breakfast?"

"Why should I? I'm not. So tell me," he said, his voice growing louder as he leaned in. Danny could smell sour coffee on his breath. "I hear you had a stroke. Unusual in someone your age. How did it happen?"

He did not want to talk about it. Especially to this asshole.

Robard muttered something under his breath. "I don't think you should—"

"Stow it, Robard. Henley's going to want all the gory details. What happened, Sinofsky?"

Danny's jaw tightened, but he was here to play along, so he answered the question. "I was hit in the head during a collar. An arrest."

"On the street?"

"In a bar."

"Really? Which bar?"

"I don't think the governor moves in those circles."

Hanson paused, then thought better of it. "Call it native curiosity. I'm from Sokanan originally. As is Andrew. You're originally from Sokanan, aren't you, Andrew?" The question sounded more like a dig.

"Yes, Marcus." Spoken with forbearance. "Twenty or more years ago." And then in a low voice for Danny's ears only, he said, "Sorry."

"So what bar was it?" The hostility in Hanson's voice set Danny's teeth on edge.

"The Dutchman on Melvin."

A moment's silence. Were the questions done?

"Hmm. Guess you're right. Never heard of it. How about you, Andrew? Ever been to the Dutchman?"

"No."

A chair scraped back. Someone tapped on a microphone. "Ladies and gentlemen."

Hanson grumbled, his words lost as the noise in the room began to settle. Voices hushed, the rattle of dishes and forks slowed. The man at the microphone began to introduce Governor Henley, and Danny's brain exploded with the sight of the Dutchman.

The picture congealed in front of him, as clear as though he'd been transported from Veterans Hall to the bar. Murray Potts polishing a glass, the huddle of people at the pool table, the blur of movement as the door to the restroom opened.

A hand shook him. "Detective. Detective!"

And like that, the vision disappeared, leaving darkness in its wake.

"Are you all right?" Robard whispering again.

Someone at his back. "What's the matter?" Mike spoke in his ear.

Danny shook his head. "Nothing."

"He turned white. Froze," said Robard.

"I'm fine. It's . . . it was nothing."

"Here." A glass was shoved in his hand. "Water."

He sat rigid, sweating beneath the vest. As if from a distance he heard applause, and then the governor began to speak. The meaning floated by in a haze of words.

Why was his brain doing this to him? Was it Hanson's questions? Did it mean anything or was it just random, as Martha had said? He tried to focus on the scene, conjuring it up in his head. It was as though his brain was clobbering him with that key moment of distraction. The restroom door opening. If he hadn't turned his head, he wouldn't have lost control of the crowd. There would have been no fight. No punch. No stroke. No blindness.

He balled his hand into a fist and clamped it hard against his knee. He willed himself to calm down, to concentrate on what was going on here, in this room. Forget the Dutchman, he was an open target now and he'd better focus on that.

He swallowed a gulp of water, slid the glass carefully onto the table. He heard his name over the loudspeaker. As promised, the governor had mentioned him in his speech. A pause, as if everyone in the room was waiting for something to happen. In the sudden stillness his heart pounded loud as a gunshot.

A low close voice spoke in his ear. "Wave," Robard said.

Danny held up a hand and the room burst into applause. For half a second he braced himself for a hit. The applause would cover any residual noise.

But the applause stopped and he was still there. No shot, no impact. Nothing.

Danny's guard bumped down, but only a small notch lower. He was still out in the open, still available for target shooting.

But the speech ended and nothing happened.

Afterward, what felt like a platoon of people ushered Danny away, pushing and prodding him into someplace past the noise of the previous room. Wherever they'd taken him, it smelled of chemical flowers, like room deodorant, and he pictured some kind of anteroom. But it could just as well have been a hallway or a broom closet. Was there furniture in the room? No one offered him a seat, which would have given him a few more clues. He heard Miller's deep voice talking low into his radio, so he knew his squadron was still with him, but he wished to hell he knew where he was, and could map out his own escape route.

"Detective Sinofsky?" He turned toward the voice. It sounded like Andrew Robard again. "This is Paul Norris. He'll take the photo."

"Good to meet you." Norris had a high Midwestern twang.

Danny nodded in his direction, picturing a tall, lanky farm boy, and realizing at the same time that what he imagined and what was true could be acres apart.

"And this," said Robard with more than a touch of pride and importance, "is Governor Thomas Henley."

At a loss for where Henley was, Danny stuck out his hand in Robard's direction. Another hand grabbed his, and Danny corrected his position.

"It's an honor to meet you, Detective," the governor said. At least he knew what Henley looked like. From pictures and news reports, Danny knew the governor was of medium build, with a flat, bug-eyed face, and a mop of light brown hair.

"If you'll just step over here a minute next to the governor . . ." Norris maneuvered him a few steps, until Danny felt someone else's body. The governor was shorter than Danny, his shoulder meeting Danny's upper arm.

Robard didn't seem to like that. "How about we put you in a chair, Detective?"

"I'm not going to look like I can't stand on my own two feet," Danny said.

"This is fine, Andrew," Henley said quickly. "Let's take the picture. I have a schedule to keep."

"Yes, sir." Robard seemed to snap to attention. "Of course."

"Detective, if you could turn your face to the left," Norris said.

Danny complied, heard a click, then another and another.

"Got what you need, Paul?"

"Got it, Governor."

"Let's go then," Henley said, immediately moving away.

"Burdock," Miller said. "See Mr. Norris out of the building."

"Yes, sir."

"Good luck, Detective," the governor said. Already his voice sounded as though he were across the room. "Agent Miller, keep me informed. Andrew will be in constant contact. I want to know the minute you have a lead on this Kokir."

"Yes, sir," Miller said.

A door opened and closed, and his ordeal was over. More or less. Now it was just waiting for it to be made public.

That thought soured inside him, leaving a nasty after-taste.

"How you doing?" Mike's overeager voice came from the left.

He hated that cheery note everyone suddenly used with him. "Still alive."

"That's good news."

Danny made a face. "No pain, no gain."

CHAPTER 18

———•———

Danny's picture appeared in the afternoon papers. He couldn't see it, but Mike told him about it, and he managed to get the article online and read it. He sat still, listening through the earphones as Mr. Ed's robotic voice read the caption under the photo: "Detective Daniel Sinofsky." Couldn't be clearer if they'd painted a bull's-eye on him.

But, like the morning at Veterans Hall, nothing came of it. No stranger walked down the street when he shouldn't, no one sneaked up to the house or drove by aimlessly.

Not that anyone thought the photo would work that fast, but the waiting put an edge on everyone. Martha wandered into the den—Miller's nominal command post—accidentally knocked over a carefully constructed time line, and Miller snapped at Burdock for letting her out of the bedroom. Newson, one of the other agents, said something under his breath about Burdock not being able to keep his women locked down, and Burdock growled at him. The atmosphere in the house tightened, and Miller had to come between the two men.

"That's enough, Burdock, get Miss Crowe back in the bedroom."

"Agent Miller"—Martha's voice was cold and severe—

"I am not a prisoner to be dragged this way and that at your whim."

"I'm afraid you are, Miss Crowe," Miller said curtly. "Burdock."

"Yes, sir."

Their steps moved toward the bedrooms, Burdock's determined, Martha's less so.

"And Newson, get on the horn and see what's going on with the SWAT team."

"Yes, sir."

More footsteps walking way.

"You all right?" Mike leaning close.

"I'm fucking fine, Mike. Stop asking me every five minutes."

Someone's phone rang and all activity stopped. Danny tensed, ears straining to hear every morsel of Miller's brisk end of the conversation until he disconnected.

"Listen up, everyone." They were all listening anyway, or at least the deep silence seemed to indicate they were. "We got a tip on Kokir."

"A tip?" Danny couldn't believe it. The news was like the sun coming out from behind the clouds. "What kind of tip?"

"Anonymous. To Sokanan PD. We should hear within the next half hour whether it's any good. A team is on its way."

Who was on the team? Where were they going? An acrid wave of frustration rolled over him. He should be on that squad. In the car. Chasing the lead.

He wasn't the only one stuck waiting. He was pretty sure Burdock hadn't cuffed Martha to the bed, though he'd probably like to. But she wouldn't have heard the latest because who would bother telling her?

Not that he cared; she'd brought it on herself. It wasn't his job to keep her informed.

And yet, ten minutes later he found himself in front of her door, cursing himself silently. "Burdock, tell Miss Crowe, we've had a tip on—"

The door whipped open. "Danny?"

Damn. He knew this was a bad idea.

"Please stay in your room, Miss Crowe." Burdock said the line by rote as if he'd been repeating it without much success for hours.

"What's happened?"

"When you need to know, you'll be informed," Burdock said with the same frayed edge to his voice.

"Danny?"

"Miss Crowe." There was some shuffling and a lot of clothes rustling.

Martha squeaked. "Take your hands off—"

Danny raised his voice. "Burdock."

"Inside."

"Burdock! It's okay. Let me talk to her."

"Jesus," Burdock said with disgust. "Be my guest."

Danny moved forward, ran into the agent, and they did a little dance, getting more tangled.

"Get out of the way, Agent Burdock," Martha barked, and underneath her breath he heard, "Idiot" as well.

Danny took a step back, Burdock stepped aside, and Martha pulled him forward. The door slammed shut.

Danny leaned against it, crossed his arms, too tempted to get closer to her. "Well, you've certainly been making friends all over the place."

"I don't see why they have to practically lock me in like this."

"Because they don't trust you," he drawled.

"That's ridiculous. I'm not the bad guy."

"You didn't stay where you were supposed to, you jeopardized on ongoing investiga—"

"All right, all right. Let's not rehash old news." She sucked in a breath as though reaching for calm. "Something has happened. What?"

Mentally, he shook himself for even being there. "We got a tip on Kokir."

"A tip? From whom?"

"It was anonymous."

"Someone just . . . ups and calls?" The skepticism came off her in waves.

"Sometimes we get lucky."

"And sometimes hell freezes over."

"Why don't we wait and see if it pans out before we roll out the gloom and doom."

"I'm not—"

"Oh yes, you are." He reached for the door. He wasn't going to stand there arguing with her about things that hadn't even happened yet.

"Wait. Where are you going?"

"Back to the land of wishing and hoping."

"Stay." Her voice was small, sweet, and he liked the begging tone.

Against his better judgment, he turned back.

But just to be sure, he stayed by the door. "So . . . did you want something?"

"I . . . wanted to say—"

"Yes?"

Another big breath. "Just that I'm—"

A rap on the door by his ear. "Sinofsky!" It was Burdock.

"Yeah?" Danny opened the door.

"Phone. I think it's good news."

Martha saw the grin on Burdock's face and despite what Danny thought about her, hope flared. He took the phone, identified himself, and mostly listened, interrupting with only a few terse comments, like "where" and "unbelievable" and "I want to be there."

He hung up at last. She was barely breathing.

"What? What happened? Was the tip good?"

Slowly, Danny nodded. He looked shell-shocked. "Led them right to Kokir's little hideaway."

"Was he there?"

"No, but everything else was. Maps, plans, explosives, ammo, and a whole lot of underwater equipment—tanks, wet suits."

"Wet suits? What's he going to do?"

Danny ran a hand through his hair, a gesture of disbelief. "Blow up Indian Point, looks like."

"What?" She stared at him, at the pinched lines around his mouth and the tension in his jaw. "That's . . . that's crazy. How?"

"Set a string of explosives under the river leading up to the plant site."

"Oh, my God." Fear and amazement snaked up her back. "Will we be able to stop him?"

"Miller is meeting on it now. Looks like Kokir was planning everything for tomorrow night."

"You're kidding. Then . . . then we got to him just in time."

"Yeah. Talk about luck."

Danny stumbled around the bedroom, arms out and groping, and she bit her lip to keep from helping him. When he found the bed at last, he sank onto the edge. "I haven't told you the best part."

The best part? She wasn't sure she wanted to hear much more.

"Kokir's command post was a room above the Dutchman."

She breathed deep. The Dutchman. Where the punch Danny had taken started the stroke that blinded him.

"Is that why . . . is that the connection to you? He thought you saw him?"

"That's the theory everyone is working on. It's what makes sense."

"Did you see him?"

He laughed, curt and rough. "How would I know? I don't remember smelling Tiger Balm, but I'm not sure I would have noticed back then."

"If that is the connection, and they catch Kokir, we'll be all right. This will all be over." She said it with a sinking feeling. She should be happy, ecstatic. She should be glad to get back to her life. But that would mean saying good-bye to Danny.

"That's right." He said it matter-of-factly and she wondered if he was thinking the same thing. But then he rose. "I gotta go. I want in on the planning. I want to catch this guy."

She opened her mouth to protest, then closed it again. She couldn't imagine he could do anything to help, but she wasn't going to say so. Let someone else burst his balloon.

She watched him go, saw the door close behind him, and retreated to the bed where she'd spent so much time during the last two days.

She wasn't sorry. She would not have been able to live with herself if she'd let Danny do this alone. But her presence had undermined his confidence, and she was sorry for that.

Not that it would make much difference. He would do whatever he would do and then this would all be over and they would say so long and that would be that.

She thought of the time they'd spent together in the apartment. They would be her memories now. At least no one could say that she didn't know what it was like to love a man. To be loved by him. Even if it was for only a few nights.

Then again, maybe her father had been right. Maybe her life did lack a certain . . . something. These last few days . . . Had Danny filled those holes? She'd been happy, when she wasn't terrified. Would she be happy again once Danny was gone?

And he would be gone. She knew that as clearly as she knew anything.

She rolled the thought around in her mind, feeling the ache it created.

Maybe that was why she wanted one last memory.

Why late that night, when the house was quiet and Burdock had been replaced by a less cautious Newson, she slipped out of her room, told the agent she couldn't sleep and wanted a cup of tea, and headed toward the kitchen. He followed sluggishly but didn't seem to notice when she put water up to boil and only pretended to turn on the burner.

"Bathroom," she said as she strolled out of the kitchen. Once out of sight, she scurried away, across the living room and down the hall to Danny's room.

Miller and the other agents were camped out in the den, which she didn't have to traverse, and the one guy stationed by the door barely looked at her when she repeated, "Bathroom."

She didn't bother knocking, just slipped inside Danny's

room. It was dark, but her eyes adjusted quickly. He was sitting up, chest bare, back against the headboard.

"What are you doing here, Martha?"

She groaned inwardly. She'd hoped he'd be asleep and she'd have a few seconds to simply enjoy the look of him before negotiating began. No such luck.

"How did you know it's me?"

"The nose knows." He crossed his arms. "So?"

She crept closer. "I . . ." Now that she was here, she didn't know what to say. Sometimes she had no trouble talking to him. Other times, like now, she got completely tongue-tied.

"I think you should go back to your room."

She fell back on the obvious. "I can't sleep."

"Try hot milk."

She reached the bed. "I want to talk to you."

"We can talk in the morning."

"I want to . . ." She paused for a breath. ". . . to apologize."

"What time is it?"

The question threw her. Flustered, she glanced at the digital readout on the clock radio by his bed. "Three twenty."

He nodded. "So you waited until the middle of the night to apologize?"

Her face heated. Why could he always see right through her? In a low, soft voice, she said, "I don't want to be alone."

He sighed. "Everything's going to be all right. You're safe."

"I'm not worried about my safety. I just don't want to be by myself anymore." She sat down on the edge of the bed.

His mouth curved ironically. "In the cosmic sense or more down to earth?"

She touched his arm. "Earth, Danny."

He shivered with her touch. "There are half a dozen men in the house," he said quietly.

"They're mostly in the den." She stroked up his arm to his shoulder, the muscles tightening under her fingers.

"I can't. I thought I explained that to you. We can't do this anymore."

"I know. But . . ." She licked her lips. "There must have been a million women you did this with who you didn't care about. What's one more?" She ran her hand across his chest. Beneath the taut skin, his heart leaped at her touch.

"It wasn't a million. Maybe half a million. Seven hundred and fifty thousand tops."

"Very funny."

"And I did care about them. We had fun. No one was ever hurt by me." He captured her exploring fingers, stopping her. "But this is different."

"Why?"

"You're different."

She knew that for a fact, but he hadn't minded before. "How? How am I so different?"

He squirmed, shifting his weight on the bed. "You just are. In every way imaginable."

Echoes of schoolyard taunts vibrated in her head. Wicked Witch. Scare Crowe. Big Foot.

She slipped her hand from beneath his and fisted it in her lap. "Ah, I see."

"No, you don't see. You never have." He turned his face toward hers, his eyes lit with fiery conviction even as they focused to her left. "It's not about your face or your body, which I can see, even if it's only with my hands. It's not even about you. It's me. I can't give you anything. All the others, they didn't want anything. Why do you think I picked them?"

"I don't want anything, either."

He laughed. "You don't even know what you want."

"But you do?"

"Oh, yeah. Like I know myself. A house. A family. A man to cook for. Laughter in the moonlight. Sweetness at dawn. You want everything, Martha. You deserve it. But you won't get it from me."

"Why? Because you're blind?"

"Because I can't see where I'm going! What I'm going to do with my life. I can barely take care of myself, how can I take care of someone else?"

"You don't have to take care of me. In case you missed the last thirty years, we women are liberated now. Betty Friedan and Gloria Steinem and all that."

"Yeah, I know first-hand what it's like to live with a liberated woman. It killed my mother."

"It won't kill me."

"I'm not going to be the load someone else sags under." His mouth was a firm, harsh line, and she opened hers to respond when a commotion burst into hearing from outside.

"I don't know! She was right here a minute ago."

"Why the hell can't anyone keep track of that woman?"

"She wanted tea."

"She didn't even turn on the heat!"

Danny shook his head. "Martha moves and chaos follows." He swung out of bed, padded to the door and opened it. "She's here," he called.

Footsteps came at a run and the door burst open. Miller, Newson and two other men glared at her. She raised her chin in defiance.

"Did you want something, Agent Miller?"

"I want you to stay in your goddamn room!" He jerked his head at Newson. "Take her back."

She threw a pleading glance at Danny, who, of course, couldn't see it. Newson grabbed her by the elbow and tugged her forward.

"You're hurting me."

"You're lucky I don't bean you one," Newson grumbled.

"I'm perfectly capable of walking without help."

"Hold on." Danny put up a hand. "It's all right. You can leave her here."

Miller shook his head. "That is not—"

"You want to know where she is, right? She'll be here. With me. No problems."

"And how the hell are you going to keep an eye on her, when you won't even know if she leaves?"

Danny's jaw tensed, and his voice crisped. "I'll know. Besides, she won't leave. Trust me."

Miller looked from him to her and sudden understanding flew into his face. "This is a federal operation, not some high school prom."

Danny grinned. "No dancing. Scout's honor."

"She's a witness. You're a cop."

"Not for long."

"You can't—"

"I won't."

Miller growled and turned to her. "Do I have your word that you won't wander off?"

"You have my word." Then added stiffly, "As if you need it."

Miller made a sound of disgust. "Newson, stay glued to that door. I even catch your eyes drifting away, I'll carve your balls off."

"Yes, sir." Newson sent her a malevolent glance. "I'll give the lovebirds all the chaperoning they need."

Martha slammed the door on him and turned to Danny. A minute ago he couldn't wait to get rid of her. Now . . .

"Why did you do that?"

He sighed, shook his head. "I don't know. When it comes to you, I don't know why I do any of the things I do." He nodded toward the bed. "Get in."

"Only if you come with me."

He snorted. "Man, you don't give up."

That struck her: she *had* given up. On so much. Her youth, her chance at life. But not Danny.

He trailed his way to an armchair in the corner, clearly comfortable with the room and the objects in it. "I think we'll be safer if I finish the night out here." He sat down.

"Okay." She crossed to the chair, sank onto the floor at his feet, and laid her head in his lap.

That wasn't what he'd intended, and she knew it. But he made no protest, just put his hand on her head, stroking the hair back from her ear.

"You're one bossy, stubborn, tenacious woman, Martha."

"It's the key to all my conquests."

Danny smiled, his fingers entwined in the silk of her hair. He pictured the long black strands, and in his imagination they showed up thick and sheened with blue. Dark and deep as the perpetual night in which he lived.

CHAPTER 19

The strategy to catch Kokir was threefold: divers were dispatched to eliminate whatever explosives he might have already set up, and two teams were sent to intercept him, one on water and one on land.

The only catch? Danny wasn't part of it.

The discussion had been brief and to the point. No one could be spared to watch out for him, and he couldn't watch out for himself. He would only get in the way.

Miller delivered the verdict, cold and final, leaving Parnell to say quietly, "I'm sorry, Danny."

Kokir would be busy that night, and an attempt on Danny or Martha seemed unlikely, so they took everyone except Burdock, who chafed at being the caboose left behind.

Danny knew the plan intimately, and as the night ticked on, he roamed the house like a ghost, his uselessness eating away at him. He knew when the divers would be in position, when the choppers would take off, when the SWAT team would arrive. The times ticked off in his head, but he couldn't connect them with reality. He still hadn't gotten a watch he could read, and he refused to ask Burdock the time every two minutes.

Burdock seemed to have given up on keeping Martha on

a tight rein, and she wandered the house at will. Danny smelled her here and there, her clothes leaving a vapor trail of flowers that seemed totally inappropriate to his mood and the circumstances. He wanted to scream at her to stay away. And yet he wanted to cling to her, too. Cry on her shoulder, weep for his lost life, his lost future.

The whole experience was a harbinger of things to come. Of other people acting for him. Of him at loose ends, not knowing what to do or how to do it.

Without the bulk of the men, the house was quiet, distressingly so. Only him and his thoughts to keep him company.

And Martha.

But she didn't say much, for which he was glad. Just sat, or roamed or sighed. And occasionally, "It's ten o'clock. What's going on?" Or "It's twelve fifteen. What are they doing now?"

And each time, he would respond. "Setting in the divers." Or "Waiting. Just waiting. Like us."

The wait was intolerable. He was stiff with tension. When the doorbell rang he jumped a foot.

"Is that them?" Martha said, and he heard his own hope and fear in her voice.

"Miller wouldn't ring the bell," Danny said.

"Get into the bedroom," Burdock said. "Both of you."

He heard the sound of a round being chambered.

"Go!" Burdock ordered. And Martha put a hand on his arm to drag him away.

"I'm not going anywhere." His heart was zooming, but he spoke with quiet conviction.

The bell rang again, and Burdock hissed, a deadly rasping sound through his teeth. "For God's sake. At least get her locked up."

"It's all right," Martha said. "I can lock myself up." Her fragrance drifted away in time to her retreating footsteps.

"Who is it?" Burdock called through the door.

"Andrew Robard. I met Detective Sinofsky at Veterans Hall during the governor's speech."

"An aide or something," Danny said. "He sat next to me."

The door opened.

"I can't let you in," Burdock said.

"We called ahead." Robard seemed distressed, a high whine to his voice. "Didn't you get the orders?"

"No."

"Damn all this red tape. Look, the governor sent me. He wanted someone to stand by, make sure everything went well and that Detective Sinofsky was all right."

Danny gritted his teeth. More babysitters.

"I'm fine. Tell Henley I'm fine."

"Please," Robard said. "I don't know what kind of mix-up there was. I wanted to be at the staging area, but I couldn't get through. I thought I might be able to wait here instead." He gave a small, confidential laugh. "It's my job if I don't at least come in until we hear what the word is on the power plant."

Silence. Danny imagined Burdock thinking it over. "Sinofsky, you're sure this is the guy at the speech?"

Danny shrugged. "Sounds like him."

"All right. But stay where I can see you."

"No problem, officer—"

"Burdock. Agent Tony Burdock."

"Thank you, Agent Burdock. I appreciate it. And so will the governor. Believe me."

And there was a zip. A pop. Danny knew that sound. A bullet.

He dove to the floor. "What the—?"

Another crack.

Danny felt around the edges of his position. Smooth and cool—the hardwood floor—then bumpy and giving: carpet. His shoulder scraped against something—a chair or a couch? He pulled himself behind it.

"Burdock?"

No answer.

"Robard?"

No answer.

Jesus Christ. Was there someone else?

Clothes rustled. A step. His ears strained. The sound came from the left. Danny dodged right.

"You can run, but you can't hide." The voice was soft, deadly. Robard's voice. Maybe ten feet away.

His brain was working so fast he didn't have time to think about the craziness of that. The only chance he had was to even the playing field. He felt for the length of the piece of furniture he was hiding behind. The couch, definitely. He pictured the room, got it mapped in his head. He inched farther to the right, took a breath, and lashed out, hitting the end table. The lamp on top went over with a splintering crash.

A bullet fired in the direction of the lamp. Danny lunged the opposite way, clawed, groped, and trailed his way to the kitchen, another bullet chasing him.

The house was old, the fusebox in the broom closet. He fumbled wildly for the correct door, flung it open, groped for the box, which he knew was on the left, but not exactly where, wasted precious seconds finding it, cursed himself and his useless eyes, and shoved every switch to the opposite direction.

He turned but not quite fast enough. Something exploded in his upper arm. Pain lanced him, but he couldn't focus on it. He dove for the ground, rolled, and another bullet hissed past him.

Martha had barely closed the bedroom door when she heard the crash. She jumped, nerves on edge. Was that glass splintering? Maybe Danny or Burdock had dropped something. No one had come to tell her who was at the door, but then no one had bothered to tell her much of anything since she'd barged in.

Instinct told her to stay put, stubbornness told her to see what was going on. While she was debating, the lights went out. Alarmed, she opened the door, peeked out.

The hallway was dark, too, and beyond it the house was black. She opened her mouth to call out to Danny or Agent Burdock but a strange, popping zing made her freeze.

She remembered that sound from the farmhouse. Gunshots.

Her blood chilled. Was it Kokir? How was that possible?

Her pulse leaped into overdrive, and her father's words echoed in her head. *Get as far away as possible.*

Slowly, she sank down to the ground and inched forward, flattened against the wall, until she could see shadows in the front of the house.

Two men on the other side of the living room, forms dim, their edges blurred into blackness. She squinted, inched closer, thought she saw Danny clutching his left arm, and someone else.

Someone with a gun.

Her breath clogged, her stomach heaved. The gunman was too small to be Kokir; he was smaller than Danny. Who was he? The question whizzed through her mind as he crept closer to Danny, arm extended, pointing, aiming that deadly machine at his head.

"Danny!" she cried without thinking, and both men turned. The gun fired, a flash in the dark, and something knocked her backward. A punch, a burn in her shoulder. She sat stupidly, stunned by the impact of the bullet.

"Martha!" Danny's voice was frantic but far away. *"Martha!"* She blinked, trying hard to stay focused. Blood was seeping down her shirt, and the gunman was coming closer.

Danny scrambled toward the sound of the last shot. Martha hadn't answered him. Pure panic took hold, a storm of fear so desperate for a minute he couldn't move.

Jake's voice came out of nowhere: *Remember the closet.* Danny shook off the mind-numbing fear. Quiet. Listen. He couldn't use his eyes, but he could use everything else.

Out of the darkness came a voice. "Who . . . who are you?" It was pinched and dry, but it was Martha. A sea of relief washed over him. She was alive.

"Governor Henley's chief of staff," Robard said politely.

Danny tried to pinpoint his position. Ahead, a bit to the right.

"What do you want?"

Good girl. Keep him talking.

"To win the election, of course." Clothes swished. Steps tramped forward. The hallway. Robard was heading toward Martha's room. Fear for her battled with silent encouragement. If she kept Robard focused on her, Danny might have a chance to creep up on him.

"I . . . I don't understand."

"The campaign staff, Marcus Hanson and incompetents like him, think winning is about issues and polls and numbers, but it's about heroes. That's what people want. And I've given them one: Thomas Henley, a man who can stop a terrorist attack. Everyone will be scared, but the governor will calm their fears and be reelected. A new Giuliani."

"The governor knew about the attack on Indian Point?" She coughed, but her voice, low and strained, expressed his own incredulity.

"Of course not. I arranged it. And made sure everyone involved got caught. Except for me, that is. And now there are only the last two witnesses."

"But I never saw you before." He heard a sliding, dragging motion. Was Martha moving backward? Deeper into the hallway? Why wasn't she on her feet? He didn't want to face the possible answer to that. Whatever she was doing it was tactically brilliant. Robard would be trapped inside the hallway, with Danny controlling the only exit.

If he could get there in time.

And if his calculations were correct.

He crept forward, slow, cautious, absorbed on his footing, on avoiding the familiar obstacles, on staying low. Fear—of the dark, of stepping wrong—enveloped him, base, black, and shuddering. His hands were damp, his neck wet with sweat.

"Yes, well, unintended consequences," Robards was saying. "I'm sorry. I really wish it hadn't come to this."

And then Danny realized what Robard was doing. Drawing him out. If Robard threatened Martha, Danny would have to move fast. And that would give away his position.

Ahead of him, clothing rustled, weight shifted. Robard was doing something . . .

Martha gasped. "God, no! Don't!"

Danny had no choice. He lunged, shoulder low, and hit something. A grunt, a body toppled. Something metallic fell and slid. Robard's gun? Martha cried out, but he couldn't pay attention to that. He grappled with a male body, tangled in hands and legs. Robard was small; Danny could feel the fat on him. Too many chicken and roast beef fund-raisers; not someone who was used to street fighting. Danny didn't have too much trouble turning the bastard on his back like a plump turtle. The minute he was pinned, Danny kneed him in the groin. A scream of agony.

Robard tried to roll over, but Danny sat on him. His hands found Robard's throat and squeezed. Robard squirmed and bucked, his arms flailed. Light punches landed on Danny's shoulder, chest, face. He squeezed tighter.

Fingers clutched Danny's arm, dug into the bullet wound. Now it was his turn to yowl. His hold loosened, and Robard broke free.

Movement. Was Robard getting to his feet? For half a second, Danny paused, listening for clues.

A kick landed in his ribs. Christ, that was clue enough. Danny fumbled for the other man, grabbed empty air. Steps running. Stop. Running. What the fuck was he doing?

And then Danny remembered the gun falling. Robard must be looking for it. If he found it, he and Martha were both dead.

"I've got it! I've got the gun!" Martha. To his left. "Don't . . . don't move." Her voice sounded weak, and he groped around on the floor and walls until he found her. She was sitting against the wall. His fingers traced her position on the floor, up her waist to her arms and out to the hand that held the gun.

"Martha. Are you all right?"

"I . . ." She swallowed. "I don't know."

"Can you hold on?"

"I'll try."

"Pull the trigger if he moves an eyelash."

Danny stumbled through the house and into the kitchen, where he felt around for something to tie Robard up with. He used to have a training rope somewhere, but who knew where it was now? He had two spare pairs of handcuffs but couldn't find them. He yanked open drawers, hurriedly tapped and handled and felt his way through the contents, but all he came up with were dish towels, rubber bands, and a pair of scissors. He was heading back with those when the gun went off.

Another bolt of panic shook him, and the impulse to dash down the hallway drove him forward. But you can't run when you're blind, so he forced himself to keep his path in his head, weave in and out of furniture, use his hands and arms to set a course. Slow. So goddamn slow it was torture.

"Martha. Martha!"

No answer. His chest nearly exploded, the blood pounding in his ears.

Still. He had to be still. Listen.

He crouched down, felt around for his position, ran into a chair leg. Traced its shape. An armchair. Left or right?

He heard the minute creak of steps. Did Robard have the gun? Terror bubbled up, fierce and paralyzing, and he shoved it away. He couldn't think about what that shot meant.

He waited for the steps to move closer, for the smell of the man's sweat to penetrate.

"Come out, come out wherever you are." Robard spoke in a high, nasty taunt.

Come and get me, you sick bastard. He wanted to say the words out loud, but that would give away his position. Who would have ever thought the darkness would be his friend?

A step scraped left. Slowly, silently, Danny moved right, keeping the chair between them. He stilled, willing everything inside him to shut down, leaving only his ears alive.

Out of the darkness came a steady wheeze—fear forcing the breath out of Robard in a hard, audible hiss. Near, then muffled. Then near. Then muffled.

It took Danny a second to realize what Robard was doing. He was turning, sweeping the room.

Danny had less than a chance, but he had to take it. With one swift move, he shoved the chair left, heard it make contact.

He scrambled to where the grunt came from, found Robard scuttling on the floor like an overturned beetle. Racing for control, Danny battled arms, found the gun hand, and squeezed Robard's wrist until he hit bone. With a squeal, Robard dropped the weapon. Danny flung it away but had to loosen his hold on Robard to do so. Robard tried to take off in the direction of the gun. Danny tackled him by the ankles, toppling him over.

They wrestled on the ground and Robard managed to get on top. This time his hands tightened around Danny's neck. He gurgled, his breath stuttering, stopping, consciousness falling away.

He groped beneath him.

Back pocket. Find back pocket.

His fingers closed around the scissors. Slid them out.

With every ounce of strength left, he plunged them into Robard's back.

CHAPTER 20

The hospital was a nightmare of smells and sounds. Disinfectant and stale coffee; gurney wheels clattering over linoleum, rubber soles squeaking, the clash of voices hollering orders: "GSW to the chest!" "Keep that airway open!" "Get her labs, then put her in OR 3!"

The sounds echoed in Danny's head as a resident cleaned the wound in his arm and slapped on a bandage.

"Heard anything about the woman they brought in with me?" He swallowed; his voice was stretched and tight.

"The other gunshot victim?"

"Yeah."

"Too early to tell. They've got her stabilized. She's in surgery."

His stomach twisted, and as if in sympathy, someone down the hall vomited.

"Looks like you're going to make it, Detective." The resident slapped him lightly on his good shoulder, unaware of the irony. "Gotta go. I'll give you an update on your friend if I hear anything." Metal curtain rungs scraped open, then closed.

A baby started screaming, a desperate high-pitched siren that pierced his brain.

"How about we find someplace quiet and go over everything again?" That was Mike. Parnell had sent him to do a first look at the house and the two dead bodies, Burdock and Robard. He'd shown up a half hour ago, sober-voiced and edgy.

"Let me see what I can score," Mike said, and the curtain whisked open again. He returned a few minutes later and tugged Danny away from the coughing and crying, the bustling swish of clothing, and the acrid smell of antiseptic. Down some kind of hallway, where he trailed walls with his bad arm and used his other in front as a barrier against random encounters with chairs and gurneys and water fountains.

"Go right," Mike told him. He felt a space that indicated a doorway and stepped through.

"Surgical waiting room. No one's here. Sit down." Mike pulled him by his good arm.

"Hold on. You want to lead me somewhere, do it right. You walk, I hold on." He positioned Mike beside him. "Give me your arm." Mike obliged and Danny wrapped his hand around it as Martha had showed him, just above the elbow. "Now you can take me to the chairs."

Mike walked him a few steps without mishap. "Nice," he said. "Very cool. Kind of like a stroll through the park. Why didn't you show me this sooner?"

He couldn't remember. Whatever battle he'd fought with pride and humiliation seemed ridiculous now. "The seats, Mike."

"Oh, yeah. On your right. All empty."

Danny felt around, found the row of plastic seats, and settled into one.

"So, let's hear it again. Everything that happened at the house."

Danny repeated the story he'd already told twice. "I

know it sounds crazy, but Robard claimed he'd set up the whole thing at Indian Point to get the governor reelected."

"And you don't remember seeing him or meeting him prior to, uh . . . to the thing with your eyes?"

Before Danny could answer, Mike's cell phone rang. He spoke briefly into it and disconnected. "They got Kokir." His voice held a note of rough satisfaction.

A wave of weak relief. It hardly seemed important anymore. "Alive?"

"Yeah. Lieutenant says to sit tight, he'll be here soon."

The waiting began. One by one, guys from the station wandered in. Bayliss was first, braving the hospital maze to find him.

"How you doing, Sin?"

He couldn't tell Bayliss he was sick with worry, so he fell back on the familiar banter that was easier. "What are you doing up this late, Sergeant?" Danny said.

"Making sure my boys are okay." The sincerity behind the words gave Danny a measure of warmth over the ice of fear.

Later, Danny Marcal and Joe Klimet, two other guys from the detective division, showed up.

"Hey, Sin," Marcal said.

"Looking good, Sin," said Joe.

They perched somewhere and fell silent. They didn't have to talk. Just being there was comfort enough.

And yet there was still the question of betrayal. Had one of these guys given him up, not once, but twice?

Then again, no one had to leak his whereabouts the second time. That had been the whole point—to get him out in the open.

Then why was he still walking around while Martha was fighting for her life? His hands started shaking, and he fisted them tight to keep them steady. It was like a bad dream come true.

Danny didn't know how long he'd been there, sweating in the silence, when Hank Bonner showed up. Bayliss had left when Dave and Joe arrived. They left when Hank did. He knew what they were doing. He'd done it himself. The hospital shift. The Waiting Brigade. One of the ten commandments of law enforcement. Thou Shalt Not Leave an Injured Officer Alone in the Hospital.

But Hank wasn't there on a comfort call.

"Got results on that APB," he said, his voice a slow steady drawl. "Tampa PD picked up Anita's sister, Bea, last night. Seems someone had threatened Anita's daughter as leverage against information on you, Sin."

A short, brief silence while Danny absorbed that shocker. "Anita was the leak?"

"Looks like it."

No one said anything. What was there to say?

"According to Bea, she was miserable after the attack on the farmhouse. You on the run, Tim hurt—"

"What did she think would happen?" Danny burst out.

"I don't know, Sin. Thing like that, maybe you tell yourself it will be all right, and then it isn't. She told Bea she couldn't do it anymore, and somehow she managed to get Bea and the kid away. Bea figures that's why she was killed."

A flare of fury raced through Danny, not sure who he was more angry with—Anita or whoever had killed her. "Kokir cop to that?"

"Not yet. Lieutenant's working on it."

Danny scrubbed a tired hand down his face. His arm hurt like a son of a bitch, but that and the rest—the leak, the case, the questions still unanswered—all paled in comparison to the biggest question of all. When would they get word on Martha?

"Mike, see if you can get an update—"

"Jesus fucking Christ, what are you doing here?" Charlie Crowe exploded into the room like a harsh, rusty saw. "Haven't you done enough?"

Beside him, Mike stirred. "Calm down, Mr. Crowe. Detective Sinofsky saved your daughter's life."

"Don't give me that crap. He's the reason she's in here." His coarse voice cracked. "You promised. You goddamn promised me she'd be okay."

Danny felt the blood drain from his face. His throat closed up. "I know. I'm . . ." He licked his lips; he was having trouble breathing, as though his lungs had caved in. "I'm sorry—"

"Sorry? Do you know she left me?" The voice grated in anguish. "Without wheels, without any way of getting home. Left me to go chasing after you."

"I know." He spoke low, not knowing if he could control his voice otherwise. "That wasn't my idea."

Hank interrupted. "Can I get you a cup of coffee, Mr. Crowe?"

Charlie ignored him, homing in on Danny. His presence closed in, a heat-seeking missile, knees bumping knees, the hot fury of his breath on Danny's face. "You think you deserve that? Deserve her?"

The words were a slap, and Danny took it unflinching. "No, sir."

"You're damn right you don't."

"Hey, Crowe, ease up," Mike said.

"Why don't you shut the fuck up? No one's talking to you."

Danny held up a hand. "It's okay, Mike. Let him have his say."

"You stay away from her," Charlie said.

That hole inside Danny's chest widened. "I intend to."

"Then why the hell are you still here?"

"I need to make sure she's all right."

"You don't need nothing. You got your bad guy."

"We have a suspect in custody," Hank said. "Detective Sinofsky killed the man who shot your daughter."

"Good. Then there's no reason for him or you or any cop on the face of the earth to be anywhere near my Martha. So get the fuck out, the lot of you."

Danny sat stiff as though any movement would crack him in two. But what Charlie was asking was no different from what Danny himself had already told Martha.

Except that down deep in the cellar of his soul, leaving didn't feel like something he was doing for her. It was something he was doing for himself. Something selfish and wrong. Running away, abandoning her. It made his skin crawl.

But he did it anyway. "One condition, Charlie."

Mike said, "Sin, don't let this guy chase you out of—"

"I ain't making no bargains with you, blind man."

"I want to know if . . ." He paused because the words stuck in his throat. "If she pulls through. Whether she's all right. If you won't talk to me, Mike can call you. But I'm not leaving unless you agree to that."

A long, heavy silence. Someone's watch ticked loudly. Someone shifted in their seat.

"All right," Charlie growled. "But you call *me,* got that? She makes it, you don't go near her. You hearing me? Ain't nothing wrong with your ears, is there?"

"No. I hear you. Loud and clear."

* * *

Mike drove to the station, and Danny held onto his arm while they walked from the car to the entrance and down the hallway to the division squad room. It was relatively quiet, no phones ringing, no one chatting up a perp or a civvy making a complaint. Then again, the morning eight hadn't started yet.

Mike led him to his desk, and Danny felt around the familiar edges for his chair.

"I'll go see where the lieutenant is."

Danny inhaled the smell. Ink and dust and layers of floor wax. Sweat and grease from old food wrappers. He absorbed it like a tonic, a rare, healing conglomeration of accomplishment and failure, of teamwork and community, a scent he already missed.

His throat tightened, but footsteps approached and he forced the emotion down where no one would see it.

"Danny," Parnell said. "You doing okay?"

He was so tired of everyone asking him that. Who cared if he was okay? It was Martha they should be worrying about. "Yeah, sure. I'm fine."

"And the witness? Mike says she was still in surgery when you left."

He nodded. "That's right."

Silence. Danny had the odd sensation that Parnell was staring at him. It was a trick Danny had first experienced when he was a kid, and a hundred and one times after that—a way Parnell had of peering at you closely with those see-everything eyes, waiting for you to cough up whatever it was you didn't want him to know.

But the power of that look was lost on a blind man, so Danny turned away. "What's the dope on Kokir?"

Something chafed and slid against the floor. A chair?

Parnell let out a small groan and seemed to sit down. "Well, he hasn't been exactly forthcoming but I sent someone to wake up the Dutchman bartender, Murray Potts. He ID'd a photo of Robard. Looks like he and Kokir met at the Dutchman several times. And, Danny, they were meeting there the night you got drilled. Potts was . . . well, a little cranky, but he finally coughed up the fact that Kokir started the fight. He's the one who hit you."

The night came back to him, not in a Technicolor memory vision, but in his head. Slowly, frame by frame. If Robard was meeting Kokir in his room, they had to come down the stairs and into the barroom to leave. They must have run right into the drug sweep. Tangling with a cop was the last thing either one of them would have wanted. When Danny turned his head, Kokir started the fight to cover their presence and their exit.

"So that *is* why they came after me. They were afraid I could ID them."

"Looks like."

"Jesus Christ. How did they think I could do that? Even if I did see them?"

"You could get your sight back. Guess they didn't want to live looking over their shoulder. Would you? Easier to just take you out. We found a blueprint of the McClanahan warehouse in Kokir's apartment, by the way, so looks like he set you and T-bone up for that shooting."

A shudder ran through Danny, heavy with irony. All this because he might have noticed something when he could actually see. If he could see now, their faces might have jarred some memory. But he couldn't see. Couldn't ID either of them. If Martha died it would be for nothing. No reason at all.

Tears crushed the back of his throat. No reason except his damned, dead, useless eyes.

A hand pressed his shoulder. "It's not your fault, Danny." Parnell had the quiet, fatherly tone in his voice.

Danny nodded, cleared his throat. "Sure. I know. It's just the way things fell out. The facts on the ground."

Parnell didn't respond. He probably didn't believe that any more than Danny did.

"I got one more thing I need from you," Parnell said.

Danny tried a smile, but it felt all twisted on his face. "Hey, my dance card's clean."

"It's about the tip. I'd like to see if you can ID the caller."

Parnell moved, made some kind of small, clattering noise. "Mike, get the tape lined up." The phone. He'd picked up the phone. "We'll see if Danny recognizes the voice."

Danny stood, and once again, instructed someone on the proper way to lead him. Parnell took to it quickly and without Mike's commentary. In a few minutes they were in one of the interview rooms.

"Ready?" Mike asked when they'd sat down.

"Go ahead."

The ON button clicked, and Danny heard someone calling in the Dutchman's location.

"Let me play it again," Mike said, already rewinding.

"You don't have to. It's Robard. I'd know that bastard's voice anywhere."

The ID confirmed what everyone had already suspected. That Robard had double-crossed his partner. The attack on Indian Point had been a setup from the first. A sick election gimmick for a campaign that was circling the drain.

"Where would Robard get the money to hire a guy like

Kokir?" Mike asked. "Shit, how would he even know about him?"

"Homeland Security is auditing campaign funds," said Parnell. "They think that's the most likely source. As for contacting Kokir, the governor is responsible for security at the state level. Through his office, Robard had access to all sorts of information and databases about terror organizations. Not too hard to get from there to Kokir."

"Think Henley was in on it?" Mike said.

Danny shrugged. "Robard denied it. Said it was all him."

"Think anyone will believe it?"

"Probably not," Parnell said.

Mike called the hospital from the car on the way home. Martha had made it out of surgery. The boulder wedged between Danny's shoulders lifted a hair.

"She's going to be okay. You'll see," Mike said, and Danny didn't reply, too afraid to hope.

"Look, your house is still a mess. Let me take you to Beth's tonight."

"No." The word came out quickly. Too quickly. He wasn't ready to face Beth yet. "I can sleep on your couch. Tomorrow, if Parnell releases the scene, I'll call a cleaning service. But I need something first. At the house."

"What?"

Danny took a deep breath. "My cane."

CHAPTER 21

The lilacs were blooming. Martha opened her bedroom window and the scent drifted in with the sun. She plopped back on her bed and looked around her room, enjoying the rawness of it. It was all so new. Her own home, her own appliances, her own furniture. Even after two months, she wasn't used to it.

Then again, she wasn't used to a lot of things yet. Being alive, for one. Not lying on a hospital bed for another. But she was learning to enjoy it. Learning to trust it was real and not the end of a dream that would never come true.

She smiled, inhaled the sweet fresh scent of the bush outside, and stretched languorously. Her body didn't even twinge in reaction. Except for the scars and the occasional spasm when the air was damp, nothing was left to remind her of what had happened there.

She checked the clock at her bedside. Nine thirty. God, she was lazy this morning. And happy. Why was that? She breathed deep. The sun, the spring, the lilacs. Weren't they reason enough?

Tossing the covers aside, she bounded out of bed. She'd promised herself a treat today. Lunch in the garden at Lilly Ridge. A trip to the Cloisters or the shops in Rhinebeck. A boat ride down the Hudson.

She stopped midway to the bathroom. The rule was she had to do something new, and she'd already gone down the Hudson. It had been dark and cold and more dangerous than she could have known. Her heart thudded as the memories flew at her. Danny in the moonlight, his black lashes thick with rain, his sightless eyes fierce and compelling.

She let out a breath. Would she never forget?

Funny how flashes of memory ambushed her. Yet she remembered almost nothing of what should have been the most traumatic event. Only Danny telling her to shoot if Robard moved and then a woozy shiver, as though she was about to faint. Did Robard move? He must have. Lieutenant Parnell thought she and Robard probably struggled for the gun and that was how he'd shot her. She had no idea. Only that when she opened her eyes she was in a hospital bed, tubes in her mouth, and Charlie was snoring in his chair.

In all those months, through all the nightmares and shrieking in the dark without remembering why, through the terror that she'd never breathe on her own again, through all the bruising, soreness, and considerable pain, Danny never appeared. He sent no cards, no flowers, no box of chocolates. The agony of her physical injuries meshed with that other agony, but when she tried to ask Charlie a few discreet questions, he practically bit her head off.

"He's alive and in much better shape than you, and I don't want to hear his damn name again."

She didn't have the strength to fight with him. Not then, at least. And as the weeks passed and she grew stronger, she still heard nothing from Danny. So she tucked that particular pain deep inside and stopped asking about him. If he wanted to see her, he knew where she was.

They released her from the hospital in time for Thanksgiving, and she went back to work in the new year. But she couldn't settle in, everything scraped against her—her office seemed dull and dusty, and she couldn't bear to set foot inside the hospital. She was impatient with her students at the School for the Blind and with her private rehab clients. She and Charlie fought over the smallest things—a glass he hadn't washed, a shoe he hadn't put away. It was as though she'd outgrown herself.

When life seemed to close in, she took to driving, taking long, soothing trips to places like Woodstock and Kingston. One Saturday, she drove by a little house with a FOR SALE sign on it. It was tiny, only a thousand square feet she later learned, but it had a round arched front with an overhang like the seven dwarves' cottage, a small turret on the right with an octagonal porthole, and under the bedroom window, a lilac bush.

She stopped the car and stared at it, her heart beating wildly. And then Danny spoke, a voice floating in her head.

"And now the two of you, you're what—an old-fashioned spinster and her father?"

That's what she was. That's exactly what she was. Or had been. And she was tired of it. So very tired of it.

She'd never done anything spontaneous in her life, but before the day was over she'd made an offer on that house. By week's end, it was hers.

She thought she'd have a battle with Charlie over it, but he was not only supportive, he was downright pleased.

"About damn time," he told her. "You just make sure to invite me to dinner. I'll even leave my smokes behind."

She'd smiled at him, unexpected tears welling up. "Thank you," she said.

Charlie cleared his throat and patted her hand. "No, Martha girl. Thank you."

He still bugged her about Arnie Gould, and much to her surprise, she finally agreed to go out with him. He was a nice man, with a neatly trimmed beard and a shy smile, and she knew she could do worse. But when she looked at him her heart didn't flutter, her stomach didn't curl into knots. How could she be happy with someone who didn't make her feel that way?

A month after she moved into the house, she was eating lunch in the cafeteria with a few students and another rehab instructor. They were talking about plans for the coming weekend and someone asked her what she was doing.

"I'm going to Hawaii." She blinked. Where had that come from? She was no more going to Hawaii than to Mars.

Some of the students oohed and aahed. The instructor said, "What? For the weekend?"

Martha put down her fork. "No. I'm going for two weeks." She swallowed. "A month, really." What was happening to her?

"That's fantastic. I didn't realize you were going on vacation."

"I'm . . . I'm not," she said slowly.

"You're not?" The instructor looked as confused as Martha felt.

And then it hit her. "No. I'm . . . I'm resigning."

"You're what?"

She gasped, laughed, and gasped again. It was out, like a genie free of the bottle. "I'm quitting."

"But why?"

"I don't know." She giggled. "I really have no idea. I just . . . I just am." And she'd picked up her tray, deposited it at the dirty dish window, and walked out.

So foolish, so impractical. So un-Martha-like.

And now, here it was a month later and she still hadn't managed to get to Hawaii. She'd been too busy buying furniture, taking herself out, gardening. Especially gardening.

She'd spent hours and hours in the dirt, absorbing the sun like the black-eyed Susans she'd planted. She loved their golden petals and dark eyes. They were tall and gangly like her, maybe even a bit weedy, but with forthright color.

This summer she'd have creamy white pansies, hot pink geraniums, and a rainbow of snapdragon to go along with the black-eyed Susans. And next spring irises and lipstick-red tulips.

And still she wasn't tired of it. Getting up when she wanted to, taking care of nothing, pleasing no one but herself.

Soon, she would have to think about a job. She'd never spent much of her salary, but even so, her savings wouldn't last forever.

But she didn't want to think about that now. She wanted only to get out in the sun, lay out a new bed for some roses she was thinking about planting, and later, take herself somewhere she'd never been before.

She opened her dresser, still amazed that it no longer contained a mound of loose knit trousers and tunics in brown, gray or navy. Not that she'd turned into a sex goddess, but she had ventured into a boutique, put herself in the saleswoman's hands, and come away with things she couldn't hide behind. There were even some floaty dresses and skirts hanging in her closet now. Okay, so she was still her skinny self and her feet were still size twelve. But she had her own kind of curves and not too long ago someone had appreciated them.

About time she did, too.

She tugged on a pair of slim-fitting jeans and a white tank top and slipped into her favorite flip-flops, the pair that were so rundown they molded to her feet. In the kitchen, the sun flooded the buttercup-yellow walls, and she sighed with happiness. She might be a spinster, but at least she was a spinster on her own terms now.

She put water up to boil for tea, popped a piece of bread in the toaster, and took out the apple butter she'd bought last weekend at Apple House, Hank Bonner's family orchard. When the toast was ready, she took her breakfast out to the patio, grabbing her gardening hat and waving it at Fred Wister, her retired neighbor who was already on his front lawn weeding.

The small wrought-iron café table and two chairs she'd bought at a yard sale perched in a shady spot on the brick deck. She sat down, munched on the toast, and eyed a corner of the terrace where the roses would look pretty climbing over a half-wall.

"Still using that sachet."

She whirled, dropped the toast, and sent her teacup flying. Her mouth opened but no words came out.

Danny leaned on the cane and seemed to peer into the distance. "Cat got your tongue? Oh, that's right, I forgot. No cats."

And still she couldn't speak. He waited on the grass, and she couldn't stop staring.

"You *are* back here? Your neighbor said you were and I'd hate to think I'm just another blind man talking to the air."

She shook herself. "I . . . yes, I'm here."

"Can I come in?"

"Yes . . . of course. Uh, there's a step—"

But he'd already found the ledge with the cane and expertly navigated it.

A thousand questions flooded her mind. Where had he been, why had he disappeared, what had happened to him. But the one pressing closest to her mouth was the one she burst out with.

"What are you doing here?"

He came toward her, the cane steering an obstacle-free course. It tapped against a chair, and he moved closer, felt its outline and sat down. All in one fluid, nonstop motion.

"I came to see you."

"Me?" She squeaked. Something had happened to her mouth. It had turned into the Sahara. Her tongue felt like sandpaper.

Danny's face was grave. "Unless there's someone else here?"

Breathe, girl, just breathe. "I . . . no. Just me."

He nodded, his expression relaxing. "Good."

What to say, what to do? "Would you like . . ." She inhaled. "Would you like a cup of tea?" *God, that was inane.*

He smiled, a small wry twist of his lips. "Only if it comes with half a bottle of whiskey."

Whiskey? Had he taken to drinking? He didn't look like a drunk, he looked fit and fabulous. A little too fabulous if you asked her. He wore a tan suit with a black crewneck underneath. She'd never seen him in a suit before. It hung on his beautiful body perfectly, as though molded to fit. His shoulders were broad, his hips slim. She looked away, her breath stuck in her lungs. Still the fantasy man.

"A little too early for the hard stuff, isn't it?"

He shrugged. "Not if you need it."

"Need it?" She scoffed. No one ever needed whiskey at ten in the morning. "For what?"

"Courage."

That set her back. She looked down at her hands as if they could tell her what to say. "Am I so terrifying? No wonder you stayed away so long."

"That's not it, and you know it."

She lifted her head, drilled him with a look that was wasted on him. "Actually, I don't know it. I don't understand. I was in the hospital, I almost died. You were nowhere."

"You're wrong. I was everywhere. I checked on you every day."

"Checked? With who? Why didn't anyone tell me?"

He shifted in his chair. "I . . . I can't say. I only know I asked. Every day."

"But why didn't you come to the hospital?"

He cleared his throat, coughing into his hand. "I . . . uh, I couldn't."

"Why not?"

He hesitated. "Lots of reasons. I wasn't here, for one."

That shocked her. "You weren't here? Where were you?"

"Virginia. The VA has a school for the blind. I trained there for three months." He looked in her direction. "I do a mean Denver omelet now."

She raised her chin, not in a mood for jokes. "So, you've been back, what, four months? Why show up today?"

"I brought you a housewarming present."

She looked around. No box or wrapped gift. He was stalling. "Why are you here, Danny?"

"I told you—"

"You could have mailed a gift."

"Not this one." He reached inside the suit jacket and pulled out a slip of paper. He slid it across the table.

"What's this?"

"Your gift."

She picked it up. It contained an address in California and a phone number.

"I don't understand. Whose address is this?"

"Your mother's."

She gasped and dropped the paper as if it burned her.

"I'm pretty good with the computer now. Not much I can't do. Skip tracing, missing persons, identity fraud, computer scams. I'm . . ." He paused and she only half heard him, still focused on what he'd said. *Her mother.* "I'm thinking about going out on my own. Specializing in computer crime. Maybe branch out if I can talk Jake or Mike into—" He quieted, as though realizing she hadn't responded. "Still with me?"

"I . . . I don't know what to say."

"You don't have to do anything with the address if you don't want to." He spoke quietly in a soft, gentle voice. "But she's interested if you are."

Decades-old resentment flooded her. "She knew where we were. If she's so interested, why didn't she try to contact us sooner?"

Danny traced the iron whorls in the table with his fingertips. "Things happen, Martha. Sometimes people need to grow up. Learn how to live with the things they've done."

"You talking about her or you?"

He smiled, and it was edged with regret. "Both." He raised his head, his gaze more or less on her face. "She was ashamed. Cried when I told her about you. Took me several phone calls to get her to agree to let me pass on her contact information."

"I hope she isn't expecting a big happy family reunion."

"To be honest, she doesn't even expect you to call. But,

I thought, someday you might want to. And now, if you do, you can."

He rose.

"Wait a minute. Where are you going?"

He pointed a thumb over his shoulder. "I've gotta get back. I'm running the department's CIs and teaching investigative techniques twice a week at Val State. I've got a squad car picking me up in"—he felt around on his wrist—"ten minutes."

"That's it? You barge in after eight months, drop my mother's address on me, and take off?"

He scratched the corner of his mouth with the back of his thumb. "I . . ."

"What do you want, Danny? Why did you really come here today?"

"Uh . . . no mystery. Your mother. I wanted to—"

"No. You came here. In person. After eight months. Why?"

"I told you."

"Why, Danny?"

He laughed uncomfortably. "Where's that whiskey?"

"Uh-unh. You're on your own. Why are you here?"

"Jesus, I'd almost forgotten how persistent you are."

She waited, heart pounding.

"I missed you, okay? I wanted to see if maybe, by some wild coincidence, you might have missed me."

There was hope in that. Hope and despair. He could have missed a friend. She didn't want to be his friend. "If I did, I wouldn't have waited eight months to notice it."

"All right. Christ," he muttered. "All right. It didn't take me eight months. But, God, Martha, I nearly got you killed. What was I supposed to do, hang around clinging to your skirts, praying you'd get well enough to take care of me?"

"I wouldn't have minded a prayer or two."

"You think I didn't pray? You think knowing I put you in the hospital wasn't a knife in my gut?" He looked miserable, as well he should.

"You didn't put me in the hospital. Andrew Robard did. You just didn't stick around afterward."

His jaw tightened. "I'm not going to argue about it. I know what I did and didn't do."

"And now I'm fine, so you can take the knife out?"

"Not exactly."

"Then exactly why are you here?"

"I *told* you." He was a study of impatience reined in. "I heard you'd moved. I wanted to give you a gift. Something to make your new life . . . fuller."

"My life is full enough. I don't want a present. I never wanted anything from you."

"That's not true. At least, I hope to God it's not."

She blinked. "You do?"

A horn honked from the street. Danny took advantage of it. "Look, I've . . . I've gotta go."

"Uh-unh. You're not running away again."

Anger flared in his face. "I didn't run away."

"That's what it looked like to me."

"Dammit, why can't you understand? I left so you could heal without the burden of taking care of me. I left to heal myself so I could come back and fucking take care of myself. I left because I promised your dad I—" He stopped in midsentence, a stricken look on his face.

"You what?"

The car honked again.

"Christ. Nothing. Forget it. This was a bad idea." He turned around and started toward the street.

She watched him absently, still reeling. What had he

said? He'd checked on her every day. With whom? He'd heard she'd moved. From whom? She could think of only one person.

She sprinted after him, got in his way. "Oh, no you don't. You and Charlie cooked up a deal, didn't you? Let me guess, you stay out of my life and Charlie lets you live?"

He pursed his lips, thought about it, gave her a grudging nod. "Something like that."

Her ears were ringing. As though someone had punched her in the head. At the same time, she wished Charlie were there so she could squeeze his thick neck in her two little hands. Of all the stupid, wrong-headed, Charlie-like things . . .

And suddenly, it didn't seem so awful. Just left-footed. Dunderheaded. She started to laugh.

Danny's black brows came together in a heavy scowl. "You think this is funny? Charlie's going to kill me for sure."

"You know, he didn't pay much attention to me growing up. All of a sudden, I'm his new mission in life, and he still gets it wrong. Poor Charlie. So, what—he finally gave you permission to see me?"

He looked sheepish. "Yeah."

It struck her how sweet that was. "So you and Charlie— you've been talking about me?"

"I wouldn't say . . . talking. More like . . . discussing."

"Arguing?"

"Loudly."

"And what did you say to convince him?"

"I told him to stuff his objections up his"— He coughed. "Well, you get the picture."

"And how did he take that?"

"He's not a calm person, your dad."

"But he said all right?"

"I didn't give him much choice."

"Why is that?"

"Why?"

"That's right, Danny." She was running out of patience herself. "Why did you go toe to toe with my dad?"

"I . . . isn't it obvious?"

"Not to me."

"Now I can make your bed, wash your clothes, shop for food and cook you dinner. I have a job, and maybe, if I'm lucky, a future."

She kept her voice cool. "That's very impressive, but I don't need a man to do that stuff for me. I can do it for myself."

"The point is, you won't have to do it for me."

"The point is, I would have liked doing it for you."

He threw up his hands. "Jesus, even proposing to you is an uphill battle."

She stilled. The blood left her body to pool somewhere at her feet. "What did you say?"

Quickly, he held up two hands. "Look, I didn't come here to say that. At least, not today. I thought we could, you know, start slow. So if you're going to freak, I'll take it back."

"I'm not freaking!" Except her voice screeched and her heart beat so fast any second it would break through her ribs. "Okay, so maybe I am. A bit." She took a breath. Tried to calm down.

"But you're not . . . you're not totally against the idea?" He looked so hopeful, she almost laughed.

"Not . . . totally."

Then *he* laughed, the jerk.

She slugged him. "You think this is funny? How many proposals do you think I've had in my life?"

"I don't know and I don't care."

She crossed her arms and studied him narrowly. "Why do you want to marry me anyway?"

His lips curved in a lazy smile. "I like the way you boss me around."

"Not much of a reason."

"How about because I couldn't get you out of my head even though I damn well tried?"

She shrugged. "An improvement."

"How about because I felt like a piece of me was missing and without you everything was boring and without purpose?"

"Better."

"How about . . ." He paused, and whether it was for dramatic effect or for courage or to get it right, she didn't know. She hung there, shoulders tense, fingertips frozen, lungs clogged while he breathed, licked his lips, and finally said, "How about because I love you."

"Ah." She sighed. She was surfing an incredible wave and hoped it never ended. "Bingo."

A uniformed police officer tramped up the walk from the front of the house. He was large, potbellied, and rolled like a teddy bear. Danny turned at the sound of footsteps.

"Hey, Detective. You coming or what?"

"I'm coming."

Martha put a hand on Danny's arm. The muscles tightened under her fingertips. "No, he isn't."

The officer looked from Danny to her back to Danny. All of which was lost on Danny. "Uh, ma'am, I take orders from—"

A smile tugged the corners of Danny's mouth. "Officer

Newman, when you're around Martha Crowe, you usually take orders from her. Whether you want to or not. Thanks for coming out."

Newman gave a good-natured shrug. "More fun than directing traffic. Nice garden you got going there, ma'am."

"Why thank you."

Newman left, and she and Danny stood there silently, awkwardly.

"I do love you," Danny said softly.

"I love you, too."

"Yeah, I think you might have mentioned that."

He reached out and she stepped into the circle of his arms. He sighed with contentment. "Now this is what I've been missing. Scare Crowe's long, lean body in my arms."

She froze. She hadn't heard that epithet since high school. *High school.* "You remembered."

He kissed her temple, where the hair started. "Spent the last eight months trying. Scare Crowe, Big Foot." His voice was grim. "Yeah, I remember."

Cold gripped her, fear crowding out all the happiness.

Danny squeezed her tighter. "You all right? I didn't mean to upset you. It's just that remembering meant so much to me. To have your face—even a fourteen-year-old image of your face—in my head. God, it was a little miracle."

His words cut through her. Of course it would mean a lot to him. It was all he'd ever see of her.

"Hey," he whispered, "where are you?"

She put a hand on his cheek. "Here. I'm right here."

And so was he. A shiver scuttled over her. Wasn't that what counted? That he knew what she looked like—and it didn't matter? He was still there.

She looked up into those intense turquoise eyes, still so

beautiful. She'd bet he'd trade their magnificence for an ugly pair of mud-brown ones that worked.

Only a fool would say that beauty didn't count for much in this world.

But only a fool would base her life on it.

Danny felt her quiver, sensed fear in her silence and stiff back. "Shh," he cooed. "Relax. It's all right. I don't want to marry your face." He held her close, whispered in her ear. "Just tell me one thing. Do you still scold in that schoolteacher voice?"

Immediately, she straightened her spine. "I do not talk like a schoolteacher," she said in her schoolteacher voice.

He grinned. "Glad to hear it." He nuzzled her neck and inhaled that delicious scent. "And you still use that sachet stuff."

"I'm used to it."

He slid his hands down from her waist. "Do you still have that dimple in your—"

"Yes!" She squeaked and slapped his hands away. "At least I think so. I haven't exactly looked."

He took her face in his hands. Beneath his fingertips her jaw curved into his palms, a bird nesting, a traveler coming home. He kissed her, long and deep and sweet. "So Martha, my dear, dear Martha, what do I care about your face?"

Martha wrapped her arms around him. Suddenly, she didn't care either.

About the Author

A native New Yorker, **Annie Solomon** has been dreaming up stories since she was ten. After a twelve-year career in advertising, where she rose to Vice President and Head Writer at a mid-size agency, she abandoned the air conditioners, heat pumps, and furnaces of her professional life for her first love—romance. *Blind Curve* is her fourth novel of romantic suspense. To learn more, visit her Web site at www.anniesolomon.com.

Read Hank Bonner and
Alexandra Jane Baker's story in

TELL ME NO LIES

In a small town in the Hudson Valley, Alexandra
Jane Baker has set the perfect trap for a murderer.
But the fatal shooting of a dear friend puts her
plans—and her own life—in jeopardy. Beautiful,
wealthy, and alone, she stirs the suspicions—and
desire—of Detective Hank Bonner, who catches
the homicide case. Counting down his last days on
the force, Hank will break every rule, cross every-
line. Because a ruthless predator is very near, and to
protect Alex and everything he holds dear, Hank
will put himself in the line of fire.

THE EDITOR'S DIARY

Dear Reader,

From an unexpected belly laugh to the perfect pair of shoes, life is full of happy accidents. But the best one is the romance you never saw coming and the one you can't live without. Just ask Danny and Annie in our two Warner Forever titles this February.

New York Times bestselling author Iris Johansen raves **Annie Solomon's** previous book is "a nail biter through and through." Postpone that manicure you've been planning—her latest, **BLIND CURVE,** is even better! Undercover cop Danny Sinofsky never needed anyone or anything. But when he suddenly goes blind in the middle of a bust, Danny couldn't feel more helpless. Now, refusing to believe his sight is permanently gone, Danny must work with mobility instructor Martha Crowe. Determined to get through Danny's wall of anger, Martha keeps one secret from him—she was the plain girl in high school who had a crush on him. But when Martha witnesses an attack on his life, they are thrown into a safe house where this man without sight starts to see the real beauty inside this courageous woman. With a relentless assassin trailing them, they must act as one, using Danny's razor-sharp instincts and Martha's eyes, if they want to survive.

The man in your life always says exactly the right thing. He never leaves the toilet seat up. And he always surrenders the remote control without a thought. Sounds like the perfect guy, right? He sure is—because Annie Long from **Candy Halliday's DREAM GUY** created him. Meet Joe Video, the most lucrative product the DVD and video game company Annie works at has ever been part of. Fresh out of her most recent disaster of a relationship, Annie couldn't help but wonder why we can't create the perfect man? So, with the help of Rico, a devastatingly gorgeous actor hired to play Joe Video in the DVD, Annie sees her creation come to life. The only problem— she has trouble resisting his charms. But is Joe Video really as "perfect" as he seems? Because Matt, her co-creator and an unforgettable romantic mistake, is proving himself to be more perfect than Joe Video ever could be.

To find out more about Warner Forever, these February titles, and the authors, visit us at www.warnerforever.com.

With warmest wishes,

Karen Kosztolnyik

Karen Kosztolnyik, Senior Editor

P.S. Watch for these exciting new novels next month: **Wendy Markham** pens the poignant tale of a widow trying to raise two children, a man who's certain there's more to life, and the heavenly matchmaker with a plan in **HELLO, IT'S ME**; and **Susan Crandall** delivers the enthralling story of a woman who's unexpectedly left a child under dubious circumstances and a man with a lot at stake who's determined to unravel her every secret in **PROMISES TO KEEP**.